SCANDALOUS ALCHEMY

KATY MORAN is the author of *Wicked by Design* and *False Lights*, published by Head of Zeus in 2017 under the pseudonym K.J. Whittaker and published as *Hester and Crow* on Kindle. After a career in the book trade, Katy now lives with her husband and three children in a ramshackle house in the Welsh borders.

Visit Katy's website to sign up for her newsletter and enjoy exclusive short stories set in the world of *Wicked by Design*.

katymoran.co.uk

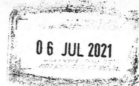
KATY MORAN

SCANDALOUS ALCHEMY

HEAD
of ZEUS

First published in the UK in 2021 by Head of Zeus Ltd

Copyright © Katy Moran, 2021

9 7 5 3 1 2 4 6 8

A catalogue record for this book is available from
the British Library.

ISBN (HB): 9781786695420
ISBN (XTPB): 9781786695437
ISBN (E): 9781786695413

Typeset by Divaddict Publishing Solutions Ltd.

Printed and bound in Great Britain by
CPI Group (UK) Ltd, Croydon CR0 4YY

Head of Zeus Ltd
5–8 Hardwick Street
London EC1R 4RG
WWW.HEADOFZEUS.COM

This book is dedicated to the memory of my grandmother, Edna Limbert

So, lovers dream a rich and long delight
But get a winter-seeming summer's night.

John Donne, 'Love's Alchemy'

Dames of elevated rank, likewise, whose doors she entered in the way of her occupation, were accustomed to distil drops of bitterness into her heart; sometimes through that alchemy of quiet malice, by which women can concoct a subtle poison from ordinary trifles.

Nathaniel Hawthorne, The Scarlet Letter

This book is set during a period of re-imagined history.

*In 1815, Britain, Prussia and their allies lose the Battle of Waterloo. The British royal family die in prison during the French Occupation, eventually leaving a young Russian princess as heir to the throne. Even once the Occupation is over, the Napoleonic War continues until 1825, ending at last with Napoleon agreeing to retreat within the original borders of France.
Here, where Napoleon once surrendered, the ancient palace of Fontainebleau plays host to a peace conference.*

Note on the text: the Russian name Nadezhda is pronounced as it is spelled; the 'zh' follows 'pleasure' and 'treasure'. In Cornwall, 'maid' is an affectionate term for a young girl.

PART 1
CORNWALL, 1820

1

Lamorna, Twelfth Night

Clemency Arwenack didn't want to look like a complete flat, but she'd never been inside the ballroom at Nansmornow before. No one had asked her to dance, so she was still wedged on a brocade sofa between her godmother Lady Boscobel and the curate's wife, both of them in mutton-leg sleeves. In Clemency's opinion Mrs Tregarthen was an idiot to have chosen claret-red silk, with that complexion. Local acquaintances and neighbours were leavened with friends from London and even a Russian poet, and the champagne flowed faster than small-beer in a back-alley tavern.

Clemency watched the chandeliers ablaze with shivering flames and calculated the cost of the candles alone; in the bindery, she'd had to save every last spoonful of lamp oil. It was hard not to stare at the arrangements of scented narcissi boated across the Cornish sea from Bryher, and the ladies in sparkling jewels and feathered head-dresses, most of them looking at her sideways. The Earl and Countess of Lamorna didn't often entertain on a grand scale, but when they did, you'd have to be sick or dead to refuse the invitation. That's what Lady Boscobel said, anyway.

Tonight, everyone else Clemency's age was charging up and down a polonaise, the musicians sawing away at their violins while she sat here like a fool. Still, if she could row out to meet the gentlemen of the free trade on a moonless night, she could equally put up with a night of humiliation as the Boscobel charity case.

Unlike the free-traders with their barrels of Chambord and brandy, Clemency dealt in information. She never had anything to carry on those nights save those messengers from foreigners, kept safe in her own head; she'd always been good at remembering things, and then passing it all on to Lord Lamorna. The fewer who knew of that the better, though, just the same as you turned your face to the wall when the gentlemen came up through Penzance with brandy and gold. You couldn't tell what you'd not seen, after all.

Grandpapa used to say she was quick at picking up foreign speech because of all that cant she'd heard in the Peninsula: all the camp brats could swear in English, Spanish and Portuguese, officers' daughters included. She'd learn how to manage in a ballroom, too, if this was the way it had to be. It was just that she was better suited to low-voiced conversation with his lordship in Grandpapa's bindery shop than doing the pretty in his ballroom, that was all. She'd cope with this awful velvet gown, so tight around her arms, and her hair all scorched and primped with the curling irons, and everyone staring, just for one night.

Except that it isn't one night, though. It's for ever. Clemency pushed that thought away. It wasn't for ever, anyway, so she should stop being blue-devilled about the whole thing. In five years, she'd be twenty-one, and she could go back to the bindery and live there just how she pleased with her own little independence, small as it was, and never mind the terms of Papa's will. She hoped he was pleased with himself, wherever he was now, wrapped in clouds in a place of unimagined blessings or whatever: ruining someone's life when you'd been dead eight years yourself was quite the feat.

Valentine hadn't looked at her all night. They'd waited in the marble-tiled vestibule at Boscobel Castle for Bough to bring the carriage around, Clemency shivering with a silver net shawl draped across her shoulders.

Pretty as a peach, he said then, pinching her chin. *You be careful now. We can't have all the young bucks taking advantage, can we?*

That didn't seem very likely, not with her hair done up in these ridiculous pin-curls, and her still unsure of the steps in anything more complicated than a country dance. As far as the law went, it was Valentine who was her guardian, not his mother, even though he seemed very young and handsome for that, not really like a person in authority. Clemency knew she'd beat Valentine at piquet if they played: he'd go in aggressive right from the start, and it would be easy to show him a weak game until suddenly she didn't. His lordship was another matter: he'd taught her every last refinement. Clemency couldn't see him now among all this silk and satin crowd: it could be he'd gone into one of the side-rooms. She'd acquired a pretty sharp-tuned awareness of his presence at all times, and there was no sign of his elegant shoulder nor his greying head.

'Of course, young Captain Helford is *quite* the scandal,' Mrs Tregarthen was saying to Lady Boscobel in a hushed whisper, reeking of champagne and gum arabic breath pastilles. 'He's been on leave for a week already, and he spent at least several days in London before coming down to Cornwall.' Her eyes narrowed, reddened nostrils flaring. 'The mail coach leaves from the Stag every Monday and Thursday, so if he arrived yesterday, he could surely have taken last week's coach on the Thursday. But instead he stayed in town.'

Clemency took a sip of her champagne.

'Oh come now, Agnes, the young people must have their fun.' Lady Boscobel spoke with her usual airy light-heartedness: Clemency had already learned that it disguised an iron will. Lady Boscobel's fair ringlets were glossy with pomade, held in place with a tortoiseshell comb, and this was her first time out since the end of her mourning. To Clemency's mind she planned to make the most of it. 'I'd be aghast if Valentine wished to remain at home with me all the time. He spends as much time in London as possible, although of course so many of his trading opportunities are there, but it's not just that, is it? I don't blame darling Kit for a little rabble-rousing in town – the company will be pretty thin on the ground at this time of year, but all the better to gamble in hells without having to be polite to us ancient old tabby cats at parties. And I would imagine that the usual social scene in London seems rather flat after serving with the Coldstream in Russia – can you imagine the glamour of St Petersburg? All that snow and magnificence.' She smiled, showing her well-kept teeth. Clemency was sure she didn't think of herself as a tabby cat at all. 'One can't help noticing that Kit's not here, though – at a ball in his own home.'

Mrs Tregarthen smiled, malicious. Her reverend husband's godliness hadn't rubbed off on her, that much was obvious. 'Yes, rather an insult to Lady Lamorna – one hears she's driven a wedge between the two brothers. It was only to be expected, of course. Rich as Croesus and very pretty, in that exotic style, but one has to be brought up to a certain kind of life. Lamorna's mother was French, of course, and even that didn't end well.'

Lady Boscobel shrugged her pretty shoulders. 'I suppose their father was no more unfaithful than anyone else's husband, God rest his soul.' She sighed. 'Sometimes it feels as if one's entire generation has gone; I remember when Mark brought her home from France, and they dazzled every ballroom in London.'

Mrs Tregarthen eyed her over the rim of her champagne glass. 'Oh, come on, Georgie, don't be maudlin. Well, if Kit hasn't fallen out with Lamorna or her ladyship, perhaps he's just got better things to do. You and I both know he was angling for a sniff of Princess Nadezhda in London. He's probably at the Wink: I doubt our Cornish girls compete with Russian glamour. Such a peculiar foreign name she has, though! It doesn't seem right for an English royal, but the reverend informs me that she will be Queen Sophia upon her coronation, so that's a good Christian name, at least.'

'Isn't Sophia from Ancient Greek, Mrs Tregarthen?' Clemency had read a lot of Grandpapa's books. 'I think Nadezhda is rather a pretty name. It sounds exciting.'

Mrs Tregarthen raised her sparse eyebrows almost all the way up into the grizzled curls at her hairline. 'Isn't the girl rather young to be out, Georgie?'

Clemency's belly lurched: Grandpapa might always have encouraged her to be inquisitive, but she kept forgetting that young ladies were not supposed to have enquiring minds or volunteer opinions. Nor were ladies meant to contradict.

Lady Boscobel smiled. 'Keeping young girls immured in the schoolroom for ever is very unwise, Agnes. If they are to be in *real* society at all, far better for them to gain a little experience in the countryside. I don't know about Kit hanging around Princess Nadezhda in London, though. I heard Lamorna does everything he can to ensure they don't meet, short of forbidding the boy to see her. I can see why Crow doesn't like it – I wouldn't want Valentine playing cicisbeo to royalty. I don't know about you, but whether Princess Nadezhda is to be finally Queen of England or not, I find it so difficult to think of her as anything but Russian and a Romanov to the bone, even if she is poor Princess Sophia's daughter, God rest her soul.'

'God rest all their souls,' Mrs Tregarthen said, darkly. 'As if anyone believes the royal family really died of gaol-fever in the Occupation. It was foul play by the French, mark my words, and no one will ever convince me otherwise. I hear that this Princess Nadezhda is odiously spoiled and pert – how insulting that we should all have to do the pretty with such a forward young puss as they say she is.'

'I thought her highness looked a trifle overwhelmed when I saw her at Princess Lieven's rout-party in the Little Season,' Lady Boscobel said. 'She's quite young, after all: no more than twenty, I believe. What do you think, Clemency, darling? Should you like to travel pell-mell across the ocean and find yourself heir to the throne in a strange land, with everyone gossiping that you'd fallen head over heels in love with Kit Helford?'

Clemency shrugged, sipping her champagne again. 'I wouldn't know, ma'am. And I haven't seen Captain Helford for years. I'm not sure I'd know him if we met in the street.'

She'd never tasted champagne before; she liked the dry sensation of the bubbles in her mouth. This was her second glass and she was beginning to feel pleasantly warm, as if everything she had been worrying about didn't matter as much as she'd feared. Clemency was sure she'd find a way to manage it all, and his lordship's expectation. She always had.

Lady Boscobel laid one lace-gloved hand upon Clemency's arm. 'It's such a treat for me to have a girl about the house. I was never blessed with daughters as you were, Agnes.'

Mrs Tregarthen signalled to a footman for more champagne. 'The worst sort of trouble, when I think of what I endured with Betsy and her acne. Quite the prettiest girl before she came out at the assembly rooms, as I'm sure you remember. The spots appeared that very morning and we didn't see the back of them for another two years.' She took a glass from the footman without a word of thanks and looked Clemency up and down as if she was a heifer on her way to market. 'What on earth do you plan to do with the girl? I mean, the child of a shabby-genteel army captain and goodness knows what else? I suppose you intend for her to be presented to Princess Nadezhda at court! You've always aimed high, Georgie.'

Lady Boscobel smiled. 'I think we need not bother with that sort of stuffiness. Clemency is already coming along beautifully with her dancing master. We'll have our fun next season. The true *haut ton* favours originality, after all, and the Arwenacks were a very old family. Should you like that, Clemency?'

'I'd like to give them all a run for their money, ma'am, if it pleases you,' Clemency said, sensing that this was what Lady Boscobel wanted to hear, and she did laugh, after all.

'Only a little pert, my child,' she said, turning to Mrs Tregarthen. 'But you see she has spirit as well as her natural advantages, which of course I should never want a young girl to think too much of.'

'Well, I wish you all the very best of good luck with that,' Mrs Tregarthen went on, in a tone Clemency didn't know quite how to decipher. 'Lord, don't look now, but Lamorna is coming this way. Such a blessing about their little girl, don't you think? I saw them all in the carriage last week and in all honesty if her mother weren't there, you'd never *know*. She has such a mop of curls – they must make sure that they keep her out of the sun, that's all. Anyway, Miss Arwenack, I'm sure you'll soon settle in and quickly begin to learn how we all go on.'

'Forgive me,' Clemency said, before she could stop herself, 'but is it the done thing to be insulting about your own host and hostess, and their daughter?'

Mrs Tregarthen's red-rimmed nostrils flared again, and Clemency felt a little elated: perhaps this was why they all drank so much champagne. Lady Boscobel turned to her with a flat expression, and thank heaven Lord Lamorna reached them before anyone could speak, tall and distinguished in his evening jacket and his white cravat, with that silvery streak in his black hair, which everyone said he was terribly young for. He talked to Lady Boscobel and Mrs Tregarthen for a few moments, so that Mrs Tregarthen flushed an even deeper shade of brick red, and Lady Boscobel adjusted her shawl to reveal her décolletage and called him Crow to his face, as though they were old friends. Then he turned his attention to Clemency, looking at her with those grey eyes she'd always found rather cold.

'My dear Miss Arwenack,' he said. 'I won't mortify you by asking you to dance with someone so old, but you'll take a turn about the room with me, at least.'

She didn't have much choice but to get up and go with him, and it was worth it for Mrs Tregarthen's purse-lipped smile; he offered her his arm and she took it, and he led her to a quieter corner of the ballroom away from the orchestra. She found herself noticing odd little details: a girl's pink satin slipper tied at the ankle with a flash of green ribbon revealed as she swept through the polonaise with unladylike energy, a footman taking a moment to mop his brow with a folded handkerchief; they came at last to stand by a bookshelf lined with old maps of Cornwall and treatises on mining and minerals and fox-hunting: Grandpapa had bound the maps for his father in red Moroccan leather.

'So how are you finding Boscobel Castle?' Lord Lamorna said, in Cornish, without relinquishing his firm yet light grip on her arm. 'Setting the cat among the pigeons, to judge by the expression on Agnes Tregarthen's face. You'd be wise to have a care.'

'The attorney said there's nothing I can do about it, not now my grandfather's dead.' Clemency didn't expect the Earl of Lamorna to understand what it was like when the butcher's wife looked away from you in the street, or going without supper, or lying awake in the dark in her attic above the bindery because there was no oil for the lamp, and no money even for tallow candles that made the whole place reek of stale mutton fat.

'I'm well aware of that. Your father's last wishes are inviolate, I'm afraid, no matter how ill-considered you and I might both believe they are. He must have felt you'd be safe with the Boscobels. I suppose he couldn't have known how Georgie would turn out. But you'll be a fool to keep running information while you're under her roof, do you understand? For me, or for anyone else, for that matter. Come on, Clemency – the odds aren't in your favour now.'

He'd taught her everything she knew, after all. She, who'd played cards and dice under his orders in a St Malo tavern. 'My aces will win more than they lose eventually, won't they, though?'

'You'll come unstuck. Stop play.' He nearly smiled at her then. 'You might have the soul of an adventurer, but for a while at least you must learn how to be something different.'

She shrugged, her eyes filling with hot, sudden tears at the unfairness of it. In another life, she'd be in Grandpapa's old attic workshop now, dipping endpapers into the coloured size, watching the sun rise over the jumbled rooftops of Penzance, gulls wheeling in a grey sky; she'd be rowing out to meet the free-traders with the dying sun on her face, carrying information for coinage and, if she was honest with herself, for the sheer fiery thrill of it. 'I don't want to go hungry but it's just that it's not the life I want. Sir.'

Lamorna looked at her: host, lord, spymaster. 'Which of us chooses that, after all?'

2

Earlier that day

Captain Kit Helford wore no hat, so that snow landed in his untidy black hair, trails of his warm breath the only real sign of a living presence. The valley beyond Nansmornow was thick with settled white mist beneath a vivid pink-streaked winter dawn. Frozen grass met the heels of his boots with silent resistance as he loped downhill through gorse and dead bracken in his grandfather's shooting jacket, quiet as the hillside itself; you couldn't hear the crashing of the waves from here. Even Kit's brother had raised an eyebrow over hot coffee in the morning room before daybreak, remarking with disgust that the ground was like bloody iron. Crow would have preferred riding to hounds, all stirrup cup and lord of the manor, but Kit was happier on foot, just him and the gorse and the red deer and the silence. Alone like this, there were moments Kit even forgot what he'd done to this place; he didn't have to wonder what the people here were thinking when they looked at him.

He had sight of a red hind now, right in the crook of the valley where the mist had risen, and the breath caught in his chest as she stepped out from a stand of skeletal birch trees. A single gold leaf still clung to one naked branch, not yet whipped free by the south-westerly that usually howled across from the headland; the wind had gone still this morning with the promise of snow. The hind's flanks were dappled with pale spots, and she was sleek in the body; it was a kindness as well as good sport to cull hinds on this barren land in winter. Neither the sea nor copper ore could sustain deer as it did men. Kit shouldered his rifle, checking first that the barrel wasn't fouled, but even as he did so he heard undisguised footfall back up the valley, well above him, as well as the jarring clatter of spurs. By God, the devil might take all civilians directly to hell. The hind froze where she stood and Kit lowered his rifle: he'd lost her. The hind went to bolt, but a shot cracked out from above him on the heathered shoulder of moorland and she was struck in the flank at a hellish poor angle, surging off down the valley and into the beech copse with lopsided panic.

Kit swore quietly and hiked back up the hill to meet his brother's ghillie. Simmens was red-cheeked in the frozen dawn air with his hand-knitted muffler, more than double Kit's age and already tense; no wonder, with his second wife nearing her time down at Nantewas and one already dead in childbed. The last thing Simmens needed was a day spent tracking every dead leaf between here and Cribba Head for bloody clots of hide, but he needed his fifteen shillings a year still more, and Kit's brother expected the beasts killed on Lamorna acres to die well, and the business of childbirth to be dealt with by women.

'I'll go after her, your honour.' Simmens spoke in Cornish, his mouth set hard as he glanced up the valley towards the group of ascending young men – Valentine Boscobel, to judge by that flash of sunlight on a crop of chestnut curls, and the casual broad-shouldered gait. Valentine and his satellites were all four or five years older than Kit himself, but to him they seemed like undisciplined children, swaggering down the valley with their vivid, cold-flushed faces. Boscobel was Sir Valentine now, his elderly father despatched by apoplexy not quite a year ago; he was accompanied by a couple of Rashleigh boys down from Oxford.

'At least you're bound to get a fuck out of this evening, Boscobel,' the shorter Rashleigh was saying, speaking in French he obviously presumed Kit could not understand. 'It's all right for some – talk about low-hanging fruit. The rest of us must be content with the bloody chambermaids. Ward, my arse. She's a tasty-looking handful, I'll grant you that.'

'Chambermaids or ball and chain,' his cousin said, and they all laughed except Valentine, and at Kit's side Simmens shifted from foot to foot, one eye on the valley below, tracking the injured young hind by sight as best he could.

'To the devil with you, Rashleigh,' Valentine said lazily. 'It's all my mother. You know how women are – no stopping them once they get it into their heads to take on these charity cases.' Only then did he speak to Kit. 'You there – better get after the beast.'

Kit laughed, and Valentine turned back with a flash of anger. 'What?'

'You're right – someone must kill her now, of course.' Kit wasn't above enjoying the surprise on Valentine's handsome face as he looked him up and down; at school, Valentine had been clever, good at cricket, carelessly decent to the younger boys.

'Good lord, young Helford.' Valentine glanced at his friends with a quick smile. 'You really must forgive me. I didn't know you at all. Been giving the French the devil of a time in Russia while the likes of us kick our heels, I hear.'

'Just as damned well, with a reputation like that,' one of the Rashleighs said. 'Been up to London yet, Helford? I hear those Russian girls are wild in bed – a sweet armful, is she, her royal highness?'

Kit smiled. 'Say that again.' He'd punch Rashleigh's teeth through his fucking throat; Rashleigh's eyes bulged a little at the look on his face, but that was no bad thing, and Kit pushed away a memory of Nadezhda's amused dark gaze, and the way she'd called him Khristofyor, naming him for her own. Using him for her own, too. One day she'd like as not be crowned if the public could be brought to accept her; Crow said they'd call her Queen Sophia then. A pretty peculiar look-out for the hoyden disguised as a soldier he'd known in Russia.

'Shut up, Rashleigh,' Valentine said with his expansive grin. 'Listen, there's a cock-fight at the Admiral Benbow to-morrow night. A few of us are going. Helford, you should come along. My groom gave me a certain tip about the ban-tam, and they've a roulette table upstairs, would you believe.'

'Good of you – perhaps I will,' Kit said, who knew exactly which wreck the roulette wheel had been salvaged from. He left them to it; there was little sense in pointing out that it had been the sort of shot only an idiot would take. Instead, he addressed Simmens in Cornish as they walked side by side away down the hill, 'I'll make after the hind, Ed. You go home.'

No matter if it took all day: he could hardly stick the prospect of the evening ahead, anyway.

3

By the time Kit got home, Nansmornow was a mass of candlelit windows just visible through the trees, the North Star a bright point of light above ancient rooftops, and he could just hear the faintest strain of music drifting across parkland now white with snow. No, it was no use: the dancing had long since started and, late as Kit already was, he must go in, shedding battered tweeds for his regimentals; all the girls would be expecting an officer tonight. They were sure to dine soon, and he was honour bound to attack the lobster patties and honeyed dates with some tongue-tied vicar's daughter on his arm, proof that there was no truth to the court gossip about Nadezhda, or her highness, or whatever the hell he was meant to call her these days, as much as for the sake of convention.

Kit had run the hind to ground in the gully behind Borlaze just before nightfall; she could no longer stand when he'd found her among the bracken. He'd finished her quickly with a hard and expert thrust of his Malinois dagger so that the light went out of her dark eyes immediately, even as warm blood splashed his face. He'd as lief have stayed in the warm fug at the Wink all night, wetting the head of Ed Simmens's new son, but Crow's men would be more at ease with him gone. Kit was no fool: he didn't have to wonder what they said of him behind closed doors. He deserved all of it. In any case, it would be insulting to his sister-in-law not to show his face at the ball. He loved Hester as though she were his mother and there was no choice but to go, no matter how little he could be bothered with it.

Reaching the furthest edge of the little lych-yard, he sensed movement near a stand of ancient yew trees and glanced up into flecks of unearthly silver-white spinning against the winter darkness, his own warm breath a frozen cloud. A trail of silver cloud slid from before the moon, and Kit found that the alcoholic tang on his lips tasted like vodka brewed outside the back of a taverna instead of the smuggled brandy he'd drunk at the Wink.

There was someone in the yew trees. *Fucking French:* the words slipped through his mind unbidden. It was years since the Occupation, when French troops had patrolled Cornwall, but instinct drove him to reach first for a pistol he wasn't carrying, and then to unsheath the Malinois again, honed blade glittering hard and bright in cold moonlight. His rifle would be no good at this range; his gaze slid across the expanse of cold, silver-lit parkland to the rambling bulk of the house, windows blazing with candlelight. Hester and Crow were inside with all their guests, the child upstairs in the nursery. Kit sensed the bastard's heartbeat over there in the yew trees; he could even see a trail of warm human

20

breath. French soldiers had killed his own sister here on this land. They'd left her hanging from the chestnut tree naked save only her shift, for all to see. Every time Kit tracked bluecoats through heavy Russian snowfall, he thought of Roza at home in Cornwall and the grotesque angle of her head as she'd hung. He thought of the blood on her thighs, too, and the blank white-hot terror she must have felt as she died, just like the hind he'd killed today. All of it his own fault.

Kit moved across the snow in complete silence, knowing that he had disappeared into the darkness, even as the shadow he approached took on living human form. Another step, and Kit had him. It wasn't until the French soldier screamed and bit his hand that Kit was aware of velvet beneath his fingertips and a warm fresh scent of Castile soap.

'Christ, I'm so sorry.' He stepped backwards, releasing and then steadying her, his heart racing as he sheathed the knife, even as he recognised a familiar dusting of freckles across a ridge of cheekbone.

'What the bloody hell are you playing at, Kitto Helford?' Clemency demanded, using a childhood name that even his own brother rarely deployed now, snowflakes landing on her velvet-clad shoulders – cool as you might choose, all things considered. 'I thought you were going to cut my throat.' She was all wide, absurdly long-lashed eyes, just as she had ever been, although now there was no sign of that faux-innocent expression that had got them out of hot water so many times as children.

'I meant to,' he said. 'I thought you were a French soldier.'

'Idiot,' she retorted, looking him up and down. 'They're

long gone. From here, anyway. Aren't you supposed to be at that ball dancing with debutantes instead of attacking innocent people outdoors?'

Idiot, he told himself. She was right. *Fucking idiot. Get a hold on yourself.* What in God's name was she doing at Nansmornow, in the ugliest ballgown he'd ever laid eyes on? She faced him directly, her eyes bright with chagrin, and Kit felt another surge of unease, recalling Rashleigh's lascivious smile as he tossed the character of the Boscobels' new dependant into the gutter. *Ward, my arse. She's a tasty-looking handful, I'll grant you that.*

Clemency flushed, her cheeks burning. Kit's forehead was smeared with dried blood, and he was dressed to hunt, not to dance; his hold on her had been absolute, one arm across her chest, his release and apology immediate and heartfelt, but he was a damn long way from the black-haired boy running at her side down a Newlyn back alley, that was for sure.

'Old Nick fly away with debutantes.' Kit let out a long breath and smiled suddenly; those deep-cut dimples were still the same, but that air of barely repressed mischief had almost completely vanished, hidden behind something watchful and dangerous. No wonder. His father's servants at Nansmornow used to say that the devil had put in his eyes with a sooty finger – they were pale grey, his lashes very dark. God, the stories she'd heard of him. Did he think she hadn't heard the rumours?

'Heaven help you if that collection of ballroom turnkeys

hears you're outside alone with me, Clemmie.' He took off his heavy jacket and drew it close about her shoulders, simultaneously abrupt and graceful in the way that he moved.

'Oh, never mind!' She breathed in the faint, sea-salt scent of his body and the blood along with some sort of herbal tincture: his shaving water, perhaps. He was so much taller than her now, broader, too. He was also right, damn him. If Lady Boscobel came to discover that she was out here alone with Lord Lamorna's wild young brother, there would be trouble. Never mind that Russian princess everyone was whispering about: gossip might fly about his entanglement at court and every hostess in London would still fight to receive him, but the rules were different for her.

'You might have a point – I'm going to get into the most awful hot water if people find out I've been out here with you alone. I'm not supposed to do this sort of thing any more.'

'Damn it all to hell,' Kit said, with a glimmer of a smile. 'I'll dress, and you'll just have to dance with me. Then no one will dare say a word. It's my ball, after all – for my sins. They threw it for me. My brother and Hester, I mean.'

'Dance with you?' Clemency demanded. They were still holding hands, and she drew her own away. 'You'll have to think again if you reckon I can manage a quadrille. I suppose you think you're doing me a favour.'

He looked down at her, serious now, more snowflakes settling in that tousled dark hair. 'God, not in the slightest. According to the old trots in my brother's ballroom, I'm a spoiled young rake and no better than I should be: I don't do favours. Will you give me one dance, though, Clemmie? Something to think of next time I'm digging a siege-trench.'

'Digging trenches? Ordering your men to do it, I should say.'

'I do take a spade myself, you know,' he said. 'It isn't all cavalry and cannons.'

'Oh, very well,' she said, looking away as if she didn't particularly care. 'I suppose it would be unpatriotic to refuse.'

PART TWO
FIVE YEARS LATER

4

London, Spring 1825

'I want Kit Helford.' Princess Nadezhda Sofia Romanova leaned back against velvet cushions in the state apartment at St James's Palace. Heir to the English throne, she was gowned in silk of a vivid tangerine, weightless fabric revealing the lean strength in her arms. Her dark curls were cropped short, a fashion now replicated in drawing-rooms across Mayfair. She sat with her legs casually crossed like a man, so that one silver satin slipper hung inadequately moored from her toes as she twitched a foot with rhythmic impatience. She had the prime minister in with her as well as the Russian ambassador's wife: as ever, Countess Dorothea Lieven was all trailing Kashmiri shawl, profuse ringlets and acute observation.

The Duke of Wellington managed, after a pause, to speak: 'I'm sorry, your highness?' Wellington was an Irishman, but he had the sort of high-coloured, raw-boned Home

Counties face that flushed easily. 'You desire Lieutenant Colonel Helford to captain your personal guard?'

'I don't know why you should both look as though I've just asked for the devil himself.' Nadezhda indulged herself in a few swift, scattered memories of Russia, most particularly the taste of sweet medovukha on Kit Helford's lips and the disreputably merry light in his eyes, always so startlingly pale against those thick black lashes. Dorothea and Wellington might stare all they liked; she had the self-control not to flush. 'Don't you want me to be safe in France? Helford is the best there is.'

Nadezhda pushed irritably at her emerald-crusted Viennese betrothal ring. The letter said it had belonged originally to an Austrian empress. That empress must have been of odalisque proportions, whoever she was, for the ring hung loose around her finger; she felt like a child playing at being queen, but in reality they'd crown her just as soon as she was married, bound into place on the English throne not just by Britain and Russia, but by the might of Austria, too. Archduke Louis Charles Habsburg-Lorraine was both Prince of Hungary and the scion of an offshoot of the mighty Austrian imperial family: judging by the fact that he'd left his correspondence to an elderly aunt, he had all the arrogance of an emperor.

'Of course it's essential that you have a personal guard in France,' Dorothea Lieven said carefully. 'No one pretends Fontainebleau is going to be straightforward: people hold on to their grievances after twenty-two years of war.'

'Idiocy, the entire affair.' Wellington spoke with such a controlled explosion of rage they were both compelled to turn and look at him. 'There's no need for a royal presence at the negotiations at all: it only complicates things. Every man is in this bloody game for himself: France, Austria, Prussia, Persia, Russia – most of them give less of a damn about Napoleon scurrying back within his own borders than they do about a nice easy route into India, you'll see. Fontainebleau's about iron and tea and Bukhara and damned bloody sea-routes, not doing the pretty with royalty.'

'The tsar will be at Fontainebleau, as will crowned heads from every royal court in Europe and beyond, as well as the Prince of Hungary. For a start, it would be peculiar if there was no *English* royal presence,' Dorothea said. 'And grossly insulting to the Austrians, if her highness didn't come to meet Louis Charles.'

Nadezhda forced herself not to glance down at the ring: she couldn't have them thinking she wouldn't come to bridle.

'Helford won't do it,' Wellington said instead. 'He's made every excuse to avoid court for years. And before he came of age, his brother shifted to keep him out of your orbit, if I may say so, your highness. Lamorna isn't without influence now.'

Nadezhda crossed her legs again with brisk impatience and a froth of scented aerophane orange silk. 'Helford's not on half-pay yet, is he? If he's given orders, he must obey.'

'Damn it, Dorothea, people will talk,' Wellington went on. 'How do you think it will sit with Austria if Helford of all people captains the personal bodyguard? In six years the boy has barely set eyes on her highness, and look at the state of this.' He flung a closely printed pamphlet down upon the table.

Dorothea picked it up between thumb and forefinger. 'Idle gossip and speculation,' she said after a swift appraisal. 'You know what these rags are like with the scurrilous rubbish they print – a basis in fact is no requirement. The Coldstream has barely been back in England a week, and I can tell you now that when Kit Helford has actually troubled himself to leave Horse Guards, it's to visit the sort of place in Soho or near the docks that I'm ashamed to discuss. He certainly hasn't danced with her highness at a masked ball, whatever these pamphleteers insinuate.' Her eyebrows shot up as she read the next paragraph. 'Danced with or worse. Good God, the impudence of these people.'

Nadezhda fully intended to contemplate in delicious frustration all the ways in which one might misbehave with Kit Helford at a ball, but not until she was in the privacy of her own chambers. She must try not to concern herself too much with the miniature portrait of her fiancé. The court artist had done his work well, capturing the golden cap of hair, an assured blue gaze, and the extremely uncompromising set of the sitter's mouth: Louis Charles Habsburg-Lorraine would just have to learn the hard way that she was not to be dominated. And if the gossip about Kit Helford had never really gone away, she might as well make use of it. 'Does the Cabinet want Austria to believe that they are to have everything as they wish?'

Wellington smiled at that, giving a reluctant snort of laughter.

'I'm sorry, your highness, but that young archduke is not a man you ought to tangle with,' Dorothea said, with a rare display of complete sincerity. 'Leave all this to the negotiation table. I really must ask you to take care in your dealings with Louis Charles. You've been protected here for so long—'

'But you can't protect me in my marriage-bed, is that it?' Nadezhda demanded quickly. 'I'm not afraid.'

'Perhaps you should be,' Dorothea said, with feeling. Sunlight streaming in through the leaded windows struck a collection of gilded Sèvres ornaments on the vast Tudor mantelpiece of carved oak, and Nadezhda fought for breath, her head spinning.

Wellington leaned back in his chair with the air of a man about to beat a tactical retreat. 'What of her highness's other staff? Is the position of Mistress of the Robes still untenanted? We'll need a sensible girl: someone without too many interfering relations.'

Dorothea waved a hand, dismissive. 'Oh, that's all decided. She's a steady girl with a good eye – a certain sort of something, you know. An old family on one side, but not fashionable. None of your Melbournes or Lennoxes to trouble us.'

Nadezhda yawned. It was more than time to bring all this to a close. 'Oh yes, the eminently forgettable Miss Clemency Arwenack.'

'Arwenack?' Wellington's eyes instantly narrowed. 'She's Cornish, then.'

'Yes, but not the Jacobin sort,' Dorothea said quickly. 'She's in France with her people already – she was Valentine

Boscobel's ward and still lives with them now. They arrived at Fontainebleau last week, and I've written to Georgiana Boscobel already. The girl must have close to half a dozen seasons under her belt and she's still single – they'll be only too pleased to see her comfortably disposed of. Which she will be, as long as she doesn't make any foolish mistakes.'

That wouldn't be the only letter Dorothea had written on this topic, Nadezhda was quite sure of that: unlike most of her English royal relatives, Tsar Alexander was very much alive, and always interested in her affairs.

'Valentine Boscobel, though: dear God,' Wellington said, thin-lipped with disgust. 'One can't go anywhere in London now that doesn't stink of the shop, even if his mother has somehow managed to make herself all the crack.'

Dorothea smiled. 'You're just as hypocritical as you are old-fashioned, Arthur, really. If you can manage a lot of soldiers, surely you can tolerate a charming Cornish ordnance-dealer for the sake of his useful dependant?'

Wellington subjected her to a frozen stare, which he abandoned in the face of her smiling amiability, shaking his head.

'Well, never fear.' Nadezhda got up, briskly shaking out her skirts. 'Clemency Arwenack at least is the human equivalent of cold porridge: it would be impossible to ignite any sort of scandal in her presence, so you may stop worrying your heads on that score. If you don't mind, I'm going to change. I must ride out before my mare kicks a hole in the stable door. And send word to Helford. If the honourable lieutenant colonel chooses not to obey this summons, he'll soon learn of his mistake.'

The Duke of Wellington could reply only with a bow, and Nadezhda went out, smiling.

5

The copper bath was draped with fine white linen, set before a roaring fire in Nadezhda's dressing-room. Branches of a silver candelabrum blazed with light, casting long shadows on the painted panelling, and Nadezhda lay back in the steaming water, revelling in the heat: a miserable summer night in London was nothing to a true Russian winter but over the years she'd grown to feel the cold, and draughts poked and prodded like thieving fingers through every cavernous chamber in St James's Palace. Rain lashed at the tall windows, grim early twilight just visible between a crack in the curtains of heavy white brocade, even as she remembered chopping onions to make pike kotleti, and how she would afterwards sit at the kitchen table to eat a great heap of the hot patties with buttered kasha, savouring the crisp crust and fragrant, salty fish. It was another life that might just as well have belonged to someone else, Nadezhda thought now, watching steam rise from her bare toes as she lifted one steaming foot from the water. Thank God there was no state affair tonight.

It was no surprise at all when Dorothea stepped into the candlelit chamber, all hovering servants making themselves scarce on the instant. Stretching in the hot water, Nadezhda gestured at the carafe of imported medovukha resting on a gilt occasional table. Dorothea poured two glasses with unceremonious competence, passing a brimming crystal glass as though she'd spent her formative years in a tavern and not an extremely select convent. Dorothea was still in her day-dress of figured muslin: she'd want to be away soon, the carriage whisking her down the paved and torchlit expanse of St James's Street so she could dress to dine with her husband.

'I do hope you know what you're doing.' Dorothea sighed and sat in the chair by the bath, glossy dark ringlets carefully arranged over one slender shoulder. At almost forty, she instinctively sat with the candlelight at a flattering angle. 'Kit Helford. Really? Sometimes I have to wonder if you're quite sane.'

Nadezhda allowed the medovukha to trickle down her throat, savouring the honeyed sweetness. 'Listen, my fiancé is under the full control of the Austrian court, and I meant what I said to the duke: we'll do ourselves no favours if Austria supposes they can have all they wish at this peace congress affair.'

'Play at politics all you like. Believe it or not, I'd actually rather you weren't hurt emotionally. I do hope you're not being sentimental about Kit. He might have escorted you to England all that time ago, but now really isn't the time for childish attachments.' Dorothea swirled the golden liquid around in her glass. 'If you're foolish enough to have an affair with a Helford of Lamorna, at least wait until after you're married, although be warned, their bastards are always unmistakable. Even so, I take no issue with a dalliance.'

'Well, you should know all about that particular danger, but don't worry your head about it,' Nadezhda said lightly. 'I know how to have my fun without scuppering a whole peace treaty. It's the new lady-in-waiting I'm interested in. Obviously, you'll already have reported every aspect of my personal staffing to Petersburg and my dear papa. It's only polite to share the details.'

Dorothea frowned. 'Don't be arch. What do you expect? Obviously, Tsar Alexander takes just as great an interest in your affairs as he always has done.'

'That's putting it mildly.' Nadezhda let the glass dangle from her fingertips, her lips honeyed and sticky with the alcoholic tang. 'Was it darling Papa's notion to plant this Arwenack girl among my staff? What does Russia have to gain from it? Come on, who is she?'

'Oh really, now,' Dorothea said, laughing. 'Not everything is a conspiracy. As a matter of fact, the tsar has nothing to do with Clemency Arwenack, although I'm sure he'd approve – *don't* refer to him as your father, even in Russian and to me only, darling.' She smiled, sipping her medovukha. 'Actually, Clemency is my own notion, and sometimes I think you ought to appreciate me a little more than you do, especially if you're nursing a *tendre* for the future captain of your personal guard.'

Nadezhda raised both eyebrows. 'Really? Isn't she rather a nobody, really, and very young? I've seen her at a couple of balls and she seems nothing special to me.'

Dorothea laughed again, candlelight catching her lustrous pearl earrings. 'Precisely – a little provincial miss. Listen, people with a long way to fall are always useful. We'll see. As far as I'm aware, Miss Arwenack has been extremely careful to avoid any inadvisable liaisons. She's *very* fashionable, but no flirt, and she's got no money of her own, either, which does make all that sort of thing less likely, even if she is rather pretty in that wide-eyed ingénue style. Unfortunate freckles, though.'

'Except that you're convinced she's not as innocent as she looks? Well, I can't fault your logic.' Nadezhda sank into the warmth again, water sliding down her slender neck in runnels as she re-emerged. *People with a long way to fall.* Only a little fool would dwell on the fact that she was one of those herself: secret bastard of a dead princess, chancer, liar, heir to the throne. And only a little fool would long for a mother she'd never known: Dorothea was the closest she had to that, watching her now with such smiling intensity.

6

Fontainebleau, Île de France

Dawn light bled rose gold across the sky by the
time Clemency's maid Bluette escorted her across
the cobbled plaza in the centre of Fontainebleau, in
disapproving silence. The Boscobels been granted the use
of a smart townhouse with green louvred shutters and a
balcony overlooking a garden stocked with lavender and
bougainvillea, not far from the elevated environs of the
Hôtel de Montausier: as ever, Georgie had made good
use of her connections. Clemency's upper arm ached and
she still felt the pressure of the Prussian courtier's strong
fingers: he'd capitulated soon enough, though, even if his
grip had left her with bruises. It was his own fault. She'd
beaten him so thoroughly at faro he'd easily conceded to
her whispered offer of a compromise; it was just a request
for information, after all, and if that information allowed
Valentine to strike an advantageous deal for gunpowder

with the Prussian court, then why not? Georgie always said guilt was a selfish indulgence, and she was right. As Clemency watched, a child skittered out from an alleyway between two of the tall, elegant houses that fronted on to the plaza, skipping ahead of her mother, who wore a red scarf tied around her head and a reed basket strapped to her back. No more than five years old, the little girl's cap was tied haphazardly under her chin: it made Clemency want to straighten it for her, and she looked away.

'Are you all right, mademoiselle?' Bluette stared at her, and Clemency looked down to find the maidservant had taken hold of her arm, her eyes now wide with concern. 'You went that white I thought you'd been taken ill.'

The child and her mother had gone, leaving only an onion skin blowing away down the cobbled alley, and Clemency forced herself to ignore a surge of nausea: it had been a very long night, and she'd drunk a great deal of champagne.

'I'm perfectly fine. There was no need for you to escort me.' Clemency pressed a silver florin into the maidservant's hand as they stepped past Georgie's superannuated major-domo, Michel, who eyed them both as if they'd been soliciting in the street. The entrance hall was dingy, the marbled floor laced with grimy cracks illuminated by a solitary oil lamp flickering on an occasional table topped with tired Breton lace.

Bluette tucked a strand of wayward chestnut hair back beneath her cap, only a little mollified by the florin, which she tucked into her bodice. 'Oh yes, what are you then, mademoiselle? One and twenty? Two and twenty? Quite the old duenna of the town. In France, our young ladies are civilised. With all these soldiers and courtiers about, who knows what might happen to a girl like you?'

'Oh, go to bed,' Clemency said, with weary resignation. Bluette didn't have the first clue, thank God, but it hadn't taken long to get the measure of one another. Even so, she didn't need looking after. Her tone brooked no argument and Bluette obeyed without further discussion, whisking herself away to the servants' quarters. Clemency heard voices drifting along the carpeted passageway before she was even halfway up the stairs: God, there really was no rest for the wicked.

Valentine and Georgie were still in the drawing-room along with a handful of guests – Lady Burford among them, to judge by that trill of silvery laughter, more was the pity. Clemency leaned on the wall opposite the door, irritated by the hum of cut-glass aristocratic chatter – not that she was in any position to judge: she'd long since lost the soft Cornish burr of her childhood. The silk wall-hangings emanated a faint reek of damp and stale cigarillo smoke, and anyone with half an ounce of sense would go straight to bed. If Val and Georgie were desperate to learn the outcome of tonight's adventuring, Georgie would soon shake her awake. The drawing-room door swung open amid her moment of indecision, and Valentine stepped out into the corridor, looking a touch the worse for wear in his waistcoat and shirtsleeves, his curls rumpled.

He gave her a rueful smile. 'I thought I heard the door.' He reeked of claret, his skin touched gold by the sun.

'Your butler disapproves.'

'As well he might, young lady—' Valentine broke off,

glancing over his shoulder as more laughter rose up in the drawing-room. 'We're still entertaining.' He raised both eyebrows. 'Louisa Burford,' he mouthed, even as Georgie's voice rang out.

'Oh good Lord, Louisa, don't tell me there's no smoke without fire. And please don't mention fire in the same breath as Kit Helford!' Georgie cried from her favourite chaise beneath the window. 'Darling, tell me that naughty girl has come home?'

Clemency couldn't help despising herself a little for the hot red flush spreading from her cheeks down to her décolletage. Banishing Kit Helford from her mind, she stepped into the room, curtseying to her aunt and the small gathering of guests. Louisa Burford had terrorised Clemency's childhood for the brief period she'd been married to Kit and Lamorna's father, but the others were strangers only recently snared in Val and Georgie's net. Marks, most likely, people with everything to lose but yet something to gain by allowing themselves to be drawn into the Boscobels' set, from that older woman with the moth-eaten peacock feather pinned to her head-dress to the young Austrian officer fretting with the silver braiding on the cuff of his jacket. Clemency sank down on the chaise beside Georgie, leaning into her scented embrace.

'It's a great injustice how you always manage to look so fresh, darling,' Georgie said, laying down her cards.

Louisa Burford raised a single arched eyebrow, elegant as ever in a gown of clinging copper silk; to Clemency as a girl, she'd seemed like a creature from another world. 'Home at this hour, Miss Arwenack? You ought to take care – I hardly think your maid is a proper chaperone, and what passes for seemly behaviour in London or Cornwall is pretty unlikely to fly at court.'

Georgie smiled. 'Oh come now, Louisa, Clemency's not exactly a green young girl just out of the schoolroom.'

'She's not quite a respectable old maid, either,' Louisa replied, sweetly.

Clemency knew better than to offer a retort, and Louisa turned straight back to Georgie, obviously more than willing to pick over a fleshier carcass. 'Either way, one has to hope there's no truth in all this gossip about Princess Nadezhda and Kit Helford. I dare say her highness's betrothed won't look too kindly on it, and so much of the treaty depends on this marriage.'

'Louis Charles?' Georgie said archly. 'No, I would imagine not. I'm much too old to say so, but Kit is a peach – the worst type of competition for anyone, never mind all the scandal. He could kill you with his bare hands, but at the same time he always looks as if he's just about to laugh. Don't you agree, darling? You were such playmates – weren't they, Louisa?'

'Oh, he's pretty enough,' Clemency said. 'And I assume he knows it, too. They always do.'

Georgie laughed. 'Wise child. Well, whether you like it or not you'll be seeing a lot more of the gorgeous lieutenant colonel from now on.' Reaching into her reticule, she drew out a folded letter, letting it fall into Clemency's lap. With a flicker of a glance at Louisa, Georgie shot Clemency a wicked look from beneath her lashes. Whatever the content of the missive, it was calculated to annoy her friend. Stifling a yawn, Clemency opened it, wondering at the creamy weight of expensive paper beneath her fingertips even as she stared in breathless disbelief at the contents.

'They can't mean it,' she said, flatly, letting the letter fall on to the card-table.

'Does Countess Dorothea Lieven ever say anything that she doesn't mean?' Georgie's gleeful smile was a bad match for the warning expression in her eyes. 'Mistress of the Robes, Clemmie. It's perfection for you.'

By perfection, Georgie meant non-negotiable; there was a steely edge to her tone that Clemency had learned to respect. She didn't trust herself to speak. Not here, not with an audience. Georgie and Valentine would expect the usual. They'd want a route to an advantageous trade deal out of this, or useful information at the very least. Clemency was good at bringing men to the brink of ruin, but if she knew Kit Helford, she would barely need to try.

Louisa Burford very nearly spat. '*Mistress of the Robes? Clemency?*' Recovering herself, she sipped her brandy. 'Well, it's wonderful how progressive St James's is becoming. When I was a young girl, court was so hidebound. It's certainly a great piece of luck.'

'Oh, fustian, Louisa! You're just cross because everyone thought it was neck and neck between the Lennox chit and your sister's girl,' Georgie said, gaily. 'One needs experience for a position at court. A habit of diffidence and discretion. Clemency isn't just up to the task, she's an ideal fit for it. Countess Lieven is no one's fool.'

'Is she, though?' Louisa asked. 'Kit and Clemency will be spending a lot of time together, if he's captain of the royal guard. Georgie's right: you did used to run about with him rather a lot as a little girl, after all.'

'Yes, ma'am, sometimes,' Clemency said, aware that Georgie was watching her closely. Kit had never given two straws for the grandeur of his home, all gold-painted ceilings and portraits of ancestors, but she hadn't liked going there when they were children, and Louisa herself had put a stop to it as his stepmother; Clemency remembered her bending down in a gown of cool silk so that her face was at the same level as her own, those glossy dark curls lacquered by light spilling in through the tall window at the end of the great hall. Louisa had smiled then, with absolutely no humour at all.

'Now then, my dear Miss Arwenack,' she'd said, her breath smelling strongly of sugary rose pastilles. 'If you have any sense at all you won't let me see you here again. You're not a suitable playmate for Master Helford. Do you quite understand? Know your place.'

Clemency had nodded, hot tears of humiliation standing in her eyes.

No, Louisa had been right about one thing, all those years ago: she ought to have stuck to her own kind, because then Kit Helford would be no different a mark to the Prussian courtier she'd shivved only that evening, delivering one more victim into Valentine and Georgie's sphere of influence, and then none of this would have mattered.

As it was, she was going to have to play for time.

At Clemency's side on the chaise longue, Georgie gave them both a triumphant smile. 'Well, I can't lie – a position at court is certainly a step up, but all the better to have an old friend close at hand. Darling Kit will show you how you ought to go on. Don't you think so, Clemency?'

'She'll have to keep her wits about her if there's any truth in all this gossip about an affair between him and the princess,' Louisa said; she was like a terrier with a rat.

Across the room, Valentine glanced up from a round of cribbage with the peacock-feathered woman and gave her a quick, sympathetic nod; sometimes Clemency felt that she and Valentine communicated without speech, understanding one another as they did. It was already decided, then: Mistress of the Robes, a position at court. Court was a route to influence for anyone; the Boscobels, as ever, would not be content with what was usual for everyone else. *Damn.*

'I'm sure there'll be so many opportunities,' Georgie said, smiling. 'I couldn't be more delighted.'

Louisa glanced down at her well-shaped fingernails. 'I'm actually rather glad that my sister's girl is to keep her distance, as a matter of fact. She's still very young, and I'm sure Clemency has both the experience and common sense to steer well clear of any possible scandal. Although I'm sure I'd be the last person to pay any attention to foolish speculation about Lieutenant Colonel Helford and her highness.'

Clemency wanted to rush to the window and throw it open, drinking in all the fresh air she could, watching the market-traders set up to trade fish, honey, lavender and preserved sausage. She wanted to be one of them, just a girl hawking baskets and Marseilles soap with nothing ahead of her but an honest day's work.

Clemency got up and walked out, all a blur of watered-silk wall-hangings, pitted brass doorknobs and waxed floorboards. In her own chamber, a wave of exhaustion rolled over her, and she sat on the floor in the middle of the rug, abundant muslin skirts billowing as she remembered: Kit hadn't been able to stop laughing, that night, running at her side through the moonlit streets of Penzance with the stink of low tide in the air, the taste of brandy still on their lips, even as Mr Jenkin from the Star caught up with them, grabbing them each by one arm with his meaty hands.

'Bloody thieving brats! I'll see you hang—' Jenkin broke off when he got a good look at who he'd caught, releasing them both with a sudden jerk as they all stumbled into the moonlight. He spat on to the cobbles. 'His lordship will hear of this, Master Helford – you mark my words.'

'Good luck getting him to understand which day of the week it is, Mr Jenkin,' Kit had said, still laughing; his fine white cambric shirt had come unbuttoned and his black hair was a tangled mess; he was always the same combination of expensive chaos. 'Look, I'm sorry,' he said, with that smile that had got them both out of trouble so many times before. 'We didn't break open your barrel, I promise. The cork was out and I thought I might as well test the quality. Better than that letting your beautiful black-market 1789 run off into the drain, isn't it?'

'You're a bloody devil. Dragging the maid down with you, I suppose, your honour?' Jenkin said sourly. 'Get out of my sight, the pair of you.' He looked Clemency up and down, shaking his head, and she didn't have to ask Jenkin if he'd tell Grandpapa or not, because of course he would, and Grandpapa would just look at her in that way he did, so disappointed. It was worse than if he'd got angry, but Grandpapa was never angry with Clemency, only with damned bloody English aristocrats.

'You ought to take care, maid,' Jenkin went on. 'His honour might be able to get away with God knows what, but you'll soon enough find there's one rule for the likes of him and another for you and me. Go on home, for God's sake. There's redcoats all over the town tonight, as if we didn't have enough to manage with the bloody Preventives.' He jerked his head at Kit. 'Your brother among them, too, from what I've heard, so mayhap you will get the hiding you deserve after all.'

Kit sketched him a mock bow and Clemency snatched at his elbow. 'Come on! I'm sorry, Mr Jenkin. We should have told you about the brandy.'

Jenkin made no reply to that, just hawking tobacco-scented sputum on to the cobbles as he hunched an angry shoulder, moving away down Chapel Street past the Admiral Benbow with that seaman's rolling stagger he'd never quite lost.

Clemency dug her elbow into Kit's ribs as they walked away. 'You didn't have to cheek him like that, did you? I don't know how you have the nerve.'

'Oh, don't worry about it,' Kit said lazily, kicking a knotted ball of dried seaweed up the cobbled street. 'Jenkin can go to the devil.' He turned, flashing her a smile. 'We weren't doing anything wrong, after all. Or not that wrong.'

'Rubbish,' Clemency said. 'Come on home with me. I suppose your father' s still got that orgy or whatever it is going on up at your house.'

'Courtesans all over the bloody place.' He spoke with an edge of false bravado that no one else would have noticed.

A quarter-hour later, after running side by side through the streets of the town, they climbed over the wall into the little paved yard behind the bindery where Mrs Teague, who did for Grandpapa, had pegged the washing. Sheets, small-clothes and nightgowns hung in the moonlight like white ghosts. The shop was dark and shuttered, but a small leaded window glowed yellow up high, with the moon risen behind the chimneys and rooftops. Grandpapa was in the workshop above the library, then.

Letting themselves in through the back door, she and Kit slipped through the little kitchen where the fire was banked down for the night; either Mrs Teague or Grandpapa had left out a cloth-covered plate and they stood at the table eating fresh bread spread with thick butter, sliced ham and sweet, salty pickled onions that burst in your mouth. Clemency knew Kit wouldn't want to go home that night at all, not with the way things were at Nansmornow, so, without discussion, they crept past the shuttered bookshop and up the creaking back stairs to the bindery where Grandpapa was standing over the worktable in his Chinese smoking jacket, a lamp at his side.

He barely looked up from his work as they hurried past, and Kit followed Clemency up the ladder up to the loft where they'd slept side by side so many times. Mrs Teague always said that one day His Honour Master Helford would go away to school and he wouldn't be friends with Clemency any more, and all to the good, in Mrs Teague's own opinion, as if anyone cared to listen to that.

They lay on their bellies side by side like a pair of mackerel in a bucket, nothing but hard floorboards beneath, looking down from the loft into the shadowy workshop, lamplight from the high shelf glinting off Grandpapa's bald head: he'd taken off his old-fashioned wig and left it on a chair where it sat like a lady's lapdog.

'I love watching him at work,' Kit said quietly. 'My father just doesn't do anything, or not that you'd want to see. What's he about now?' he went on, nudging her.

'Double endpapers, by the look of it. He showed me how the day before yesterday.' Clemency frowned. 'He doesn't normally bother to do them himself, though.'

'*Look!*' Kit said, snatching hold of her arm.

She followed Kit's gaze as her grandfather took up a slip of thin foolscap, no bigger than her own little finger, concealing it between the marbled endpaper and an endpaper signature. The foolscap was so fragile and Grandpapa so clever with the paste that the hidden scrap would be almost invisible to the naked eye once the book was finished, just the faintest outline, and even that disguised by the coloured marbling. Even so, the tiniest imperfection would be a cost to Grandpapa's pride. Kit and Clemency turned to stare at each other in mutual shocked silence.

Alone in her bedchamber at Fontainebleau, Clemency sat on the floor, staring with numb fixation at her satchel, slotted neatly between the bed and nightstand, lamplight catching the battered brown leather. She reached out for it, and her hands really were shaking now.

You're a damned little fool.

Her fingers closed around the strap, but she didn't press the old brass clasp, knowing so well what was inside: the small nipping press Grandpapa had given her when she was very young and her pillow was wet with tears every night; those spools of thread; a ream of unstitched paper; the small pot of wax; her box of colours; her paintbrushes; her pots of ink; the quill that needed repairing; her awl. All that was left of her old life; very nearly all that was left of her old self, saving that which it hurt too much to examine. Hadn't she long since given up every part of herself that still bore any value or importance?

1

The fire had long since sunk down to an orange-sized ball of glowing embers, even as morning light flooded in – Bluette knew by now that Clemency never went to bed with the shutters closed. Staring up at the embroidered bed-canopy, she swore softly; there was still one taper burning low, the flame rendered almost invisible by judgemental daylight. Sleep was hours away, if it came at all. God, how that Prussian's face had crumpled when she laid down her final card. There was something sacrilegious about it, watching a grey-haired, distinguished sort like that brought almost to tears.

Allowing her thoughts to wander when in a maudlin frame of mind was a risk too far. Clemency sat up, leaning back against a mound of feather pillows and creased linen. *Move.* Swinging her legs out of bed, she hugged herself against the morning chill and left the room barefoot.

She let herself into the tiny library, nightgown billowing

out behind her, and found the two entire walls lined with books, gilded spines catching the candlelight – Leviticus, Dante, Madame de Lafayette, *Les Liaisons Dangereuses*. It was almost as if Grandpapa were still here with her, his fingers glittering with gold leaf. At least he'd never know what she'd become, all the things she'd done for Georgiana Boscobel, and for Valentine, too. Outside, one of the gardeners was early to work: she forced herself to listen to the faint snick of the shears every few moments as he began to deadhead the roses. Better that than daydreaming like a fool about what could not be helped or changed.

Sunlight dappled the faded Indian carpet, striking the gilt frame of a Parisian landscape scene, and even as Clemency reached out for a battered copy of *Glenarvon*, she heard voices. *Low* voices, coming from the drawing-room next door: Valentine and Georgie had still not gone to bed, then, and glancing at the carriage clock on the mantelpiece she saw that it lacked but a few minutes before a quarter to six. Hurrying across the carpet barefoot, Clemency sank into the armchair nearest the adjoining wall: eavesdropping might be a pretty low habit, but where the Boscobels were concerned it was a matter of self-preservation. Staring at the cracked and peeling green paint on the panelling, she heard Georgie quite clearly, her voice rising a few notes.

'I'm just concerned that you've promised too much, that's all. Shouldn't you have held back at this stage?'

'Don't be a fool, Mama,' Valentine said briskly. 'The practicalities should be easy enough to manage, especially with Clemency's new position.'

'She'll be squeamish about it, darling, mark my words. She's exactly the sort to be sentimental about Kit Helford and that kind of childhood attachment, and we may very well find that she baulks at blackmailing him – dress it up how you may: it is what it is.' Georgie let out a spurt of laughter. 'Don't be surprised if you weren't her first romantic hero, that's all.'

Clemency drew her bare feet up beneath her, hugging a tapestried cushion to her chest; the silence in the other room crashed and clanged like pots and pans dropped on a flagstone floor. It was worse hearing it spelled out in plain English.

'Sometimes I think you read too many novels, Mama,' Valentine said, with all his usual smooth ease. He sounded so convincing that Clemency could easily picture Georgie's puckered brow, and how she would be feeling as Valentine smiled: of course she was a little fool, making something out of nothing. Of course. There was nothing to do but go back to bed.

Late morning sunlight shafted into the room along with a welcome stream of fresh air tinged with the reek of the marketplace: old fruit, high meat and animal dung. She'd only slept for a handful of hours at the most, thank God. It couldn't be more than half past ten – the tea on her bedside table was still hot; Georgie wouldn't take her chocolate in bed till almost noon, and even Valentine wouldn't emerge from his own room for a while yet. Forcing herself out of bed, she squatted over the chamber pot to pass water. Legs aching, Clemency yawned as she cleaned herself with a linen cloth and cold water from the jug, scrambling into her clothes. It was Bluette's morning out, which was just as well: she couldn't face the maidservant's all-knowing glances. Thank God for front-lacing stays, that was all. Her head pounded as she tipped powdered hartshorn into the tea cooling at her bedside, draining the cup in one. Clemency knew she was lucky: these days, the wine never, ever made her slip, even if it did help her forget.

Dressed in velvet-trimmed cambric and an ochre spencer cut to her exacting requirements, she found Michel already at his post by the front door, redolent of camphor and disapproval in a dour black jacket worn greenish at the elbows. Georgie's economies with the servants were such a useful barometer that her latest request hadn't come as a surprise: *Darling, there's a Prussian courtier who really ought to be of use to Val.* It was all so bloody sordid.

Clemency stepped outside into the little front garden, breathing in the soft warmth of the lavender hedges, the sun upon her back; she had to grasp at these little moments of pleasure that had nothing to do with the Boscobels or their never-ending requirements. Letting herself out of the wrought-iron gate, she found shaded market-stalls crammed on to the cobbled plaza: baskets of huge, misshapen red tomatoes, bolts of printed muslin, embroidered tablecloths, eels in buckets and hanging rabbits dripping blood from their eyes on to the cobbles, the great palace resplendent on the far side of the plaza, all red brick and vast, glittering window. If Val and Georgie had their way, she'd be moving into new rooms within the royal quarters, all the better to serve her highness – alongside Lieutenant Colonel Kit Helford. It couldn't happen: not yet.

Moving swiftly through the crowd, Clemency turned her back on the palace and made for a quiet side-alley: she knew where to come. Even after five years, his lordship was always meticulous in ensuring Clemency knew how to contact him, should the need arise. Now she had no choice. The narrow townhouse had shutters painted a faded shade of blue, and wizened geraniums competed gamely with dandelions in a neglected window box. Clemency had the key safe in her reticule, cold iron at her fingertips. Turning it in the lock, there was a moment's resistance before the door swung open, revealing a dark passageway leading to a flight of stairs. Clemency let the door swing shut behind her: if she'd been seen, it was already too late to do anything about it.

My dear, always behave as if you are meant to be precisely where you are. That's what Lord Lamorna had always told her, so long ago, and he was right: taking a look over her shoulder would only make her look suspicious. With the tiny window shuttered, the tiled passageway and staircase were dark and gloomy, and she had to feel her way with one hand resting on a well-used banister greasy to the touch. She heard the birds before she saw them – a throaty, warbling song that reminded her of waking in her old attic bedroom at the bindery shop when Grandpapa was still alive, before she'd made the first of so many mistakes, but she couldn't think about that; you had to move on, you couldn't dwell on the past.

Clemency let out a long exhalation of relief as she

opened the door to find a row of pigeons sitting on the windowsill, shutters flung wide open to the blue summer sky. The neglected bedchamber was draped in dust-sheets, which was all to the good – the birds had left their mark, coming in and out, the sheets were streaked white with their leavings. She went to the dressing table and found all she needed in the drawer: pen, ink, lightweight paper. Sinking down on to her knees, Clemency composed her message in the numerical code Lord Lamorna had taught her so long ago. Folding and rolling the paper, she inserted it into the tiny brass cartridge and let the silver-grey pigeon hop on to her outstretched wrist. Her first message to his noble bloody lordship in five long years. Was he still looking out for them? Would he even read it? Burning nausea rushed up her throat at the thought of Valentine and Georgie finding out, but there was no choice. She had to take the risk. Briefly, she closed her eyes.

Here we go again.

Clemency allowed the bird to fly away, watching it hurtle across the hot blue sky above the market square, and only then did she breathe – or that was how it felt, at least, a merciful release of pressure.

8

In London, several hours earlier, two black-clad footmen heaved a butt of water up the Hellfire Club's back stairs, sweating and grimacing as they gained a lamplit landing tiled in green and white marble. A servant in identical livery held open a door, his expression unchanging even as water slopped on to his polished shoes, and the two footmen edged into a drawing-room where the capital's most dissolute elite engaged in ruinous entertainment.

Despite the lateness of the hour, a small crowd had gathered between tables arranged around panelled walls hung with oil-painted pornography in heavily gilded frames. Heaving the slopping butt between them, the footmen set it down where the Marquis of Dereham's groom knelt upon the carpet. They were both well trained enough to ignore the aristocratic young gentlemen calling out jocular advice. The water stank; it had come from the pump in a squalid cobbled yard behind the club. The kneeling groom remained motionless. Head bowed, he wore the expression of a man who despite everything could still not believe this was really happening to him.

'Ten to one he can do eight minutes. Eight minutes under water, Dereham, or I'll see you damned.'

'Twelve, man – I said twelve. Twenty thousand says he can breathe for twelve minutes under water.' Dereham gestured expansively towards the Hellfire's discreet maître d', Wesley, who had the betting book laid out on one of the baize side-tables. 'Wesley, is not the bet already entered into the book? Twelve minutes.'

'Yes, milord. It is.' Wesley coughed, carefully not looking at the groom kneeling on the floor barely three feet away from him. The fellow had a military bearing, likely one of the many decommissioned soldiers so desperate for work since the peace that he'd take a post with a vicious young greenhorn like Dereham. It was a crying shame, but not worth Wesley's position to speak up: he was no fool. It wouldn't be the first time a night at the Hellfire had ended with a corpse going down the back steps, not – in Wesley's experience – in an establishment frequented by violently rich and aristocratic young white men who could get away with what they liked.

Dereham smirked at his audience, obviously relishing the attention as one of his satellites spoke up from the crowd.

'Wait, wait, wait. Has anyone even asked the fellow if he consents to breathe under water? No one can deny it's a bold claim.'

Dereham tossed off another glass of champagne, all paid for on his father's account. 'Oh, what does it matter? Very well, no one could call us brutish, could they, Gillings? My good man, do you agree to breathe under water for eight minutes – no, twelve minutes?'

'Milord!' The groom's eyes had taken on a wild expression.

'See, he's perfectly happy with the notion—'

'*Leave it.*' A voice carried across the room from a window-seat, addressing the Marquis of Dereham as though he were a badly trained spaniel. The habit of command was unmistakable, the insult eye-popping. The speaker chose not to move from his seat; in low candlelight it was only clear that he was tall, his long legs crossed at the ankle, with a glimmer of gold braiding at his shoulders. He was with a small group of intimates, all in the mess jackets of various very smart Guards regiments.

Young Dereham smiled, but couldn't help betraying a slight shifty nervousness, which was only too understandable in Wesley's view, now that he saw who had spoken. You didn't want to mess with that.

'What the devil do you mean by interrupting a wager, Helford?' Dereham was on the fret now, no two ways about it, and you couldn't blame him, either.

'Milord—' Wesley ventured, but no one listened to him. Of course they didn't. They were all too busy carefully not looking at Lieutenant Colonel the Honourable Kit Helford. There could be no quibbling about the glittering military career, or the fortune that had come to him from a grandmother, or the string of high-end mistresses, the latest one only recently cast off with all due charm. Helford was that rare creature: a second son just as filthily rich as he was spoiled, and the target of every canny matchmaking mother since the day of his own come-out, never mind that he was also a gazetted arsonist and had once escaped a hanging rope in the middle of a riot during the French Occupation. He had history, all right: Wesley knew his regulars, and Helford was gallows bait ten times over, had his honour been born to a poor man and not a Cornish earl, of course.

Now, though, Helford continued to deal for his companions as though nothing had happened, and young Dereham gave a nasty smile, casting a quick look about for his own friends who, to their credit, remained crowding around the silent kneeling groom and the butt of water soaking filth into the Aubusson rug. The Aubusson hadn't been cheap, in point of fact, a black-market affair from the crooked captain of an East Indiaman, but Wesley had got worse than stagnant water out of his carpet before now.

Dereham sneered again, addressing the corner of the room, which was all he could do because his challenger hadn't even bothered to look up, let alone get out of his seat. 'What's the difficulty, sir? Are you afraid to watch? Why else would you interfere with another man's wager? *It's in the book.*'

The room went very quiet then, but there was no more acknowledgement from the table by the window that Dereham even existed.

One of the marquis's friends spoke up into a ringing silence: the short one with thick fair hair. 'I dare say Dereham is right. Once a wager's in old Wesley's tome, it's a matter of honour. Gillings can't back out. Nor can Dereham. Best get the thing done, Helford.'

An audible sigh. When the reply finally came, it held a

note of suppressed amusement. 'But it's not a wager, it's a fucking idiotic charade.'

Another hush fell, thicker and deeper than before, and Wesley was just aware of a ripple of nervous mirth from somewhere near the door. This night was going to cost him, going to cost the club, too. Dereham turned to his friends with the smiling expertise of the schoolroom bully.

'What, is Helford some sort of coward? Surely not.' Dereham addressed him again – unwisely in Wesley's opinion, not that anyone cared to hear it. 'My good man, if you can't bear a little tension, then have you really come to the right club? The bet has already been laid.'

'Darling, wagering is for grown men and women.' The laughter hadn't quite left Helford's voice, and neither had he adjusted his luxurious long-limbed sprawl, nor had he even looked up from his hand of cards. Briefly, Wesley closed his eyes: Christ, what a mess.

Dereham threw a theatrical glance at the nearest of his friends. 'How *is* her royal highness, Helford?' With sudden and shocking violence, the marquis took his groom by both shoulders, plunging him head first into the water.

The pistol shot rang out, deafening. Thick, yellowish smoke filled the room. Wesley choked on the stink of gunpowder, and then a lot happened at once: Dereham's groom surged away from the water butt, rocking back on his heels as he spewed green water across the room. The marquis himself was stretched out upon the floor in a spreading pool of blood amid a sharp, hot stink of urine. By the time the smoke had cleared, Helford still hadn't got to his feet, although in point of fact he was the only person in the room who moved at all, quietly dealing cards. No one made a sound: Wesley felt as though he were witnessing the entire thing from a vast distance. Of course, any sort of panic seemed ridiculous considering that Helford himself was now absorbed in his round of piquet, talking to his fellow Guardsmen without even bothering to look up, as though he shot to kill every other day – which, Wesley supposed, he usually did, a man on the battlefield more often than he was off it, until that devil Napoleon had agreed to treat for peace, anyhow.

'Shall we have more claret?' Helford asked, lazily. 'I don't mind moving on to brandy.'

He didn't even bother to tell Wesley to clear up the mess.

9

A day later, Kit Helford crossed Hay Lane in the clear light of dawn, idly considering rooms at the Albany; was it wrong to go home with a head full of equal parts bhang and green goddess and the scent of ambergris all over his cravat? Such considerations had never stopped his father or his brother; in those days, the courtesans were all over the house. But there had not been a mistress at Lamorna House then, or a seven-year-old girl spreading pressed violets all over the drawing-room table. Berkeley Square basked in the sunlight, and thick heads of yellow pollen drifted from the plane tree in the railed oval garden, all so damnably run of the mill and familiar, and yet so far from what he was used to: the rattle of camp kettles; men cleaning weaponry and bartering with camp-followers for scavenged chickens or to sew on a button; the fug of woodsmoke; gallows humour instead of all this finicking two-faced politeness. It was so early that even old Mowbray wasn't up yet and an alarmed young housemaid let Kit in with a silent curtsey, a green linen apron pinned to the front of her faded gown.

'Good morning, Greta.' His smile made the girl flush right down to her neck, but he hardly registered that; the scent of fresh coffee drifted from the breakfast-parlour, and he found that the shutters were open but the yellow silk curtains still drawn, the room suffused with heavy golden light. Lady Lamorna herself reclined on the chaise beneath the window; his sister-in-law was still in her nightgown, a rust-red silk scarf wrapped around her cloud of light curls. Propping herself up on one shapely elbow, she dismissed a clearly terrified Greta, and then Hester was on her feet in moments, facing him with her dark eyes blazing and an ancient christening blanket of knitted lacework clutched around her shoulders; normally a rich light-brown, her face was almost grey, her cheeks alarmingly sunken.

'*Two minutes,*' Hester said, taking a swift, unsteady step towards him. 'I don't care how many battalions you've got under your command – you have precisely two minutes to explain yourself.'

'Hets!' Kit took her in his arms, alarmed. 'You look damnably hipped. What on earth are you doing in here at this hour?'

Hester broke away, still furious as she gesticulated with wordless frustration at the silver dishes of gooseberry and quince jam laid out on immaculate pressed linen. 'Oh, never mind that. It's the only room that doesn't have the most nauseating smell of carbolic, or if it does the coffee overpowers it.'

He stared at her in sudden understanding, grinning.

'You're increasing, aren't you? Been casting up your accounts over it, by the look of you. Never seen anyone look so green, you poor darling.'

Hester waved away this revelation. 'Never mind that. The whole of London is in an absolute uproar, and I for one should like to know just exactly what you have to say for yourself.'

He yawned, releasing her. 'Oh, did Dereham die, then? Awful man. Will you tell Crow I shall go to Manton's with him later, but not until after twelve? I'm for my bed.'

'No you are not!' Hester hissed, collapsing back on to the chaise with a stifled groan as he turned to pour himself coffee, all servants having wisely absented themselves. 'The Marquis of Dereham isn't dead yet – or he wasn't when his father came here last night. Not but that it wouldn't serve you right if he did die. You just shot him and then went raging around every opium den and fleshpot in London, by the look of you, cool as a pineapple-ice, and for the whole of yesterday, too. Oh, Kitto, what have you done?'

Kit raked both hands through his hair, a little alarmed by her diminished state. 'Well, I'm sorry for that, anyway. I should not have troubled you and Crow with Bloxworth for all the world. But come on, Hets, Dereham was drowning his own groom and the fellow was a Guardsman. Or he had been, anyway. Either way, he didn't deserve to die like a dog. Dereham does, though.'

Supine on the chaise, Hester stared at him, her eyes narrowed. 'Nonsense – you just enjoy killing people, in point of fact, and you're not meant to. Anyway, I suppose you don't know the prime minister is waiting for you in the library with your brother.'

'What?' He paused, still holding the silver coffee pot, steam issuing gently from the spout. 'The Duke of Wellington?'

'He *was* the prime minister last time I checked.'

He glanced at the brass carriage clock that had crowned the mantelpiece in here for as long as he could remember; it was a quarter to seven in the morning.

'Would you like some brandy in that coffee?' Hester asked with awful precision. 'There's still some in the carafe in the drawing-room if you do.'

Kit laughed, bent to drop a brotherly kiss on her forehead and went out with his cup.

Twenty minutes later, washed, dressed and shaved by his imperturbable valet, Phelps, Kit let himself into the library. He found the Duke of Wellington at the desk and his brother the Earl of Lamorna sitting on the fire surround, smoking a cigarillo with their father's very old Dalmatian dozing at his feet. Sailor, soldier, spy, tattooed polyglot, expert liar, Crow looked much as Kit remembered Papa: tall and dark, with that streak of grey behind one ear, and his very own air of unruly éclat. Eleven years Kit's senior, Crow still dealt in intelligence when called upon: he had the lion's share of the family's subtlety and could be devastatingly unreliable when he felt like it; Kit knew very well that, of the two of them, he was the blunt instrument. He'd weathered the sharp end of Crow's tongue often enough to be certain that 95 per cent of his brother's barely concealed fury was directed at the Duke of Wellington: what was he doing here? Surely the Dereham affair was far below the notice of the prime minister?

'Good of you to join us,' Crow said mildly, tapping ash into the grate.

'The pleasure's all mine,' Kit retorted. Actually really longing for his bed now, he dropped into a crouch at the Dalmatian's side, rubbing her behind the silky black-spotted ears, and allowing her to brush his fingers with her warm tongue. 'Who's my good girl, then?' He spoke to her in Cornish; then he rose to cross the room, leaning on the bookshelves by the long sash window to address his brother. 'Well, sir?'

Crow didn't bother to suppress a flash of sardonic amusement. 'I'll leave that to the duke, you chaotic young nightmare.'

'In point of fact, I have two items of good news, Helford,' Wellington said. 'Number one, Dereham survived the night, which is a good sign, not that it appears to concern you in the slightest. Secondly, you're not to join the ranks of my half-pay officers after all, not that you need the money. You're to accompany Her Royal Highness Princess Nadezhda to the peace negotiations at Fontainebleau as captain of her personal guard. That's what I came here to say, or part of it. However, it's more complicated than that. Obviously, her highness is going to require a highly expert level of protection at Fontainebleau, but there is also an element of diplomacy.'

'I should rather think there is,' Crow said. 'Whose idea

was it to declare her highness's suitor before the treaty? Surely not Fred Robinson and Canning?'

'Bloody factions at Whitehall,' Wellington said; it was as close as he would get to admitting he had been temporarily outflanked, Kit realised. Crow was a Whig to the bone, though, and politically opposed to Wellington on almost every issue, so there was a limit to what the duke would tell him, formally at least. God only knew what they discussed off the record when it came to matters of intelligence. As ever, the duke would retreat until he could be sure of a victory. 'The princess's personal guard is to be a collaborative force,' Wellington went on. 'It's a matter of smoothing ruffled feathers, but your second-in-command is to be a Frenchman of Napoleon's choosing.'

For a moment, Kit stood very still; Wellington stared back. Crow just looked infuriatingly entertained by the whole affair.

'No,' Kit said, throwing up the sash window; he stood for a moment and leaned out, watching tufts of yellow plane blossom drift from the trees behind the wrought-iron fence in the middle of the square, so that neither of them could see the expression on his face, although Crow could likely guess at it, damn his eyes. 'I'm sorry,' he said, 'but I must disoblige her highness, and you too, sir.'

'It's not a request.' Wellington looked as if he wished he was enjoying coffee and devilled kidneys, far away from Lamorna House.

'I have no wish to renew any form of acquaintance with the crown princess,' Kit said abruptly.

'*Doucement*, Kitto,' Crow said, with a below-the-belt deployment of his Cornish childhood name.

He took hold of the windowsill, looking down at his own long, hard fingers gripping the painted wood. 'I'm sorry, but no,' he repeated. 'I'll sell out first.'

'Oh, for God's sake,' Wellington snapped. 'We have no need of your tantrums, Helford.'

'Bloxworth is an obstacle,' Crow said, 'which leaves you with a small difficulty now.'

'How should it?' Kit said, turning to look at them both. 'Dereham was drowning a man for a wager.'

'Look,' Wellington cut in. 'There's enough scurrilous gossip about you and the princess already – that at least is not your fault, I'll warrant you, but my God this hasn't helped. Christ knows I'm only too well aware what those bloody pamphleteers are like. And at least ten men who were in the drawing-room at the Hellfire that night swore directly to me that you only fired once her highness was mentioned by name. No one will ever believe it was really about saving the life of Dereham's groom, whatever your own motivations were.'

'So what are you saying, sir?' Kit asked, with forced calm. 'That if I don't accept this command, the papers will only print more rubbish about me? I really don't care.'

'Yes, well, it's not only about you, unfortunately,' Crow said, tossing the end of his cigarillo into the fireplace. He was all laundered white linen and impeccable tailoring, his black hair touched with that distinguished silver and still a little damp from the morning wash basin; Kit by comparison felt even more dishevelled in the regimentals he'd been wearing since Thursday.

Crow glanced at Wellington. 'With respect, Duke, I couldn't give a damn about Nadezhda's reputation, or the Crown, or her marriage negotiations, or the Whigs or the Tories or the Ultras, or any of it.' He turned back to Kit, speaking now in Cornish. 'Listen, giving in to your murderous instincts was an error of judgement. You're a Helford of Lamorna. You might be as good as above the law, but the rumours and scandal ought to concern you. Who do you expect to be damaged by that? It's Hester and even Morwenna who will suffer for this, not you.' Crow glanced at Wellington and switched back to English. 'It's nearly the end of the Season, but that's actually worse, as you really ought to know: a few weeks for discussion to mount before you dish up an entire summer and autumn's worth of gossip to every house party between Cornwall and the Highlands. You must be out of sight and out of mind now, not in three weeks' time. Number one, you will go to France as her highness's bodyguard so that everyone is far too busy dissecting that information to care if Dereham dies or not. Number two, you will discharge that duty with such rigid decorum that everyone in London and Paris comes to utterly disregard the notion of any other connection between you and the princess.'

Kit's grasp on his temper had only been fragile to begin with. 'You're actually no longer in a position to compel me to do anything. I'm not a child.'

'Well, then stop behaving like one,' Crow said.

For a moment, they faced each other across the room,

Crow with infuriating calm, Kit with perfectly restrained anger, the Duke of Wellington completely forgotten by Kit if not by the head of his family. Crow was right. It was the height of childishness to defy his brother's expressed wishes like some sort of idiotically wilful debutante just because he was no longer obliged to obey his every last word. He'd never excelled at doing that, at any rate, and had paid the price for it on more than one occasion. Now there was no price to pay – only the knowledge that Crow was right. He thought of Hester on the chaise in the breakfast-room, turning her face away from him. How could the natural order of pregnancy make a woman so ill, nearly all of her vitality drained away? And that was before you even got to the birth. What if she died then, just as his own mother had done?

It took every effort to address his brother and Wellington with something approaching calm. 'Fine. When shall I go?'

10

That evening, Kit sat in the drawing-room at Lamorna House in his shirtsleeves, sketching a collection of freesias and blowsy late tulips, a carafe of claret at his elbow. Mowbray had insisted on a fire in the grate and heat filled the room with the scent of freesia, which only made him feel more tired: he still hadn't been to bed. Kit knew Hester had come to watch him long before she spoke, but with her own artist's sensibility she didn't interrupt. He turned to face her, smiling but appalled at how drawn she still looked. She stood in her wrap of Japanese silk with one hand on the mantelpiece, head cocked as she glanced down at his preliminary sketches, her hair loose in an abundant mass of light curls.

'Very nice,' she said. 'I have a whole new package of charcoals if you want some. I find that sketching makes me dizzy and I can't bear the smell of paint.'

'How damnable for you, Hets.' He knew very well

that without the solace of painting or the distraction of adventure her mind was apt to fix on anxieties. Of those there were plenty, and in no small part thanks to his own actions.

'I dare say it's worse for Morwenna – her governess has just gone off to be married to a shipping clerk, you know, and here I am, no company at all.' Hester sighed. 'The worst of it's that it actually makes sense to listen to your great-aunt – Thérèse insists that Morwenna should spend the summer with her at Fontainebleau. I do hate it when she's right: she only becomes more insufferable. You know how I feel about us being apart, let alone the prospect of a sea voyage, but Morwenna adores her.'

'I don't know why: the woman's a martinet. What are you doing in here, anyway? You ought to be lying down in your bed. What would Crow say?'

'The sickness eases off a little in the evening, for some reason, and never mind your brother. He's gone to Brooks's. Did you work off all that angry spleen at Manton's? Better you shoot at targets than at awful young men, I suppose. Crow says your aim is so acute it's genuinely rather frightening: your eye has got no worse, at least.'

Kit set down his pen. 'One has to be competent at something. God, we really must be in dire straits if Jack is given to socialise.'

Hester just smiled at him. 'It's peculiar: perhaps it's because you're apart from us for years at a time, but sometimes when I look at you I'm still shocked to find you a grown man, and yet in so many ways you don't change at all. You always used to do this when you were angry and troubled – sketching flowers, I mean. No, I'm increasing and disgustingly sick with it – you must allow me to be sentimental if it pleases me.'

He turned so they were sitting face to face and poured another glass of wine from the carafe Mowbray had solicitously left for him, sliding it across the polished walnut table towards her. 'I'd do anything to please you, as you well know. Come to the point: it's not like you to prevaricate.'

'Oh, very well. When you go to France, I must insist that you do exactly as Crow has asked; he told me what he said to you.'

'I know. I'm to head off a scandal.' Kit looked at her across the table. Crow was right; never mind Dereham himself: this was the worst of what he had done. 'I've been inexcusable, Hets. I should have used my head and thought about how my own idiotic behaviour might affect you. And Morwenna, too. I know things are different for you. Not as easy.'

Hester took a sip of her wine, fixing him with a steady gaze over the rim of her glass. 'Well, yes, I suppose you could put it that way. Ten to one some gossip will find a way of attaching blame for this to me, and to Morwenna by extension, which is another reason to have her out of the way with Thérèse. Her smallest indiscretion will otherwise become even more of a target for malice. You realise, of course, that she and I are held to a far higher standard of behaviour than most other women and girls that you know. Morwenna looks white, but she'll still be harshly judged to an extent.'

Kit hadn't known shame like it. 'I know it won't change

what I've done, but I'm deeply sorry, Hets. I can't begin to tell you.'

'No, I should think you can't,' Hester said, with simple but devastating anger. 'That's not all, though. I won't have you making Crow unhappy.'

'What? Much he cares!' Kit swerved from shame to incredulity: one never knew which way was up, being taken to task by Hester. Crow himself had once tersely confided that it was akin to swimming into a ten-foot wave.

Her eyes shone, dark and expressive. 'No, listen to me – I've known you long enough to read you like a book, Christopher Helford. I expect you find it pretty sickening that Crow is holding you to account when what you've done is far less bad than the worst he ever managed. I bet he gave orders that you go to France for my sake, in that infuriating way as if he were your colonel. Well, listen: it's not just for my sake that you must go, or even Morwenna's, but for his as well as your own. The thing is, he wants you to be content.'

'Oh come on, I deserve it with both barrels on your and Morwenna's account, but now you're just being mawkish.' Kit had gone into battle enough times to understand that she was only being so frank because there was every chance he might not return before her time came with the child; this could be one of the last evenings they spent together, but he'd be damned if he had to accept it.

'And wait while one of you does something idiotically self-destructive instead of actually facing up to whatever has caused the upset?' Hester said in her own relentless way. 'You know very well that I can't allow you to cut up your brother's peace – it was hard won. And believe it or not, when you're miserable, it makes him very unhappy indeed. What on earth will you do now that the war is over? Lurch from scandal to scandal and then try to forget it all in majoun shops like the one you were in last night and the night before?'

'I don't know. I suppose my regiment might go to India, but I've no interest in that sort of damnable sanctimonious warfare. Napoleon was an honest fight, at least, but that's finished. It's all grasping over trade routes now. I know Crow wants me to manage Oakhurst, but to tell you the truth I've no interest in Kent, either.'

'All these estates and big houses you're encumbered with, how exhausting.'

'Well, it's only one in my case, but I know, I know.' He could hardly tell her now that all he really wanted was to go home to Cornwall. Not when the child in her belly would likely disinherit him or more likely his own children if he had them.

'You really did have a good war, didn't you?' Hester said, reading his mind as she so often still did. 'Sometimes I wonder if it wasn't a bit too good. Don't forget you have skills other than exterminating people.'

He smiled, then. 'Like drawing and painting? What would Crow have to say about that, I wonder? It's all very well him owning mines and shipping fleets, but I don't think it would go down very well with his lordship if I set up as a shabby-genteel portrait painter.'

'As I recall he didn't want you to join the army, either, but here you are, one of her highness's most decorated young officers,' Hester said at her most acerbic. 'Whenever you disobeyed your brother's most expressed wishes, you always did it with such spectacular attention to detail.' Hester swirled the dark red wine around in her glass. 'Just remember how miserable Nadezhda made you, all that time ago – her highness, or whatever they're calling her now. I don't care who she is, but she's not the girl to see you happy.'

She was the only person who could say such things to him, and so Kit smiled at her again, pushing away a six-year-old memory of Nadezhda Romanova riding before him, her body pressed against his, so long ago. There had been no saddle then, just a golden Turkoman mare and a wide-open expanse of Russian grassland. That girl no longer existed, and neither did the freedom they'd tasted, all that time ago. His only task was to shield and protect the woman she had become, and this was all that mattered.

With a frustrated sigh Hester held out her arms to him. He held her close. She was so much smaller than him now; for such a long time the nearest he'd had to a mother. 'I will. I won't fail you, I swear. I'm sorry,' he said into her hair, knowing only too well that it was not enough.

Returning to the drawing-room the following morning after a solid nine hours of depthless sleep and a large plate of beefsteak, eggs and quince jam, Kit found his small niece Morwenna now battling her father over a complicated game involving pots of ink, quills and quantities of discarded foolscap paper. She was sitting on Crow's lap in a cloud of sashed white muslin, green satin slippers discarded on the Turkey rug, her fair curls bent low over the table, fiercely engaged in writing something as Crow watched her with a slightly abstracted air.

'Papa,' Morwenna said, turning to look to him. 'Papa, you don't attend – you have to make the poem rhyme in the order that I wrote all the words on my list. You can't just mix them up.'

'I'm afraid I'm very foolish at it,' Crow said, with a smile in his voice Kit hadn't heard since his own childhood.

'But you're not; normally you're even better at *bout-rimés* than Mama!' On seeing Kit, Morwenna got up and rushed to him. 'Will you play?'

Kit laid a hand on Morwenna's head as she clung to his legs, her curling hair soft beneath his fingertips. 'Later I shall,' he said. 'I haven't had enough coffee to thoroughly beat you yet.'

'Off you go, my heart,' Crow said, in French, 'we're about to become boring.'

Morwenna had been reared strictly but with a great deal of kindness, so she slid off her father's lap, made a well-taught curtsey and went out with quite a creditable attempt to hide her chagrin, Kit watching her go. There was little gentle about Crow's expression as soon as the new footman closed the door behind her: they hadn't been alone together since Wellington had swept off back to Apsley House the morning before.

'You realise the whole of Brooks's was humming with your antics last night, or it was until I arrived. And if it's all over Brooks's, you can be bloody sure it's everywhere else, too.' Still seated, Crow leaned forwards on his elbows, watching him.

'I'm sorry, Jack. Must you do the rounds until the gossip dies down?' Kit knew very well just how much Crow disliked going out in society.

'It looks an awful lot like it. One doesn't murder marquises, Christophe – not in Mayfair, anyway.'

'I suppose it's perfectly all right to exterminate the lower sort in one's club for entertainment. It's the hypocrisy I can't stand.'

'Kill anyone you like, but just do it south of the river and be quieter about it next time.'

'Oh God, must you always be so downright withering?' Kit said, leaning on the mantelpiece, still feeling the effects of all the narcotic stimuli the Port of London could offer. In that moment, Crow looked so much older than his four-and-thirty years that Kit felt the urge to protect him, to tell him to go home to Cornwall and not worry about anything.

'And must you always be such a damnable hot-headed idiot? Bloody young fool.'

'Look,' Kit said, 'I quite understand it's wiser for Morwenna to be out of London and even Cornwall in the middle of my own damned scandal, but I don't like the sound of Fontainebleau. Wellington and the Cabinet think they've been clever presenting the peace congress with this fait accompli of Nadezhda's marriage, but the truth is they'll have antagonised everyone except Austria, will they not?'

'Very likely,' Crow said. 'It's certainly not what I would have advised, put it that way. Wellington was a fool to have allowed it to happen.'

'And a fool to allow the princess to insist that I captain her personal guard? The gossip about us is bad enough, but it'd be a pretty mess if anyone actually knew the truth.'

'Which bit of it?' Crow said, with a sardonic twist to his smile. 'That Nadezhda's Tsar Alexander's bastard, not his cousin; that her mother Princess Sophia was never married to anyone, let alone a Romanov? Or the bit where Nadezhda ran away from her foster home and lived disguised as a Semenovsky Guardsman for months, riding in your company across half of Russia?

'Actually, the gossip alone will be bad enough if it escalates beyond all this tuppence-ha'penny tragedy about you being hopelessly in love with one another: fucking a female heir to the throne is technically treason. Which is why, my boy, you will squash any form of talk about you and Nadezhda by being nothing but utterly professional in her royal presence, particularly when there are witnesses.'

Kit went over to the sideboard and poured steaming black coffee from the silver pot, draining the cup: it was either that or strong drink when Crow was in this sort of mood.

'If Morwenna's at Thérèse's and I'm at the palace, I'm afraid I may not be able to protect her as she ought to be – not if the whole affair goes badly, as any fool can see it will.'

'You won't have to: you must know I would never allow Morwenna to be placed in the slightest danger,' Crow said. Getting up to pour himself a glass of brandy from the cut-glass carafe on the sideboard of polished walnut, he poured one for Kit, too, handing it to him.

Kit drank, cognac blazing down his throat. 'All right, I'll do it. No one will be talking about Dereham, but I won't kick up a scandal about Nadezhda, either. Don't worry.'

'I don't know how it is, but I find it highly unlikely that I won't be fretting myself into a hernia on your account for the rest of my life.' Crow swirled the brandy around in his glass. 'At least I'm used to it. Listen, you should know that one of my informers was compromised five years ago.'

Slowly, Kit set down his glass. 'That's your side of things, not mine. I don't want to know the first thing about that sort of affair. And if it was so long ago, why does it matter a damn now?'

Crow raised his eyebrows. 'Do you really think I'd bring this up if it wasn't essential?'

Kit sighed. 'What, then? It had just better not be anything that will get me shot for treason, that's all. Why are you so certain that this informer of yours has had their cover blown to hell, anyway?'

'I'm sure of it,' Crow went on, 'because it's Clemmie Arwenack, and she's been living with the Boscobels since not long after Gloyne died – her grandfather.'

'I know who her bloody grandfather was.' Kit failed to disguise his anger: even now – doting husband and father and careful landowner – Crow could still be guilty of such profound amorality that it took one's breath away. 'If you must recruit children with no protection or fortune then by all means continue do so, but I fail to see what such a damned bloody awful thing has got to do with me.'

'Push aside your moralities for a few moments and listen,' Crow said. There was no servant in the room, which ought to have been enough to set anyone on guard, and so Crow filled Kit's glass himself, again. 'Clemency Arwenack might once have been your childhood accomplice, but these days she's a blackmail artist and extortionist *par excellence*, like all the most fashionable women. She's also now your partner in office.'

'What?' Kit said, angrily draining his glass.

'She's just been appointed Mistress of the Robes and you are the captain of her highness's personal guard.' Crow spoke with the flicker of a smile. 'Take care, my dear boy, that's all I'm saying. Against my expressed wishes, Clemency ran information for me exactly twice after she went to live with the Boscobels. Then, out of the blue, she stopped. Valentine and Georgiana are holding something over that girl that frightens her even more than I do.'

11

The formal gardens at Fontainebleau were an ordered riot of ornamental waterways, espaliered trees and shaven lawns, and Clemency and Valentine were walking that morning by the Grand Canal, the sun hot on her back through layers of light muslin and padded linen corsetry.

'He's here already, you know – Helford, I mean,' Valentine said. 'Strolled into a party at his aunt's late last night, I believe.'

She'd grown used to the way people watched them when he was with her – Val had always attracted attention, with all that lazy glamour. Even now, a group of Austrian diplomatic wives observed him from where they stood by the clipped topiary, smiling behind their fans.

All she could do for now was to change the subject. 'I'm more concerned about this Belgian of yours. I heard that he only came as part of their royal escort. He'll be going home to Brussels soon, won't he? What do you want out of him?'

Valentine bent to pick up a stone, throwing it out across

the glittering expanse of the Grand Canal, where it tossed up a small, greenish splash. 'Count de Mercy-Argenteau? I thought the old lady had explained this already. Argenteau has court links to the Master of Ordnance in Brussels. Good ones, too.'

Clemency examined the nearest rose bush, sprays of blowsy, open-headed crimson blooms. 'Isn't that line going to be rather a dead duck now peace has been declared?'

Valentine smiled down at her in that teasing way of his, always waiting for a reaction. 'Come, you're not that naive. There's already a bone of contention between Belgium and the Netherlands. They could still go to war even if Britain and the allies agree something with France, and Napoleon stays within his own borders like a good boy. In which case it might as well be me supplying Belgium with rifle parts and ammunition as anyone else. It's going to be useful if Argenteau loses to you in a pretty big way.'

He spoke then without looking at her, his gaze resting on the fractured sunlight on the waters of the ornamental canal, a slight smile twitching at one corner of his beautifully sculpted mouth.

'Come on, you enjoy this, Button – admit it. God, it used to make you so gorgeously wet.'

Clemency breathed in the expensive scent of his cologne, brewed especially for him at an atelier in Paris. 'I think it's pretty tawdry now, really. Don't you?'

For such a long time, she'd hoped he was better than this.

'Stop changing the subject.' He spoke with lazy affection. 'It's her highness and the so-handsome Kit Helford that we need to get to the bottom of, don't we?'

She'd heard nothing at all from London, not even so much as an acknowledgement of her message. Fine. She'd risked more than Lamorna could ever know, sending word after all these years, asking him to come. She wasn't even sure if she'd dare warn him that the Boscobels planned to compromise and then blackmail his brother. The Boscobels, after all, knew far too much about her. There was only a silly childlike hope that if Lamorna were here, he could help her somehow. But if he didn't care even to reply to her message, what more could she do?

'Why stir things up this much when there'll be opportunities at court anyway?' she asked. 'There'll be all sorts of contracts and dealings open to you now, at any rate. Why do you need Helford and her highness so beholden to you? Apart from anything else, it's a pretty huge risk to start trying to manipulate people at that sort of level. It feels like playing with fire to me.'

'Alive to every suit, aren't you? It makes sound commercial sense, that's all.' Valentine gave her the tilted smile that had destroyed more debutantes than she cared to count; he was, as she knew very well, one of the most sought-after prizes on the London marriage mart.

He really is a catch, as Georgie was so fond of saying.

Clemency stared down at the gravel beneath their feet; why should she still feel that surge of pleasure at his approval? 'Surely it's better to tread carefully?'

Valentine stopped to examine one of the rose bushes, snapping off a flower with brisk efficiency before letting it fall to the gravel. 'Look, what harm can it do? Everyone's already gossiping about Helford and the princess enough as it is – you'll be stoking the fire, not starting it. All you need to do is watch and wait until they commit some indiscretion and then make the most of it. I doubt you'll be waiting long. From what I hear, her royal highness and Helford will hand it to you on a plate within the first week. By the end of the first month, they'll both be eating out of your hand.'

'I've known the man since I was seven years old and you're asking me to set him up for a fall.'

'Oh God, don't tell me my bloody mother was right,' Valentine said, turning to her with all the intensity of his full attention. 'I swore blind to her you'd never be such a goose. Look, if Helford remembers you at all, it's as a wharfside brat. I doubt he even took as much notice as that.'

'It's a risk, that's all I'm saying. And Kit Helford has seen the world. He's no flat. It won't be easy to take him in.'

Valentine knew her, after all, better than anyone, even Georgie.

'They're all flats. You just need to forget any childish attachment, that's all.' He spoke with sudden brutal precision. 'You owe Helford nothing.'

'I know that. You're right. I'm refining too much upon the whole thing,' Clemency lied. With a light-headed sense of detachment, she watched a girl in white muslin dart like a fish between the serried ranks of trees barbered into conical shapes. As if pursued by an imagined foe, the child paused to take cover behind the topiary and for a brief, idiotic moment, Clemency fought a wild urge to cry. Breaking her cover once more, the little girl landed heavily on her hands and knees in the gravel, right at Clemency's feet. Valentine stepped aside without so much as a glance;

Clemency withdrew her arm from his and dropped into a crouch, her hands shaking as she helped the child to her feet. She couldn't have been more than seven, dressed in ill-advised white muslin, already grass-stained.

'I wish I were so brave!' Clemency briskly brushed down the girl's skirts. 'That was a real tumble.'

The child dropped into a speechless curtsey and fled, leaving her alone with Valentine once more.

He took her arm again and in that moment she couldn't breathe. 'You're always so natural with children,' he said.

Side by side, they looked out over the glittering expanse of water, the force of nature contained by ornamental waterways and clipped topiary, and Clemency's heart clenched in her chest like a bloody fist.

12

On Kit's first day at Fontainebleau, he woke late to the perfumed body of a stranger. Her dimpled arm was draped across his naked chest, and the silk skirts and lace-trimmed petticoats he had ruthlessly pushed up around her waist last night now pooled across his own legs. He had been thorough in his attentions, and she not quiet about receiving them. He lay supine for a moment, staring up at the gilded and embossed ceiling: despite the entertainment, he'd have preferred bivouacking out in the open with his men to this damned bonfire of the vanities; doing the pretty at the Hôtel de Montausier last night had been bad enough, and yet unavoidable, delivering Morwenna into his great-aunt's care. There was only more of it to come.

Washed in cold water and clad in clean linens, and leaving Phelps to deal with the girl, Kit refused to break his fast with anything save honeyed coffee. For that he received his valet's outraged commentary about the unwisdom of going out on the march fair clemmed, and could only assuage it by letting Phelps help him into his jacket, which had aired by the window overnight. Fully civilised once more, or at least to a cursory glance, Kit left the palace, crossing the sun-soaked plaza to the house of his great-aunt. He paused only to buy a handful of strawflowers and late mimosa in the marketplace for his small niece, who had plagued him so relentlessly on their journey from London to France that at times Kit had wished himself tracking French snipers through frozen boreal forest.

Napoleon had restored the ducal townhouse to Kit's great-aunt several years before, after her exile in Russia. He found Thérèse de Saint-Maure still entertaining at the Hôtel de Montausier in lavish style and the intended recipient of the strawflowers out with her maid. The vast reception chamber had been designed for the sort of crowd it now held, and so although the walls were hung with landscapes and portraits in heavy gilded frames, including several of his mother, decoration had only really flourished on the domed ceiling where Venus received Mars on a plump velvet couch, painted in earth colours on fresh plaster.

Thérèse's gathering this morning was of the highest ton: international, almost entirely female, and very exclusively bejewelled. It also included Joséphine Bonaparte Tascher de la Pagerie, the emperor's former wife and mistress of twenty-five long years, who was drinking champagne steaming with ether as she sat by the fire, her elegant clustering curls just touched with grey. It was already too late to beat a retreat: the history between Joséphine and Kit's own family was so scandal-ridden that everyone within a six-foot radius had abandoned any pretence of not settling down to see who would take the first shot, even as Kit inwardly cursed. Joséphine hated him, with reasonable justification.

'Angel, you do look so glowering and cross, pacing there before the fire. What on earth is the matter?' Sitting decoratively among tasselled cushions, Joséphine cast a faux-conspiratorial glance at her companions. 'Do you know,' she went on, 'a little bird told me that our gorgeous young Helford pines for a certain royal childhood sweetheart. Take care you don't get your fingers burned, won't you, darling?'

'Who have you been listening to, ma'am, the town dressmaker? I didn't think Bonaparte was so badly dipped as all that.' Kit yawned: she wouldn't be the first to attempt something of this nature, so he might as well get used to it.

Joséphine got to her feet, lithe and sinuous in silk that clung to her perfectly preserved figure, smiling as she moved in for the attack. 'Dear me, *what* could possibly make you glower and sulk in such a manner, my sweet?'

They stood face to face, Kit wishing her at Jericho. Stepping closer, Joséphine ran the tip of one elegant finger down the gold lacing on his Guards jacket and he suppressed an angry shudder at her touch. Kit was just aware that the room had now fallen completely silent around them both. There was still no sign of his great-aunt, the devil take her eyes.

Joséphine smiled, looking up at him from beneath lowered lashes. 'Oh yes – *now* I recall what must be making you so out of reason cross. Your brother's wife is in the family way again, is she not? Dear Lady Lamorna. What a wonderful surprise after all these years. Never mind, you know – perhaps it will be another girl.'

Kit turned and walked away, leaving Joséphine to enjoy her victory, a stunned silence in his wake.

'*Christophe!*' Thérèse de Saint-Maure advanced upon him, clad from head to foot in black bombazine and lace like a vulture done up in corsets.

'Ma'am.' Kit stooped to kiss his aunt, breathing in the unfashionable but oddly comforting scent of her orange-flower eau de toilette. Exiled from France during the Terror thirty years before, Thérèse still considered herself part of the Ancien Régime, and very nearly everyone else completely beneath her notice.

Accepting a glass of the 1811 Le Courvoisier from his aunt's liveried footman, he obeyed a wave of her lace-gloved hand and they retreated to a quieter part of the room where he collapsed beside her on the chaise nearest the window.

'You're supposed to be suppressing gossip, not raking it up,' Thérèse went on, giving him the look she usually reserved for depressing the pretensions of the *outré*; he really was in trouble.

'It's nothing, ma'am.' Kit forced away a memory of Papa's old library at Nansmornow, now Crow's: the rows of books with gilded spines, the faded rug, a painted map of the Cornish sea two centuries old. *Home*. It was damnable that he was considered to be jealous of an unborn child. Kit leaned his head against the back of the chaise and stared up at the cherubs on the ceiling before turning to meet his aunt's unwavering gaze, her eyes exactly the same shade of pale grey as his brother's.

Thérèse glanced over the back of the chaise, casting a critical eye over the fashionable throng. 'Never mind your bloodthirsty behaviour in gentlemen's clubs, the knives are out for you. You do like to dance with your demons, don't you?'

'I just enjoyed my war, that's all.' Kit smiled, but in such a way that another expression of swift concern flitted across his aunt's face, and he changed the subject. 'You may as well tell me how the land lies at this bloody awful court.'

'Oh, may I? Would you have an old woman perjure herself with treachery to her own nation?'

'Nonsense, you're not under oath. Anyway, am I not your favourite?'

'You're worse than the most shameless young hussy, and I should know just what to do with you if you were a girl under my charge.' Thérèse glared at him over the rim of her own brandy glass. 'Nevertheless, if you want to know, there is consternation already about the Sublime Porte, of course. The Spanish and Dutch are insisting that there is no place at a European peace congress for an Ottoman emissary, which is laughable when you look at the implications for trade routes via Russia and the Ottoman Empire.' She glanced out of the window. 'Odd, isn't it? I wonder if England will find Tsar Alexander is no longer quite so invested in placing his little half-Russian princess on the English throne. Peace with France does rather throw up different opportunities for the Romanovs, doesn't it? They may not have to suck up to the British any more to get across Afghanistan and into India. These things almost always come down to trade, in the end.'

'Don't think,' Kit said carefully, 'that the same point had not also occurred to me.'

Thérèse let out a sharp burst of laughter. 'Of course it did. You're no one's fool, I'll grant you that. Anyway, what you may not know is that the Dowager Queen of Württemberg has defied her stepson the king and is travelling by easy stages to Fontainebleau. Fool of a woman! Worse than her mother. I don't know what she hopes to gain by it, at her age.'

'The Dowager Queen of what?' Kit said, running a mental tally through every middle-European kingdom and principality he'd campaigned in. '*Oh.*'

'Indeed! The former Charlotte, Princess Royal of England and Wales. Nothing could be more absurd – she must be sixty if she's a day,' Thérèse said, without much justification: she had to be easily the wrong side of seventy herself, although Kit had no very exact notion of her age, and in any case she showed no sign of retreating into genteel retirement from society.

'She was married off out of England long before you were born, of course – the only one of her sisters not to be kept at home with the Queen, I might add, with predictably dreadful results. The silly fool would have done better to marry off the entire pack of them, and then you might have better than a Russian minx as heir to the English throne.'

Kit watched her: Thérèse always knew more than anyone expected. She'd survived a revolution and thirty years of exile, but no one ever took much notice of an old woman. More fool them. 'Surely you're not suggesting Charlotte's a threat to Nadezhda's claim? Württemberg was allied to Napoleon for at least four years in the war. It won't fly, or they'd have had her on the throne for years by now.'

'Yes, well, darling, you may not have noticed but we're in the middle of negotiating a peace treaty *between* England and France.' Thérèse shrugged. 'Who knows? Let's hope your Russian chit gets married to her Habsburg princeling and safely crowned before too long, shall we? These negotiations have scarcely begun and already I can't bear it – the whole town full of damned fool courtiers with about as much breeding between them as a back-street trollop.'

'Outrageous, I'm sure,' Kit said: once Thérèse got on to social position there was no stopping her. It was no less boring when you considered that along with his own mother, she was the only Saint-Maure to have escaped the guillotine.

Thérèse gave him one of her sharp looks. 'Young dog! Joséphine is disgustingly full of herself about your second-in-command, so if you've any sense in your head at all you'll tread carefully there, too.'

Kit glanced across the room. 'Where Joséphine is concerned I'm always careful. She hates me worse than the devil.'

'Hardly surprising, darling,' Thérèse said, mildly. 'You did, after all, set fire to a palace with her inside it. But youthful folly is youthful folly and such matters don't bear discussion.'

'Indeed.' Kit drained his glass, the brandy scorching his throat as he tried not to think about the flames and the grain of the wood on the gallows-steps. 'Did she say who my second-in-command was going to be? I got to know a few of the French officers in Paris once the peace was declared.'

Thérèse raised a single sparse eyebrow. 'Consorting with low females all over the Left Bank, I shouldn't wonder.' She brushed an invisible defect from the black bombazine skirts of her gown. 'But as for your second-in-command, no – Josa kept that very close to her chest and was vilely smug about it, too.' She sighed, addressing him now with candour all the more devastating for its rarity. 'Listen to a woman for once, my dear: you were made for the battlefield, not for the cut and thrust of court life, and you'll have to rein in that fighting spirit you displayed just now if you want to survive here, especially now you've been given this utterly ridiculous command: head of the crown princess's personal guard, of all the absurdities! Don't allow this – that person to be the ruin of you.' Thérèse reached out and took his hand in her own, her thin, fragile fingers cobwebbed with lace gloves, so that it was impossible to be angry with her.

'I always listen to you, you know that,' he said.

'Much good it will do you. I would not for all the world have had you anywhere near Nadezhda Romanova, or whatever they call her nowadays, let alone in her company all the time as captain of her personal guard. I'm at a loss to understand why Lord Lamorna has allowed this to happen – you may be of age, but Crow's no fool, even if he does want everyone to stop talking about that young man you did your best to exterminate in London.'

'Maybe my brother believes that I might behave differently now than I did as a boy of seventeen? I don't know why you can't do the same.'

Thérèse frowned. 'She's no longer your Nadezhda, do you understand me? Don't be a fool, that's all I ask. I've no right to request that you treat your own family name with the respect it deserves, but I beg you not to expose your poor mother's to comment and gossip.' She sighed again, this time with the air of giving up on a lost cause; Thérèse had his brother's gift of reading one like a book: had any of them ever really believed he would emerge from all this with his honour intact?

13

Towards the disreputable tail end of that evening, Clemency played Pope Joan with two Spanish officers and a Belgian count in an anteroom to the state apartments, the stakes dizzying enough to attract a small crowd that included Valentine Boscobel. This would have to be the last game she played at Fontainebleau, or people would begin to talk. She'd chosen her gown and directed the dressing of her hair for tonight's gathering with all the strategy of a well-judged military campaign: muslin of the palest green with a touch of gold embroidery at the bodice and a suggestion of gilded spangling at the short sleeves, unremarkable braids coiled and pinned atop her head in a demure crown.

Clemency sat with the count and her two Spanish officers in a quiet corner furnished with carved panelling and Louis XI chairs upholstered in duck-egg Savonnerie tapestry. It was increasingly hot: Empress Marie-Louise's receptions were notoriously stuffy and even most of those who played deep had long since given up and gone to bed, leaving the air thick with heat and shivering candlelight. She was aware of Valentine behind her, deep in vivacious conversation with a pretty Austrian countess, but still watching, of course. Clemency reached across the staking board for her champagne, hands visibly shaking. Even at this hour of the night, it was exceptionally well iced, lead glass crystal cold relief against her lips.

Across the table, Count de Mercy-Argenteau gave her a considering smile as she drank, his shirt points so high that they obscured his profuse sideburns. Avoiding Argenteau's eyes, Clemency fixed her gaze on the emerald pin nestling in the folds of his white cravat. The two Spanish officers had begun play with a great deal of gallantry, directing the footmen to top up her glass just a little too often. Now both looked as if they wished themselves elsewhere, sensing scandal. Clemency leaned forwards to look at the staking board, resting both elbows on the table like the cottage-bred scavenger of a soldier's daughter she was – but only Valentine knew anything at all about that.

'Dear girl, you must not try to peek at my cards.' Argenteau smiled at her, his eyes cold. 'I ardently pray you're not hoping to cheat.'

'Do you always speak as though you've swallowed a dictionary, my lord?' she asked.

Argenteau shrugged. 'Insolence doesn't blind the world to bad play, Mademoiselle Arwenack.'

Behind her, one of their audience said quite distinctly, 'Would we have arrived at this pass if you didn't have a nasty habit of challenging greenhorns for hideous stakes, Count? This is a bad business, mark my words.'

'Come, come, my lord – if I were a man, I'd call you out!' Clemency spoke with a rakish slur. 'You can't assume we ladies don't care for our honour just because we're not perpetually exterminating one another in duels.' Her elbow slipped off the table, knocking her champagne to the floor where it soaked through the satin slipper beribboned at her ankle. *Perfect.*

No one spoke. The Spanish officers glanced at each other across the table, and a prickle of alert awareness climbed the length of Clemency's spine as she looked up to find a French officer watching her from by the window. Unlike everyone else, he didn't wear the hungry, almost gleeful expression of a witness to impending disgrace. Just below medium height, he was dressed in the blue ceremonial mess kit of an elite division of dragoons, his hair cut and brushed into the *coup au vent*, dark curls tumbling rakishly over his forehead. Clemency met the Frenchman's gaze with her most innocent expression before turning back to the board. Napoleon had intelligence agents all over Fontainebleau: if this dragoon was more than just a casual observer, there was nothing remarkable in it.

Across the baize table, Argenteau gestured theatrically at the painted staking board and leaned back in his chair with a leisurely display of menace, sleek and well-fed in his close-cut jacket. He hadn't long succeeded to his late father's estates near Bruges: the sprawling twelfth-century castle, a townhouse on the Rue de la Roi, and an almost unrivalled position at the summit of Brussels society. The count had had a bad war, though. He'd made mistakes with both investments and loyalties, more than once. He smiled at her, still waiting, that emerald cravat pin catching the candlelight once more just as a swift, sudden hush fell upon the groups of people nearest the entrance. It was so late that the imperial footmen were no longer announcing anyone who chose to come in, and Clemency felt another unsettling prickle of unease.

This time she had no need to turn in her seat: she had positioned herself to maintain full sight of the wide, gilded double doors topped with Napoleon's imperial crest. All she had to do was look up from the board to see Lieutenant Colonel Kit Helford walk in, tall and dark in a scarlet Coldstream mess jacket glittering with medals as he dealt out that dimpled smile to all and sundry, so very much at ease that it was not possible to square this laureled sprig of the nobility with the vagrant child she remembered, or the fact that less than two weeks ago he had shot a man in cold blood at his club.

The room fell silent at his entrance; even Argenteau tore his gaze from the board. Clemency sipped her champagne; a servant had replaced her glass at a gesture from one of the Spanish officers. Kit Helford gave a curt nod to Valentine, crossing the Aubusson carpet to one of the tall windows and slipped into easy conversation with the Prince of Orange, apparently insensible to the stir he had created. Clemency risked a glance over her shoulder, catching sight of the tolerant smile Valentine dealt out in return, as if Kit were still that much younger neighbourhood stripling who deserved the occasional patronising show of friendliness. Valentine really could be a bloody fool at times. She was about to turn back to the business of play when she sensed

Kit look up from the group of intimates now gathered around him; he stood out from the rest like a wolf among lapdogs. He was tall, of course; paying no further attention to Valentine, he met her gaze over lacquered and pomaded heads; managing, in fact, to look her up and down, very quickly, so that Clemency's heart raced, even as he saluted her with a sardonic and unsmiling lift of his glass.

Clemency turned away, ignoring the tightening sensation in her chest, as if she had been laced by an enthusiastic maidservant. She'd drunk enough champagne to fell a prize fighter: sometimes it made her jump at shadows like a spooked horse, that was all. There was nothing anyone could do to help her now, least of all a spoiled young rake who was welcomed with a smile by all after shooting a man at the Hellfire. Clemency felt a hot surge of dislike and turned back to the board, staring at the painted counters.

'Your turn, Mademoiselle Arwenack.' Argenteau smiled again, ignoring a murmur of disquiet from the audience. She had to take a hold of herself and concentrate: she stood to lose not only all she'd won from the Spanish officers but Boscobel Castle, too. The latter wasn't actually hers to stake, but play was play, and no one could put a stop to this now even if they'd wanted to. All the same, the atmosphere had soured, thick with stale breath, brandy and the swelter of overheated bodies.

Clemency's gaze flicked down to the cards in her own hand once more, sweat seeping through the fine linen of her shift and into the thick cotton padding of her stays. Her voice shook: good. 'I'm at your service, my lord count.'

Argenteau's smile took on a rigid quality and Clemency

laid down her final card. One of the Spanish officers swore softly, under his breath. Among the spectators, someone gasped. Across the room, the French dragoon watched with the flicker of a smile, and Clemency felt an unexpected rush of pity as Argenteau's face collapsed like a waxen witch's poppet held before the fire. She held his gaze. He would have ruined her without thinking twice about it, and she was wicked enough to enjoy her own victory: Argenteau's disbelief, followed by a shielded blaze of naked hatred and a flash of self-pity, a sheen of perspiration breaking out across his forehead. Even the points of his shirt collar drooped a little. He mastered himself, getting to his feet, turning to offer a sarcastic bow to the stunned spectators.

'I offer you my most profound congratulations, Mademoiselle Arwenack.' To Argenteau's credit, his voice didn't shake as he spoke, even though everything he owned now belonged to her – wealth accrued over eight centuries, as the Boscobels had been certain to ascertain before identifying him as her mark. Argenteau bowed again as she got to her feet, smoothing out the creased skirts of her silk gown; she sensed Valentine's presence directly behind her, and he placed one hand at her waist.

'That's my girl,' he spoke quietly, his voice rich with promise that once would have rendered her unable to think of anything except the warmth of his touch. Georgie had put a quick end to all that.

She didn't turn to look at him, addressing Argenteau instead as she stepped away. 'Will you gratify me with a turn around the room, my lord?' Clemency asked, with all the calm placidity she could muster. 'There's much to discuss, and I should like to make matters more convenient for you where I can.' She lowered her voice, leaning so close to him that she had no choice but to breathe in the smoked trout and stale brandy on Argenteau's breath. 'An arrangement, perhaps?'

'I'd be honoured,' Argenteau said, with a thin-lipped, furious smile. 'The formal gardens will be tranquil at this hour.'

'I've a fancy to remain indoors, sir.' Clemency had no desire to end the evening with a dagger between her ribs, and she held the driving whip, anyway: it was her choice, not his. Argenteau submitted with a gracious bow, but the smell of his sweat was now overpowering: he'd lost everything, he was in a state of panic – exactly where she wanted him. The Spanish officers made their escape, chairs pushed back a little too quickly. Clemency didn't blame them: it was always difficult to know what to say to someone when their better options now included a bullet in a quiet room. Argenteau held out his arm to her and she took it, aware that their audience including Valentine himself had drifted away to observe other games or to flirt on velvet chaise lounges. She was playing with fire by walking alone in Argenteau's company. Desperate men did foolish things: she hadn't needed Lord Lamorna to tell her that, either, although of course he had, long ago. She couldn't resist glancing across the room towards the window again, searching for the tall, louche figure of her former spymaster's brother. Kit Helford was gone.

14

The temple of Venus was overgrown with tumbling wisteria in a neglected corner of the palace gardens: there was even a cobwebbed trestle table that must have been left behind after some long-ago garden party. With a linen apron knotted over her gown, Clemency could play the part of her old self, laying out her needle, thread and the small pot of beeswax alongside the little nipping press of polished walnut that Grandpapa had made for her when she was small. The endpapers she'd coloured at home in Cornwall were safe in the press, marbled cerulean and vivid emerald green, as if finishing a book for a client was all she need concern herself with. The silence out here was sweeter than cold almond and orange-flower ratafia: Clemency couldn't face Valentine and Georgie this morning. She and Valentine had arrived home in the early hours to find Georgie still entertaining again – a smaller, more select party this time, nothing but a blur of unfamiliar faces. Valentine had come to her bedchamber once Bluette left her installed in a fresh nightgown with the covers drawn up. He'd leaned in the doorway with brotherly informality.

That was well done, Button. The smile again. *I take it Argenteau will be calling on me tomorrow to reach an arrangement?*

Of course, she'd said. They both knew she was obliged to them, that there was really no choice about any of this.

She'd almost finished stitching the signatures now, pulling waxed thread through holes in the thick paper deftly pierced with her awl, taking respite in her own dexterity. There was always another deal to strike, someone else to compromise with a bad debt or the promise of a fatal rumour withheld. High-flown ethics are for the privileged, Georgie always said, and anyway, even if she shafted Kit Helford and her royal damned highness right up to the hilt, it would make no difference to Kit. He'd still be invited to every last tonnish party; he'd still ride home along the coast road beyond Newlyn to keep Christmas at Nansmornow, all the windows lit up for his arrival. He'd survive a scandal, even if Clemency herself met the edge of a cold blade one night at the behest of his brother. She wouldn't put that past the Earl of Lamorna. She'd be disposed of without a second thought. Everyone knew that Lamorna and his young brother had endured a fraught relationship over the years; everyone knew that, despite this, neither would tolerate harm or insult to the other.

With a jolt of awareness, Clemency knew she wasn't alone.

Forcing herself not to jump, she caught a glimpse of crumpled white muslin and caught her breath, a short, painful gasp. The girl was even more dishevelled than she had been yesterday, watching Clemency's every move with large dark eyes as she clung to one of the lichen-stained marble pillars, grass in her heap of fair curls. Turning away, Clemency looked down at the thick pile of folded cream-white paper, her sight momentarily blurred. Aware of the child behind her overcoming hesitancy and sitting down to watch, Clemency threaded her needle and began to sew a fresh signature to the book block, stitch by careful stitch. What harm could it do to let the girl be? She'd made a nuisance of herself around many a campfire, watching Papa's men cleaning muskets or wiping kit-belts with linseed oil, but it didn't pay to think too much of that, either, or of what might have been.

Clemency drew the small walnut nipping press from her satchel, unscrewing it with deft, calming movements; pulling out the endpapers, she set them ready on the table, already glued to the guard sheets. She'd marbled them in the stillroom at Boscobel Castle, gathering seaweed to boil for carrageenan jelly and mixing the size, adding colours from the paintbox Grandpapa had made for her before he died – cerulean blue and sea green. With the little girl watching her in shy, curious silence, Clemency sewed the guard sheets to the signature block, stitching and pulling waxed thread until she could almost believe that she'd never left Grandpapa's bindery shop in Penzance, that she'd never taken the first of all the steps that had led her to this place.

'Morwenna Helford, what the devil are you doing?'

Clemency froze at the sound of a very male voice, lazily cultured and disconcertingly familiar. Turning, she set down her needle and thread, watching as her silent audience of one fled to the tall young officer leaning in the doorway, scattering faded wisteria petals as she went. Sunlight caught the gold lacing at the epaulettes of Kit Helford's crimson Guards' jacket, picking out strands of copper in his tousled dark hair as he bent to catch the child in his arms, lifting her so high that she let out a shriek of laughter: Morwenna. Such a pretty name: his niece, then, Lord and Lady Lamorna's child.

Oh, Christ.

Holding the little girl with unthinking competence, Kit didn't look like a man to be taken for a bubble or a flat. He turned his attention to Clemency now, but without the slightest flicker of recognition, dealing her a direct cut that he had no idea how much she deserved. He cut her now, no doubt, because she gambled and cheated and drank; how would his face twist with disgust if he knew the rest of it? Her sight blurred and the breath caught in her chest with an unpleasant twisting sensation; all she could do was look down at her needle and thread.

A stitch in time saves nine, Georgie had said. *No one need ever know, darling, but we simply can't afford for this sort of scandal to get out.*

The child's well-rehearsed courtesy was lost in an unmannerly shout of delight as Kit twitched her up into his arms once more, sitting her side-saddle upon on one shoulder. Ducking, they went out into the heat of the spreading lawns, leaving Clemency alone in their wake, in a ringing silence that she couldn't bear.

15

With Fontainebleau heaving like a nest of maggots, it was Jacques's duty to be sure where all the best quarry might be sprung ready for when the English princess arrived, and the hunting started off. They'd not catch him on the hop: bloody ignorant pack of would-be aristocrats that they were, as if the Revolution had never happened. Walking with Porcelaine leashed at his heel, Jacques kept a weather eye on the girl as she went on ahead of him down the deer-track through unfurling bracken, her cap of dark hair glossy like a new chestnut – she didn't crash about and shout like some children did; quick and seemly she was, pacing along so quiet in her pinafore and striped pantaloons, treading nice and light even in those hobnail boots handed down from a cousin in Barbizon. It wasn't ideal, being saddled with the bairn when his mother died, but a promise was a promise, and at least Alie was sturdy and strong as well as quiet; she kept up with the beaters all day.

To Jacques's mind, that lot up at the palace didn't deserve the honour of a fine chase, but it was a matter of pride to give them good hunting, and he'd heard talk of a white hart with antlers as wide as a barn door. It was the Boussion lad that swore to it, four parts drunk at the time, but the thing was Jacques had noticed signs of a stag in this part of the forest when there had been none for two summers now: there was scat, and a good lot of undergrowth broken off shoulder-height to a man. A stag with a fine set of antlers had been in these parts, you couldn't deny it. It was Alie herself who'd first found the branches snapped clear off, coming to tell him with her face so small and smudged and serious; bless her, he'd had to have words about not straying too far from the cottage after that. She was much too young to understand for herself, but there were some bad types about. You heard all sorts.

Sensing movement, Jacques signalled to Porcelaine with one hand on the back of her elegant white neck, his fingertip brushing the wide leather collar he'd tooled for her himself. Alie turned and looked at him over her narrow shoulder, a question in her serious dark eyes. Jacques nodded, holding up one hand, a signal she understood without question or complaint. If he and Bluette were blessed with a child of their own, there might even be a son, a brother of sorts for the lass: after all, there had been Pelletiers in the huntsman's cottage since the time of the troubadours, or so his mother always liked to say. The girl might not be his own by blood, but he and Bluette would see her right. Bluette had promised to stitch her new gown for their wedding, and Alie was that giddy over it – the first new dress she'd ever had, he shouldn't wonder. Porcelaine was a good lass, too, knowing her business so well that he didn't even have to leash her, not even when she scented quarry as she did now, her long lean body quivering with the thrill of it, her bloodline bidding her chase even as loyalty to him told her to wait.

And then, as they watched – Jacques, Alie and Porcelaine – the great white stag stepped out from between the beech trees like a beast from the other place. Oh, by heaven, he was a big one too, a great, noble creature, with antlers easily six feet across, and all of him purest white; a true lord of the forest he was, standing there so still and quiet and unafraid. Jacques could hear nothing but his own breathing, and the girl's, too, as if all other sound had been drained from the world. Oh yes, if they wanted it, those idiots up at the palace, Jacques would give them a chase the like of which they had never seen before.

16

The following morning, Kit arrived at the Duke of Wellington's Fontainebleau headquarters with a full fifteen minutes to spare, waving away both the duke's nervous young ADC and his offer of cognac.

'Off you go, Russ.' Kit hardly noticed Captain Russell's grateful smile at having his nickname recalled to mind. 'I'll see to myself; I don't doubt you've reams of paperwork to wrestle.'

'You're not wrong, sir.' Russell saluted with one fist held to his forehead and retreated to the baize-topped desk in the corner. Kit went to stand by the ceiling-height window that looked out across the palace gardens, gazing discontentedly at the view. Ornamental pools in unnatural shapes ignited a spark of longing for home, for gorse-covered cliff-tops and the stink of the sea, and the shabby, comfortable familiarity of the drawing-room. It was just so damnably queer how quiet everything was here, save the interminable scratching of Russell's quill and the rustling of paper, enough to give anyone a fit of the megrims.

Restless, he sensed the promise of movement in the room beyond and got to his feet a bare half-moment before Russell scrambled up and saluted again as the large, gilded double doors at the far end of the reception chamber were opened from within by a footman. Kit was announced by full name and title to a vast drawing-room beyond, far too large a space for the small group of people seated on chaises and armchairs arranged by an incongruously cheerful fire. Wellington was habitually neat in his blue jacket with that forbidding expression on his weathered face, sharing the same chaise longue as Joséphine, who oozed venom and éclat in plain dark blue muslin. This was meeting was strictly unofficial, then. Two courts operated at Fontainebleau, synchronised like polished brass cogs inside a pocket watch: the foremost run by Napoleon's unloving and opportunistic wife Empress Marie-Louise, much addicted to protocol and overheated receptions. The second was a court of shadows, operated by Joséphine to deal with the sort of delicate but essential courtly business that couldn't formally be acknowledged, such as providing a guard to a princess who was a personal guest of Napoleon, and therefore ought not to need one.

'Darling!' Joséphine said. 'Goodness, I see Claire in you today – so like your dear mama. I believe you know Miss Arwenack, of course?'

Clemency Arwenack turned, smiling in polite feigned ignorance of his discomfiture, all that long straight hair swept up into a crown of braids on the top of her head to reveal the elegant curve of her neck. Her cheekbones were still dusted with freckles, but she'd chosen well with that gown of jonquil: she was all the greenish gold of new hay, clear-eyed and refreshing. What in God's name had she been playing at, knifing the Count de Mercy Argenteau at Pope Joan? Kit recalled Boscobel's lazy smile as he'd walked up to her afterwards, one hand at her waist as though she were his doxy.

She looked at him dead in the eye with a slight lift of one arched eyebrow, as if this was the very first time they had crossed paths. 'I'm delighted to see you, Lieutenant Colonel. I understand we are to be working in close collaboration.'

Kit crushed a surge of annoyance. He'd deal with her when he was well ready, and not before; he offered a slight bow and nothing more, ignoring the sardonic tilt to her smile. A young French officer in a gilded blue dragoon's uniform occupied the chair beside her, all curling black hair and large dark eyes of a peculiarly expressive brilliance, and Kit swore with silent blasphemous precision. At Bayonne, the fellow had led his men in an impressive rearguard action. It had only needed this: they'd actually fought one another. Afterwards in Paris, with peace declared, they'd even crossed paths a few times in the Café des Aveugles in the crowded cellars of the Palais-Royal. Now, the French dragoon sat in an armchair furthest from the fire with one leg crossed over the other, observing them all with well-concealed but complete and utter mistrust.

'Good afternoon, Duke.' Kit spoke with all the calm respect he could muster.

Joséphine smiled. 'This is the Commandant Thomas

d'Harcourt of dear Napoleon's finest regiment of dragoons – I believe you've both met, although were not perhaps properly introduced. Thomas, this is Lieutenant Colonel the Honourable Christopher Helford.'

'I'm charmed, sir.' D'Harcourt spoke with smooth, polite assurance, accepting a glass of champagne from a footman. One–nil to Joséphine, then: Kit knew she'd forced him on to his back foot.

'Well,' she went on swiftly. 'Now, it'll take less than a week to reach Calais if you change horses often: rather a fast and uncomfortable journey, I'm afraid, Miss Arwenack. But most of our other royal guests are already in residence at the palace, and I'm sure we'll all agree that the sooner her highness reaches Fontainebleau, the more comfortable we'll all feel. The roads can be dangerous, even at this time of year, with these long evenings.'

D'Harcourt crossed his legs. 'What delayed her highness, if I may ask? Since her captain and her Mistress of the Robes are already here in France? It seems odd.'

'Helford and Miss Arwenack were already in or en route to France when their appointments were arranged,' Wellington said repressively. 'And her highness, I believe, needed to look over a horse in Newmarket before her journey could begin.'

D'Harcourt raised his dark brows. 'A horse. I see.'

Kit glanced at the doors, sensing movement in the room beyond; Clemency immediately looked away; she had an air of streetwise awareness, and he recognised a fleeting glassy expression in her eyes that made the hairs on the back of his neck stand up, reminding him of Crow in the aftermath of Waterloo. She didn't fit – that was it. It wasn't that he didn't know what she'd become. The leaders of the *haut ton* deemed Clemency Arwenack an original. That certain sort of something, they called it. She'd been admitted into the first circles on the strength of it, as well as her father's very old name – despite the trade in her mother's background – all under the Boscobels' wing. So why did she have the look of a man who had seen hell on the battlefield? He didn't miss the frisson of surprise passing between Joséphine and Wellington, either: clearly, neither of them had been expecting anyone else. D'Harcourt sat back in his chair, both eyebrows raised, and Clemency watched with slightly studied calm as the gilded double doors swung open once more. Kit fought the instinct to reach for the pistol holstered at his belt; he was not on the front line now, but God only knew that it felt like he was.

The newcomer walked in with an air of supreme self-possession, all golden hair and immaculate tailoring, waving away the terrified footman who was trying to announce him. 'No, no, don't worry about all that.' He turned to face them all, unsmiling. 'They all know who I am, after all.'

Joséphine and Wellington rose to their feet on the instant; there was no choice but to follow suit, and Kit went through the motions of making a formal greeting to Louis Charles Habsburg-Lorraine, Prince of Hungary, Archduke of Austria, internally repeating his brother's directive like a priest reciting the catechism.

Number one, you will go to France as her highness's bodyguard so that everyone is far too busy dissecting that information to care if Dereham dies or not. Number two, you will discharge that duty with such rigid decorum that everyone in London and Paris comes to utterly disregard the notion of any other connection between you and the princess.

Kit had the advantage of height alone; with a dismissive glance, Louis Charles cast himself into the armchair, crossing one leg over the other, displaying flawlessly polished boots.

'Really,' he said, 'don't mind me in the slightest. Do go on. I assume you were discussing my fiancée's journey to Fontainebleau, and how you plan to ensure her safety?'

Josephine gave a wild smile. 'Every arrangement has been made, your grace. Commandant d'Harcourt and Lieutenant Colonel Helford are among our most highly decorated soldiers, both of the utmost competence. Of course, there will be other guards taking care of the baggage-train, but of her highness's personal safety you can be absolutely assured.'

'She'll not go out of our sight, your grace,' Kit said, ignoring an alarmed glance from d'Harcourt.

The archduke smiled. 'How fortunate we all are that you're already acquainted with her highness. Old friends, as it were.'

'I'm certain that her highness will feel perfectly secure with both Commandant d'Harcourt and Lieutenant Colonel Helford at the helm, your grace,' Clemency said brightly. 'I understand that her highness has never before travelled to France: I always think it's so much nicer to have familiar people about when one is in new circumstances, and of course as a Frenchman Commandant d'Harcourt will be able to regale us all with local detail.' She smiled at Prince

Louis Charles with the air of a nursemaid placating a difficult child. 'Let's only hope that we are not to be too troubled by the weather.'

She hadn't been ill-mannered or even forward, exactly – more just repressively sensible in a way that no one could object to, and so far Kit was the only person in the room who saw she'd adopted that schoolroom-mistress guise with as much ease as she might toss a shawl about her shoulders before a ball. Manipulative little baggage. Louis Charles glanced at her without a flicker of interest, deeming her unworthy of a response, more fool him. Joséphine smiled at Clemency, obviously amused by her wide-eyed countenance.

Ignoring her, Kit addressed the prince with careless courtesy. 'You might join us, your grace. Commandant d'Harcourt and I would welcome your direction. You could then be personally assured of your fiancée's safety.'

Kit was more than aware of d'Harcourt's expression of suppressed fulmination; he ignored it, fixing his attention instead on the golden-haired Louis Charles.

The prince looked up with a faint, enquiring smile, and very little expression in those cornflower-blue eyes. 'Helford – I do have that right, don't I?' he went on gently. 'Soon to be disinherited by a happy event, I believe? You have my sympathies. I thank you but no – I don't know about you, but on my own account I find that a little anticipation lends savour to a dish, don't you?'

Kit forced himself not to reply, only too well aware that he was not expected to. Instead, he remembered cleaning a gunshot wound on Nadezhda's belly long ago, standing up to his shins in a Russian river. How much it had cost her to trust him; did it still frighten her to be touched unexpectedly?

'Anyway,' Joséphine went on, still smiling too much, 'as I was saying, I'm afraid it will be a fast few days to Calais. You must be there before the royal yacht docks, of course, and we believe her highness will be ready to sail on Tuesday, which even with a fair crossing should allow time enough to establish yourselves at the Coeur de Lion before a rendezvous with the royal party. I'm sorry about the prospect of an uncomfortable journey.'

'Oh, I'm sure we shan't be upset by a brisk pace, ma'am,' Clemency said, as if she addressed the mistress of an emperor every other day. *Shit.* Once again, Kit fought off the heightened sense of awareness that always rose up within him before an attack. And Prince Louis Charles just watched and smiled.

17

Sunlight streamed into the palace stables, the wide doors flung open so that Alie could see swallows wheeling and tossing in the hot blue sky outside. She liked coming to Fontainebleau with Jacques: he'd get her a twist of barley sugar in the market afterwards because she was never a trouble, even though he was sad because his sweetheart was going away with her fine English lady. Alie always sucked the barley sugar till it went thin. If she wasn't careful she'd end up with black teeth like the birds of paradise at the palace who, Jacques told her, did nothing but make idle talk and eat sweetmeats all day long. Bluette said it was all true: in one afternoon the lady's friends had eaten a whole dish of lemon and lavender confits, licking the thick white sugar from their fingers. It had been a long time since Alie had finished her bread and honey that morning, though, and she wished Jacques would stop talking so that they could go and get the barley sugar: Jacques said she ate more than he did and soon she'd be bigger than him, but that couldn't be true, because he was taller than a tree in the forest.

It wasn't just the barley sugar today, though; Alie swallowed a hot flame of excitement. Bluette had said she should have a brand-new dress for the wedding. She was even to choose the cloth herself from Madame Herbert's stall on the market, where rolls of flowered lawn and spotted cotton were piled up in a heap, and there were reels of bright ribbon, and Madame Herbert's scissors flashing in the sun. Bluette had one of Alie's old dresses that was worn to threads so she knew how to cut all the pieces to the right size, and then she would stitch it herself. Alie could tack the hems because she knew how to do that if she was careful. Bluette said her real mama must have had a rare hand with a needle, because she was very young to be so careful and steady. Or my papa, Alie had said, he might be a tailor who makes clothes. *That's as may be, child,* Bluette had said, with one of those looks at Jacques where they sort of talked to each other without speaking.

If only Jacques would stop talking now, they could go to the market: she'd hold his hand and look at the big heaps of silvery fish and the apricot pastries and the strings of sausages; she loved the market. But Jacques was still leaning on one of the stall doors with dust all over his boots, talking in his low rumbling voice to that man Alie didn't like, the one with the nasty face who always told her not to fret the horses when she wouldn't do that, anyway. Alie was never frightened of the hounds but the horses were huge, with their glossy coats and their heavy iron-shod hooves always so loud upon the cobbles.

Jacques was talking about the coverts; soon the empress and all the kings and princesses would ride out just like in one of the old stories he told her when they lit the lamps at night. At her side, he shifted his weight from one foot to the other, raising his voice a bit now; he was going to be a long time and if she mithered him he'd turn and look at her with that little frowning crease between his eyes, not angry but just sad. There was no point in trying it on. Alie picked up the skirts of her pinafore – her favourite, with those thick stripes yellow as a lemon – and jumped from one patch of shadow to the next until she reached the big doors. She wouldn't go far or Jacques might not get her the barley sugar. A flash of green caught her eye and Alie crouched down on the dusty cobblestones just outside the stable door, touching the arrangement of soft white rose petals and fresh green beech leaves with one sun-browned fingertip.

'It's a house for the beetles.' The other girl was bigger than her, maybe even seven. She had bouncing curls all piled up on her head and threaded with a blue ribbon; her jacket was that bright cloth the rich people wore, her skirts made of fine white stuff that looked as if it would blow away on the wind. Alie jumped, drawing her hand away from the arrangement of leaves and petals as if it was red hot like a pan in the fire; she wanted to run away but she was too afraid to move.

Crouching down, the girl smiled, a curl tumbling loose: she didn't even notice how her fine white skirts were trailing in the dust and dead leaves. 'It's all right. I don't mind if you look.' She spoke so fine that Alie was struck dumb like that bad milkmaid who wouldn't draw water for the fairy by the well. What if she opened her mouth and toads and vipers came out? The girl smiled, holding out a handful of bruised white rose petals.

'My name's Morwenna. What's yours? You can play if you want.' The words tumbled from her lips like bright flashing diamonds. 'You just have to build a little house like this. Maybe yours could be for the butterflies?' She laughed. 'But you might have to build it high up in a tree, if it was for butterflies. Let's do one for the ants instead.'

Alie waited, uncertain, but Morwenna's smile was so friendly that she couldn't mean any harm, even if you did have to be careful with her sort, because they'd always get you into trouble.

'My name's Adeliz, but everyone calls me Alie.'

'That's a nice name.'

Alie reached across and took a single petal from Morwenna's clean hand, propping it up with a scrap of straw; it was a bit like Jacques had shown her how to make a shelter in the forest out of spreading branches. It would be all right to play for a little while, because she was a good girl and he wouldn't mind.

A lot of folk said Jacques Pelletier was a hard man, living out in the woods all alone, not fit to look after a child, but they didn't know him as Bluette did. He was that soft on the little girl, bless him, resting one big sun-browned hand on the top of her head as Madame Herbert waited behind her market-stall with an indulgent smile, her shears at the ready.

'That one, please.' Alie pointed shyly at a bolt of muslin printed with a pattern of flowers and cherries.

'And a few yards of that stuff,' Jacques said, pointing at Madame Herbert's basket of bright trimmings. 'Whatever it is.'

'Ribbon,' Bluette supplied, longing to put her arm around his waist, although it wasn't proper to do that yet, or not in the marketplace, at least, for all that his child was growing in her belly. 'The green ribbon, madame, if you please.'

As if sensing Bluette's need, Jacques gave Alie a centime and sent her off in search of barley sugar, and they walked arm in arm behind her, Bluette holding the paper-wrapped package.

'I wish I could kiss you now the way I want to,' Jacques said to her, dark eyes glinting with promise.

'Well, you can't – we'll have tongues wagging from here to Avon.' She'd miss him so much; the way he looked at her, his touch. They reached for each other in the same moment: everyone knew they were promised, it couldn't hurt to just be in his arms for a moment. She closed her eyes, pressing her face into the rough linen of his shirt. 'Two weeks at least, they're saying. A week to Calais and then another back here – and that's if we're not kept waiting for this English princess.' She sighed. 'At least I'll have time to stitch of an evening, or at least I hope so.'

Jacques kissed her forehead. 'I hate the thought of you being up at that bloody palace. Lady's maid to an English girl is one thing, but all this court business is something else. I don't like it.'

Bluette sighed. 'We've been over this a hundred times, sweet. It's not what I was banking on, either, but Lady Boscobel says I'll get an extra three *sous* a week if I go with Miss Clemency. It's not as if we couldn't do with the nest egg, is it?'

Jacques looked at her, and then shrugged. She loved that about him: the way he never rode roughshod over her, respecting her will. 'They say all this will be over by autumn. You won't have to work in service then, not if you don't choose it.' Jacques toyed with a strand of hair that had escaped from her cap, his thumb brushing the delicate skin behind her ear. 'Listen, don't worry,' he said. 'I know you were left wanting when Jean died, but I've no plans to die soon.'

'Neither did Jean.'

'I know he didn't,' Jacques said. 'We'll be all right, though, my love. I'll keep you well enough.' He was such a big man, not lean and wiry as Jean had been. When Jacques spoke, his voice rumbled deep in his chest like rising thunder; you couldn't help but feel safe with his arms around you, even though Bluette knew too well that there was nothing safe about this life. Jean's last hours hadn't been peaceful: he'd been in too much pain, taken by the black bile. Even then, he'd told her over and over how much he loved her. She must be running mad to even think of risking another loss like that.

'Better to live while it's in our giving,' Jacques said quietly, still holding her close.

'How do you always know whatever it is I'm thinking?'

'I know how you are, that's all, can't take a step without

thinking it through from every direction.' Jacques was smiling still; she knew that, even though her cheek was pressed against his chest and she couldn't see his face. 'I love you,' he said. 'Come back to me soon.'

18

'You really must join us this evening.' Commandant d'Harcourt handed Clemency out of the carriage, steadying her a little as she stepped on to the wet cobbles. Kit had dismounted without a word to her and was already loping away across the stable-yard in that imperious way of his, spurs rattling as he dealt out swift orders to his valet, his groom and anyone who stepped across his path; they had barely exchanged two words in the four days since he'd handed her up into the carriage outside the Horseshoe Steps at Fontainebleau.

'So kind of you, Commandant, but honestly I'd better just retire,' she replied, glancing up at the tavern, warm lamplight glowing around shuttered windows. 'I don't know how it is, but I always find travelling so exhausting, even though all I'm doing is sitting still.'

'Oh come now,' d'Harcourt said, with that calm smile of his. 'Helford and I will begin to be offended if you forsake our company again.'

'I'm sure that's not true.'

'How can you doubt me, Mademoiselle Arwenack?' D'Harcourt released her gloved hand: had their fingers been entwined for a moment too long? 'In just a matter of days, we're going to join forces escorting an extremely spoiled princess across France, but anyone would think you were trying to avoid us. Her highness is already a fortnight late attending an international peace congress just because she wanted to look over a new horse. And yet we've scarcely gone beyond the civilities. My man rode ahead: the private parlour will be prepared. You won't be subjected to the rigours of the taproom.'

She manufactured an obliging smile with the perfect edge of harassed civility. 'Very well, Commandant. How kind.'

Half an hour later, Clemency subjected herself to a critical examination in a pockmarked looking-glass, smoothing out her skirts of watered aquamarine silk as Bluette sat on the truckle bed in a voluminous nightdress, combing out her plaits even as she exuded disapproval. In fairness, the cut of her gown was a risk but one she was willing to take; was this how men felt waiting to go into battle? Up until now, she'd dressed with almost Presbyterian propriety, but now her small, rounded breasts swelled up to the grosgrain-edged neckline of her bodice; her fine gold necklace and pendant drawing attention where it needed to go.

'Hoping to catch the commandant's eye with that get-up,' Bluette said with her usual acerbic precision. 'Unless it's that other one you're after.'

'For goodness' sake, don't be pert,' Clemency said. 'I'm

not exactly after a tumble in the hay. I'm dressing for dinner: it's what we do.'

Bluette rolled her eyes. It was the first time Clemency had ever seen her without a cap pinned firmly to her head; her hair was rather pretty, falling in enviable auburn ringlets as she packed away her stitching into a blue linen bag. It had looked as if she was making a small dress, and Clemency turned away.

'I'm just not sure I'd call it actually sensible, mademoiselle, going into that bear-pit.' Bluette punctuated herself with firm strokes of the hairbrush. 'I don't know what taverns are like in England, but I call it very unwise, if you please, to go downstairs into all that mayhem.'

'I didn't ask for a lecture.' Clemency leaned on the window-sill, looking out across the stable-yard; she really was a fool to let Bluette be so impertinent with her, but it was a novelty that anyone particularly cared what she did. A strain of bawdy singing drifted up from the taproom below, and lamplight from one of the open stalls threw an oblong of yellow light across the cobbles: stable-lads sitting up to share a flask of brandy, no doubt. Like it or not, d'Harcourt had her in a corner, so it was just as well she needed to get the measure of him – as well as the Honourable Lieutenant Colonel Helford. 'I don't mean to go into the taproom, anyway,' she said, lightly. 'Commandant d'Harcourt has bespoken the parlour, so you needn't worry about the proprieties on my behalf.'

'I'm sure, mademoiselle,' Bluette said, tying her nightcap firmly beneath her chin and revealing a pale flash of freckled shin as she swung her legs into bed, tugging the horsehair blanket up over the sheets.

Leaving Bluette to enjoy her disapproval, Clemency stepped out on to the quiet landing, waxed floorboards glowing by the light of an oil lamp left on a sideboard of carved oak. A young maidservant in a starched white cap emerged from another chamber and gave her a surprised glance but she ignored that, making for the narrow stairs. As she gained the flagstoned passageway, the muffled sound of male voices drifted from the taproom, a burst of laughter suddenly louder as the heavy oak door flew open and two men surged out into the hall behind her.

She heard no spurs, though, no strong yet lightweight tread, only the scraping of hobnailed boots against flagstones worn smooth by the passage of centuries. Two men: both strangers. Cold fear washed through her: she wasn't the first girl to be caught unawares out here and neither would she be the last. The parlour was less than six feet away, the door of waxed and polished oak illuminated by the glow of a lamp set on an occasional table. She forced herself to walk with brisk and unafraid purpose, the heels of her brown jean boots striking well-worn slabs; her two unwelcome companions had fallen silent, ribald laughter echoing away into nothing as she felt the heat of their gaze. *Damn. Damn, damn, damn.* One let out a long, low whistle, but she knew better than to turn and look. Even as fear jolted through her, the door to the private parlour swung open to reveal d'Harcourt himself leaning against the doorjamb, his regimental jacket a vivid blue in lamplight that caught his highly polished boots.

'Miss Arwenack.' He bowed, sweeping her into the room with a basilisk stare over the top of her head. Of the two men behind her, Clemency was left with only a brief impression of wine-sour breath, homespun and pipe-smoke. D'Harcourt gestured at a young maidservant to close the door, and with a tumbled impression of crimson-painted panelling and Delft chinaware on the mantelpiece, she passed a table laid with covered dishes, already outmanoeuvred.

'Goodness, what a lovely blaze.' Crossing quickly to the fireplace, she held out both hands to the fire, her voice steady.

'I must apologise; I ought to have sent my man to escort you.' Once again, d'Harcourt ignored her attempt to redirect the conversation. The maidservant held out a chair at the table and d'Harcourt waited by his own place, watching her with mild surprise. His implication was clear: she had a maid of her own, after all, but coming downstairs alone was exactly the sort of foolish, inexperienced mistake she wanted him to believe that she would make.

Taking her seat, she looked down at her lap as if disguising another flush. 'The fault's all mine, in fact – I should have come down with my woman, but she's so fatigued by the journey I thought it better to send her to bed.'

D'Harcourt paid no attention to the barb, unfolding his napkin with a brisk snap. 'Would you prefer claret or Rhenish? The claret is reasonable enough but the Rhenish is exquisite: Monsieur Herbert must have struck a very commendable bargain with the gentlemen of the free trade. Marie here will be your chaperone, and in my opinion, women and girls are not to be blamed for the fact that men make it unsafe for them to walk alone.'

'Rhenish, then, I thank you. And that's an unusual view, Commandant.'

The table was laid for three, but if he wasn't going to mention the empty chair, she certainly wouldn't.

'A logical one, though, I hope.' D'Harcourt smiled, ushering her into a flow of easy conversation, adjuring her to taste all the dishes on the table – steaming garlicky potage, a rich bouillabaisse, jellied beef, hot rillettes in a terracotta dish; it wasn't until Marie brought in the removes and d'Harcourt had helped her to a slice of pear tart with Chantilly cream that he remarked Helford's valet had sent his apologies.

'How curious that he should be delayed,' Clemency said, watching d'Harcourt's eyes widen just a fraction as she finished her fourth glass of wine.

'I collect, however, that you and the lieutenant colonel are already quite well acquainted?' d'Harcourt said, leaning back a little in his chair to watch her.

It was common knowledge, easily discoverable: she could admit to it. 'Yes, we knew each other as children. Or rather, I knew him. Kit Helford can give me two years, so I expect I was rather beneath his notice.'

'In Cornwall, I believe? You must both be of the foremost families.' He gave a wry smile. 'Of course, in France we're supposed to advance upon merit alone, not that it works quite like that in practice. Anyway, here we all are, a fine royal retinue.'

He spoke with an edge of sarcasm: was that just a Frenchman's disdain for the divine right of kings and queens, or did he mean to imply something else? 'Well, as for foremost families, that's certainly true of Lieutenant Colonel Helford,' Clemency said, biting into a forkful of pastry, pear and sugared cream. 'The Lamornas are a very old family indeed. My father's people are similarly ancient but *very* impoverished. My mother's family were in trade in a very small way, though, and my guardians are in it in a very big way, so you see we are making progress towards a more equitable way of life, even across the Channel.'

'Do you have a very revolutionary turn of mind, Miss Arwenack?' D'Harcourt signalled to the maidservant and a moment later Clemency's glass was brimming once more.

'Actually, I think it's perfectly shocking,' she said, with a calculated, wild little giggle. 'Cutting off the head of your king and then a few years later exterminating ours. No one really believes our royal family died of gaol-fever in the Tower during the French Occupation, do they?'

'Oh come now, we French and English are supposed to be putting all this behind us.' D'Harcourt sat back in his chair, crossing his legs. 'It's a peace conference after all.'

'Well, do you really think I'd have been appointed Mistress of the Robes to the crown princess if I did have a revolutionary turn of mind, as you put it? We're not so forward-thinking as that in England.' D'Harcourt didn't need to know just exactly how badly it stuck in her craw to call herself English instead of Cornish.

D'Harcourt shrugged. 'You're right. The Cabinet and the rest of the princess's staff would be more careful, I'm sure. Countess Lieven is certainly not a woman I'd choose to cross.'

'I don't know why on earth you'd wish to,' Clemency said; of course, she only felt so cold in that moment because there was a draught, or the fire wanted building up. 'Can I have some more wine?' Laughing, she signalled to Marie. 'I'm such a goose,' she went on, with a confidential air. 'I was only twenty-one in February. Sometimes I forget that there are some things I may order just as I choose. Where do you come from, Commandant?'

'Avon, actually,' he said. 'My father's estates were restored by Napoleon after the Revolution. We're very close to Fontainebleau itself. I was living in Paris on guard duty until this came up. Believe me, I much preferred the Quartier des Célestins to my stepmother's notion of hospitality. Before that, Cairo. My mother was Cairene.'

'Egypt! How exciting!' Clemency knew quite well that she sounded a breathless little fool; all the better to knock this self-assured Frenchman off his perch.

'Not really when you live there. Then it's just home.' D'Harcourt spoke with a flare of emotion in his eyes, as brief as it was sudden. 'But to return to your earlier point, I don't think you should fear being thought gauche. You appear a very capable young woman, Miss Arwenack. Count de Mercy Argenteau lost to you in rather a big way not long ago, and yet you've managed to escape the vulgar round of gossip. That's quite a feat.'

'Everyone plays all the time. I may be young, but there's nothing extraordinary in it.' Clemency paused, waiting, letting him fill the gap even as her heart raced.

'Really? I should say that winning a thousand-year-old fortune and a castle was quite something. Unless the Spanish officer who played at your table that night was mistaken or exaggerating.'

D'Harcourt spoke into a sudden silence, and Clemency could do nothing but sip her wine, allowing a little of it to slop from the glass, trickling cool down her wrist. D'Harcourt was still watching her expectantly: there was no choice but to admit that she'd reached an arrangement with Argenteau and he knew it as well as she did. Likely that had been the sole aim of tonight's cosy, wine-sodden supper: thanks to d'Harcourt and her own stupidity, all Valentine's dealings with Argenteau would now take place with the knowledge of the French court, and bile rose up her throat as she understood the enormity of her mistake. She opened her mouth to speak, but in that moment the door opened with a sharp, jarring burst of movement and Kit came in, stopping where he stood. He was in his waistcoat, his shirtsleeves rolled up, his black hair a little damp as if he'd just washed directly at the pump. She felt the heat of his gaze, shocking and direct, and grasped the stem of her wine glass, light-headed.

'Forgive me,' Kit said, acknowledging her now with the barest of nods. 'I'm sorry about your supper-party, Thomas. Monsieur Herbert's mare had a difficult foaling.'

'Good Lord, is there no end to the skills of the English giant?' D'Harcourt poured him a glass of Rhenish without the slightest sign of discomfiture: he had her in a corner, after all.

'Cornish, you devil: there is a difference.' Kit went to stand by the fire with his wine. 'My brother once had an Arab in just the same fix. Herbert got a fine chestnut filly tonight.' He smiled easily, with infectious joy at a new life.

'How fortunate then for Monsieur Herbert,' d'Harcourt said. 'Will you dine? I'm afraid we didn't wait.'

Kit's gaze rested briefly on Clemency once more. 'I can see that. I thank you, no – much to the disgust of Madame Herbert, I took bread and meat with the stable-lads just now; I'm afraid I'm still not out of the habit of eating whatever I can find whenever I get the chance.'

'That's wartime,' d'Harcourt said, with an elegant shrug. 'We've all learned habits that will prove hard to shake.'

'Indeed,' Kit said, and with another single dispassionate glance he took in the rakish cut of Clemency's gown and the flush staining her cheekbones. And yet when all was said and done, she knew why Kit ate whatever he could find whenever he got the chance, and it wasn't the war. After all, she'd known him best in the days when his father was always drunk, his brother away at war, and not a respectable servant would stay at the house. Then, Kit ate only when a thieving footman or a courtesan took pity on him, tossing him cheese rinds or half-eaten sweetmeats from their own platters. That was only when he was at home, of course. There were times when he'd lived with his half-sister and her mother in their cottage in the woods. Clemency remembered Roza and Nessa. She remembered how they'd died, too.

Kit Helford might cut her and look at her with disgust, but he had his own fair share of past sins.

A sudden, thin pause stretched out as the maidservant cleared away the last of the covers, all the more dissonant in the face of the camaraderie between d'Harcourt and Kit: she was the fly in the ointment here. No, if it wasn't for her, they'd be settling down to a comfortable talk about horses or the war, no matter if they were most likely informing on one another at the same time. Kit turned back to the fire, holding out his hands to the blaze; his black hair was a little unruly, curling against the starched collar of his shirt and the fine white linen of his cravat.

'Do you like to play, Commandant d'Harcourt?' Clemency said then, looking up at him from her fifth glass of wine: he wouldn't be fool enough pursue her further about Argenteau with Kit in the room. 'We ought to do something, if Lieutenant Colonel Helford doesn't care to dine. I must take care, though – I'm afraid that I've a reputation as an incurable gamester.'

D'Harcourt stared at her. 'No more than anyone else, I'm sure, Mademoiselle Arwenack, for all your skill.'

'Oh, beginner's luck, in reality. Well, we're honour bound to entertain ourselves,' Clemency said with a flick of her fingertips at Marie, who really couldn't have been more than fourteen and only just managed to conceal a yawn. 'I suppose there are some cards in the tavern. Bring them, if you please. I should like to play.'

19

'I'll play you with pleasure,' Kit said, without bothering to look at her, the candlelight casting flickering shadows across his face.

There was something in his tone that made Clemency feel light-headed, and the young maidservant froze in the act of stacking dishes on a lacquered tray.

D'Harcourt yawned. 'As you wish,' he said. 'I had the most godawful losing streak in Paris. I'm for my bed.'

Clemency caught her breath just in time. 'Goodness, how ill-mannered of me to force my preferences on the room.'

'Not at all.' D'Harcourt got up, pushing back his chair. As he bowed, Clemency fought an absurd wish to call him back, to not leave her alone with Kit Helford, above anything, but Marie closed the door behind him, and he was gone.

'Well,' Kit said, turning at last. Clemency pushed back her chair and stood up, and he gave her another considering look, tall and infuriatingly graceful in his close-fitting breeches and fine white cambric. The fingers of one hand flexed as he watched her, long and lean in the firelight; there was no sign of that dimpled smile now, not a hint of the laughter that with him had always seemed only a moment away. It was only she and Kit, and the silent young maid, who laid a fresh linen cloth upon the table and then went to the sideboard and set a deck of cards before her. Kit took his seat; she felt a strange sort of elation at the heat of his presence. He granted her a single, steady look as she took a hold on herself and sat down again to cut the cards. There was no need for discussion: it would be piquet.

'I suppose I should count myself lucky that you're not planning to cut me like you did in the garden. Twos or threes?'

'Threes.' He shifted lazily in his chair, watching her deal, refusing to be goaded; she'd play the younger hand, he the elder. 'I'll admit I was disconcerted to find you in the company of my niece. She's only young. Who knows what you may choose to teach her?'

Clemency shrugged, sipping her Rhenish; she was hardly about to allow herself to be stung by his words, however well calculated they might have been. He'd known her very well indeed, a long time ago. She laid down the talon – eight cards face down upon the table – and they began to play, both with aggression, each making rapid calculations. Turn by turn, they laid down their cards, his fingers long and elegant in the candlelight. The tactic she usually reached for first was already out of the window and in the gutter: there was little point in pretending to Kit that she was going to let him dictate the terms of this game. Lord Lamorna, after all, had taught them both: *Go in tight and keep your opponents under pressure.* They played for hours, expensive white candles burning low; she couldn't deny the pleasure of pitching her mind against an opponent who was her match. She was looking at a narrow win when he went in for the attack.

'So, what do the Boscobels hold over you, anyway?' Kit spoke without looking up from his hand, idly toying with the stem of his wine glass.

'Hold over me?' Clemency said, smiling. *Oh, holy God.* 'I'd have thought you would have seen more of the world by now, Lieutenant Colonel. Without funds, it's impossible to purchase shelter or food. There's nothing genteel about poverty, destitution or starvation. What have my financial affairs to do with you?'

'Carte blanche,' Kit said, laying down his cards and earning a ten she'd rather he hadn't, signalling to the maid to fill both of their glasses once more. 'Your grandfather despised Valentine's father. A damned bloody lapdog of the English, Gloyne called him, as I recall. It's funny – I always thought you felt the same, even though I know your father was loyal to the army and the Crown before anything else.'

'Very likely Grandpapa did say that,' Clemency said, calculating the impact of his own hand against hers. 'He was fiercely Cornish, as you know, whereas the Boscobels have always sought influence in London. Unfortunately, Papa named Valentine's father and Georgiana as my guardians in his will if Grandpapa were to die before I came of age. There wasn't much anyone could do about the arrangement once Grandpapa was dead. Private feelings and Cornish loyalties didn't come into it.'

'And yet you're twenty-one,' Kit said. 'Of age, and still living at Boscobel Castle. You were pretty hard at work when I found you with Lady Morwenna. Clearly, you still have a taste for binding books. Why not just go back to the bindery?'

She fought a flash of anger: was he using his niece's title as a weapon? *You're not one of us, get back to where you came from.* Just in time, she steadied herself. He was trying to rile her, that was all, and he'd very nearly succeeded. She looked up, holding his gaze across the table: cards and fresh linen and the carafe of straw-gold Rhenish. If he thought she was about to let him ride roughshod over her, he'd have to think again. She considered her next move, laying down her cards, at which he cocked one eyebrow with sardonic approval.

'It's so abundantly clear,' she said, calmly waiting for him to play his hand, 'that you've never had to contemplate surviving on a very small income – the uncertainty when prices go up or down. And actually, it's boring, too. Mind-numbing, in fact, because you can't think about anything else.'

'And it ought to be abundantly clear to you that the French are very interested indeed in this habit you have of playing deep. What arrangements do you reach with your victims? I'm assuming you're at least aware that d'Harcourt is obliged to spill every detail of this journey to Joséphine, no matter what strategy you're attempting. He'll repeat every last word of your conversation just now.'

'Doubtless,' Clemency said. 'I should think d'Harcourt is also charged with keeping a weather eye on your relationship with her highness, too. Everyone seems to be talking about that. If either of us has been unduly busy since we last met, I rather think it's you.'

Kit drained his glass. 'Why, are you jealous?'

She laughed at that. 'Oh, a direct hit, Lieutenant Colonel. Well done.'

He smiled. 'D'Harcourt was a dog to give you that Rhenish. It's halfway to rum. You've drunk enough to fell a sailor, but you're very damned close to stone-cold sober, aren't you? Having a hard head must help when you're fleecing influential courtiers at cards, I'll warrant you.'

She was intensely aware of his height and strength, even as he sat at his ease before her.

'In essence,' he went on in savagely quiet Cornish, 'what in the name of bloody fuck do you think you're doing, Clemency?'

It was the first time in five years that anyone except his brother had addressed her in her mother tongue.

'Carte blanche,' he said again, laying down another ten.

'My job,' she said simply. 'An alien concept to you, I see.'

He smiled at her. She'd got him now. 'I've served eight years, but I wouldn't expect you to understand that.'

'I'm sorry: you're highly skilled, of course, at killing people, including at your club. Anyone else would have hanged by the end of the week.'

'Dereham? He's not dead yet, more's the pity. But, yes, let's discuss your new position. Mistress of the Robes? Did the Boscobels arrange this?'

'How should I know?' Clemency asked lightly. 'I'm just the poor dependant who does what she's told. It's not my place to ask questions.'

He let out a sudden crack of laughter. 'If you expect me to believe that, you're way out. You're up to something. Come on, what's it all about? Valentine Boscobel's trade dealings?'

She turned on him, speaking with furious enunciation. 'You don't know anything about me.'

He looked at her across the table, the light in his eyes now wholly dangerous. 'Oh, yes I do. You've changed, I know that much. And not for the better.'

Clemency got up, pushing back her chair so that it shrieked across the floorboards. 'Congratulations,' she said. 'You've learned how to be both patronising and judgemental. I'll try my hand at the same, shall I? You've been very much occupied since we were children, too. I might look at the wrong person the wrong way across a ballroom and never receive another invitation, but oddly enough every hostess in London would consider your presence a victory. Let's see – you set fire to Carlton House during the Occupation and were almost hanged. Quite the hero, but let's not forget that you caused chaos in Cornwall, too, dynamiting the French garrison so that their troops made sure the entire district paid for it.' The words flew from her lips, unstoppable. 'Perhaps it didn't matter to you that your own sister hanged because of your heroics, and your old wet-nurse, and your father's old butler. But they were all only servants, weren't they?'

He got up then, his cards abandoned, shoving back his

own chair. '*Stop it.*' He enunciated each word with savage care, and then a light came into his eyes that really did frighten her.

You fool. You've gone too far.

With a clear effort, Kit regained self-control. 'My dear Miss Arwenack, have you no idea just how many other things I'd rather be doing than acting as bear-leader to her royal highness? I'm sworn to protect her, after all. I may not like this duty overmuch, but I shan't let anything stand in my way, and I'm always extremely thorough in everything I do. Do you understand? Everything.'

She took a step towards him; she wasn't afraid, but he didn't move, which as a gentleman he ought to have done. They were less than a bare inch apart, he with a kindling expression on his face that had her momentarily lost for words and all too aware of the low-cut bodice of her gown; she was, for once, utterly out of her depth. 'I fail to see what your conscientious habits have to do with me. What do you want, a campaign medal?'

'No, I've already got several of those.' He smiled again then, his eyes hard. 'Let me make myself clear. I'm captain of her highness's personal bodyguard; I'm on my way to Calais to escort her to Fontainebleau. Naturally, I don't intend to let anyone stop me. You have your own agenda, which at the moment I don't fully understand. Frankly, I'm not sure I want to. If you won't deal honestly with me, you'll learn that I'm not in the habit of granting any quarter to those who get in my way, that's all. I can't be any clearer about it. Is there anything you wish to say?'

Clemency looked him up and down: God, he hadn't

changed. He was still just as arrogant as ever, just as oblivious to the limitations faced by anyone who wasn't the hopelessly spoiled second son of an earl.

'Well?' Kit said, lordly and now really furious all in one, and she restrained herself from dealing out the slap he so richly deserved.

'I have nothing to say to you, Kit Helford. Nothing at all.'

Turning before he could reply, she left him there, walking straight out of the room. Kit sent Marie scurrying after her, the young maidservant lighting her way up to her bedchamber; at first, she thought Kit might follow, but she was on her own.

20

As the carriage slowed, tall thin houses gave way to wharves of dilapidated warehouses and the rain intensified, drumming on the roof. At last they drew to a halt, and when Clemency looked out of the window she saw the dark bulk of the royal yacht alongside the quay. At an abrupt knock, her carriage door swung open. Instead of a groom to hand her out, Kit stood waiting with one ungloved hand outstretched, tall and dark in his long greatcoat. D'Harcourt squinted through the rain, looking askance at the chaos of shouting pursers and dithering well-dressed passengers.

'Miss Arwenack?' Kit addressed her with one eyebrow cocked, waiting. Beyond the most basic pleasantries, they had exchanged not a word since parting in that lamplit parlour, three nights ago now.

Clemency took his hand. She at least was gloved in kidskin, aware of the warm, lean strength in his fingers. 'How kind.' She stepped down on to the rain-washed cobblestones with dismissive courtesy. 'Thank you so much.' She turned to d'Harcourt, aware of Kit's gaze on her. 'Has her highness disembarked, Commandant? My woman knows to have the furs and blankets prepared in our carriage: I expect her highness will be ready to enjoy all possible comforts after a crossing in this weather.'

'I'll look into it.' D'Harcourt spoke with weary resignation, rain streaming from his crested hat. 'It looks like exactly the typical sort of nightmare that unfolds when a simple task is left to civilians.'

He strode off into the downpour and Clemency turned to Kit; in the same instant, they released each other's hands. 'Tell Bluette to have your own baggage ready,' he said. 'You're going home. You've had your chance to spill; I don't care what the hell sort of game you want to play, but if you think I don't see pretty clearly that you intend to get in my way, then you're mistaken. I don't allow people to ambush me with petty bloody court intrigue.'

'You don't allow it?' She laughed, so furious in that moment that it was impossible to do anything else. 'I can't help but admire your cheek, Lieutenant Colonel, but I think you'll find that my royal appointment has absolutely nothing to do with you.'

He smiled, but even in the moonlight she saw that uncharacteristically hard gleam in his eyes again. It unleashed a breathless plummeting sensation in her belly, as though she'd just missed her footing on a cliff-top path. 'All I need to do is inform Dorothea Lieven that you're compromised and you'll be on a return trip to Dover,' he said pleasantly. 'Don't make the mistake of thinking I can't contrive it.'

'Of course you can contrive it when Dorothea has known you since the hour of your birth,' Clemency snapped. 'But that doesn't make it a sensible or a rational plan. Have you stopped to consider that you might be interfering in something you don't have the least comprehension of?'

He had already turned, though, and was walking away towards the chaos on the dockside, leaving her standing, presumably to await his orders.

'Haven't you learned by now not to rush your fences, Kitto Helford?' She allowed her voice to carry over the widening distance between them. He stopped, turning to her once more with such an expression of repressed force that it was as if only a thin cloak of civilised social nicety prevented him from carrying her to the royal yacht with his own bare hands.

'What?'

She had one chance. 'It's always been your besetting sin and obviously it still is,' she said. 'Dynamiting French garrisons in the Occupation. Torching palaces. Shooting marquises in gentlemen's clubs. *Acting without bloody well thinking.*'

He strode swiftly back towards her. 'What the devil are you talking about?' He spoke with such quiet and arousing menace that she felt a startled awareness of her clothing: lace-edged stays, trimmed silk bodice and undergarments, skirts that now felt shockingly insubstantial. 'I entirely fail to see what the hell has that got to do with you, or with this situation now.'

'It's got everything to do with me because you haven't changed; you never learn,' Clemency said: if he thought

she was about to succumb to his charms, he ought to think
again. 'Rushing in, sure as damnation that you know best
when you're not even in full possession of all the facts, and
never mind the consequences.'

'Fine.' Kit's eyes darkened. 'If you think I'm going to
defend my considerable charge sheet to a quayside Newlyn
brat, you're quite out, but I'm very sure that I don't have
time to play your games now. Stay, if that's what you wish.
But if you cross me, you'll be very sorry indeed, do you
understand?'

Clemency watched him walk swiftly towards the quay,
the tails of his regimental greatcoat whipping out behind
him as he went, knowing what she'd see if she turned her
head to face the rain: a whisk of starched pinafore, an
unreachable girl, always just out of sight.

Kit Helford didn't begin to have the smallest notion how
far she'd go, no matter how long a game she must play.

Kit knew she was watching him as he walked away. Jesus
bloody Christ, the way she'd looked at him with purest
anger, her eyes dark with desire he couldn't be sure she'd
even admitted to herself. She knew the worst of him, damn
her. Clemency Arwenack might be an abandoned little
criminal, but if her methods of extortion didn't extend
to seduction it was only because she didn't care about
the considerable effect of her very direct stare, those rare
flashes of sincerity, and that habit of occasionally swapping
prudish high-necked gowns for exquisitely cut confections
that only barely concealed her breasts. It was a battle not

giving in to the instinct that had kept him alive on countless battlefields: she was in danger, too. It wasn't the extortion of Count de Mercy-Argenteau, either: she'd barely flinched when confronted with that at the coaching inn. She was up to something else and they both knew it, hustling for her Boscobel friends, pushing for influence at court like a damned little card sharp. Doubtless she meant to knife him just as she'd knifed the count. Either way, if Miss Arwenack chose to cross him, she'd very soon regret it, even if she had spoken no more than the truth tonight: he was in danger of rushing his fences. If he didn't squash this white-hot burst of rage and rapidly summon his wits, he'd deal very badly indeed with Nadezhda Romanova, that was certain.

Kit wiped the scowl from his face and approached the chaotic jumble of stevedores, sailors and arguing servants with well-trained calm. God, d'Harcourt had been right; it really was the sort of unholy mess only civilians were capable of making: harassed pursers shouting, upturned valises spewing furs and undergarments, bolts of cloth falling into noisome puddles. Pickpockets darted like minnows, and a maidservant went off into hysterics at the sight of a panicking mare unloaded in a sling from the foredeck of the royal yacht. The mare screamed as it rose into the air, dropping horseshit over the assembled crowd, and Kit snatched hold of the nearest infant thief by the collar just as the brat was taking a dip into the pockets of a parson who had formed part of the crowd for reasons better known to himself.

'Fuck off unless you want the chop.' The filthy child froze and then fled; every last one of his criminal colleagues in

Kit's vicinity stopped what they were doing and scattered. Kit raised his voice. '*Stop*.' Everyone on the quayside immediately halted and Kit turned to the nearest stevedore with a stream of orders issued in a tone that his own men would have recognised all too well; the scene was cleared in a matter of ten minutes. The crowd melted away, leaving only a bucking, rearing horse now released from the sling and a small knot of onlookers that surely included Nadezhda herself, a cloaked and slender figure breaking away from the small gathering, moving towards the Arab mare with swift confidence. The Arab bucked, but Nadezhda went straight to her head just as Kit had known she would. In moments she had the horse calm, handing her over to a servant.

He could do nothing then but watch as Her Royal Highness Princess Nadezhda Sofia Romanova walked towards him with all the ease of a woman who was well versed in the art of making others late. For the first time in more than half a decade, they faced one another: he and Nadezhda, all the quiet efforts of his brother and her courtiers quite undone, so that he became only dimly aware of the rain. He said nothing, waiting for her to speak. Nadezhda shrugged back the hood of her cloak in a movement so familiar that he wished he could turn around and walk away; the flash of diamonds at her white throat should not have been a surprise. Of course she wore diamonds now.

'I suppose I should be grateful that you haven't stormed in with an ill-informed attempt to take control as every other man would have done,' Nadezhda said at last, impervious to the rain beading her cropped curls. She watched him with that dark, intelligent gaze he had never forgotten, not in every last ballroom and whorehouse from Russia to Vienna and London and back again.

Kit only shrugged. 'Why should I have done? You had the situation perfectly well under control. The only difficulty is that your staff are cold, wet and exhausted, and I'm sure there's a good reason why there was no one on board with the necessary skill to manage this horse except for yourself. Your highness, I beg you will allow me to escort you to the carriage.'

She smiled. 'But I have no intention of travelling in the carriage after being cooped up at sea for two interminable days, Lieutenant Colonel. Why on earth would I have troubled to bring my new horse if I didn't intend to ride her?'

Kit crushed a flare of irritation, aware that Clemency, d'Harcourt and Dorothea Lieven had approached and were waiting for them both in the rain. 'With respect, it isn't safe, your highness. Even if d'Harcourt and I were to ride ourselves, we couldn't guarantee your protection on horseback.'

'I can ride as well.' Clemency spoke up so suddenly that everyone stared at her. She dropped into a clipped curtsey, rain dripping from the neat spray of feathers on her hat: she'd just shattered a yard-long list of royal protocol, so that Dorothea Lieven visibly winced. Kit didn't miss the flare of challenge in Clemency's fine, long-lashed eyes.

'Well, I certainly don't mean to go on horseback,' Dorothea said, rain dripping off the fur-lined hood of her habit. 'I'm fagged to death. I intend to fall immediately asleep beneath a fur in a nice, well-sprung carriage, but if Miss Arwenack rides as well, I don't know what more you could object to, Christophe, darling? It's adorable that you're so concerned by the proprieties, though: your papa will be spinning in his grave, I shouldn't wonder.'

'Where to begin?' Kit said, correcting the flash of temper with a bow. 'I doubt that the average French highwayman will care if her highness is accompanied in spiritual cleanliness by a female companion.' He cast a quick glance at Nadezhda, who looked more amused than anything else. 'It can't be done unless you ride with me, actually with me in the saddle, which is out of the question, of course, because that would be so very damnably improper.'

'I do believe that's your problem, not mine,' Nadezhda said, with a glimmer of flirtatious laughter in her dark eyes. 'It's been such a long time that I'm afraid I can't resist. Anyway, aren't you going to kiss me, Khristofyor?' She smiled, and Kit knew he had not quite managed to hide his expression of swiftly subdued anger, even as he obeyed, raising her gloved hand to his lips.

21

Nadezhda closed her eyes as they rode into the rain, weightless and free. Day after day on the road had passed in a blur of sensation: Helford's torso warm and hard against at her back, his lean muscled limbs entwined about hers as if they were already lovers; instinct had long since warned her to let him take the reins, and he did this one-handed with an arm around her waist in shocking intimacy. The downpour had intensified into a constant waterfall, but ahead she could just make out Miss Arwenack mounted on a chestnut mare, utterly straight-backed in the saddle as if the rain didn't touch her. Clemency had a neat figure, a surprisingly beautiful seat that looked as if it was probably natural, and had so far displayed only reserved competence. There was no hint yet of what Dorothea had promised in her bedchamber at St James's Palace all those weeks ago: a girl who went to parties with Lady Boscobel, gambling long into the night. A girl with secrets, not to put too fine a point on it. There wasn't much use in having a Mistress of the Robes at all unless one could compromise the little fool right up to the hilt, and Nadezhda fully intended to discover exactly what Clemency had to hide. She hadn't made a single complaint about riding for a fourth day, or even the weather, and Nadezhda was only too well aware that the royal insignia embroidered in gold across the bodice of her velvet riding habit was the single thing protecting her from the tongue-lashing that Kit Helford would not have hesitated to deal out as a hot-tempered seventeen-year-old captain.

The dressing-down he so clearly longed to unleash would have been justified, too: *if*, of course, one had no understanding of her situation.

Gossip this hot moved faster than fire: she'd leave it to Louis Charles Habsburg-Lorraine to imagine Kit Helford holding her with such firm possession, his fingers occasionally grazing the narrow curve of her velvet-clad waist, even though he moved with the most intoxicating angry restraint. Unwittingly or not, Kit's occasionally lingering touch made it only too clear that there was a price to pay if she wished to use him in this way: he would leave her wanting more while she did it. No, Prince Louis Charles had better very quickly come to understand who was to hold the riding crop in their betrothal. Alone in her cabin on the royal yacht with the oil lamp flickering and swinging, she had studied the miniature portrait hour upon hour. The golden-haired Prince of Hungary had already offered her the set-down of not actually even writing to her himself, leaving that to a Habsburg-Lorraine aunt who had littered her correspondence with so much religious homily that Nadezhda would have laughed had she not been so angry.

'We've arrived.' Kit leaned forwards a little, speaking into her ear in clipped French as he reined in, halting the horse, quite obviously savouring the movement of his body against her own. He was right: the lights of a château glowed across a flattened expanse of sodden wheat. Yet another French aristocrat with his lands and title restored after the Revolution; yet another evening of tolerable food and provincial conversation. He was annoyed that she was forcing her party to ride in this weather; it was rather satisfying that he had no way to express it.

'I can see that. Did you have another point to make beyond stating the obvious?'

She felt a shiver of tension pass through him: whether it was anger or amusement she couldn't tell; he made no reply and just spurred on the Arab, squeezing her a little between his thighs as he adjusted his position in the saddle. He had glorious legs even if he was in a colossal sulk. The Arab cantered up the long, sweeping driveway towards a puddled courtyard where the carriages were already assembled: her own staff were everywhere, riling the comte's liveried footmen with sarcastic sotto voce civilities that drifted across the courtyard.

Kit dismounted and she felt the lack of his warmth, cold air at her back as he swung himself out of the saddle with practised grace. She couldn't help noticing how his gaze lingered on Miss Arwenack's slight figure; she had dismounted too and was issuing a stream of instructions to an elderly major-domo who was attempting to shield her from the rain with an umbrella of oiled Aurillac silk, even as she strode from one heap of corded trunks and damp bandboxes to the next. She stepped out from behind the carriage again with the white-haired major-domo still at her heels, one arm around the shoulders of a tearful young woman of the bedchamber whose named Nadezhda couldn't even recall.

'Yes, precisely, that's what I said – a mustard footbath. It's exactly the thing for a head cold, and I'm afraid I do think the poor girl is feverish.' Miss Arwenack's voice carried across the courtyard, competent and collected.

'Do you not tire of this yet, your highness?' In the rainy gloom, Kit's eyes were a silvery grey, very pale against the darkness of his lashes. What could he say, after all? She was Princess Nadezhda Sofia. Those eyes darkened now, betraying his arousal.

Nadezhda dismounted then, splashing into the mud so that they stood face to face in the downpour. 'What exactly is that supposed to mean?'

'The carriages,' he said, with restrained patience. 'It may suit you to ride with me day after day, your highness, titillating your future husband with a bit of forward-going scandal about it, but are you sure that your new lady-in-waiting has a reputation that can stand up to this?'

White-hot rage shot through her. 'Don't make the mistake of believing that familiarity entitles you to impertinence,' she said calmly.

'Indeed, I'm sorry,' he said. 'Of course there is no familiarity at all.'

22

At dinner in the great hall at the Château de Sigy, the Comtesse de Sigy laid a roguish hand on Kit's thigh beneath the table; she was at least four parts drunk. To top that off, they had invited the curate, who took the opportunity to treat the table to a homily about the forgiveness of past sins even in wartime, which was pretty awkward when Kit had exterminated more Frenchmen than he cared to count. Worse, the curate's badly dressed wife stared with unabashed interest at d'Harcourt across the lamb with stuffed tomatoes and the sea bass with hollandaise sauce and the saffron orange cream, exactly as though he were a curiosity at a circus. Thomas himself was doing his best to field a series of increasingly impertinent questions from the comtesse about his family in Cairo whilst Nadezhda behaved with predictable childishness. Dressed in white satin with the royal sash across her breast, she refused to allow the red-faced Comte de Sigy at her left-hand side to draw her into conversation; Clemency, meanwhile, held up a one-sided conversation with the comte's boorish son. Selecting a cherry from a silver dish, she glanced across the table, meeting Kit's gaze over the array of silver dishes and crystal glasses with a sudden flash of humour, as though all this were a joke they shared.

'Tell me, dear Commandant, is it very hot in Egypt?' The comtesse turned to d'Harcourt with an over-familiar smile, resting one hand upon his arm. 'For a man of African descent, you're very pale, aren't you? One might almost believe you to be purely European.'

Thomas smiled straight ahead at the candles. 'Cairo is hotter than Orléans, ma'am, I grant you.'

'And what about your religion? Do we have a Mussulman among us?' she persisted, with a shattering burst of laughter. 'Goodness, if we're not careful we shall find ourselves witness to a theological argument between you and our dear Father Valmes. I must admit, I do find other cultures so fascinating.'

'I'm sorry to disappoint, ma'am,' d'Harcourt said evenly, 'but I'm afraid I was born into the Orthodox Christian faith.'

'How *so* tremendously exotic, all the same,' she went on, brushing the back of d'Harcourt's hand with one plump white fingertip.

'I couldn't help noticing your rose garden, Comtesse,' Kit said, giving her no choice but to leave d'Harcourt alone and grant him her full attention. 'My mother started one at home in Cornwall before I was born, and I notice you have many of the same varieties. Are they specifically French?'

'As a matter of fact, they are.' She looked up at him from

beneath lowered lashes; as she reached for her wine glass he couldn't help breathing in the sickly scent of the perspiration soaking into the underarms of her satin evening gown. 'And are you specifically French, Lieutenant Colonel Helford? I actually knew your mother through her aunt. Claire de Saint-Maure was quite the beauty, you know. Tall as a reed and such a sweet smile, she had – very like your own, with those dimples. I can understand why your father was minded to spirit her away out of France. But doesn't that leave you feeling rather compromised at these negotiations? French mother, English papa. How difficult that must have been for you during the war.'

In the silence that followed, Kit was well aware that Clemency was watching him in some amusement, even as he fought the desire to inform the Comtesse de Sigy that his sire had been Cornish down to the eleventh generation with scarcely an English bone in his body. Nadezhda just looked bored, toying with her wine glass, d'Harcourt politely stunned. Kit shrugged. 'It's not uncommon to have a few French relations, ma'am; I served in the British army, after all, and I swore allegiance to her highness.'

The clergyman's wife stared across the table; even Valmes had been momentarily silenced, sweating into his curate's robes in the heat of the fire and the blaze of candlelight.

'How wonderful to hear it, Lieutenant Colonel Helford,' Nadezhda said, with an openly flirtatious smile that Kit knew only too well would likely wash up in Fontainebleau and Paris as a full-blown affair. London, too, in all probability, where doubtless someone would find a way of blaming Hester for it. *Christ.*

The sweating clergyman launched into a soliloquy about the weather, but the comtesse just spoke straight across him; she was clearly a lot more drunk than she looked. 'I must say, but surely at least it's rather awkward at court with your history, Lieutenant Colonel Helford – Christophe, if I may?' She broke off into a peal of shattering laughter, moving away from Kit, thank God, as the footmen began to remove the covers. 'I mean, the fire at Carlton House—'

'—took place eight years ago, my dear Comtesse,' Nadezhda said, leaning back in her chair so that the candle-light struck the royal insignia on her sash of blue silk. 'I would say there's more than a single act of youthful vandalism to forget between our two nations, and so we had all better practise the art of forgiveness as soon as we may. The ladies will retire now.'

'What a charming idea,' Clemency said with a bright smile. 'May I trouble you for a tour of the gallery, Comtesse?'

In the lengthening silence that followed their departure, d'Harcourt silently slid the brandy across the table; Kit accepted it without question.

Hours later, Kit woke in darkness, hearing only the distant call of an owl and d'Harcourt's steady breathing in the other bed: despite the Comtesse de Sigy's groaning supper-table, the footman had apologetically admitted that the fourth-best guest-chamber had a hole of considerable size in the roof. As the two gentlemen were both military men, he hoped they would not mind sharing quarters. Kit didn't, even if d'Harcourt had lain on his bed writing meteorological observations in a leather-bound notebook, only once looking up to survey Kit's scattered trail of shirts and cravats. His own top boots had been neatly lined up at the end of his bed before his valet even came in. *Good Lord, Helford, doesn't your man despair of you?* D'Harcourt didn't know Phelps, who would have been mortally insulted if Kit picked up his own cravats.

Damn it all to hell, though, had he really imagined that sound? The soft tread of footfalls in the corridor outside?

Unless the curate had something going on with the comtesse, this wasn't the sort of house party where you expected migration between bedchambers. The room was lit only by embers glowing behind the brass fire screen, and Kit leaned on one elbow, listening. No, he wasn't mistaken: he heard it again – a soft creak, weight placed upon a floorboard. Reaching for his breeches, Kit pulled them on rapidly along with his boots; God only knew he had no intention of confronting an intruder naked as the day he was born. D'Harcourt was already sitting up, shedding his nightshirt and scrambling into his clothes, revealing a flash of dark underarm hair. By the time Kit reached for his pistol, the footfalls were by now unmistakable and they moved to the door as one. After a shared glance in the firelit gloom, d'Harcourt reached out and opened the door: the hallway was dark and quiet – a creak sounded away to their left, in the precise direction of the comtesse's bedchamber where Nadezhda had been accommodated with Clemency in the dressing-room next door. A bolt of awareness slid down Kit's spine as if someone had just dragged a stinging nettle slowly down his naked back. Slowly, slowly they made their way down the pitch-black corridor, passing an occasional table laden with a bowl of dried rose petals that filled the stale air with their scent, Kit sensing d'Harcourt behind him: if the man's loyalties left anything to be desired, now would be the time to find out.

At the sound of faint footfalls, Clemency got out of bed, signalling wildly at Bluette not to move from her truckle bed. Thank God Bluette had the sense to keep quiet; she sat up, clutching the covers to her chest, her eyes glittering in a shaft of moonlight sweeping into the room between the curtains. A deep, ingrained instinct warned Clemency that this wasn't just the princess moving about in her own chamber next door. Nadezhda was small and slender: these footfalls spoke of a heavier weight. Crossing the room quickly, carpet warm underfoot as she passed by the glowing embers of the fire, she reached the adjoining door, which had been left ajar. Nadezhda had complained earlier that the room was badly aired, which was true; she'd insisted that the curtains were left open, the window slightly ajar. Reaching the door, Clemency froze where she stood, terror coursing through her.

There was a man in Nadezhda's room, his outline framed by the moonlit window. Unable to move, Clemency's gaze slid to the left; Nadezhda was crouching on the pillows of her bed in her nightgown. Reaching beneath a bolster, she motioned minutely at Clemency to stay where she was. All the same, she found herself inching backwards into her own bedchamber; in thick, terrified silence, she held a finger to her lips, signalling at Bluette to keep quiet. She hadn't moved. Crouching, Clemency reached out for the chamber pot between her bed and Bluette's, her fingers closing over the chilly enamel handle.

Then she ran across the room, quick and silent. She made sure not to look at the fire this time, and by the time she reached Nadezhda's room her eyes had grown used to the dark. He looked so ordinary: heavyset, only a little older than her, Nadezhda and Bluette, with nondescript brown hair and a shaving cut on his lower jaw. With a grin, he turned to face Nadezhda, who smiled back and shot him with a small pistol she must have concealed beneath the bedclothes. Nothing happened: a misfire. In a surge of movement, Clemency stood up with the chamber pot in both hands and brought it down as hard and as fast as she could on the back of their assailant's head so that black blood ran in a thick sudden river down the back of his freckled neck.

With a roar of pain and rage he turned around to face her, his face twisted with fury: he'd dropped his pistol, though. Nadezhda reloaded and fired, but the shot only caught him in the shoulder, and now he turned on her and grasped her around the neck with both hands, pushing her backwards on to the vast canopied bed. Clemency scrabbled to reach the pistol he'd dropped, but then couldn't remember how to reload let alone fire it, and their attacker now was on top of Nadezhda, bearing down upon her, his shoulders twitching with the effort of choking her. Gasping, Clemency tried to scream but no sound came out; all she could hear was Bluette shrieking for help from the next room.

*

Kit heard the familiar click of a misfiring pistol, followed by a shot, and covered the remaining distance to the comtesse's bedroom at a sprint, moving so quietly with d'Harcourt that they took Nadezhda's assailant by surprise. He'd been throttling her, his meaty shoulders hunched over the task. Now he turned, drawing a dagger, blade glinting in the moonlight – but all the same a man who used his bare hands as a weapon before anything else.

Nadezhda's face was frozen in a rictus of enraged fear and she had scrabbled backwards against the ornately carved headboard of the canopied bed. Even as her attacker whirled around to face them, Kit sprang forwards with his curved Mameluke dagger out. Feinting with the knife, he snatched at the man's injured shoulder, eliciting a spittle-flecked roar of agony. Spinning him around with violent speed, Kit got one arm around the man's throat, see how he fucking well liked it. Kit squeezed and choked as he crushed his assailant's wrist, forcing him to let go of the knife; he was distantly aware of d'Harcourt scrabbling across the floorboards for it.

The attacker was quick and damned strong with it, writhing like a salmon, hooking one foot around Kit's ankle in an attempt to bring him down, but he was alive to that, even as he felt the sudden, quick hot shock of burning pain in his lower belly: the little shit had got another blade into him, hopefully not into anything too important. Kit's head spun with the burning shock of it, but this wasn't the first time he'd been stabbed; he didn't have long to react. With a shriek of table legs across waxed boards, they crashed to the floor, and Kit was just aware of d'Harcourt covering Nadezhda with his pistol, and a door flying open, lamplight spilling into the room.

Kit felt another sharp burst of pain and then the resistance as he forced his dagger through skin, shoving it home with impatience even as blood spattered his face. He pushed the bastard away before the usual hot piss of a dying man went everywhere, kneeling on his chest to make sure he was really dead, not even bothering to crush the quick hot flare of satisfaction. Kit was just aware of frantic voices around him but paid no attention to any of it until he saw the life go out of the attacker's eyes – the fucker really was dead.

'*Sav,* Helford!' *Stop!* He looked up to find Clemency standing over him in her nightgown, hair loose down her back, speaking in Cornish. 'Jesus bloody Christ, you're not supposed to be enjoying this.'

Hands on hips, she looked him up and down. Kit was just aware of d'Harcourt helping Nadezhda out of the room with Clemency's lady's maid Bluette, the dissonance of barefoot women with loose hair and nightgowns, d'Harcourt's shirt unbuttoned down to the chest and untucked.

He laughed. 'Dear God, what a state we're all in.' The words came to him in Cornish, his first tongue, but that didn't matter, not with her.

'If anyone's a state,' Clemency said, tartly and still in Cornish, 'it's you. Honestly. Sit down on the bed; I've rung for hot water. You're spewing blood like a stuck pig, you idiot. Better you ruin my sheets than her highness's – what are you waiting for, the Second Coming of the Lord?'

'Never mind the hot water,' Kit said, ignoring the waves of pain. 'We need to know if there's any more where he came from. Wait here – I'm serious. D'Harcourt and I need to search the grounds.'

23

Kit and D'Harcourt quartered the gardens and demesne in driving rain: they found nothing and no one but between them had to manage the well-meaning but useless efforts of Sigy and his son. Thank God it had been clear at a glance that the head stableman and gardener roused from their beds were both former military men and could be relied on to make a proper job of the rest of it, and of stationing a guard around the house.

'Whoever it was, they like as not acted alone,' d'Harcourt said, expressionless in the moonlight as they walked back to the house, even as dark tendrils crept across Kit's field of vision. 'You're about to swoon like a debutante in the Café des Aveugles. Come on, we may as well go back to the house. Georges and his man will watch the grounds.'

'Never mind that. Can we trust Sigy with her highness?' Kit said, squinting at the lamplit windows of the château through the rain. 'He's made a show of helping us, but how the devil do we know he's not behind this himself? This is insane: two months ago, this would have been enemy territory for me and for her.' Kit laughed, which was agony, blood seeping through his fingers. 'I'm honest to God escorting an English princess through French territory, with a Frenchman. Whose idea was this, anyway?'

D'Harcourt marched along at his side; their boots crunched into the gravel. 'Come on, do you think our every host wasn't thoroughly investigated before we set out? Napoleon doesn't want to be blamed for a princess with her throat cut. Look, Helford, we've been given this detail. We're going to have to trust each other to an extent.'

Kit said nothing; his every instinct told him he could trust d'Harcourt as a man, but men were often given orders that conflicted with their true nature: such was life.

D'Harcourt sighed. 'Well, you assured me it was safe to leave the princess with your valet, after all, and like a fool I took your word for that.'

'I wouldn't trust her with anyone else, if I'm honest, Thomas. Phelps is just as good with a garrotte as he is with my top boots, fortunately.'

Clattering up the wide front steps of the château, they were greeted in the cavernous black-and-white-tiled vestibule by the comtesse in a quilted dressing gown and curl-papers, and a phalanx of night-capped servants in varying states of undress. Looking at Kit, the comtesse screamed and dropped her night light, and Clemency elbowed her way past a housemaid with a nightgown set on fire by the comtesse's candle, ignoring the shrieking.

'Come on,' she said to Kit, with a complete lack of sentiment. 'You're causing chaos.'

He was light-headed enough to allow d'Harcourt to stalk away to assure himself of Phelps's competence; bowing, he followed Clemency upstairs, doing his best to observe the pain as if from the outside. The shock of the wound had worn off, and it was no longer coming in waves but a constant battery; they were in Nadezhda's room now, coverlets spilled over the bed, the dead body of her assailant still sprawled upon the Comtesse de Sigy's Turkey rug: that was unfortunate.

'For goodness' sake,' Clemency said, and he allowed her to back him against the panelled wall, staring up at him with such ferocity. 'Look at the state of you.'

'Never mind me,' he said. 'You hit an assassin over the head with a chamber pot.' He laughed, which hurt like hell. 'Dear God, Clemency.'

'Oh, be quiet and *lie down*. Come into my room. I don't feel much like mopping up blood with a dead body on the floor, although I see that you're not in the slightest bit particular about these things.' She took one of the folded linen cloths from the pile left on the bedside table and took a bowl of steaming water from a speechless footman hovering in the doorway.

He followed her as she stalked through into her own small bedchamber, which led directly off Nadezhda's: clearly, it was usually the comtesse's dressing-room, still redolent with the scent of her perfume. The windows in here were unshuttered, the heavy brocade curtains had not been drawn and moonlight slanted in, revealing the outline of Clemency's curved and slender form through the fine lawn of her nightgown. There were two beds set up in an awkward space between the window and the comtesse's dressing-table; Bluette, thank God, was nowhere to be seen.

Damn it, why did it feel like the most natural thing in the world that he should go up to a bedchamber with Clemency, like man and wife of twenty years? Why did it feel so entirely right that he should want to tug at the ribbons of her nightgown so that the entire frilled confection slid down over her shoulders, and the devil take the consequences?

She set down the basin and cloths with furious economy, opening the window so that cool night air flooded in, scented with that afternoon's cut grass.

'*On the bed!*' Clemency hissed, and so he sat down just to silence her; when would she deign to share her secrets with him, the damned little shrew? His head spun and he lay down on the mound of pillows, and she sat beside him, wiping with methodical care at the blood so that warm water ran warm down the side of his torso and on to her bed.

'God, such a fuss, as if this were even the worst I've ever had. I'm making a damned mess of your coverlet.'

'Oh, do be quiet. It needs more pressure. I'm going to unbutton your breeches.' Unabashed, she climbed on to the bed so that she straddled him in her nightgown, her loose hair brushing the naked expanse of skin at his belly.

'The devil you are.' He swatted at her behind with one flat hand as she bent over him, but all she did was tell him to spare her the melodrama.

'As if it's anything I haven't seen before: we used to swim naked, if you recall. Don't worry, I'm not going to ravish you.'

He didn't stop her although he could have; she undid

the buttons, quick and deft, folding down the top of his breeches just a little, as she'd promised, pressing a folded wet cloth against his hot and ruined bloodied skin so that he let out a gasp of relief as their eyes met. It was hard to say who moved first, but either way she kissed him back with such ferocity, pinning one hand above his head so that he wasn't about to stand for it, and despite the hot waves of pain, a moment later he was teasing her neck with kisses of his own. It felt preordained, as if he had been waiting for years just to do this.

'I expect,' he said, looking up at her, 'that you think you're trying to throw me off guard while you suppose I'm at a disadvantage. Do you know, it's really about time that someone gave you what for.'

'Not if you get it first.' She kissed him again, one hand in his hair.

'We'll see about that,' he said, running one hand up her leg; he would have that damned nightgown out of the way. 'You tell me, my dear. Shall we see?'

'Get on with it, you insufferable bloody aristocrat.'

'With pleasure, my little extortionist.' With one merciless tug, Kit loosed the thick satin ribbon at the neckline of her nightdress so that the fine white lawn slipped away, revealing her right breast, and he teased the hardened nipple in a ruthlessly gentle circling motion so that she cried out in unalloyed pleasure, arching her back. He kissed her again, and the taste of her was better than the bloody elation of coming through a battle still alive even when everyone else was dead around him, but then all of a sudden she pulled away, with such desolation writ all over her face that he released her. Kit absorbed all the shock and pain as if it were a physical blow, exactly as if he'd taken a hit after all.

'I'm sorry,' she said, breathless, eyes wide. 'I'll send for a servant to help you. This was really very wrong of me, truly.'

It was the first honest thing she had said to him since he'd set eyes on her dispassionately delimbing Count de Mercy-Argenteau in a candlelit antechamber: he could see that. 'For God's sake, never mind the moralities. Clemency, do you honestly believe I'd kiss you like that or even at all if I wasn't going to make it right?'

She just shook her head, scrambling away and clutching fragile linen about her as though his touch burned her; did she think he would pursue her if she didn't wish it? All he could do was watch as she walked swiftly from the room with her hair in tangled coils down to her waist, nightgown billowing out behind her as she fled, leaving him with the words dying on his lips: *Marry me and have done with it all, you little witch*. One sinner might deserve another, but the worst of her crimes were nothing to his.

'Get that end tied off, will you?' Kit said, four fingers down a very large glass of hot rum, and now a stranger to courtesy.

D'Harcourt snipped the catgut suture with a pair of steel shears that flashed in the candlelight, raising his eyebrows with sarcastic sincerity. 'Tidy enough for you, my lord?'

'Oh shut up, you're just as much of a seigneur as I am, d'Harcourt, if not more so, considering you're the oldest son and I'm a mere spare.'

172

'Tell that to my stepmother. She spent the entire war hoping one of your lot would finish me so my father would be succeeded by one of her own children instead of a boy from Cairo.'

Kit winced. 'What a bitch. What did Bluette say – Miss Arwenack's servant?'

'Her highness is sleeping, and your man Phelps is looking like he'll eat anyone who comes near her. Can you raise yourself? I need to pass the bandage underneath you. You were lucky that knife didn't hit anything important.'

'I've always been lucky.'

'Yes, a regular gallows-cheat: I remember the newspaper reports from London in the Occupation. I read all about your escape from the scaffold in *Le Moniteur* over breakfast with my tutor. And now I'm working with a notorious rebel: delightful, I'm sure.'

'I was only a rebel because you French had invaded my country. Now we're on the same side, you may just consider me efficient.'

'Indeed,' d'Harcourt said, pinning the bandage with calm competence, 'so efficient that the one person who might have told us who is trying to kill her highness now lies dead as a doornail. As if your countrymen have the slightest leg to stand on when it comes to invading others, either.'

'Oh please, you are no better,' Kit said, glad of the searing-hot rum; he would just have to put up with how much this hurt and pray for sleep – laudanum was too much of a risk. And yet he could not escape the certainty that it wasn't even Nadezhda who needed salvation, but Clemency and perhaps himself, too, considering the quick hot flare of satisfied enjoyment he had felt on plunging his dagger into the dead man who now lay in the Comte de Sigy's wine cellar.

They would have to send ahead word of the attack; part of Kit wished he was still the young soldier who would be tasked with a mud-splattering gallop over several days, nothing to do but ride like the devil and change horses, without thinking too hard about who exactly had sent an assassin to kill the heir apparent to the English throne before she had even reached the peace congress, or how many more times this was likely to happen, and who was behind it.

24

Three days later, Nadezhda's cavalcade and baggage train crept ever closer to Fontainebleau; she had ordered the carriages to continue overnight at a decent clip, changing horses at every possible staging-post. The Arwenack girl had fallen asleep with her head against the curtained window after allowing Nadezhda to win at both travel chess and two hands of piquet: Clemency played just as well as Nadezhda anticipated, commanding her features with iron-hard self-control, despite the desolate expression in her eyes that even she couldn't conceal 100 per cent of the time.

In the course of six long years spent at a foreign court, Nadezhda had knowingly used all her charm to win over the right people. Now, when she visited provincial market towns in unpronounceable parts of the rain-washed English countryside, she was greeted by smiling local gentry and little farmers' daughters presenting her with bouquets, instead of silent suspicion. That had taken time. It had also taken years of close observation: watching, listening, noting all the little things that people gave away about themselves without even realising.

Clemency Arwenack was an intriguing puzzle.

This evening, she had engineered her own loss with a deft combination of self-denial and sleight of hand, tucking loose strands of plain brown hair behind her ear and flushing across those freckled cheekbones. The fragile skin beneath her eyes was bruised purple with exhaustion as though she tended to sit awake most of the night until sleep finally caught up with her. Nadezhda was close to sleep herself when Clemency's hands began to move. In the grip of a dream, she plucked at the plaid blanket with fretful speed, as if searching in vain for her last banknote. Her eyelids flickered rapidly and she began feeling along the seat cushions, the blanket slipping off her lap, and that was when she tried to scream. First it was just a formless sound, coagulating into distinct words in a tongue Nadezhda hadn't heard since she'd last seen Kit whispering to wild horses, long ago.

Ow flogh vian. Ow flog vian. The distinct words tailed off into a yell that the postillions must have heard; questions would be asked if it happened again, and with swift efficiency Nadezhda leaned forwards, clamping her hand over Clemency's mouth. Clemency opened her eyes in staring panic, disorientated, her face drained of colour so that the dusting of freckles stood out in sharp relief.

'Be quiet,' Nadezhda said softly, not moving, still with one hand over Clemency's mouth and another resting on her rigid shoulder. Removing the hand from the girl's mouth at last, she rested it on Clemency's knee, instinctively reassuring as if she were dealing with a wounded young horse.

Clemency turned her head sharply to the side and let out a pained and wordless exhalation; in that moment a queer, tell-tale shiver passed between Nadezhda's shoulder blades and she felt unthinkingly across the mound of furs for the spangled reticule lying beside her on the velvet cushions. *Not again.* Kit and d'Harcourt had scarcely needed to warn her that this might happen. There were too many horses: hoofbeats in the distance grew louder with every breath she took as the horses neared. Drawing the reticule towards her, she pulled out the six-inch pistol and the velvet cartridge bag, priming and loading the small firearm with well-drilled efficiency.

Clemency's eyes widened a little as she caught sight of the pistol, but there was no time to react: the first gunshot from outside the carriage interrupted the call of an owl, and Nadezhda and Clemency were flung together in an ungainly heap: one or more of their own horses had jerked between the carriage traces, the carriage lurching in response. Battling furious frustration at not having her own hands on the ribbons, Nadezhda staggered to her feet and leaned against the wall near the curtained carriage window, turning her head to the side so that she could see outside but without presenting her own silhouette to the attackers. She swallowed a sharp intake of breath – there was a dark figure at the window; below the low brim of his hat, the attacker's face was concealed by a scarf and moonlight shone silver from the barrel of his pistol.

Nadezhda raised her own, but in the half-moment before she touched the trigger her attacker's head disintegrated before her eyes in a shower of blood and skull-fragments. Brain matter flew and stuck like a platter of scrambled eggs dropped by a hapless footman.

Clemency had already ducked, hauling Nadezhda down with her, even as she swore in Russian.

'Stay down!' Nadezhda hissed, shoving her downwards as she rose just enough to catch another glimpse out of the window. Kit rode into view, controlling his own startled horse with effortless expertise: she knew how much that would have cost him, too, with the wound in his belly. He ducked, narrowly avoiding a return burst of musket-fire. Nadezhda's stomach lurched as the carriage flipped over, and all was a blur of airborne velvet seat cushions and flashing shards of broken glass until with a final, teeth-crushing jerk the carriage settled on its side, the door now beneath their feet.

For a moment, all Nadezhda could do was lie in her cloak among the broken glass and disordered upholstery. This was going to hurt, but not yet. Then, clinging to the seat, she hauled herself upright and stepped past Clemency, who was on her hands and knees amid the shattered glass, her eyes glittering in the darkness.

Breathing in audible disordered gasps, Clemency staggered to her feet, her neat feathered hat askew. 'If you'll allow me, your highness?' Wrapping the folds of her thick woollen cloak around one hand, she reached up, smashing away the shards of glass still clinging to the window frame, with no sign at all that she'd just woken from a screaming nightmare only to be shot at. Irritated by her composure, Nadezhda elbowed her out of the way and climbed up on to the seat, then out of the upturned carriage's window, sliding down on to the track below. Shaking her skirts and fur-trimmed habit free of more broken glass, she gestured down at Clemency not to move, breathing in the scent of mud and trampled grass, just aware of a swirl of motion behind her; movement with a quiet and decisive familiarity to it. Helford was right behind her. He didn't lay a finger on her; even so many years later, he still understood that it frightened her to be touched unexpectedly. Even before he spoke, she sensed his laughter rising to the surface like bubbles in champagne, irrepressible: at last.

'Your highness, may I suggest that you *get down*—' Together, they dropped, even as she heard the queerly distant sound of several pistol shots, one after the other. Long-preserved instinct had led her to lie face down, still ready to fire her own pistol, and Kit lay on top of her, shielding her body with his own – the warm pressure of *him*; she could still breathe, so he was obviously taking some of his own weight. She sensed a hesitation, too – a sort of cognitive or emotional distance – but doubtless that was down to his injury. Even so, his presence was overwhelming alongside her own need to fight their attackers or flee. Squinting in the moonlight, squirming beneath him, she glimpsed a figure on horseback, hunched in the saddle, but still just within range. Her sight was as keen as it had ever been; her own guards wore bearskin-trimmed cloaks, the horseman did not, and so she raised her loaded pistol and fired. The fleeing figure tipped immediately sideways out of the saddle and she breathed in a rush of chilly air as Kit rolled off her, getting to his feet in a sudden rush of economical movement. He just looked down at her, very briefly, then turned and spoke in rapid French to his second-in-command, who was staring at Nadezhda as if she had just sprouted wings.

'D'Harcourt, see if he's dead, will you?'

D'Harcourt was already sprinting towards the body, leaving Nadezhda alone with Kit once more.

'Well?' She got up, speaking with even, measured calm, tilting back her head a little to look up at him. In the near distance, women's voices rose up to the moonlit clouds, and someone was sobbing. It didn't matter. They didn't matter.

'Madam,' he said, when he should have given her a royal honour. 'May I suggest that you wear my jacket?' For a moment, the years fell away between them and she was once again a lying, cheating girl dressed as a boy soldier, and he a disgraced young captain who would have done anything to recover his reputation. Kit let out a long breath, and looked at her from beneath those infuriatingly thick, dark lashes, and before she knew what she was about, he'd removed his regimental jacket and the warmth of it settled about her shoulders.

'Your royal highness,' he said, 'much as I admire the accuracy of your aim, that was a regrettable choice.'

'I must look to my women.' Clutching the jacket about herself, Nadezhda ignored the fact that he was no longer smiling and what that might mean. She turned and twitched the trailing hem of her gown out of the mud, picking her way across the rutted track to where the ruined carriage lay.

★

Breathing hard as the gunpowder smoke cleared, Clemency crouched among wet bracken, clinging to the splintered remains of the carriage wheel, the dead man less than a foot away. The princess had walked straight past their attacker's body with brutal, seasoned disregard, Kit's crimson jacket casually tossed about her shoulders. Clemency squeezed her eyes shut, forcing herself to breathe, remembering the faint, spicy scent of the princess's skin as she held her hand over her mouth. *What had she said?* And yet there was no time to even consider it now: dark blood trickled through rutted mud, and there was a stink of human ordure. Clemency pushed away a memory of flyblown corpses left by the side of a sun-baked road in Portugal – soldiers, women and children – knowing that if she closed her eyes now, alight with this white-hot terror, she would allow herself to remember things that were better left alone. Had Mama and Papa been left to rot in that condition on some frozen mountain pass, both of them dead on the retreat to Corunna? Mama had been with child, she knew that much, unable to keep up with the fleeing British army, with the French in pursuit. *Captain Arwenack chose to remain with his wife,* the letter had said.

She couldn't die here, any more than she could allow herself to recall the sweetness of Kit's lips against her own and the way he had looked at her, his eyes so light a grey that they were almost silver, with those dark lashes black against his pale skin, as if his eyes had been outlined in kohl just like a courtesan. Good God, what had she been thinking? In the days that had passed since that kiss, they hadn't exchanged a single word beyond essential courtesy. Covering her mouth and nose with a handful of her cloak, she let go of the carriage wheel and stood up, still unsteady as she stepped past a pale heap of something that could only be brain matter. Creeping around the outside of the upturned carriage, she heard just the ragged rhythm of her own breath, unable to look away from the corpse: a rough jacket, a homespun waistcoat, legs flung out like those of a sleeping child, and a slick of awareness slid down her spine.

If the moon had not slipped from behind unspooled cloud, she would never have caught sight of the medallion: pewter grey, flashing in the mud. The dead man's fingers reached gracelessly for the night sky, the pistol lying yards away. Stepping past his hand, she wasn't able to quite look at the mess where his head had been. Dropping into a crouch, Clemency reached out for the chain and pendant, her fingers clasping cold metal; all she could hear was her own disordered breathing. The medallion was only small, no bigger than a halfpenny, but there was enough moonlight to make out the rudimentary face of Christ, clearly marked with a halo and a pair of scratched initials impossible to decipher in the darkness.

Side by side, Kit and d'Harcourt emerged from the fading smoke at an economical run, d'Harcourt's face the picture of consternation as he signalled to her for silence. D'Harcourt turned to Kit, nodding after Nadezhda towards the cavalcade; swift, silent communication passed between them, and d'Harcourt went after her, away through the trees, leaving Clemency with Kit; he was shot through with a predatory awareness of their surroundings, not quite human, as if he could read the darkness. She couldn't die here today: that was all, the only thing that mattered.

'You're quite safe,' he said, stepping swiftly towards her. 'They're dead.' Then he simply opened his arms to her so that she stepped into the protection of his embrace, her hot tears leaking into the front of his waistcoat. 'It's all right,' he said, without the smallest understanding of what she wept for. 'I promise you're safe.'

It hurt so much that he made no demand of her; with exquisite tact he made no allusion even to what had passed between them, or the awful accusation she'd levelled at him. *But they were only servants, weren't they?* She couldn't move, couldn't speak; if he knew the truth about her, he'd turn around and walk away. She could bear to think of the way he would look at her. For a moment she was aware of nothing but the warm solidity of his chest, her face turned sideways against it, breathing in the faint air of laundry soap that clung to his cravat, and the other, more familiar scent of his body that her own recognised on a deep, low level. Gently, he cupped the back of her head in his hand, so that she felt his long fingers moving through her hair.

'I'm sorry,' she said. 'Oh, Kit, I'm sorry.'

'It's all right, *caradow*,' he said, slipping into Cornish. *Beloved.* He'd actually called her beloved. 'It will be quite all right, you know.'

In his arms, Clemency almost believed him, just for a moment.

25

In Fontainebleau several hours later, Kit and d'Harcourt left the dead men in a munitions wagon in a narrow side-street leading off the plaza and went into the Chat Rouge by the back steps. In lamplit gloom, d'Harcourt passed Kit the tall glass of frothing green bhang lassi garnished with candied rose petals, leaning back against the upholstered settle. In the past fortnight, neither of them had slept for more than a few short hours at a time.

'These attacks are going to get pinned on the French.' A muscle in d'Harcourt's jaw twitched as he failed to control his exasperation. 'She's just as much of a hell-born babe as you. She damned well shot him. Shot him dead right there and then. I mean, what kind of woman does that? Now how in the devil's name are we supposed to find out who they were and who sent them? Christ, what do they want?'

'Other than to kill the heir to the English throne?' Kit took a draught of bhang, savouring the cool, cardamom sweetness before passing it back to d'Harcourt; he wasn't about to think of Clemency, and the way she had come to him for protection beneath all those dark branches. 'It could be anyone. Think about it: her highness's suitor was meant to be chosen at Fontainebleau, not before. The British presented the whole conference with a fait accompli – an open alliance with Austria via Louis Charles Habsburg-Lorraine. Obviously, the alliance with Russia already stands. With peace declared between France and the allies, everyone's eyeballing Bukhara and Afghanistan and the way into India. France stands to lose out, as do Ottoman concerns, as well as Spain, Portugal and Prussia.'

'And India, I would imagine,' d'Harcourt said drily. 'The Prussians no doubt feel you've sold them down the river, too. A bloody cheating lot, you British, aren't you?'

'Factions at Whitehall – Wellington was furious,' Kit said, since it wouldn't hurt for the French to know that, if indeed they didn't already. 'I can't help thinking that you and I have both been left out for the wolves with this command.'

D'Harcourt gave a hard-edged smile. 'I wondered how long it would take you to reach the conclusion that you and I are considered expendable. All I had to do was be not quite white enough, whereas you had to shoot a man in his club. We don't even know their nationality,' he went on, with quiet, furious emphasis. 'And now the one man who might have been useful to us is dead.'

'I'm sorry. I had no choice but to finish one of them, really.' Kit took a long, steadying breath. Walking away in the night, wrapped in his own jacket, Nadezhda had looked at him over her shoulder with a sparkling challenge in her eyes that he'd never forgotten, not in all the years of their separation. 'As for her highness, when you come to understand her a little better, this sort of thing won't surprise you. Her background is unconventional.'

'Oh come now, do you really think Joséphine didn't make sure I knew every last detail?' d'Harcourt said; in two weeks they had discussed everything save this. 'She's one of the tsar's bastards, isn't she? She's not the child of some Romanov cousin. He's her father. Served as an ensign in the Semenovsky dressed as a boy, but we'll gloss over that chapter. You escorted her to England; six years later there's still a groundswell of gossip about it. Well, she's got a half-decent aim still, I'll give her that, even if all this doesn't appear to have left her with much common sense.'

Kit yawned, but he was going to have to make sure Wellington realised exactly how much the French already knew. 'He'd likely have put a bullet through his own head before giving himself up.'

D'Harcourt turned to face him then, with swift and unsettling perspicacity. 'Are you defending her? Doubtless I shouldn't say this, but I like you, Helford: you'd better tread carefully. If there really is anything between you, for the love of Christ, knock it on the head. I can't afford a scandal any more than you can, and I've seen the way you look at her Mistress of the Robes. This really isn't the moment to divide your favours between Mademoiselle Arwenack and the woman you're supposed to be protecting. Use your head.'

'Believe me, I mean to,' Kit said. 'We'll have to take both corpses back to the palace. With any luck, someone there may even be able to tell us who they were. The servants may at least recognise them if they're local.'

'Recloses, not here,' d'Harcourt said.

Kit turned to look at him, battling a wave of frantic exhaustion. 'What do you mean? There's nothing in Recloses. It's just a small village.'

D'Harcourt shrugged. 'I certainly found it quiet after Cairo. We need Father Honfleur, though. If anyone can help us find out who these men were, he can. I doubt you've been here long enough to hear of the Belleville affair, but an apprentice was killed at the tannery a few years ago. Everyone suspected his master, but it was all ready to be swept under the rug as you'd expect. Father Honfleur proved it murder – something to do with fragments of cloth: Belleville hanged himself in the barn before they could get him to the guillotine.'

'Well, Christ only knows what the hell else we're to do with two dead men, but how discreet is he? Saving your presence, but whatever your man finds out, we don't want it all over the cantonment.'

D'Harcourt yawned, taking another sip of the bhang lassi. 'Oh, we can trust Honfleur to keep whatever we may learn close to his chest. He was my tutor – almost from the day I came to France I spent more time at his house than at my father's. Odd though it may be to ask you to trust me, I can tell you now that Honfleur won't broadcast our affairs.'

'Well, all right.' Kit suppressed an unexpected rush of pity. His own childhood might have been pretty damnable in its way, but for all the times he'd eaten only when a courtesan fed him sweetmeats from her plate, Lamorna House and Nansmornow were still home, never just his father's house. D'Harcourt's stepmother had not appreciated the presence of her husband's eldest son, that much was obvious. Kit thought of his own former stepmother, and suppressed a shudder. Hester had warned him about Louisa Burford. *She's never forgiven you for hating her – she wanted the world to believe her a maternal paragon.* At d'Harcourt's side on horsehair cushions, the bhang ushered him gently towards rest and even now he thought of Clemency, and the slight warmth of her body as he'd held her in his arms in the forest, her braids dishevelled and unpinned. As a girl all that hair had hung down to her waist, wet and tangled with fronds of seaweed, her eyes flashing with dark humour when she ran down the beach at his side, always keeping pace, fearless with every step.

An empty china cup of warm milk infused with laudanum sat on the dresser, and Clemency found Nadezhda kneeling at her prayers before an icon set up on the marble-topped bedside table. Gilded wood caught the candlelight, revealing fragments of Cyrillic lettering.

'Don't tell anyone, will you?' Nadezhda got up briskly, shaking out the voluminous skirts of her nightgown, her eyes already glassy. 'I'm supposed to have converted.'

'Of course not, your highness.' Clemency curtseyed, retreating. Her own bedchamber was starkly simple by comparison to the royal apartment: red tiles upon the floor, her familiar satchel sitting on the narrow bed containing all of her binding tools and equipment. The pair of high-backed silk brocade chairs repurposed from some state apartment had been angled before a sulking fire that failed to penetrate the damp atmosphere. Closing the adjoining door behind her, she leaned on it, closing her eyes. Opening the window and turning to the log-basket, Clemency saw an elegantly gloved male hand resting on the arm of the blue chair, its occupant otherwise concealed. She swallowed an airless scream as Valentine spoke.

'Button.' He didn't move, didn't stand, leaving her to force one foot before the other, walking around to the fireplace, facing him as he sat in elegant cross-legged contemplation of the flames.

'What on earth are you doing here?' She had to fight not to sound foolishly high-pitched.

Valentine smiled and gestured to the other chair, ignoring the scandal of his presence in her bedchamber at night. She sank into the chair, the travel-stained skirts of her riding habit spreading out as she sat.

'I just came to see how you are, that's all.' He paused, raising one eyebrow. 'Naughty girl: I hear you had quite the journey. Riding outside the carriage with those two young men doesn't seem especially proper, does it? Gossip travels fast, as you ought to know.'

Clemency shrugged. She could have been killed in two separate attacks on the royal cavalcade, but to him that was just an irrelevance. 'Her highness insisted on riding with Helford until we were attacked for the first time. She's up to something – stirring the pot with her fiancé, I should think. Bluette heard from one of the palace under-maids that the Prince of Hungary never wrote to her, even when the betrothal was arranged.'

Bluette herself came in at that moment with Clemency's valise, opening it up on the bed, unfolding chemises and nightdresses with calm complacence, so that she was flooded with relief.

Valentine scarcely glanced at her, speaking now in English. 'Wouldn't it have been that little bit more infamous had her royal highness ridden alone with Helford? Why did you offer to give up your place in the carriage?'

Clemency swallowed a jolt of fear, offering a light shrug. 'Dorothea Lieven is no one's fool, even if the princess is more concerned with riling Prince Louis Charles than anything else. It's got to at least look as if I'm doing my job. Come on, Val – we always play the long game, you and I.'

'Will there be anything else, ma'am?' Bluette dropped into a clipped curtsey, ignoring Valentine with all the training of a seasoned professional.

'I thank you, no.' Clemency knew she sounded calm, unconcerned, but God only knew how much she'd have to tip to keep this nocturnal visit from the ears of other servants. Bluette curtseyed again and swept out, leaving a clean nightdress folded upon the bed, the servants' door clicking shut behind her.

Valentine looked up at her with the ghost of a tolerant smile. 'Button, just don't leave it too long before her highness is compromised, will you? You've been gone a fortnight: the treaty negotiations didn't just stop while you were away. I'm sure it's nothing, but Princess Charlotte arrived last week from the Kingdom of Württemberg.' He shrugged. 'I mean, she's an old woman, but I've heard a few people say that she finds life at Gochscheim quite chafing.'

'What are you getting at?'

Valentine smiled, yawning. 'Don't waste your time, that's all I'm saying. Make the most of the Russian chit while she's still a real contender to the throne. It's easily possible that she'll be outmanoeuvred here at this very conference. Just do as you're told, Clemency.'

She couldn't breathe, her fingers turning white as she gripped the back of the chair. He left by the servants' door. When he had gone, Clemency stood at the window for a long time.

In the cold darkness of the icehouse, very early the following morning, the two dead men were laid out on wooden tables, side by side, one headless. Kit, Father Honfleur and d'Harcourt gathered, surrounded by blocks of glistening greenish ice; oil lamps had been lit, casting long shadows. Kit was already regretting breakfast: fresh bread, salted ham and thick, black, sugared coffee from a silver pot kept warm on the vast range in Father Honfleur's kitchen.

D'Harcourt glanced down at the dead man who still had his head. 'Not looking his best, really, is he?'

'I'm afraid we know very little about them, God rest their souls,' Father Honfleur said with a swift sign of the cross. With that crown of wild white hair, he must have been elderly even when d'Harcourt had come to him as a boy. 'All we can safely say is that neither of these men are likely to be local – I certainly don't recognise the fellow still in possession of his head and neither did my housekeeper Madame Boussion or – crucially – Madame Étienne at the Chat Rouge. Between Madame Étienne's area of specialism and my own, we know men of every sort in a considerable radius of Fontainebleau.'

'And Madame Boussion, your housekeeper – why does she know everyone?' Kit asked.

Honfleur shook his head. 'Is there not a Boussion in every town, Lieutenant Colonel? To begin with, she's related by birth or marriage to most of the lower orders in the cantonment.' He sighed. 'And doubtless those who consider themselves of greater birth, too. At any rate, we can be reasonably confident that this attack on the English princess wasn't carried out by local thieves – which would seem unlikely, in any event, after what happened at the Château de Sigy. Of course, we can only say that with any certainty about this gentleman here—' He waved one thin, veined hand at the corpse that still had a head. 'Whether or not they were French or foreigner is another matter.'

Kit reached for one of the musket-balls that sat on a tin plate beside a small leather pouch, holding it up to the light with a practised eye. It was a fraction smaller than the balls in his own cartridges. 'Well, these are French, at any rate – not that it means anything. Any man can get hold of a Charleville if he wants it and can pay, English or French. Damn it, even if they were only common criminals with no intention beyond holding up the princess's carriage, they'd scarcely carry anything that might identify them.'

Father Honfleur coughed. 'If I may show what I have

discovered?' he asked. 'Or rather, what my housekeeper found when she helped me to lay them out.' With great care, the priest took up the leather pouch and reached into it; holding out a scrap of linen fabric, he let it fall on to the table between them all. 'The gentleman who, ah, lost his head wore a shirt with cuffs that had been removed and replaced. This was found caught in the new seam on the right-hand cuff of his shirt.'

D'Harcourt looked down at the curl of linen, frowning. 'Thieves usually begin as poor men – is it really so unusual he wore a shirt that had been repaired a few times?'

'The pattern of embroidered flowers,' Kit said, at last. 'It's Russian. I've seen this style a thousand times. It can't be proven, of course, that *he* was Russian, or on whose command he was acting.'

'Her highness is due to marry Louis Charles Habsburg-Lorraine, after all,' d'Harcourt said. 'What if Russia see a British alliance with Austria as a threat rather than an advantage?'

'They would have been party to that arrangement, though. You can't take a piss at St James's without Dorothea Lieven making sure the tsar knows of it,' Kit said, ignoring a prickle of creeping unease. He'd as lief face French cavalry than this sort of hidden, sneaking threat. 'That marriage makes a mess of everyone else's trade routes – there's scarcely a court at the congress that doesn't now have a motive to get rid of Nadezhda and scotch the Russo-British alliance with Austria. Either way, it's all only suspicion.'

'Sigy aside, it's still possible that this pair were just ordinary criminals,' d'Harcourt said, a little bleary-eyed: he looked as tired as Kit felt. 'That road through the forest is notorious for highway robbery.'

'An unlucky pair of criminals, in that case, to encounter her royal highness,' Honfleur remarked drily.

It was impossible to argue with that, at least.

26

The headless man reached towards Clemency through a cloud of gunpowder smoke, his outstretched fingers blackened. When she dared look at his face again it had become Valentine's, smiling at her in the way that he always did. She awoke with a stifled cry to grey dawn light probing between faded crimson brocade curtains that had been left slightly open; Bluette knew she couldn't sleep in a room with the shutters closed. She slipped her hand beneath the pillow, her fingertips brushing cold metal, even as a floorboard creaked in the adjoining royal chamber. The medallion would have to wait for closer inspection: after less than four hours' rest, her highness was up. Swinging her legs out of bed, Clemency suppressed a gasp as her bare feet hit the tiled floor, snatched at her wrap and ran swiftly to the door. Stepping into the carpeted magnificence of the royal bedchamber, she found Nadezhda's bed empty, the heavy gold and crimson coverlet in disarray, and the princess herself in nothing but a pair of silk stockings gartered with red ribbon; she was on her knees before an open travelling chest that spewed crumpled silks, satins and sarcenets.

'You need not look so surprised.' Nadezhda sat back on her heels. 'I suppose you think it pretty odd that I'm up so soon after all that laudanum. Well, the fact is it doesn't seem to soothe in the way it once did. I wasn't born to spend my days sitting endlessly in carriages and council chambers, keeping my thoughts to myself. It's untenable. Thank God. I thought I'd never find it.' She turned, standing up and tossing a crumpled riding habit on to the end of the bed; Clemency was determined not to be parochially embarrassed by the smudge of dark hair between her legs, or her rose-pink nipples. 'Well, if you must be useful then you can render that habit as respectable as possible in five minutes,' she said. 'And if you dare so much as offer to ring for a servant I swear to God I'll see you back in your irrelevant Cornish province next week, never to leave your friends the Boscobels' house again. Do you understand?'

'Perfectly, your highness.' Clemency smiled, but she had never been less certain which card to play. 'Should I send a servant for your guards, ma'am?'

The princess was still unabashed by her own nakedness as she turned and stepped into her shift, revealing the neat, boyish curve of her rear. 'Oh, I don't think there's any need for that, is there?' Nadezhda flipped through a heap of discarded clothing, selecting a set of lace-trimmed stays. 'I'm very sure you'll find that rousing either would be like trying to wake the dead, and in any case they're more likely to be at some disreputable tavern by now than in their own quarters. Will you attend to my dress or not? I can tell you now that riding without stays is very uncomfortable indeed.'

Clemency thought of Kit in that lamplit tavern, assuring her that he wasn't in the habit of granting quarter to those who got in his way, and also – as she sometimes allowed herself to do – of Valentine's unmistakable tread outside her old bedchamber at Boscobel Castle.

She took up the dangling silk corset ribbons. 'Of course, your highness.'

Hoofbeats sounded in the cobbled street outside the Chat Rouge, forcing Kit awake just as the maidservant came in with a coal scuttle. He and d'Harcourt lay sprawled upon the large settle, d'Harcourt still asleep with one arm flung across his eyes; some unknown person had taken pity and tossed a reeking moth-eaten blanket over them both. Kit breathed in a nauseating combination of inexpensive perfume and stale smoke as dawn light teased the shutters, lancing across dusty floorboards. D'Harcourt groaned.

'Christ.' Sitting up, Kit rested his head in both hands, signalling to the grinning young chambermaid. 'Bring some coffee, if you please.'

'Whatever you say, sir.' She got up, ineffectually brushing a smear of soot from her striped apron, obviously big with news. 'Only I thought as you might want to look at the princess riding past, that's all. Everyone in the kitchens says as it's her.'

Kit and d'Harcourt moved on the same instant, hurling off the blanket as they rushed to the window, throwing back the shutters just in time to see Nadezhda and Clemency on horseback, each sitting to a well-trained trot in the street outside.

Nadezhda rode alongside Clemency at a smart pace, subjecting her to a quick appraising glance as early morning light pointed fingers between the tracery of branches overhead. The princess seemed the sort to leave a less well-equipped companion on a docile palfrey trotting headfirst into a cloud of dust; instead, she'd presented Clemency with an embroidered side-saddle to match her own, ingeniously wrought with a second pommel so that she could even take fences like a neck-or-nothing huntsman, the riveted leather still warm with the scent of linseed.

They rode side by side, and Nadezhda looked her up and down, taking in every aspect of her seat. 'Did you learn to ride with Kit Helford?'

Clemency fought off the uneasy sensation of Nadezhda rummaging around inside her own mind in exactly the way that she had carelessly searched through that clothes trunk, discarding whatever she didn't need. She shortened the reins, bringing her gelding up to a canter. 'We were neighbours until my grandfather died, and as quite young children we did used to rather scramble about on the moorland ponies.'

He'd kissed her at Sigy as though it were the most natural thing in the world, bloodied by his kill, alight with it and yet so gentle, accepting her rejection with cool good manners that she knew he'd learned at a cost.

Like it or not, she had to betray him.

Nadezhda jumped her Arab over an outcrop of moss-covered rock, giving Clemency an expectant smile as she caught up – a born chess-player waiting for her opponent to make a slip. 'I dare say those moorland ponies taught you how to ride just as they began to teach Helford,' she went on. 'I was the one who really made him learn, though; we were in Russia together, you know. It was quite shocking, really – we rode hundreds of miles, just me and him. You do get to know a person that way: he hasn't changed, I can tell you that. Do keep up, will you?' She took off then at a gallop, the Arab horse kicking up a cloud of dust from the wide, sandy track.

Clemency cursed with quiet precision as she kept her gelding on a half-loose rein, not wanting him to start to think how he might get away from her. Why on earth should she care about some yard-long list of indiscretions her royal damned highness and Kit Helford had committed together in Russia? She had to think of Valentine and his requirements, not the way Kit Helford had kissed her in the dark, even after all the awful things she'd said to him. It wouldn't be long before Kit and Princess Nadezhda Sofia gave her everything she needed to hand them both over to the Boscobels. She felt pulled along by an invisible thread. Beech trees and shoulders of rock shrouded in bile-green moss flashed past as Clemency urged the gelding to a gallop, even as memories rose like the tide, unstoppable: Valentine's beautiful, lazy smile as he drew back the heavy velvet curtains around her bed, and then, much later, taking her hands in the rose-garden at Boscobel Castle.

Button, you must know we can't be together.

It never paid to think of that. Any of it at all.

Giving the gelding his head at last, Clemency caught up with Nadezhda, taking care to remain half a length behind; she could scarcely throw down the gauntlet and race her. Nadezhda was so very much at one with the Arab that it was left to Clemency to perceive that there was a stranger on horseback two hundred yards ahead, waiting in the middle of the wide, dusty track. She called out, her hands white on the reins, her voice snatched away by the wind. Nadezhda threw a glance over her shoulder, but instead of slowing the mare or even turning her around to see if they might get away at speed, she leaned forwards over her horse's neck and galloped towards the stranger.

The wind whipped tears from Clemency's eyes, and much as every instinct screamed at her to charge away in the opposite direction, there was no choice but to keep up. With the sun at his back, the horseman waited for them both to meet him, easily controlling his restless horse. Clemency could only pray that Nadezhda would at least have the sense to stop well out of range of a pistol shot. But instead, the princess gathered the Arab's paces and barrelled towards the stranger with her own pistol drawn, and in that moment the stranger's horse sidestepped, swiftly brought under control just as a skein of cloud slid from before the sun, and fresh light gilded a cap of golden hair so that Clemency knew exactly who he was: Louis Charles Habsburg-Lorraine, Prince of Hungary, Archduke of Austria.

'Your highness, don't shoot!' Clemency called out, in sudden, sickening awareness that whilst she had met Louis

Charles, the princess herself had not. Nadezhda reined in then at Clemency's side, so that she saw the elevated angle of the princess's finely moulded chin, and the spark of nihilistic amusement in her dark eyes. At that moment, a small group of horsemen emerged from the trees, all dressed in dark green livery; they came up behind the prince, close and watchful. He had his own guards, then, even if they didn't, and Clemency knew that Kit and d'Harcourt would be made to suffer for this indiscretion just as much as she would herself.

The prince was smiling now, raising both hands above his head in mocking subjection, as though he were tolerating a game of highwaymen. 'Indeed,' he said, 'I would so much prefer it if you didn't shoot me, your highness.'

Nadezhda lowered the pistol, but not before Clemency saw her suppressed expression of humiliated anger. The prince merely managed his horse with dismissive grace; he said nothing about their lack of guards. He looked Nadezhda up and down, observing her short curls, windblown and disarranged, and the dusty folds of her riding habit.

'Shall we reserve the pleasure of our formal introduction for another time, my dear?' Louis Charles smiled again, giving her Arab a considering appraisal. 'Nice, but not enough bone, don't you think? Now, if you'll excuse me, your highness, this beast is rather fresh, and I must gallop off his fidgets.'

Without another word, Louis Charles turned and rode away down the track, followed in well-drilled succession by his six liveried guardsmen.

At her side, Nadezhda only smiled, holding the reins

of her horse with an ease that didn't fool Clemency for a moment. 'Honestly, how dare he?'

'He certainly seems very sure of himself, your highness—' Clemency broke off, she and Nadezhda both turning at the uneven rhythm of approaching horses. Riding neck and neck, Kit and d'Harcourt rounded a bend in the rock-strewn forest trail, thundering towards them both, their horses kicking up clouds of dust and whirling, spinning pine needles. Clemency heard only the ragged rhythm of her own breathing, holding fast beside Nadezhda as they approached; her eyes met d'Harcourt's but he looked away with a disappointed shake of his head and she crushed an exasperating surge of shame. She owed them nothing.

'Your royal highness, may we escort you?' Kit spoke in a tone Clemency had never heard him use before: even Nadezhda flinched as d'Harcourt stared steadily ahead.

'Well, really – if you must.' Nadezhda spoke with a careless smile.

Kit let the reins fall, turning his attention then to Clemency. 'You should have prevented this. I'll deal with you later.'

'I'm very sure you will not,' Clemency snapped before she could stop herself; what did he know? 'Later, I will be very much occupied choosing gowns for her highness's formal presentation to court. I suggest you cool your heels and think on your own plans for the presentation, Lieutenant Colonel, considering the evident danger we're all in. How dare you speak to me as though I were a child? You're nothing but an overindulged aristocrat with enough scandals of your own to contend with, and self-made ones at that. You haven't a clue how other people must live their lives, and I'm afraid your explosion of temper will have to wait.'

'Oh, believe me, it can certainly wait,' Kit said; his grey eyes were cold and flat, and he spoke to her as if they were quite alone, so that a hot, angry flush seared across her face. 'I leave you to anticipate it, Miss Arwenack. In every detail.'

She sat still, reins wound tight about her fingers, watching as he rode away with Nadezhda and d'Harcourt in a cloud of dust that stung her eyes.

27

Courtiers had flocked outside in the early morning sunshine, women in this season's heavy watered silk with attendant men sweating into their cravats; Kit couldn't do much but endure the curious glances and half hidden smiles as he and Nadezhda walked in silence from the stables, skirting the formal water gardens. She'd reached for his arm and he had no choice but to offer it as they passed beneath the spreading branches of a horse chestnut tree alight with sprays of blossom like so many white candles among the green. He shouldn't have lost his temper with Clemency like the spoiled brat she so clearly thought he was; he shouldn't be this bloody disappointed. It would have been the work of a moment to send servants for him and d'Harcourt. After the journey they'd had, how could her failure to do that be excused as oversight?

Kit briefly closed his eyes, battling another surge of exhaustion; at the back of his mind he saw hanged corpses swinging from the horse chestnut trees at Nansmornow:

the truth was, after all these years at war and all he'd seen and done, chestnut blossom still made him want to vomit. *Wait here,* Crow had said, into the unending silence, before running up the steps to the house holding his pistol. Nothing Crow had ever said since that day could erase the first unspoken but unmistakable accusation: their half-sister Roza had died because of him; he might just as well have knotted the hanging rope around her neck with his own hands.

'You're very quiet this morning,' Nadezhda said with her most teasing smile.

'Trust me, you don't want anyone else to hear what I have to say to you.' She was as much to blame for this mess as Clemency – more so – and he had to measure out every last word.

When they had reached the cool darkness indoors and gained the wide staircase to the state apartments, Kit stopped dead in the crimson finery of the Pope's state salon. He turned on Nadezhda so that she had to take two swift steps, backing up to the richly painted wall, looking up at him with that teasing expression he used to find so irresistible.

'For God's sake, what the devil do you mean by all this, Nadezhda? It's so childish. What are you trying to prove?'

'It was just a ride, Khristofyor.' She laughed, and he wanted to tell her that he wasn't hers to name for her own.

'You know it was not. You were unguarded and it's going to cause no end of trouble, especially after Sigy and what happened in the forest.' She was really starting to bore him. 'You're making it impossible for any of us to follow our orders: d'Harcourt and Miss Arwenack as much as myself.'

Nadezhda smiled up at him again, running one finger along the row of ribboned decorations at his breast. 'What are these for? I know that gold one; that's for valour. How can you be so brave upon the battlefield and such a coward with me? Come, don't be so patronising, my dear.'

'I've never patronised you.' He was really angry now, his voice rising up to the embossed and gilded ceiling, not that he cared. 'If I wanted to do that, I'd shower you with flattery and kiss your hand at dances so that it looked to everyone as though I were in your power, and raise just enough gossip to please you, but I happen to believe that both of us are better than that.'

She turned away then with a flash of pique, all that bright humour gone; nobody was of any importance at all except herself. 'I can't possibly expect you to sympathise with my position, being married off like a prize heifer. To understand what it's like to be used.'

He laughed then, looking down at her, a scarce few inches between them so that he felt the heat of her body. 'Can I not, Nadia, when I'm your own favourite toy?'

'Things should have been different between us.' The words burst from her lips. 'Things should have been different but they're not.'

Kit let out a quick exhalation, even as he briefly closed his eyes.

She grasped the lapels of his jacket, her fingers white with tension. '*Please.*'

He didn't have much choice, that much was clear, even as

she traced an outline of his lips now with one fingertip, and in any case, Clemency had made her desires, or her lack of them, only too clear.

You're nothing but an overindulged aristocrat with enough scandals of your own to contend with, and self-made ones at that.

Fine.

'Helford,' Nadezhda said. 'Don't make me beg.'

'Very well.' He really did kiss her this time, with one hand in her short hair and the other cupping her rear as he tasted the sweetness of her mouth, still the same after so many years. They were only barely concealed from the footmen, and his touch was as tender as it was ruthless, so that when they had both finished her eyes were hot with salted tears. Their foreheads touched, resting together, but he was the first to pull away; understanding immediately that this was why Nadezhda went on to say what she did.

'By the way, I wonder if you can know, but Miss Arwenack has regular nightmares. Isn't that strange?' She spoke rapidly, a little flushed. 'What does *ow flog vian* mean?'

Kit barely flinched, watching dust motes float in a stream of sunlight flooding in through one of the tall windows.

Ow flog vian. My little child.

He feinted with all the skill he had. 'Did you think she was talking in her sleep? I'm not sure you can have heard correctly. That doesn't mean anything to me.'

'I dare say,' Nadezhda said; she'd recovered her equanimity by now and was smiling again. Crow had always said Kit was a terrible liar, often in the moment just before enacting merciless retribution for whatever misdemeanour he'd failed to conceal. 'Perhaps I should just ask Miss Arwenack what she dreams of?'

'If I were you, I'd be more concerned about the mess we're all in now,' Kit said lightly, and, without another word, he turned and walked away, leaving her alone.

Alie was playing in the dust at the stable door again when Morwenna came running across the cobblestones in a pale green gown embroidered all over with small flowers; Alie wanted to touch the little silk stitched roses, but she didn't dare.

'I thought you'd never come back!' Morwenna smiled, pushing back her straw bonnet. 'Sylvie says I may stay, but not for very long.' She frowned. 'My aunt says that the stable-yard isn't at all a proper place for me to be, but I think that's silly. Mama and Papa never mind me going to the stables at home. We're looking at the globe this afternoon, and I'm having my dancing lesson, but I can play now.'

Alie flushed with pleasure, leaning up against the stable door. 'Jacques doesn't come up the palace very often, but there's going to be a hunt soon so he's here today.'

Morwenna's maid, Sylvie, was watching them both with what Bluette would have called half an eye. One of the stable-lads walked over and started talking to her, making her smile. That was good, because it probably meant Sylvie wouldn't take Morwenna away before too long, although Alie couldn't imagine having a lady in a smart gown following her about all the time, telling her not to run or to laugh too loud.

'Is Jacques your brother?' Morwenna said, squatting down at her side. They were going to make houses for the beetles and ants again; they didn't talk about it: Alie just knew exactly what they would play, gathering up fresh beech leaves from the hedge running up one side of the stable-yard. 'Or is he your uncle?' She laughed. 'I suppose he can't be: my uncle Kit is the best in the whole world, but I would never call him just Kit: he still calls my papa sir, sometimes, when they're annoyed with each other and they think I don't know.'

'No, Jacques just looks after me because Madame d'Arblay died and then so did Jacques's mama.' Alie shrugged, tipping leaves into the pile.

Morwenna's face fell. 'Oh, I'm sorry. That's sad.'

Alie didn't think it was sad: she only had wispy memories of an old lady with white hair who made her stand and wind wool for hours, even when she was tired; she couldn't even be sure if that had been Jacques's mother here at Fontainebleau or Madame d'Arblay in Paris. It was all a long time ago. 'I like Jacques. Shall we make a pond?'

Morwenna smiled, happy again, her eyes sparkling. Alie didn't like it when her friend was sad; it made her feel sad, too. 'That's a good idea. We can take some water from the trough. What shall we use to hold it?'

'There's no horse chestnut shells. I'm not sure. What about a petal? We could find quite a big one.'

Morwenna looked across the yard at Sylvie, but she was still laughing at something the stable-lad had said to her. 'That's a good idea. Let's go and pick some of those roses. There's so many, no one will mind.' She held out her hand and Alie took it, so that they ran together across the stable-yard.

28

Kit found Phelps waiting for him outside Nadezhda's
quarters with a summons to attend the Duke of
Wellington at the Hôtel de Montausier. 'Which is a thing
that doesn't seem right to me, your honour,' Phelps added
with dour gloom, 'you facing a dressing-down from Old
Douro and a female relation both at the same time.'

It seemed excessive to Kit, too, as he went across the
courtyard, clouds of insects hovering above the immaculate
box hedges trimmed into intricate forms and patterns;
surviving without sleep for days at a time was easy when
his blood was up and the campfires of enemy French troops
carpeted the far side of a valley like a trail of stars, but
in this condition he would have as lief faced a troop of
partisan soldiers than his great-aunt Thérèse on her uppers,
let alone Wellington.

Thérèse's ancient major-domo admitted him with a smile
of avuncular disapproval; amid the fog of exhaustion and
the throbbing ache of the wound in his belly, aggravated

by so many days in the saddle. Kit was just aware of the black-and-white-tiled marble floor and the Louis IV gilded occasional table bearing the weight of a silver dish of scented freesia and vivid blue and violet delphinium. Running upstairs with a bitten-back curse, the waxed oak banister felt cool and smooth beneath his left hand; instinctively, he reached for the pistol holstered at his waist and had to force himself not to draw it: he was not approaching a battlefield now, even if every nerve screamed that he was. As if from far away, Kit heard the major-domo announce him to his aunt's drawing-room, and walked in to find Thérèse de Saint-Maure in her habitual swathes of black bombazine and the Duke of Wellington, both in livid occupation of the same sofa.

At the other side of the fireplace, on a chaise of pale silver brocade, Kit's niece Morwenna played cat's cradle with her father. Crow sat very much at his ease, long legs stretched out before him and crossed at the ankle, his boots still mired with dust from the road. Morwenna leaned into Crow's side in crisp skirts and embroidered pantaloons, her green satin slippers discarded on the Aubusson rug; a length of bright blue wool twined between their fingers.

'Papa,' Morwenna said to him. 'I was telling you about my friend at the stables, but you don't attend!'

'How should I, *petite*, with all this entertainment?' Crow absently plucked a piece of golden straw from Morwenna's hair and disentangled himself from her, getting to his feet. He and Kit embraced; Crow's familiar scent of tobacco and laundry soap was still the same as it had ever been, but Kit felt the usual sense of dislocation at the reminder that he was now half an inch taller than his brother. 'My God,' Crow said, in Cornish. 'You look terrible. I take it this is all under control?'

'Not in the slightest, sir, as you can see,' Kit replied in the same tongue, suppressing an overwhelming longing for the shabby comfort of the drawing-room at Nansmornow: faded brocade curtains, worn Turkish carpets, Hester's father's astrolabe on the table. Kissing Nadezhda just made him want to go home and to take that damnable Arwenack hellcat with him: home to Cornwall where they both belonged. And yet home was a place he could never go back to: home was where his own half-sister had been hanged from the chestnut tree by French soldiers who had come looking for him.

Crow gave him a searching look; there were times Kit still felt as if his brother could read his mind. 'Someone get him a drink,' Crow said.

'Oh, for goodness' sake, enough of all this,' Wellington said, very much with the air of a man at the end of his tether. 'Lamorna, this is no time for children.'

Morwenna made her well-taught curtsey and fled with one of Thérèse's maids, even as a footman announced Clemency along with d'Harcourt. The Frenchman looked as harassed as Kit felt, but Clemency just wore an expression of polite enquiry, as if she had stepped into a circulating library to choose a novel.

Of course, she'd learned to live like this, like an actress on stage playing a part – and yet Kit knew now what she called out in her sleep.

Ow flog vian. My little child.

With breathtaking force, Kit remembered the stuffy, perfumed stink of that antechamber in the palace, Clemency drinking harder than a midshipman on shore leave as she fleeced the Count de Mercy-Argenteau. And Valentine Boscobel with his hands all over her as though she were his whore. He allowed himself a brief moment to imagine crushing Boscobel's windpipe; God, it would be good to watch the light go out of his eyes. But now was not the time to allow emotion to cloud judgement.

Thérèse accepted d'Harcourt's bow with an indulgent smile and a rapid series of enquiries about his grandmother and family, before desiring Kit to present Clemency to her. Clemency curtseyed before them with all the self-possession of a seasoned card sharp, acknowledging Crow's sardonic bow with respectful nicety. Her hair had come loose from the pins, snaking down to her waist in heavy unwinding coils.

'Well, Christophe!' Thérèse spoke from her own end of the chaise, ignoring Wellington's precedence as she held out her hand to be kissed. 'You may be sure that the gossip hit my drawing-room faster than a dose of typhoid, and very disagreeable I have found it. Never have I heard the like, and I weep to consider what your poor mother might have thought of all this indiscretion: riding with that Russian strumpet in the saddle before you for a week. You might just as well have ravished the girl in this very drawing-room. Lamorna, I really can't comprehend why on earth it took you so long to get here. Let's be honest: you're the only person the boy has ever remotely listened to, on any topic.'

'I'm sorry I wasn't here sooner for your satisfaction, my dear,' Crow said. 'And if you really wanted somebody to talk sense into my brother, you'd need Lady Lamorna, not me. I don't know why you think I should have the hypocrisy to lecture anyone about really very basic drawing-room gossip, or why you suppose anyone else cares to listen to our family squabbles.'

Thérèse just responded to that with a flat gaze, and by taking up a purse she was netting.

'Helford,' Wellington said, with dangerous restraint, 'if there's anything at all that might render your own actions over the past several days less reprehensible, then you had better share it. I've just endured a half-hour with Metternich and Louis Charles himself that I hope never to repeat.'

Clemency spoke into the silence. 'I'm so sorry, your grace, about this morning, but I'm afraid the fault was really mine, not Lieutenant Colonel Helford's.'

Ignoring the room, including his brother, Kit turned to Clemency, speaking in rapid Cornish. 'God knows I should have put you straight on the royal yacht at Calais. Why did you not stop her?'

In truth, he already knew the answer to that, understanding the extent of what the Boscobels held over her. An illegitimate child, just as his own sister Roza had been. But if Clemency wouldn't admit it – and of course she wouldn't – then how could he help her? If she even wanted his help, to begin with.

She didn't reply, and he gestured with furious economy at d'Harcourt, who was doing his utmost to fade into the bookshelf. 'You do realise this isn't just about you and whatever racket you're running for the Boscobels? If anything happens to Nadezhda, it isn't just my reputation at risk, or even yours. What about Thomas? How well do you think the Egyptian son of a local nobleman is going to come out of this? You realise that his own father barely acknowledges him in public?' Kit broke off, only too well aware that all of this anger was really deserved by Nadezhda and the Boscobels, but it was too late.

'Stop being so painfully dishonest!' She flung the words at him. 'Of course I don't blame d'Harcourt for his stepmother and just how bloody awful people can be, but if you weren't in the habit of stirring up such scandals yourself none of this would matter quite so much to you, would it?'

'I quite agree, Miss Arwenack,' Crow said, speaking in languid Cornish himself; Kit had rarely seen him look so furious nor yet so simultaneously amused; for once, he didn't know the half of it.

'Well, you should agree as well that he ought to get that wound dressed again, then,' Clemency said in French, fierce as ever, and showing no signs of bowing down to Crow's position. 'Has it been looked at since Sigy?' She turned to Kit. 'Has it?'

Kit ignored Crow's raised eyebrow, but he couldn't ignore Thérèse, who was still netting her purse with methodical disdain. 'If Christophe has been injured, of course he is just disregarding it. The height of foolishness, considering the feverish habit you both have, Lamorna.'

'He'll have it dealt with, ma'am, never fear,' Crow said.

Wellington just stared straight ahead, as if by doing so he might find himself elsewhere. D'Harcourt was still absorbed in the bookshelf, as though any of this mattered, anyhow.

Kit turned to the duke. 'Your grace, I can only apologise for my own part in this morning. It won't happen again, although God knows her highness does little to help herself.'

'I take it Princess Charlotte has come in full regalia from Gochsheim to attend Nadezhda's formal presentation?' Crow said, swiftly. 'Dear bloody Christ, like Sleeping Beauty's wicked fairy godmother. I heard that Württemberg did all he could to dissuade his stepmother from bestirring herself, but the seclusion of dowager life doesn't suit her.'

'More fool her,' Wellington said, punctuating himself with stiff fury, a finger jabbing at the brocade-clad arm of the chaise. 'Miss Arwenack, if the former Princess Charlotte intends to establish herself as a competitor for the throne after all these years, these treaty negotiations are going to be dragged into even more of a mess. All you need to know is that Her Highness Princess Nadezhda must be seen to behave herself until her marriage and coronation is concluded. I fail to comprehend why this is so difficult to understand.'

'With respect, sir, we have the identity of our attackers under investigation at least,' Kit said, and it pained him that she looked so surprised at his coming to her rescue.

'They're not local, your grace, we know that much,' d'Harcourt offered, turning away from the bookcase. He looked at Kit. 'Helford, we've just had word from Sigy. Her highness's attacker there was from Saint-Sauveur-lès-Bray, so very local to the château, in that case. All we know is that he'd recently been discharged from his regiment, and had really considerable gambling debts. Of the attackers in the forest, we still don't know much at all. Your grace, we took the corpses to Father Honfleur in Recloses. Between him and the proprietress of the Chat Rouge, we can be sure they're not from this cantonment.' He paused. 'That doesn't mean they weren't also French, of course, I will admit. One of the men had a cuff embroidered with a Russian pattern.'

Wellington made a quick, dismissive gesture. 'Any camp-follower between here and Petersburg could have sold him a shirt stripped from a dead man.'

'I found this by the carriage after we were attacked. I thought you all ought to see it.' Clemency reached into her riding habit, pulling a silver medallion over her head. She passed it to his brother without so much as a glance in Kit's direction. Crow let it swing from his fingertips: a rough disc of lead worn smooth, polished to a white gleam. Kit didn't miss the quick flare of approval in Crow's eyes: misdirection was probably one of the first things he'd taught her. He felt dislocated; he hadn't quite shaken off the youthful habit of seeing his brother as omniscient. And yet Crow didn't know the truth about Clemency. *Valentine and Georgiana are holding something over that girl that frightens her even more than I do.* Who wouldn't be afraid of shame and ruin?

D'Harcourt eyed the pendant critically. 'It looks like a musket-ball hammered flat more than anything.'

'A good-luck charm,' Wellington said. 'I don't know a soldier who doesn't wear one, for all the good they do. Foolish superstition and likely irrelevant.'

Crow turned it over, examining the initials carved into

the back of the medallion. 'XB? That's unusual, at least. X is hardly a common initial.'

'It's not unknown in France,' d'Harcourt went on. 'I've a bore of a cousin called Xavier, but even if the man's name and direction were engraved on here it would make no difference. All that would tell us was who he was, not who compelled him to attack us, and even if he was a soldier that doesn't help us much: there must be any number of sell-swords between here and Moscow since peace was declared.'

'It's not XB as we understand it,' Kit said, reaching out to take the pendant from his brother, holding it up so that it caught the morning light streaming in through the window. 'It's the Russian Orthodox symbol for Easter: Christ is risen.'

In the silence that followed Kit thought of the curl of embroidered linen that Father Honfleur had shown him in the gloom of the icehouse, and Nadezhda with diamonds flashing at her throat, and all that laughter in her dark eyes, and could not help thinking of what Crow had told him, long ago. *The tsar cares for flesh and blood only as long as it is useful.*

29

Thérèse de Saint-Maure kept a formal garden in the old Bourbon style, all parterre and serried ranks of white lavender. Refusing his great-aunt's sarcastic offer of tea, Lord Lamorna walked there with Clemency, drinking cool white Sancerre from the Saint-Maure cellar as they trod shaded, gravelled pathways. She'd risen from two hours of black, dreamless sleep to a bedchamber half filled with sunlight and the scent of wisteria in full flower drifting in through the open window, and a maid to help her wash and dress, arranging her hair with long strokes of a silver brush. It was the first time in almost five years she'd been able to tolerate going to bed in a room with closed shutters: as sleep came, she was ready to call out and ask that they be left open, but the usual tide of fear hadn't risen, and instead she'd sunk into sleep on clean linen in the cool gloom, in an unfamiliar cocoon of safety.

They walked for quite a long way through the garden

before Lamorna finally spoke; he looked older than she remembered, with that streak of silver in his dark hair. In her eyes, he was still a young man down at the quay with his shirtsleeves rolled up, revealing those Otaheitan tattoos that ran all the way up his arms. He was impeccable now, though, in well-polished boots and a cravat of fresh white lawn. He wouldn't look at her with that surprising light of fondness in his cool grey eyes if he knew what she'd done. The sort of girl she was.

'I was intrigued to hear from you after so long, Clemency. When your bird arrived in London, it took me quite by surprise.' He paused where they stood on the neat gravelled path, stooping to pick up a wooden cup and ball that his little daughter Morwenna must have dropped; they were near the house now, all golden stone. 'I don't suppose you wish to tell me why that has been?'

With casual expertise, he caught the ball in the cup, glancing across at her as he did so. The heat was stifling, and even with a blue, cloudless sky there was a heightening pressure in the air that heralded a storm.

Now he was here, what could she tell him? How could she describe those fingernails smaller than the tiniest flake of soap, the thatch of dark curling hair, just like her own half-forgotten mother's, or the airless, shuttered bedchamber in a strange house outside Paris where the heavy curtains smelled of mutton fat and the sheets were damp? She'd been brought there in secrecy, in the middle of a war, all the better to conceal the result of her behaviour. Did the Earl of Lamorna really think it was possible to make him understand how it had felt, calling out in the agony of birthing to find Georgie holding her grasping, convulsing hands? So forgiving of her mistake.

Georgie said it was better not to know where to look. Out of sight and out of mind, least said and soonest mended: these things happen, unfortunately. Young men can't help their inclinations, and she'd been willing enough, had she not, relishing every lingering look across the dining table? Georgie had held her as she wept. *You'll understand a mother's love one day. You've made a mistake, but I know you're too good a girl to want to ruin his chances. When Valentine marries, he'll have the pick of all society.*

You'll get over it, Button, Valentine told her, back in Cornwall, but not for a long time later. He hadn't come with her to France, or even home from London once they returned; he'd never even seen their baby. He wasn't there when she woke in a nightgown soaked with milk to find the linen-wrapped bundle gone. No, in Valentine's eyes, all this was of no more importance than an accidental litter got on a sheepdog by one of the hounds, resulting in a litter unfit for any purpose and better drowned. The child would be looked after. *I blame Valentine just as much,* Georgie told her. *I find it brutal the way young girls are turned out of doors for a little mistake, so you mustn't worry for a moment.*

Lord Lamorna stood watching her with such a flash of patience and compassion that she wanted to tell him everything. 'Needless to say, this conversation would be easier if you stopped keeping secrets. Why did you send for me, Clemency, if you had no plans to explain why?'

'It's Kit.' The words left her mouth in a rush. She could

tell him this, at least. 'When I was given my new position, the Boscobels wanted me to make the most of it.'

'Blackmail?' Lamorna said; he looked more tired than angry. 'That dear boy would certainly have given you plenty of material, I'm sure. The Boscobels should be more careful – people are starting to take note of their friendships and business dealings. And yet you were concerned enough to ask for my assistance. What did you suppose? That I would ride in like a knight from a fairy tale and save my brother from your clutches?' He smiled, but there was such a hard light in his eyes that she had to catch her breath. 'It would be unpleasant for both of us if I felt I had to do so, wouldn't it? Still less so than it would be for him. Luckily, Lieutenant Colonel Helford is neither a child nor a fool. Do you really think he isn't already well over half aware of what you're doing, even if he doesn't know every last sordid detail of your intentions?'

Clemency felt hot, and then very cold, recalling in agonising detail Kit's warm scent of starch, soap and salt. Had he held her so close in the forest, really understanding all along that she meant to betray him? *It will be quite all right, you know.*

She couldn't speak for cold shame, and Lamorna saved her the trouble.

'Believe me, I understand just how mortifying it is to realise his capacity for sheer nobility of character,' Lamorna said. 'Surely you must know what my advice to you will be?'

'But I can't stop,' Clemency said, agonised.

Help me. The words formed, waiting at her lips, but it really was impossible to tell him the truth.

Lamorna watched her for a moment, shrugging at her silence. 'Can you not, then? He thinks it pretty shabby that I let you spy for me. You were a brave little baggage, I'll give you that. How old were you?'

Kit *knew*: he knew what she'd done in her past – some of it, although not the worst. Clemency felt dizzy: the more people who knew about those moonless sailings, those nights of scurrying along clifftops paths with a message held tight in her mind ready to be obediently repeated, the more dangerous it was, only increasing the likelihood that someone might stumble on the truth about why she had stopped.

'I was twelve when I rowed out to meet the Portuguese sailors,' she said, forcing her voice not to shake. 'A long time ago now.'

Lord Lamorna caught the ball again, letting out a sigh. 'Yes, a long time ago. The best that can be said of my career is that I've always done what was necessary, but sometimes I wonder if I shouldn't take a leaf out of my brother's book and adopt a more black-and-white approach to morality. Against my expressed wishes, you continued running information for a while after you went to live with the Boscobels, didn't you?' he went on. 'There was the night you passed on a message about a rebellion in Cornwall, and that cognac-running affair on Scilly. You weren't concerned that the Boscobels might discover your activities, even after you went to live at the castle – you were too clever for them, by a long way. And then you broke off communication entirely. Why was that?'

He was, as she knew, an expert in the art of extracting information. Diversion, unexpected questions: he was well versed in every tactic. *Stay with the facts. Give nothing away.*

No one had let her hold the child, the midwife only looking at her with disgust as she reached out, her face hot and wet with exhausted tears. *You careless girls aren't fit to give a mother's love.*

Lamorna watched her, unwavering. 'Let me be frank, Clemmie: this is your chance to ask for help. You sent word and I'm here. You can either tell me everything, or a half-baked percentage of the truth. If I receive the latter, I can't promise you'll emerge unscathed.'

What if she told him the whole, just as she'd so nearly told Kit?

They know where my baby is.

You're always so natural with children, Valentine had said, tossing a pebble into the glittering expanse of the ornamental carp pool. She smoothed out her skirts, avoiding Lamorna's steady gaze just long enough to collect herself. As if he could possibly understand her position: if she had wanted to see her child again, she must dance to the Boscobels' tune for as long as it pleased them. She wasn't an idiot. Valentine wouldn't suffer if the truth came out, but she'd be turned out of society, rejected, without a penny to her name. There was nothing romantic or noble about dying of starvation in a back street. Whilst her child was in this world, she must remain in it, too. Now that Lamorna was standing before her, it was impossible to tell him what she had done, what the Boscobels held over her.

A sudden peal of well-practised pianoforte rang out from one of the upstairs windows, followed by giddy childish laughter: Morwenna was with her own family, her own people. She was safe. No one could or would hurt her here.

'I've told you all I can, my lord.' Clemency almost spat out his honorific; he had at least one bastard of his own: for a start, everyone knew that Louisa Burford's daughter had the unmistakable Lamorna black hair and grey eyes.

Lord Lamorna made no reply, his face an unreadable mask, but he did insist that she allow Thérèse de Saint-Maure to escort her back across the plaza to the palace, sheltered beneath not only a superannuated parasol that smelled strongly of camphor, but also Thérèse's inviolable position at the top of French society, which was already far more than she deserved.

30

Nadezhda had never really forgotten how to move like the partisan soldier she'd once impersonated. Silencing a second set of footmen with a gesture, she found Dorothea Lieven and Napoleon's elegant, grey-haired mistress Joséphine at the marble-topped table alongside a tall, slender man who had arranged himself in one of the gilded chairs with unconscious elegance.

Tsar Alexander wore a close-cut jacket of black superfine that blazed with his imperial insignia in a riot of gold braiding, and he sat back in his chair, looking at her from head to toe, taking in every detail of her dishevelled appearance. He was always so impeccable himself. Even after so many years, she still felt that he saw immediately beyond the tissue of protective lies, even those he had not personally ordained. Nadezhda felt like a clockwork toy as she curtseyed before him, even as she accepted his blessing in the silence of the room.

The angry sweetness of Kit's farewell kiss remained on

her lips. Had she not long since learned to conceal every emotion, tears would have slipped freely down her face, because her very own angry, beautiful boy of so many years ago was in love with Clemency Arwenack, even if he couldn't yet see that for himself. Nadezhda didn't let a single tear fall. Instead, she knelt before Alexander and he placed a kiss of his own upon her forehead, his breath scented with sage pastilles, still lightly holding her hands in his own, his fingers encrusted with emeralds.

'My dear,' Alexander said, looking her up and down as she stood. 'So very like your poor mama that it makes me feel quite nostalgic. But you are to be married soon and crowned Queen of England. Why do you present the appearance of a disobedient child escaped from the schoolroom? Already I hear that you are to be found riding alone through the forest with only your woman, and no guard. Louis Charles is right to be concerned.' He turned to Dorothea and Joséphine. 'May I ask why my most dear cousin has been allowed to risk herself hours since her cavalcade was attacked, and days since the disaster at the Château de Sigy?' Alexander spoke now in perfect, fluent French with barely a trace of a Russian accent. 'I would have thought that her royal highness's importance to the procedures of the peace process merited a great deal more care, even if she must be exposed to such a lack of attention on her personal account.'

There was nothing to do but tell him the truth, as much as she dared. 'Sometimes I long for the freedom of a hard ride so much I'm afraid I'll run mad if I can't do it. It's no one's fault save my own, and I admit the error.'

Joséphine smiled with a look of sympathy that might even have been genuine; Nadezhda envied her éclat in heavy folds of thick green silk, those silvered curls gathered in a velvet riband. 'I am sure we can allow for the unchecked spirits of youth, your highness. We all make mistakes, and this is not irretrievable. Her highness's safety is of the utmost consideration to Napoleon, and I assure you that nothing could happen to her royal highness within the confines of the palace itself. Here, the princess's safety is utterly sacrosanct – although even the Emperor of France cannot account for the criminal element in forests at night, it would most unfortunately appear. I care for her royal highness as if she were my own daughter.'

'Yes, but really you haven't answered my question,' Alexander said. He gave Dorothea a swift glance, which she answered with the tiniest shrug: he might be the tsar but they had grown up in the same nursery, Dorothea's mother attendant to his own. His criticism of her, if it came at all, would come in private. 'Never mind my cousin's indiscretion this morning. What happened in the forest last night? And at the Château de Sigy?'

'Of course, we all want to discover that as soon as possible,' Joséphine said. 'I understand that Lieutenant Colonel Helford and Commandant d'Harcourt have already begun to make enquiries. As far as possible, descriptions are to be circulated of the two men who were killed in the forest. His Excellency Napoleon ordered a small force to be despatched to Sigy as soon as we heard of the attack there: every possible enquiry will be made, I can assure you.'

'A pair of simple French criminals, perhaps?' the tsar said

lightly. He turned to Nadezhda again, giving her one of the faint smiles she'd always hated herself for clinging to. 'So, Lieutenant Colonel Helford? Lamorna's young brother, is he not? In Russia, there's a place in Siberia for arsonists and rebels of his stamp. Such people never grow steady: they never become safe. I'm given to understand that Helford shot a man in his own club only a matter of a few weeks ago. Would you not have done better to select a guardsman from a more unexceptionable family?'

Dorothea raised a sculpted eyebrow. 'Perhaps it's my own misapprehension, sire, but I view ruthlessness as a desirable trait in the captain of her highness's personal guard. He killed her highness's attacker at Sigy, and saved her life in the forest.'

'But he's a criminal,' the tsar said, simply.

'Ought we to judge a man by the actions of his youth?' Dorothea smiled: she was one of the few people alive who could risk questioning him. 'Sasha, I've known Kit Helford since he was a very young child; Lieven and I were both close friends with his father. He might be wild unless kept occupied, but, as Joséphine says, he's also loyal to a fault. He's served his country with prime distinction for eight years, after all.'

'That shooting in London *did* take place only a month or so ago. Have the rigours of campaigning really worked the devils out of our charming Christophe, I wonder?' Joséphine said, but Nadezhda forgave her this sweetly venomous volte-face; as a hot-headed criminal boy, Kit had, after all, set fire to an English palace with Joséphine inside it.

'We need waste no more time on this matter,' Tsar

Alexander said. 'Naturally, there will be no further incidents that might be misconstrued in this way.' He looked at Nadezhda in a way that frightened her a great deal more than she cared to show.

'After all,' Dorothea went on with an air of suppressed hysteria, 'I don't know what your aunt would think of such licentious behaviour, Nadia.'

'My aunt?' With the force of a blow, Nadezhda recalled swimming out of her depth in the slow, green river at her foster-parents' dacha, long ago, the panic as she'd tried to settle her feet on algae-slick pebbles only to find cold bottomless depth and the water closing over her head.

31

Gravel dug into the soles of Nadezhda's feet through her thin silk slippers as she walked arm in arm with the former princess royal, now Dowager Queen of Württemberg; so far, her aunt Charlotte was all immobile ringlets and unreadable amiability, but that meant nothing. Still side by side, they stopped to admire a butterfly gaudy with flecks of vivid violet.

'*Apatura ilia*,' Charlotte said. 'The lesser emperor: rare in this part of France, I believe.' She turned to Nadezhda, smiling again. 'You must forgive me my botanist tendencies – it's awfully bluestocking of me. When we were girls, my sisters and I had little else to do but admire the garden. I suppose you know that my mother kept us all at home on rather a permanent basis. I was the only one of my sisters allowed to marry – an abominably stupid decision and one which caused all manner of difficulties.'

Knowing herself to be one of the difficulties, Nadezhda focused her gaze on the butterfly; it was just as vividly purple as the tall spikes of delphinium interspersed with the lavender. 'My own parents' marriage was unrecognised at the time, of course.' She dared not guess at how much Charlotte knew: was she aware, for example, that Alexander was really her father, that she was illegitimate, and the marriage of her mother to Alexander's relative nothing more than a complete confection, as was her claim to the English throne?

'Ah yes,' Princess Charlotte said. 'Sophia and that Romanov cousin, of course. I had left to marry Württemberg by then. I did feel for my poor sisters so very much: it seemed so unlikely at that point that any one of them would be allowed the freedom and happiness that I attained upon my own marriage.'

'It's not for me to judge, I know, only I can't help but think your parents were cruel,' Nadezhda said, carefully.

The butterfly took to the wing once more, zigzagging away beyond the lavender hedge. 'The irony is,' Princess Charlotte said, 'that had all my sisters married, it would have been so much easier to find a suitable heir for the English throne after the Occupation. Not that any of us could have anticipated so much loss and tragedy.'

Silence thickened in the hot, still air; implications fluttered like bats darting across the garden at twilight.

'I find it hard to be here in France,' Nadezhda said, the words tumbling forth from her lips in a sudden rush, 'affecting civility towards Joséphine is bad enough. I dread my first encounter with Napoleon and the empress. I don't know how I should look him in the eye. Surely he gave the order for our family to be killed?'

'And now we're Napoleon's guests.' Charlotte shrugged, her shoulders encased in heavy black satin. 'I'm afraid you'll soon become familiar with this sort of predicament. My late husband allied with France for years at the height of the war – my own father was furious. But such has ever been the lot of women who are born into our sort of rank. I believe in archaic times we were known as peace-weavers – a role you're shortly to take upon yourself. The Prince of Hungary seems a sensible choice: Louis Charles is adjacent enough to be useful and powerful, but not of the main Austrian branch of the family. I suppose that neither you nor Britain would wish to contend with that on a regular basis.'

'I'm grateful for the arrangements that have been made for me, of course.' Nadezhda walked on at her aunt's side, lying with the smooth ease of long practice, but really all she could think of was the intoxicating suppressed anger in Kit's fine grey eyes in the aftermath of their kiss, and the almost drunken thrill of looking up from the flying mane of her Arab horse at a hard gallop to see Louis Charles Habsburg-Lorraine waiting for her on horseback, right in the centre of the forest trail, still as a golden statue. She'd kissed Kit before, but all those years ago he had been merry with it, his hands in her hair and then running down her back, pulling her closer to him with such sweet force.

'A very proper attitude, my dear,' Charlotte said, 'but if you're anything like your mother, you'll have your own views which I don't doubt you're wise enough not to share.' She stopped on the path as sun beat down on Nadezhda's back, facing her as they stood upon the warm gravel. Reaching out, she tucked one crooked finger beneath Nadezhda's chin, tipping back her head just a little, then from side to side, examining her face from all angles so that Nadezhda could only breathe in the scent of the clove emollient this ruthlessly practical aunt used to smooth the appearance of age from her hands.

'Yes,' Charlotte said. 'You really are your mother's daughter. It almost feels as if I see Sophia looking back at me – she'd be laughing at us all, no doubt. She always did enjoy pulling the wool over people's eyes. Luckily for you, the resemblance is unmistakable.' She stepped back, wiping her fingers on a loose fold of her black bombazine widow's skirting. 'You're no one's fool, my dear. You understand, of course, that from where I stand you might have been anyone – a real cuckoo in the nest: the English were so desperate for an heir that I wouldn't have been surprised to have a complete imposter thrust upon me as a niece; for such a long time I was discounted as a contender, thank goodness, because of my husband's changing loyalties during the war.'

Nadezhda fought for breath at this brutal dispersal of Charlotte's cards on to the table: frank honesty had always left her feeling as though the carpet had been whipped out from beneath her feet, but two could play at that game. 'I never met her,' she said. 'I've seen portraits but that's it. I was hoping you might look like her but you don't.'

If Mama really loved me, if she had really cared, she would have found a way to keep me.

'There was one day,' Nadezhda went on, the words surging to her lips like vomit, uncontrollable, 'when I was sixteen years old, and my foster-mother Countess Kurakina had visitors. She always wanted to impress the

Rumyantsevs, and so we had pineapple ices. She sent me to the kitchen to help the maid set candles about the tray as we brought them in; we had the silver dishes out. I stepped into the drawing-room with the tray and when I looked out of the window, there were geese were flying over the lake in formation – you know how they do. And I knew, I just knew in that moment that my mother had died. I dropped the tray and the ices went everywhere, but I felt it: I felt the very moment of her death, as if something inside me had been snipped with a pair of shears. I was sure. Afterwards, you know, I told myself I was being a little fool and making things up. But when I came to England, I learned that my mother really had died on that day.'

For a moment, Nadezhda heard nothing but the blood beating in her ears as she looked into Charlotte's face, unable to stop herself searching, just for a moment.

Charlotte laughed and began to walk again; arm in arm, Nadezhda had no choice but to follow her. 'Perhaps it's just as well that Sophia never overly resembled me,' Charlotte said. 'I'm no mother figure, my dear: just ask my stepchildren. Listen – it ought to be as obvious to you as it is to me that there are vicious tongues already wagging here at Fontainebleau that will set us against one another. If you have any sense, you'll see me as an ally, not a threat.'

'I quite agree, your majesty.' Nadezhda silently prayed that reminding Charlotte of the throne she'd once held in that tiny irrelevant kingdom would convince her that she didn't need another, just as she herself needed no mother.

32

Jacques swung his axe, sun beating down upon the back of his neck. Sweat streamed into his eyes as the log split, bouncing away across the leaf dirt and pine needles, pale against the forest floor. Alie looked up from the basket of fresh green peas, hair clinging to her forehead in damp curls, popping one into her mouth whenever she thought he wasn't looking.

'Porcelaine has got a sore leg,' she said, frowning across the clearing. Jacques mopped his forehead with his kerchief and leaned on the axe, watching his white lymer with a critical eye as she limped from the sunny patch in front of the byre to drink from the stream: the girl was right, her leg definitely still wasn't sound. She must have sprained it somehow on the long walk home. When this lot was chopped, he'd boil water for a poultice. The girl would be hungry soon, too: she'd grown like wheat this spring. Bluette had her half-day, released early from her English mistress up at the palace, and they'd be able to spend the early part of the evening together before she was needed again.

God, how he wanted her with him; she'd made little of those attacks on the English cavalcade, brave as she was, but he didn't like it, not at all. He wanted to wake with her beside him every morning, but it wouldn't be long now until they were married. Then she'd be away from that godawful palace, and Alie could wear that new dress of hers. For now it was wrapped in brown paper, the parcel in pride of place on the dresser beside the jars of picked mushrooms and the strings of garlic and dried apple. Jacques couldn't help smiling to look at her sitting there with her basket of peas: daft little creature she was, couldn't stop touching the parcel every time she walked past it. *It's just for me,* she kept saying.

'Can I watch you make the poultice?' Alie said. 'Bluette says you're as good as the apothecary.'

'Fetch me some water from the stream and you can.' Jacques went into the house and found the basket of herbs stored on the shady window-ledge. Pulling a small sharp knife from the wooden block, he set to work chopping faded mallows and roots from the basket. Next he sliced up the white lilies, crumpled now like the silk handkerchief a lady had once dropped at Jacques's feet as she breakfasted at the curée after the hunt. The fire was already hot, so it was short work to fill an iron ladle from the bucket and hold it to the flames. Some might say it was the iron in the ladle that did half the work, keeping witch's evil at bay. Damned bloody hound, she was, that lymer, but she was his best, too, and stayed always at his side when he commanded it; he never even had to leash her when the hart was near or the scent of a boar so strong on the wind that Jacques could breathe in the muddy, piggy rankness of it himself.

The poultice came to a boil, and he began to wonder where the child had got to with fresh water from the well; it didn't do to let the bucket run dry. Tipping the green steaming mess of herbs on to the board laid out on the table, Jacques cut them fine with his knife. Alie would sit with the hound to keep her still while the poultice settled on the beast's leg, drawing out the sickness within; she could finish shelling her peas at the same time.

'*Petite!*' he called. 'Come in with that water! Didn't you want to help?' She didn't reply, and he was adept at recognising that thickening of silence in the moment of a child doing something it really shouldn't. Jacques stepped outside and found Alie squinting up at a person he'd never seen before: not Benoît from the palace, but a young gentleman well dressed in expensive riding gear. A huntsman like his father before him, Jacques had a hunter's instinct, and a cold slick of sweat thickened down the length of his spine.

'Steady, girl,' he said quietly to Porcelaine at his heel; he didn't recognise the newcomer at all – well dressed and obviously nobility or adjacent to it, judging by the quality of the white lawn cravat at his throat, and the high-bred horse steaming at his side, hard-galloped through the forest by the look of it, although the dismounted rider himself looked cool and collected enough in his fresh linens. Jacques didn't like how close the fellow stood to Alie, or the way he looked at her, but you had to take care with this sort: you really had to be careful not to offend.

The strange gentleman smiled, revealing well-kept white teeth. 'Jacques Pelletier, Master of Hounds?'

'What can I do for you, sir?' Jacques could only pray that he'd navigate this conversation without losing his position: Bluette was always saying that one day his face would get him into trouble.

The stranger made no reply for now and instead knelt down by the girl, so that he was eye to eye with her. Jacques forced himself to hold his ground.

'What a pretty little girl,' the stranger said to her. 'It must be so dangerous living out here in the forest – there are so many different ways that you might be hurt, after all.'

Alie stood in silence; she knew not to talk back to this type of person.

Still smiling, the stranger turned to Jacques. 'I've come for a word in your ear, my good man,' he said, and began walking off past the well towards the trees: they both knew that Jacques had no choice but to follow, which he did, telling Alie over his shoulder not to move, and to finish podding the peas, and not to touch the fire. She stood watching them go.

'This'll be far enough, sir,' Jacques said, knowing it could easily cost him his job. 'I can't leave the child alone too long.'

'Yes,' the gentleman said, 'it's quite the wilderness out here in the forest, isn't it? Anything might happen. When the royal hunt takes place, you must understand that there is one who won't survive the chase.' He smiled again, so unsettling. 'I don't mean the hart.'

Jacques swallowed, hard. 'I'm not sure what you do

mean, sir.' Dirty politics, plain as the nose on his face. Well, he'd have nothing to do with it. 'I'm only the huntsman. When I get word from the palace I'll summon the lads and we'll set the coverts, of course, but beyond that it's nothing to do with me, you see.'

The gentleman smiled, his eyes bright with frank amusement. 'I'm afraid you're quite wrong about that, Jacques. This has everything to do with you. Nadezhda Romanova is a pretender to the English throne. She must not be allowed to survive the hunt when it takes place, and she won't. Do you understand? No, don't look so dismayed. It's an easy matter, after all. Her highness is impetuous and arrogant, and everyone knows she longs to cast off the restriction of court life. If she sees a chance to bring down the white hart herself, then she will, riding off on her own. When the coverts are set, you'll ensure that she's separated from her guards. I don't care how that happens, but it will happen.'

'And what then?' Jacques asked, even though he already knew the answer, as if in a night troubled by indigestion and costive dreams, he saw the future playing out before him: firing the rifle, the young princess dead on the forest floor among all of last year's fallen leaves, then silence, and not long afterwards climbing the steps up to the scaffold, sunlight shining on the blade of the guillotine.

The gentleman laughed. 'I believe you understand me very well already. You're a tolerably good shot, I take it? You're Master of the Hunt, after all – used to finishing off stags or boar left wounded by inept members of the aristocracy. This won't be any sort of trouble to you, now, will it? She'll never even know what happened.'

Jacques felt curiously calm, as if he were watching all this happen to a stranger, not to him, not to Bluette, who surely would be left without a man for the second time in the space of a single year. Not to Alie, who had no one else but him to call her own. What would happen to Alie and Porcelaine when he was imprisoned first, then led in shame to the scaffold? The poultice would have grown cold on the table; left to another, Porcelaine's leg would never be sound again.

'Sir,' he said, 'I'm afraid it will be trouble. You're asking me to do evil. To commit a crime.' How could he kill anyone, let alone royalty, in plain daylight?

The stranger only smiled again, and cast a glance over his shoulder at Alie, who was sitting down with her bowl of peas, methodically podding and eating a few as she went, always so trusting. 'I'm afraid, Monsieur Pelletier, that we really have no choice. I'm sure you wouldn't want any harm to come to your pretty child, would you?'

'No, sir,' said Jacques.

33

'Certainly the emerald green – your highness has the colouring to carry off these jewel-like shades,' Clemency said, stepping back to examine Nadezhda's slender form from every angle. She was softly lit by the glittering chandelier almost as large as herself. Light from a hundred shivering candle-flames picked up elaborate gilding all over the ceiling and walls so that the room itself shimmered with life. Nadezhda paced from corner to corner, her skirts of emerald silk catching the light as she emanated a dangerous, watchful energy like a caged and hooded leopard.

'What do you think I should do?' she demanded, turning on Clemency. 'You've got secrets of your own. How would you behave in my shoes?'

Clemency swallowed, hard. 'I'm sure I don't know what you mean, your highness.'

Nadezhda only laughed. 'Liar. But never mind that. You're tactical, Miss Arwenack. Wellington says our attackers could have been Russian, even if the man at Sigy was French. Tell me: how ought I to proceed, regardless of whatever that bloody old woman wants? Should I confront the tsar and demand to know if he's tired of me, and that's why they want me dead? I must say, it's charming but very predictable to know that I'm worth less to my own family than a trade route to the Ottoman Empire.'

'There's just no proof, that's all,' Clemency said, quickly. 'Thomas d'Harcourt was right when he said that every city between London and Moscow is heaving with mercenaries since the peace was declared. A lot of officers can't afford to live on half-pay, Russian or otherwise. There's not enough evidence to lay any sort of charge or challenge.'

Nadezhda laughed, bitter. 'As if they'd bother: it wouldn't be very diplomatic, would it? No, they'll just wait until I'm dead and deal with the aftermath then. The English will take that scheming Württemberg tabby cat as their queen and have done with it.'

'If I may say so, your highness, I think His Grace of Hungary might have something to say to that.' Clemency caught her breath, but Nadezhda just watched her with sudden sharp-eyed dawning interest. 'His grace will be here soon. He's exactly the sort of individual to benefit from being firmly taken down a peg or two, in my opinion, which he certainly will be when he sees you this evening.'

'Well, you're very much right about that, and I've never been afraid to stand out, so it would be a foolish thing to start in with it now. God, pour me a drink, will you? You may as well have one yourself: I owe you that much after the dressing-down I don't doubt you received on my account this morning.'

Clemency let the silence stretch out and went to the little walnut dressing-table set out near the window. She poured two glasses of brandy, passing one to Nadezhda.

'I suppose I'm grateful you didn't go off into hysterics.' Nadezhda's fingers tightened as she clutched the glass in both hands. 'It might be that Louis Charles can help me after all, but I still don't want to get married, you know.'

'I'm sure it would be possible for someone in your shoes to hardly ever see their husband, your highness,' Clemency said, turning to examine the selection of earrings in a jewellery box inlaid with a floral pattern of lapis lazuli: rubies, diamonds, sapphires, pearls set in white gold. In the mirror, she caught a glimpse of movement, blazing candlelight from the chandelier striking the brightness of the emerald silk gown; Nadezhda set down her glass, putting both hands up to her face, her shoulders heaving. On an instinct, Clemency laid one hand on Nadezhda's slender arm, immediately withdrawing it as if she had been burned. It wasn't her place.

'Ma'am?'

'As if you care!' Nadezhda turned to face her with a tear-streaked, bitter smile. 'Oh, very well – what does it matter if I tell you anything? I've waited twenty-four years to meet someone from my mother's family – I suppose that doesn't mean a thing to you – and *nothing happened*. I thought I'd feel better, you understand? Less hideously bloody incomplete.'

'I'm sorry, your highness,' Clemency said, forcing herself

not to look up from the jewellery box. 'I lost my mother at a young age, but I did know her, at least. It must be very difficult indeed not to even have memories, only questions.'

She turned away quickly, sipping from her own glass; she must think only of the brandy blazing down her throat, and which earrings would best set off the princess's emerald satin: diamonds or pearls, something clean and simple. Then Clemency made the mistake of looking across at the bed, and among the scattered heaps of satin and unspooled lace, she saw a wriggling bundle wrapped in fresh linens; the baby was as clear and as real as her own hands: unable to stop herself, she stepped closer, but when she looked down at the child from above, her face was perfectly blank, smooth and round as an egg. She reached out, grasping one of the bedposts to steady herself, forcing herself to look away. *Idiot.* It wasn't as if it was the first time this particular nightmare had seeped into the waking world.

'I just don't know how she could have done it.' With a surge of savage movement, Nadezhda strode to the window, gripping the sill as she stared sightlessly out at the manicured ornamental trees, shadows lengthening across the spreading lawns. 'If that had been me, in the position she was in, I should have found a way to keep my baby. I wouldn't have sent her away to another country to be brought up by strangers.' She turned to face Clemency, tearstained in all her finery; what did she know of any of this, and how much had she had to drink, to unleash all these confidences without a thought? 'I suppose there's something wrong with me. Something just lacking inside, that made her want to give me up.'

'I'm sure that's not true.' Clemency forced her hand not to shake as she reached for the diamond pendants. 'And I'm sure that Princess Sophia never once forgot about you, your highness, not in all those years. Would you prefer the pearl earrings, or the diamond? If your highness permits, I think the pearl would make a nice contrast to the necklace. A little restraint is no bad thing.'

Nadezhda let out a long breath, feverishly picking up one of the long silver satin gloves draped over the end of her bed, running it between her fingers with all that restless, dangerous energy. 'You're right, Miss Arwenack. Restraint it shall be.'

'In that case, your highness, may I make a suggestion?'

'What?' Nadezhda didn't look up, fretting with the silk-covered buttons on her glove.

'Black coffee,' Clemency said. 'Unless you want the Prince of Hungary to get the better of you tonight, your highness. I don't wish to be impertinent, but the brandy is strong. You want to use him to your advantage, I'm sure, but in my opinion he'll be a dangerous man to manipulate. He's not an easy mark.'

'If I might give you a hint, Miss Arwenack?'

Clemency froze in the act of accepting a glinting diamond necklace from one of the maids, but did not reply; she only fastened the piece around Nadezhda's slender white neck, knowing quite well that the question had been rhetorical.

Nadezhda smiled wolfishly into the mirror. 'I know you're staff, but I do actually like you, darling, which is why I must warn you – no, there's no need to protest. I'm afraid it's blindingly apparent: trust me, I understand the pitfall. It goes without saying that he's devilishly beautiful, and so charming: I think it's probably the laughter in his eyes, isn't it?' Nadezhda turned to her and smiled again. 'Honestly, the last thing I want would be for you to suffer the hurt I did, Clemency. Everyone knows Kit Helford is wonderfully adept at making one feel like the only woman in the world, but somehow it's always easier to consider oneself the exception. I know I did. I see it as my duty to warn you off.'

'Your highness is so kind,' Clemency said. 'But I'm under no illusions about Lieutenant Colonel Helford. He's a very accomplished flirt, of course. We've known each other a long time, which perhaps gives a false impression of intimacy, when really it's only familiarity, and contemptuous familiarity at that.'

Clemency, do you honestly believe I'd kiss you like that or even at all if I wasn't going to make it right?

If she hadn't stopped him, what would he have offered that night? Never to have mentioned it again, needless to say. It wouldn't have been the first time she'd been promised marriage. Only a fool made the same mistake twice. And yet he'd held her in the night, in the darkness of the forest, in the full understanding that she planned to betray him.

Nadezhda glanced away from the mirror. 'Just accept a warning given in good faith if you've any sense at all.' She turned back to the glass, adjusting the necklace herself. 'He's not exactly particular with his favours, you see. I'm afraid he kissed me. Would you believe his cheek? It's been years, but I was almost shocked to find it as good as I remembered. He's so thorough about it and so competent, just as he is at everything else, and I've been quite desperate ever since. He knows very well how to please a woman – not all of them do. The first night he was here, I'm told that you could hear his paramour's *petite mort* all the way down the corridor.' She smiled, her sharp white teeth flashing in the candlelight. 'You do know what that means, don't you, darling? It's when a man brings a woman such pleasure that she loses control of her wits. I'm pretty certain I'd like to take him as a lover once I'm married.'

34

Nadezhda set down her coffee cup, half wishing that Miss Arwenack hadn't withdrawn to her own bed-chamber with such an uncharacteristically poor attempt at concealing her own anger: that hard exterior shell of hers was starting to crack, and one couldn't help wondering what would be revealed when it did. Blazing candlelight rendered the state apartment airless and she went to the window, pushing back the heavy curtains, opening the window. It was a relief to do something for herself, but even as she did so the door opened with no announcement. Just a servant, no doubt, some footman summoned to escort her to the François I Gallery, all heavily carved walnut wainscoting, fresco and stucco ornamentation. The long table would be groaning with food that she had no appetite for: roasted plovers, Provençal fritters and heaped pastries glistening with peach jam. All the real meat of the treaty was picked over by the men in hushed, quiet rooms where she was never invited. The coffee might have reversed some of the effects of the brandy, but her mouth tasted stale and bitter, and she plucked a sugared almond from the silver filigreed bowl on the mantelpiece, angrily chewing through the explosion of sweetness.

Before this summer ended, she'd be the legal property of Louis Charles Habsburg-Lorraine, even if she was also his queen. She wouldn't think about that, or being pushed on to her back in the snow so long ago, and the boy's heavy, thrusting weight on top of her, the sweating male rankness of his breath in her mouth, her eyes and nose, even as she tried to turn her face away from his, and yet she could not help thinking of that, whenever she remembered that soon she was going to be married.

'Your highness?' *Kit.* Kit, who had always understood why it frightened her to be touched unexpectedly, whose own touch had been so understanding, and so pleasurable.

He'd come in with d'Harcourt, both resplendent in their mess jackets alongside the Prince of Hungary himself, and Nadezhda swallowed the Russian profanity that flew to her lips. This was the closest she had ever been to Louis Charles: he was slender and graceful, clad like a civilian in breeches of light tan, immaculate boots and a jacket of dark blue superfine cut with such severity that his golden hair looked like a deliberate adornment. He took in the elaborate scarlet and gold interior of her bedchamber with a raised eyebrow, as if in mockery of the ostentation.

'Your highness, will you receive his grace?' d'Harcourt asked; Kit looked as if he didn't trust himself to speak, which was no surprise given how thoroughly he had kissed her at their last meeting, leaving her with nothing but unquenched desire and an irritating sense of regret.

Louis Charles ignored them both, looking straight at Nadezhda. Then he smiled, exactly as if the two of them were sharing the same joke.

'Good Lord,' Louis Charles said. 'Well, considering that there's no one here with the precedence to introduce us, I suppose we'll just have to introduce ourselves.' He bowed, and she showed him a hint of a curtsey.

'I suppose we will.' Nadezhda watched with an odd tightness in her chest as he stripped off his white kidskin gloves, letting them fall one by one on to the tapestried ottoman at the end of her bed. 'I'm late already; by this time His Excellency the Emperor Napoleon will be waiting for us in the François Gallery. Doubtless they're already swilling the champagne. They ice it well here, don't they?' She broke off: she was talking too much, but what advantage did he even seek to press by coming here alone like this? She glanced around a little wildly: Kit and d'Harcourt stood like statues of themselves, beating a full retreat into expressionless professionalism: she might as well have been alone.

The prince just smiled again, candlelight bronzing his bright hair, lending a golden tinge to the fine-grained skin at his cheekbones, shadowing the fine white lawn of his cravat. 'I thought your highness might prefer a more informal evening.' He spoke French with a slight accent that she couldn't place, realising she had no idea what the mother tongue of this Habsburg princeling might even be. 'So I came here,' he went on simply. 'Of course, I'm at your highness's disposal. We can join our elders should you prefer to dine in state.'

Another look at d'Harcourt and Kit proved beyond doubt that she wasn't going to get any help from either of them unless Louis Charles tried to stick a knife between her ribs; both stood with rigid military immobility, as if they were a pair of cadets awaiting their first inspection on the parade ground rather than the highly decorated seasoned killers that they both actually were. Louis Charles showed no sign of demonstrating a threat; he just walked with loose elegance over to the chessboard set out on the occasional table beneath the window. Idly, he picked up a white ivory pawn, examining it with apparent unconcern. Did he think she was afraid? Did he think this intrusion would intimidate her?

'Well, all right,' Nadezhda said. 'I don't see why we can't remain here. Helford and d'Harcourt: you will stay and have my apologies sent to the François Gallery. I'm sorry to inconvenience the empress and sorrier still to disappoint my relations, but I'm feeling indisposed tonight; I fear a headache, and I wish to dine with the Prince of Hungary alone.'

Kit just raised both his eyebrows, black as flecks of ink.

'Might I suggest that you can guard her highness effectively enough from the room next door?' Louis Charles suggested, lightly.

D'Harcourt and Kit looked at one another, expressionless. 'I don't think so,' Kit said, with his sweetest and most disarming smile. 'I'm quite sure you understand our position, your grace.'

'Just as you wish,' Louis Charles replied. 'There are some chairs by the window, I apprehend.'

D'Harcourt spoke quietly to a servant and took a seat, crossing his legs, Kit disposed himself with his usual long-legged sprawl, and Nadezhda turned to face her fiancé as if there were no one else in the room.

'With whom do you play at chess?' Louis Charles turned the pawn over, letting it swing between his fingertips; his hands were slender and elegant.

'Myself, for the time being,' Nadezhda replied, gesturing at him to sit. He did, which surprised her a little, leaning back in the gilded chair and looking up at her with a flash of genuine curiosity. She sat down before him; the table was only small and they were rather close together. She felt too hot, suddenly aware of the weight of her silk gown against her leg.

'It's hard not to choose a side, playing in such a way,' Louis Charles said, replacing her pawn and accepting a glass of champagne from the servant who melted into view with a tray.

'For the uninitiated, perhaps.' Nadezhda moved her white queen, only then looking up at him. 'It's an excellent way of improving. I was taught as a child to contest myself. Were you?'

'Yes. It does rather force one to look for the best moves in the position.' Louis Charles looked up at her then with a flagrant courtesan's glance that knocked the breath from her lungs. He had very long eyelashes for a man, she noticed, even as with practised appraisal she assessed the strength in his well-trained body. 'It teaches a tactical approach, rather than playing from the heart, even if it isn't as predictable as people might think.'

'We're all susceptible to mistakes: there's no guarantee of a draw.' Nadezhda rested one fingertip lightly atop her queen, rocking the piece backwards and forwards on the ivory-inlaid square. 'Would you care to play with me, your grace?'

Louis Charles watched her over the rim of his glass. 'Why not? Could you bear to start afresh?'

'It's always preferable to begin at the beginning, is it not?'

They rearranged the board, lining up each set of pieces to commence battle, ivory and ebony. Candlelight cast shadows across his finely moulded cheekbones, catching the emerald set into his signet ring; he let out a small exhalation as he picked up the queen, his lips were parted a little, his eyes cast down at the board, those thick lashes brushing his pale skin. Nadezhda signalled for champagne and played first, setting down her ivory pawn; in the fireplace a log collapsed into a heap of bright embers, throwing up a shower of sparks; outside the window she heard the call of an owl in the twilight.

'The Sicilian Defence?' Louis Charles spoke lightly, countering it immediately; as he did so, the back of his hand brushed her fingertip and the breath caught in Nadezhda's chest. 'This will be an interesting game, your highness.'

36

The following morning, sun beat down on the silken canopies set up on the clipped lawns of the grand parterre. No one mentioned the primordial stink rising up from the glittering expanse of the imperial canal, although many of the women carried oranges studded with cloves and tied with red ribbons. Platter after platter had been laid out upon the long tables: beef rump studded with coloured jellies, fried carp roes, Silesian lettuce stuffed with forcemeat and simmered in cream, ragout of thrushes slow-cooked with lardons, *petits pois à l'ancienne* swimming in butter, yolk and cream. The entire international court had gathered: women were gowned in the first style of elegance, and men wore the mess jackets of elite regiments from all over Europe, Persia and the Ottoman Empire, mingling with their civilian counterparts.

Nadezhda had been seated between Tsar Alexander and a Swedish Bernadotte princess in alarming Prussian blue satin who was trying to converse with her about

Napoleon's collection of Mameluke scimitars, but she was only really aware of Kit and d'Harcourt standing guard at a discreet distance away; stealing a look, she allowed herself a flicker of satisfaction: they were both so handsome, each wore the mess jacket of his own regiment, but both were marked out as hers with the heavy white cloak tossed back from the epaulettes. Only little fools were afraid: Alexander was such a real and solid presence at her side, the black superfine of his jacket, the lean strength of his arm, and his subtle scent of leather and clove pomade, in all likelihood wanting her dead because she wasn't useful to Russia any more; she wouldn't think about that, or of marriage, or of Louis Charles's hand brushing against hers last night, and the thrill that had shot through her body.

She turned to the tsar, words flying to her lips. 'I'm afraid I didn't ask before: I do hope your journey to France wasn't too tiring.'

'Oh, not too arduous, my dear,' Alexander replied with light conversational ease. 'It was just a matter of a few weeks on the imperial yacht. The cherry blossom was out in Petersburg before we left.' He smiled, turning to her with his implacable blue gaze. 'Perhaps you might visit Russia again once your marriage is completed?'

'I would hope to, your excellency.' Had that been the right thing to say? Anything not to think about that night she had been pushed into the snow, long ago now, hot spit landing in her face, even into her mouth, those hands tearing at her gown.

'You should smile more, dear child,' Alexander said. 'Did you enjoy your little tête-à-tête last night? That was tactically astute of you, even if it was also disastrously ill mannered.'

'It was instructive enough, your excellency: his grace will make me a civilised opponent, in his way.' Nadezhda looked up, forcing herself to breathe: the crowd had parted to reveal her immaculately tailored betrothed standing a matter of a few feet away in easy conversation with Napoleon himself and the whey-faced Empress Marie-Louise, the imperial couple encased like a pair of hermit crabs in the sashes and insignia of royalty. Marie-Louise had the air of a provincial matron who had invited summer guests but before champagne capillaire on the first day was already wishing them all gone. Together they reminded Nadezhda of the merchant couples she used to see at the summer ball in Kazan, bound in mutual dislike. Slanting sunlight caught Louis Charles's shining cap of golden hair and she took a careful sip of champagne. The empress was smiling already: the Prince of Hungary had the gift of charm, when he chose to use it.

'My word,' Tsar Alexander said, softly, just in her ear. 'Someone really has just laid his cards upon the table, my dear. For you, I believe.'

Holding her breath, Nadezhda followed his swift gaze to two liveried guardsmen emerging from the trees leading a glossy black Arab mare. She got to her feet, commanding instant silence along the long, damask-covered table: she'd moved too quickly and now everyone was staring. The black mare sidestepped, and one of the green-clad servants took a quick pace backwards: she recognised that livery with an unsettling jolt. Further down the table, Louis Charles sat at the empress's side, circling the rim of his wine glass with the tip of one finger. The hubbub of chatter died away, and Nadezhda had never felt more exposed; why had she got up? The mare tossed her head, fretting a little at the bridle; could the fool holding her not see that he needed to walk her? She wouldn't turn to look at Louis Charles again; she refused, supposing that after last night he thought he'd won her over, like some little sixteen-year-old debutante on her first evening at Almack's. One had almost to laugh.

'I hope her royal highness approves of my poor gift, that's all.' Louis Charles's tone was light, almost mocking; it ignited a susurration of laughter and chat that quickly faded when Nadezhda spoke herself, although for the first time she wondered if it wasn't she that aroused his mockery and contempt but rather the world that they both lived in.

'How good of his grace to have taken the trouble,' she said. 'The Akhal-Teke bloodline, I perceive, from her conformation if not her colour? I should like to show my gratitude and ride now, if that doesn't inconvenience everyone too much?'

She didn't wait for a reaction, stepping down from the petal-strewn dais in thickening silence; the grass was lush and still a little damp, rapidly soaking through her thin silk slippers. She crossed the lawn to where Louis Charles's attendants waited with the horse: the mare really was beautiful, her ink-black tail flicking a little. Nadezhda was sure she would jump well, but now wasn't the time to try that, not with the embroidered saddle-cloth and the scarlet breastplate; to the mare, she herself was the predator.

She walked up to the horse, approaching from the side,

keeping her body soft, no threat: she knew how it felt to be hunted. *I won't hurt you, my soul.* The mare lowered her head, ears flickering backwards and forwards, prancing to the side, and little wonder, with all these bright silk flags fluttering in the hot breeze, and all the noise and chatter gradually falling silent.

Louis Charles' Habsburg servant removed the lead rope from the bridle, handing the reins to Nadezhda, who dismissed him with a single gesture. Eyes down, she walked the mare away from the tented dais and the colourful throng, aware even as she turned of a stillness within the crowd surrounding Louis Charles himself; he was forever in repose, just like a cat in the sun.

In that moment, it felt as if he were the only one watching her as she stood alone on the lawn, hot breeze tugging at the full, wide skirts of her muslin gown, leading the shining black mare: oh God, why was it that one could trust a horse when one might never trust man or woman? Stopping, Nadezhda reached out her hand, just a little: *Are you afraid of me?* The mare investigated her fingers, warm lips against her skin, and without servant or block, she reached up to grasp the pommel and mounted in one Cossack rush of graceful movement, never forgotten in six long years, to an audible gasp from the crowd. Arranging herself with brisk economy in the embroidered side-saddle, Nadezhda twitched great handfuls of muslin skirting out of the way, took up the reins, and asked the mare to carry her back to the dais, a request she obeyed with beautiful precision.

Even as the silken tent rang with applause, the first

explosion tore straight across the heat of the afternoon and Nadezhda felt the great rush of movement as the Prince of Hungary's considered gift to her reared into a spreading cloud of gunpowder.

Nadezhda was scarcely aware of the second or third explosions, or those that followed them in rapid succession, or the screaming from the silken tent. The mare reared again, and Nadezhda leaned forwards, praying to God that she wouldn't go over on top of her. Ignoring her own fear and the instinct to use both hands as the mare's front hooves hammered into the grass once more, she drew in hard with the right-hand rein, bringing the mare's head around so that it was impossible to bolt. Instead, she tried to buck and Nadezhda had to use all her skill and nerve to bring up her head, keeping her going forward with some semblance of steadiness; she took a risk then and eased her into a piaffe, only dismounting when she had calmed. Nadezhda let a panicked guardsman hand her down from the saddle as Clemency came hurtling out of the smoke, running with surprising grace across the lawn in her gown of straw-coloured muslin.

'Your highness, are you all right?' Clemency was wide-eyed with real concern, and sudden hot tears started to Nadezhda's eyes: she'd come like a friend, as if she actually cared, but Nadezhda wasn't fool enough to fall for that; this was a matter of raw ambition and a generous salary.

'Of course,' Nadezhda snapped; there was no sign of Louis Charles, and she felt his lack as if some malign force had just whipped away all of her clothes, leaving her naked. What in hell's name was he doing, watching and laughing from the safety of the crowd? She turned on Clemency, savage. 'You're a damn fool of a girl – how could you be sure you wouldn't get kicked?'

'I'm sorry, your highness. You're so good with horses.'

'If you want to survive at court, never be foolish enough to assume so much as a single thing!' Nadezhda turned her back on the girl, leading the mare away from the crowd; Kit and d'Harcourt at least had the sense to stop their headlong sprint a safe distance away, even as they covered the area with their pistols.

'Fireworks.' Kit holstered his Gribeauval, coming closer once he saw she had the mare well under control. 'It was fireworks.' Nadezhda didn't miss the flash of heat between him and Clemency; so much anger and barely concealed longing, the pair of damned little fools. Whoever had engineered this trap for a horsewoman of her known standing had intended to humiliate as well as injure her.

'I'm afraid we don't yet know who lit them, your highness – we can't yet be sure if it was an accident or malice,' d'Harcourt said.

Nadezhda looked away as d'Harcourt fixed her with an expressive dark gaze: she couldn't stand the sight of their faces, all so concerned.

'Thomas is right,' Kit said quickly. 'The gift itself will cause suspicion: anyone could have guessed that you'd want to try her paces.'

'Perhaps it really was an accident – or at least a prank,' Clemency said. 'The fireworks will be for the hunt ball

– isn't setting them off the sort of thing foolish aristocratic young men do for a wager?'

As one, they all turned to Kit.

'Not here,' he said, with the ghost of a wry smile. 'Not like this.'

Louis Charles's name hung in the air, unspoken, his absence notable, but even as they all turned to look in his direction, another run of explosions tore through the air with the staccato rhythm of gunfire, accompanied by flashes of coloured light washed out by bright sun, and the mare shied again, instantly accepting Nadezhda's gentling touch. Kit and d'Harcourt fared little better, visibly wincing and unable to quite stop themselves ducking a little, as if dodging grapeshot on the battlefield. Who set off fireworks accidentally, hours before it was even dark? They all pitied her, that was the worst of it. Everything was a nauseating blur: the mare's black glossy flank, the silver braiding on d'Harcourt's blue dragoon's jacket, the courtly throng beneath the silken canopy of the tent.

Without a word, Nadezhda handed the reins to Kit; despite everything, she would have trusted no one else with them. Turning her back on them all, she walked over to the royal group: courtiers, emperors and soldiers all exchanging lies and flattery in the dull heat of the waning afternoon; they were already beginning to gossip about her headstrong passion and her horsemanship, perhaps even to laugh at her. Mounting up in her morning gown and silk slippers, she'd been a future queen proving to them all that the trappings of womanhood couldn't stop her. But now she felt only bedraggled and foolish, like a child after showing off at her name-day. Waving away smirking compliments and solicitous enquiries alike, she took a glass of champagne from the nearest servant, forcing herself to focus on the gathering now swelling across the lawn: a small crowd had grown around the slender, leonine form of Louis Charles Habsburg-Lorraine, so that she felt an unpleasant twisting sensation in her belly.

'Oh, for goodness' sake,' Clemency said, flushed beneath the golden spray of freckles across her cheekbones, tendrils of hair clinging to the pale skin at her temple. 'He's going to give a speech – as if now were the moment for that. He ought to be apologising or at least seeing if you're safe.'

She was right, of course, as she invariably seemed to be, but the Prince of Hungary was now holding up one hand, commanding silence among those closest to him.

'Let's go,' Nadezhda said, and Clemency ducked to shake out the abundant skirts of Nadezhda's muslin gown: yes, she would damned well look her best to hear this. As one, without further discussion, she, Clemency, Kit and d'Harcourt began walking towards the dais, all in grim silent unison, and Nadezhda knew that it would be safer by far to ignore this fleeting sensation of camaraderie, as if they were all four of them in this together, because the fact remained that she could trust nobody, and certainly not them; as d'Harcourt moved alongside her, she caught sight of the heavy white folds of his ceremonial cloak, pale as ivory against the vivid green grass, and she felt trapped in time, reliving the same moment for ever. As they all drew closer to Louis Charles, the crowd parted, all bobbing feathered head-dresses and ringlets arranged in elaborate confection.

The air grew hotter, heavier, as if before a storm, even though the scorched blue sky above the silken tent remained cloudless, until at last Nadezhda and Louis Charles faced each other at a ten-foot distance, with Clemency, Kit and d'Harcourt at her back and the gathered court watching from all sides in heavy silence.

Nadezhda looked up to find Louis Charles smiling at her as if no one else was there, just she and he in all this quiet and tense expectation. The sun caught his hair again, bright gold, his breeches and jacket alike cut close to his form, his cravat a drift of folded white muslin, and Nadezhda felt as though she couldn't grasp at the fabric of the world, as if the magnetic poles of the earth had shifted.

'Do you know, I think we should just get married here at Fontainebleau,' Louis Charles said with the now-familiar edge of self-mockery. 'Love and unity as a tribute to lasting peace. Really, I couldn't be more delighted that we have so little time to wait. I look forward to her highness hunting the white hart at my side.' He turned away, glancing at the silent crowd. When he spoke again, it was to Nadezhda alone. 'We ought to call it a celebration.'

Nadezhda dropped into a curtsey, her gilded muslin skirts billowing out, catching the breeze, even as she felt that the grass beneath her feet had been whisked away, leaving her plummeting so far and so fast that she could not breathe.

37

The stink of gunpowder still hung on the air and Clemency felt as if she'd been laced too tight, breathless and a little crushed, her skin alive with tension. Crossing the wide expanse of shaved lawn, she moved swiftly among the clipped trees: it didn't take her long to find the patch of scorched grass where the fireworks had been let off. Careless of her gown, she dropped to her knees, her fingers brushing the grass, but there was nothing to be found, no scrap of proof that might add to that precarious but undeniable scaffold of evidence against Nadezhda's own countrymen: *XB, Christ is Risen.*

'Do you ever tire of putting yourself into dangerous situations, Miss Arwenack?' Kit spoke with his habitual sweetness, laced with a thread of some other emotion that she couldn't quite identify.

She sat back on her heels and he stood watching her from the shade of a clipped box tree; she was on her feet in a moment, alarmed at how quietly he could move. The sun had bronzed his skin, picking out dark copper lights in his black hair, and she thought of Nadezhda smirking into the mirror last night. *He's not exactly particular with his favours, you see.*

She couldn't forget his brother's cold smile, either. *Do you really think Kit isn't already well over half aware of what you're doing, even if he doesn't know every last sordid detail of your intentions?*

'Is it a habit of yours to sneak up on women alone?' She forced herself to sound light, unconcerned.

His mess jacket was undone, his officer's gorget glinted gold in the sun. 'I wouldn't alarm you for the world; I took no care to be quiet.' He ran one hand through his hair. 'I'm sorry I frightened you.'

'Then it's just as well you didn't.' She looked up at him again; all his usual insouciant merriment was now gone.

'We still haven't spoken about Sigy,' he said, with brutal simplicity. 'It's tactless of me to bring it up, but worse to pretend it didn't happen. Clemency, I don't do that sort of thing to girls in your position.'

She laughed: she'd heard this one before, from Valentine. 'Except that you did.' God, how she'd moved beneath him at the heat of his touch: the fact that he'd quite clearly wanted it just as much was little consolation now. 'It's my fault. I shouldn't have given you the expectation that I might accept any sort of carte blanche.'

'Oh, for God's sake, it will be my name or nothing.' His words hung in the air between them: he'd spoken with utter sincerity, his long fingers tracing the holster of the pistol at his belt.

'What?' Clemency laughed again, bitter. God, how she wanted to scream at him not to do this. 'You can't be serious. As if you'll be allowed to marry anyone other than a debutante selected by your brother or Thérèse.'

'No. This is no one's choice but my own. Listen,' Kit said, never looking away from her. 'You're right: I'm an overbearing aristocrat scarcely aware of his own good fortune, and the whole world works in my favour. If you marry me you'll find that the same goes for you. Just let me get you out of whatever hellish mess you're in.'

For a moment she was unable to believe what she had just heard; she had to fight for breath before she could speak. There were so many things she could have told him, but in the end, despite the fact he was the only person who had ever made her feel safe, she only said, 'What, so you can continue your affair with the future Queen of England?'

If he knew the truth about her, he would never have asked in the first place.

He let out a quick breath, raking his hands through his hair once more, a habit with him that she recalled with blistering force; they had shared too much for this not to hurt.

'She doesn't mean anything to me,' he said, taking a breath. 'You do.'

'If she doesn't even mean anything to you, then quite frankly that only makes it worse.'

Clemency turned and walked away from him, the loss of his touch a shock deep in her bones.

★ ★ ★

'*Clemmie.*' He spoke her name like a supplication in church, and she stopped, much as he didn't deserve it.

Of course Nadezhda had told her about the kiss: of course she had.

Ow flog vian. My little child. She would tell him the truth when and if she was ready and not before. God, she just looked so bloody desolate, as if there was simply very little that now mattered to the bold, brave girl that she had been; one day he would make the Boscobels suffer for bringing her to this pass.

She stood with her back to him now, her gown dusty around the wide hem, her slight shoulders squared, wisps of hair escaping the pinned coils bright as copper in the slanting light. How could she think he would judge her for this as the rest of the world would when she knew how much he had loved his own sister? In the back of his mind, Kit saw Roza in her mother's cottage, kneeling down before him with a bowl of porridge dotted with fresh blackberries, dark hair hanging over her shoulder in a thick braid. She'd died by the rope, left hanging in only her shift, blood staining her pale thighs. Kit had to shut his eyes, catching his breath. Little wonder Clemency had refused him. Papa had never married Roza's mother; Kit himself had loved her all the same. And yet Roza had died without the protection of their father's name. What did those conventions and rules and pieties matter, so many lives spoiled for the sake of them?

'You don't deserve a lie,' Clemency said, with shattering clarity. 'It's not because of the princess. Or not just.' And then she looked up at him. 'And don't go thinking it's about your sister, either—' She bit off the end of the sentence even as the shock hit him with the force of a blow: she read him like a book. Had always been able to do so, in fact. 'I'm sorry about what I said on the way to Calais. That wasn't fair – bringing up what happened to Roza and Nessa Carew, and Mr Gwyn.'

Kit's head was full of gunfire. 'Yes, it was fair,' he said, when he was able to. 'I did care, though. It wasn't that I didn't give a damn because they were servants.'

She looked up at him, her face white and sharp, freckles standing out in bleak relief, and he couldn't escape the sense that for weeks they'd both been moving inexorably closer to this reckoning, that what was to come was unavoidable.

'Then what did happen?' she asked.

'You don't want to know.'

'I do. It's why you never come to Cornwall, isn't it? Once or twice in the last eight years, and yet it's your home; your first language, even.'

He sighed. 'Twice. I've been home twice. All right then. It was in '17, in the middle of the Occupation, as I'm sure you already know. The worst of it, really, when there were French soldiers all over the place. I ran away from Lamorna House in London, back to Cornwall. I don't need to tell you how much of an idiot I was.'

'No. But why did you?'

'Because I'd found out about Crow and our stepmother. He had something going on with Louisa. Papa wasn't long dead, and I took it badly, like a fool.' Everyone knew about Crow and Louisa's affair; it had been the talk of London, and it was hardly a betrayal to bring it up. 'It was the Season, so we were all up in town when I saw them together.

I left London and came home to Cornwall without telling anyone. It took me weeks; I stole some banknotes from the library, but they were all gone pretty quickly. I walked for quite a lot of the way.'

Clemency just watched him for once without calculation; he'd never told anyone this before, his own side of the story, no excuses, just the bald, unpalatable truth.

'By the time I got to Cornwall, I was starving. There were French troops and Cornish rebels everywhere. The whole place was like a powder keg – but you'll remember that. Harry Trewarthen said he'd share his supper if I did what he told me, and so like a bloody fool I blew up the French garrison at Newlyn.'

Half a meat pie. Three lives taken as a result of what he'd done, all in exchange for hunger and his own stupidity. He looked up, expecting scorn, but Clemency's expression was free of judgement.

'Crow followed me down to Cornwall. He was my guardian, then, but even so I wasn't expecting that at all. He was bloody angry, too; God, he was raging – that was a nasty shock, as well. You know what my father was like. He never minded what I did. He wouldn't have even noticed that I'd gone.' Kit stopped talking, briefly closing his eyes. 'The French meant to hang me, but Crow got me out of prison. I wasn't what you'd call grateful, put it that way. What I remember mostly is being really furious that he was going to drag me over the hot coals when we got home. He was in the wrong as I saw it, having an affair with Louisa. And then we did get home.'

A lone blackbird wheeled in the hot blue sky.

'We got to Nansmornow,' Kit said, 'and when we arrived, we found Roza and the others hanging. The French had gone there looking for me. Hester saw it, too. For all the world, I would not have wanted her to. I know what some people say of me, but I cared about Roza very much indeed. She was my sister, legitimate or not.'

For a moment neither could speak; Clemency might have her own secrets, but he didn't judge her for them. How could he?

'Obviously the fact that Roza died was the worst thing about it,' Kit said. 'But she should never have been at Nansmornow anyway – not working as a scullery maid. She was my father's daughter.' He broke off. 'Crow wanted to arrange a marriage for her – one of the tenant farmers. She ought to have had her own house, her own place, at the very least. It wasn't fair, Clemency.'

This was as close as he'd get to telling her that he knew about her own child. He wasn't Crow, happy to extract information from people when they didn't choose to give it. She was looking at him, expectant, and in truth it was a relief to just tell her all this.

'What I've never understood is why you set the fire at Carlton House after that,' Clemency said, quickly, and he thought he saw a real flash of her old self, all curious assessment. 'I mean, it was the official French residence during the Occupation. Napoleon's brother was living there, and Joséphine. Of all the targets you could have chosen as a rebel, it wasn't the most subtle.'

'Or the most sensible.'

'Well, no.'

Kit sighed. 'At fourteen, I was the polar opposite of sensible in just about every possible way. It should never have happened. I wasn't acting for anyone, not officially. Crow was obviously leading the rebellion against the French at the time, more or less, but I didn't know that then – not many people did. I thought he was a coward, not getting involved. I was just disgusted. The Cornish rebels wouldn't go near me, though – Crow didn't want me to have the slightest part in it. He'd warned them off and made me swear I'd stay away from the whole thing.'

'I take it you didn't?'

Kit offered her the ghost of a smile. 'You know me too well. Eventually, Crow found me with gunpowder and clouted me halfway across the hall at Lamorna House. So I threw the affair with Louisa in his face.'

Clemency winced. 'For someone with a really poor sense of self-preservation, you've survived an awful lot of battles.'

'I know.' He didn't tell her that whenever he ran into gunfire, it was because he deserved it; he didn't tell her that at times sheer bloody luck felt more like a curse. 'It didn't go down well.' Kit paused. It was difficult to square that morning with the man Crow was now. 'He's a hard man, my brother, when he wants to be, although perhaps it was no more than I deserved, after Newlyn, too.' He'd spare her the details. No doubt he'd earned every last blow, but to judge by the stricken expression on Clemency's face, her old spymaster was only just still in firm possession of his pedestal. Let him stay there.

'I don't think,' Kit went on, 'that I've ever been so angry. I ran away again. I had no gunpowder, and no sense, so I got myself into the servants' quarters at Carlton House and set fire to the coal-cellar. Obviously, I was caught. You'll have read the rest in the newspapers.'

Clemency let out a long breath. '*Kit.*'

She didn't need to know about the condemned cell at Newgate, or the sheer, white-hot terror at stepping up on to the gallows, the shadow of the noose against rough-hewn boards, and then disbelief as the guard beside him was shot, giving him time to jump. In Kit's mind, he heard the roar of the crowd again: *Run, run, run.*

And, in that moment, a hot slick of instinct warned him not to tell her it was Hester who had fired that shot. Neither Crow nor Hester herself had ever wanted that to get out. Society judged Hester twice as hard as any other woman already: she couldn't afford to make herself notorious. Kit stepped away from Clemency, taking off his hat and raking his fingers through his hair. Damn, it was hot. And, damn, why had the instinct which had never failed him just screamed in his face that it wasn't safe to tell Clemency about Hester's part in his own notoriety?

'It wasn't really your fault,' Clemency said, watching him. 'The French were all over Cornwall then. And I'm not surprised you thought Crow was a coward. It must have looked as if he was as good as collaborating with the Occupation. You couldn't have known. I'm not surprised you were furious about him and Louisa, either. We always hated her.'

'It was my fault entirely,' Kit said. 'All of it. We have our burdens, and that's mine.'

Clemency's gamester's mask dropped then, so that he saw

every last disconsolate emotion writ clear upon her face: even if he couldn't trust her, she despised herself because of it. In the shade of the tree, she put her hands up to his face and kissed him, the sweet almond taste of her on his lips, so that he wanted to gather her up in his arms, for it never to end, and it was only the risk to her of being seen like this that made him stop.

'It's the helplessness I can't stand,' Clemency said, flushed.

'What you need is a pistol, maid,' Kit said in Cornish, when he was able to speak again. 'Come here.' Unholstering his Gribeauval, he couldn't keep the habitual note of command from his voice, even though of course he knew well that she wasn't one of his men, and had certainly never been his to command. Her eyes blazed, for once that quick and ready tongue with nothing to say. In one swift movement, Kit held the Gribeauval out to her.

'It's a damnable mess we're all in, but you'll feel a sight less powerless.' The six-chambered pistol wasn't part of his regulation kit, but along with his Mameluke cutlass he always carried it regardless, a gift from Hester the summer he came of age. 'It's not loaded. It's got a percussion lock so you don't have to prime it like a flintlock. Take it.'

She stepped towards him, swift and sudden; for a moment he thought she might just walk straight past him, but instead she stopped, her chest rising and falling, her voice tight and breathless as she spoke, her lips a little reddened from the kiss. Her hands shook, her eyes widening a little as her fingertips inevitably brushed his own. The Gribeauval was light, with a narrow stock fashioned from polished walnut; she held it with great care.

'May I?' He waited at her side and she nodded: he passed her a cartridge from the leather pouch on his kit-belt; he felt stripped to his nerves.

'You may as well start from the beginning.' The familiarity of the task was like a rock to a man swept out to sea: he clung to it. 'You'll have seen men do this before, your father even, maybe. Bite off the end of the cartridge and pour a little of the powder down the barrel.'

She did so, her eyes widening at the taste of the powder. 'The ball next?' she said, her upper lip now blackened with gunpowder: he brushed it off with the edge of one fingertip, so that she let out a very small sigh.

'Tap the side of the pistol opposite the lock first, just a little. You want to settle the powder into the vent. Now the ball: twist the cartridge paper around it and ram it all down the barrel – that's it, nicely done.'

She had a craftswoman's hands: strong slender fingers lightly dusted with freckles. Deft in her movements, she returned the ramrod to its housing beneath the barrel, and he breathed in the scent of her body, still a little warm and all mingled with the freshness of Castile soap.

He passed her a cap; conscious of a sudden heat as their fingers touched; neither were gloved. She turned to look at him, her eyes wide and clear. It was an effort to breathe as he ran through the familiar motions of preparing the gun, made unfamiliar by her presence. 'Very well. This is where you'd go full cock and pull the trigger. You'd have a beautiful clear shot at that plane tree.' Kit broke off; he was talking too much when he had no desire to talk at all. Then, on a sharp intake of breath, Clemency raised the pistol and lined up her shot with the sight bead. For a sickening moment he thought she was angry enough to fire, and to hell with consequence: the court would stampede like wild horses. Lowering the gun, she turned to him, her lips parted.

'You're quite right,' she said, all of her devastating even calm recovered, for now at least. 'I bet it does feel good, but the satisfaction would probably last for about as long as your affections, I suspect.'

She handed the pistol back to him. Kit knew there was nothing else he could say.

38

'Sometimes I think you're avoiding me, Button.'

Catching her breath, Clemency didn't turn immediately to face Valentine. Even in the silken shade of the dais, the mid-day heat was sweltering by now, and the stink of gunpowder still raked the back of her throat. She wished Kit would come back, or d'Harcourt, but d'Harcourt was guarding Nadezhda step for step as she conversed with Princess Charlotte and an avuncular Napoleon, all three of them making light of the incident with the fireworks. She couldn't put off facing Valentine any longer. She summoned up a smile, turning to find that he was waiting for her to compose herself; he had always been like this, anticipating her next move according to his own prediction, taking enjoyment in her reactions, relishing the fact that she had needed to collect herself like this in his presence. No doubt he was just as aware as she was of the pair of Prussian women watching him from behind their fans, taking note of his well-cut jacket and his glossy auburn curls.

Clemency forced a smile. 'Of course I'm not avoiding you, Val. It's just been a busy morning, as I'm sure you saw.'

'You and Helford looked very cosy just now. Mama and I feel quite abandoned.' He smiled in return. 'I hope you don't forget old friends now you're moving in court circles, Button.' He held out his arm and she took it; there wasn't much choice. 'So how do you go on? Everyone knows her highness rode out without her guards. People are talking already, and it's definitely damaged her reputation, but we're going to need something with more flesh on the bones than that. She's got to be hiding something, surely? People like her always have secrets. You can cause trouble for the princess after she's married, but it won't be nearly as effective.'

At the back of her mind, Clemency saw their newborn daughter wrapped in fresh linens, as clear and as real as her own hand held before her face.

It's a great pity, of course, Georgie had said to her. *It's painful, but we must learn our lesson, must we not? Least said and soonest mended.*

She hadn't learned her lesson, though: instead, she'd kissed Kit and enjoyed it, twice. Her punishment was only to grow as the years went on, with all she missed: first steps, first words; that kiss with Kit was just a taste of another joy that must remain out of reach. There was no choice but to join in the pretence that none of it had ever happened.

Valentine was looking at her, expectant, angry that she'd taken this long to answer to him. 'You know you can trust me. Rumours don't take long to spread once they've started,' she said.

'Well, get on with it, then.' Valentine tightened his grip on her arm with such a pinch that she had to hold her breath. He released her, making a smiling effort to control himself, leaving red finger marks around her forearm.

'Of course.' A gambler to the bone, Clemency read him in that moment as if he were the newest country booby out on the town for the first time: Valentine didn't just want her to blackmail Kit and the princess with threats of scandal and exposure, he needed her to. Yet he had no losses of his own that she knew of, and in any case, she'd delivered a Prussian courtier and the Belgian Count de Mercy-Argenteau into Valentine and Georgie's curated web of obligation. Georgie had her losses and subsequent embarrassments, but between the Prussian and Belgian dealings Clemency had secured for Valentine, even Georgie ought to be fairly plump in the pocket now.

If money wasn't the issue, then what was?

Valentine smiled yet again, rueful this time – he did, after all, believe that he was a good sort of man. 'I shouldn't let you arouse my passions, should I? We're both worried about you – Mama and I. If you're not careful, spending all this time with Helford won't do much good for your reputation. People might start to talk.'

We were all nearly killed twice and I hit the man who tried to murder a princess over the head with a chamber pot. And yet if the Boscobels were concerned, it was only because they needed her to be an effective asset; she battled a sudden wave of anger that she had to listen to this barefaced disingenuousness.

'I'll manage it, Val.'

280

Valentine's expression intensified; he'd convinced himself that he was doing good, that he really cared about anything other than himself, but it was a very long time indeed since Clemency had stopped believing in him.

'I've always agreed with Mama that allowing you to see it would be a misguided cruelty,' he said.

She couldn't breathe. *It*. 'What do you mean?'

'I'm starting to think we've been wrong all this time.' He smiled. 'I don't think I'm infallible, Clemency: far from it. Perhaps you would keep a steadier hand on the reins if you saw the child. We're in France, after all. It wouldn't be difficult to arrange, in fact. Ruin Helford or the princess, and preferably both, and I'll see that Mama looks after the situation.' Valentine reached out and crooked one finger beneath her chin, tilting it so that she had no choice but to look him in the eye. 'I know I can always rely on you to make the right choices in the end, my beautiful.'

He turned and walked away, moving off into the crowd, sliding effortlessly into conversation with a group of French and Austrian ambassadors' wives, unaware of the hostility with which he was observed by their nearby husbands. He never could understand why people didn't like him.

By the time Clemency found Georgie sitting with Louisa Burford in the shade, sweat poured down her back. They both wore white muslin in a concession to the stifling heat, but on Clemency's own advice their gowns had been cut according to the new style, with abundant sleeves and a lot of ruffling at the hem: she must force herself to focus on small details. This was no time to lose her head.

'Darling, you must sit down!' Georgie addressed her

with genuine concern, signalling to a footman for champagne. 'What an appalling shock with those fireworks. Whoever would do such a thing with horses nearby? Her highness did astonishingly well to control that mare – I knew she was considered quite the horsewoman, but it's another matter to actually see it. How mortifying for the Prince of Hungary, though.'

'Did you hear what he said?' Louisa Burford smiled, arch as ever, as Clemency took her seat, accepting the glass of cold champagne. This was going to be easy: there was no love lost between Kit and his former stepmother. Now she knew the extent of their hatred for one another, thanks to Kit's own honesty. 'Marriage before the end of next week!' Louisa went on. 'That'll set the cat amongst the pigeons, surely. I never heard of anything more shocking. These things take months to arrange.'

'Not in France, not necessarily,' Clemency said, the champagne cool against her lips. 'You didn't hear it from me, but perhaps his grace knows which side his bread is buttered upon. If he wants her highness without a stain upon her reputation, he'll need to get her sooner rather than later.'

Louisa's carefully shaped eyebrows shot up, and Georgie leaned forwards, with a quick, secret smile that Clemency didn't miss, not for a moment.

How long would it be before this long wait was over? Weeks? Days?

She had to close her eyes, just briefly, holding tight to a memory: the warm, wriggling bundle in her arms, the sweet pull in her breast of the milk letting down that first time, running to the door when she woke to find the crib empty, only to find it locked, the cold doorknob immobile.

'What on earth are you talking about, darling?' Georgie said, fanning herself slowly.

'You must promise not to breathe a word of this to another soul,' Clemency said; would she know the child, when she saw her? 'But they've already kissed at least once, Kit Helford and her highness. It's only a matter of time before it becomes more serious, in my opinion. They're both playing with fire.'

39

Bluette's rust-red skirts were dusty from the journey and strands of her long curling hair escaping from the braids neatly pinned beneath her linen cap when Jacques met her outside the cottage, mechanically kissing away a smudge of grime from her cheek. She'd stopped at the market, riding side-saddle through the shaded forest on the mule with both baskets full. She laughed and kissed him back, her lips warm against his as she handed him a basket of pigs' trotters and a jar of pickled pears. In her presence, everything felt normal again, and the smiling stranger who had asked Jacques to murder the English princess seemed like just a terrible dream, as if he'd imagined the whole thing.

Of course he couldn't do such a thing. He couldn't kill anyone.

Side by side, they walked into the cottage where a sleepy Alie lay on the wooden settle strewn with patchwork cushions sewn by Jacques's older sisters, long ago. Wrapped in the striped blanket his mother had knitted, she was nursing Porcelaine, who lay curled up beside her, and sketching. She drew rapidly with charcoal on a sheet of paper resting on one of the chopping boards; Jacques had always supposed one or both of her real parents must have had an artistic eye. Mother hadn't known much about who they were when she took the girl in from her sister in Paris; his aunt had been unable to keep the child when her mistress died, not on her chambermaid's wages, and that was all he knew.

Bluette smiled at the sight of them and stood on tiptoes to kiss his cheek. 'You're growing soft in your old age, Monsieur Pelletier. Dogs on the settle: whatever next?'

'Alie's a good nurse,' Jacques said, 'she'll have that lame leg sound again before long, won't you, sweeting?'

Bluette frowned a little as she watched the girl. 'I know it's foolishness, but when that child puts her mind to something, she makes me think of Mademoiselle Arwenack – you know, when she's considering what gowns to lay out for her highness, or fooling around with that bookbinding kit she carries about with her. How a girl from trade ended up at St James's Palace, I'll never know. Stinks to high heaven, if you ask me.' She turned to smile at him. 'Listen to me – I've spent too long at court. Talk about addled in the head.'

Bluette laughed at herself and reached into the basket she'd just set down on the table, tossing a fresh madeleine at the little girl, who caught it with quick, sun-browned hands and a deft smile, and Jacques breathed in the scent of sugar, butter and nutmeg, which again made him feel as though surely nothing could be wrong.

'Good girl!' Bluette said. 'Now, will you lead poor Mina to the trough? She's carried me all the way home from town, the dear old lady, and we must give her some oats as well. Take your cake outside or we'll have that rat in here after the crumbs again.'

Alie fled outside in her skirts and pantaloons, and Bluette put her arm around Jacques's waist. 'You're gentle with children, for a fine huntsman,' she said.

Jacques didn't know how to begin. 'Did you bring any wine?'

Benoît from the palace stables hadn't been to see him yet. If there was no official order to set the coverts for a hunt, then surely that gentleman visitor wasn't worth worrying about? He could hardly make ready to hunt Napoleon's own forest without direct orders from the palace. Perhaps it had all been some sort of trick, the kind of foolish joke moneyed young gentlemen played to win wagers? Was that gentleman now sharing absinthe with his friends in one of the smart cafés in town, all of them laughing about how foolish and frightened he, Jacques, had looked, when given his task?

Bluette frowned at him. 'Wine? What's wrong? You do look troubled. I did bring some, but I went to Valois this time, not that vinegar merchant Émile from Barbizon.'

Jacques went to the sideboard and took down two of the green glass cups that had belonged to his grandmother, prized possessions on her wedding day, and Bluette dug into the basket for the earthenware bottle, corked and stringed, pouring them each a glass of the thin local red Grenache.

'Oh,' she said, 'I passed Benoît on the way. You know,

from the stables. He's very up on his high ropes for a man whose grandmother worked her way into a gentleman's bedchamber from the Chat Rouge. Anyway, he told me to tell you that the empress hunts tomorrow after all. I suppose you know they want to go after that white stag everyone's been talking about. He said you'll know where to find it.'

Jacques set down his glass; the wine he'd swallowed cold in his gullet. 'What?'

'I'm serious, would you believe it?' Bluette said, shaking her head as she took onions from the basket, placing them carefully one by one in the earthenware bowl on the dresser. 'God, but Benoît's so lazy. Such an important matter, and he couldn't even trouble to come all the way out here. When I said he ought to speak with you himself, he only called me an impertinent trollop, as if we don't all know he's dosed up with mercury for the pox half the time.' She rolled her eyes. 'I suppose you'll have to ride into the village to raise the men or Georges and the others won't be ready – it'll be an early start, I shouldn't wonder, now the weather's set fair for it. He's such a fool – surely Benoît should know by now that these things take more planning than this.'

Jacques set down his glass, forcibly composing his features. Bluette turned to him, suspicious; she sniffed out trouble with him the way he sensed the passing of game in the forest. 'What's wrong? What are you mixed up in?'

'It'll be a long day, that's all, with those fools hunting in high summer.' That much was true: the sweetness of flowers and herbs would draw the hounds' noses from the scent of the hart: this was better done on an iron-hard winter's morning.

Jacques couldn't help thinking of his father and older brothers, all dead now, long dead in the wars: they'd taught him everything he knew. *A hunter should never be the herald of his craft.*

40

The following morning, Clemency hurried across the grand cobbled plaza to Val and Georgie's townhouse; they'd all return from the hunt before long. It was better this way, keeping busy: wisest to steer her mind towards the many times Nadezhda would change her mind about what to wear for the ball, as if she hadn't kissed Kit in the way she had been longing to since that night at Sigy, just as he so thoroughly deserved. As if she hadn't sent a whisper running through the court that was already spreading faster than typhoid.

You didn't hear it from me.

She'd been a fool not to look for Bluette before coming out, though: those young men of the court who weren't invited to hunt had spilled forth from the confines of the palace and the streets of Fontainebleau were gaudy with officers in gilded mess jackets and young political attachés who allowed their gaze to linger upon her for too long. Many were drunk despite the early hour, staggering arm in arm and lounging by the fountain wielding tankards and bottles of wine; she quickened her pace even as a well-dressed attaché lurched out of a café and leered in her face, his lips glistening with saliva as he slipped one arm about her waist.

'Don't hurry away so soon, darling. Why don't you run away with me? I'll take you somewhere nice.'

Clemency leaned closer and whispered in his ear, unsheathing her knife, holding it close to the crotch of his wine-stained breeches. 'Get your hands off me before I geld you like a year-old hogget.' She allowed him to feel the edge of the blade so that he backed away, eyes wide, even as he spat insults, turning to shout a lewd offer at a frowzy-headed girl who stepped out on to a balcony.

Clemency twitched her skirts out of his way and hurried on across the plaza, swerving around young men and girls from the town in cheap muslins; she didn't have time for this.

Well, get on with it, then, Valentine had told her.

She would be nearly five by now, a little girl. Four years old and eight months. Clemency didn't even know what she liked to play with: dolls, balls, sticks in the dirt? She didn't even know her name. *Least said and soonest mended.* Could she have passed her in the street, maybe, and not even known her?

Nothing else mattered, and so it was best to forget how Kit smiled with his eyes, and the fact that with him she always felt as if nothing could harm her any more, never mind his appallingly high-handed manners. As if she mattered to him, anyway. She couldn't forget the malicious laughter in Nadezhda's eyes: *I'm afraid he kissed me. Would you believe his cheek?*

Arriving at the house in equal parts breathless and annoyed, she was admitted by Georgie's disapproving major-domo, Michel, and found Georgie upstairs in the sun-filled drawing-room, flicking through a book of Parisian fashion plates as though she didn't plan to commit blackmail right at the heart of court. Or rather, to sit back and watch Clemency do it for her.

'Darling!' Georgie got up, fragrant in blue watered silk, kissing her on both cheeks as sunlight streamed into the room. 'What a gorgeous surprise.' She laughed. 'I'd started to feel quite neglected! Aren't you busy preparing for the ball? I thought you'd be horribly overrun. I'd imagine her highness is fickle about her gowns.'

'It's all under control,' Clemency said, sitting down. Georgie rang for another cup, and they spoke of common-places until the young maidservant had retreated with the tray. When she'd gone, Clemency watched Georgie pour milk into her tea. *Least said and soonest mended.* 'Valentine said you'd arrange for me to see her if I set people talking about Kit and the princess.'

'Who, darling?' Georgie spoke without looking up from the fashion plates. 'Goodness, they're taking it too far with these mutton-leg sleeves – I don't doubt it must be a boon for girls who aren't blessed with a neat little figure like yours, though, but some of this volume is just absurd.'

Clemency's hand shook, spilling tea into her saucer.

Georgie looked up, frowning slightly. 'Oh, I see.' She paused. 'My dear, I'm not sure you fully understand.' She smiled then, tucking one pomaded golden ringlet behind her ear. 'Listen, darling: a mother's love – well, Valentine is big enough to look after himself, of course, but I'd still do anything for him. I can promise you that the little girl is very happy where she is. Have you considered that some things are best left in the past?'

'But I didn't stop loving her just because you took her from me,' Clemency said, sure even as she spoke that it had been a terrible mistake to show her hand in this way. 'What harm can it do, just to see her? She wouldn't even have to know it was me. Of course I wouldn't want to spoil things for her.'

'Darling, it's just that it was all for the best.' Georgie frowned again. 'I do think Val has been rather selfish, dangling this in front of you as an option. I'm really not sure it was a good idea.'

'He promised.' Even as Clemency spoke, she realised the flaw in Valentine's request, now that her judgement was less clouded by the immediate shock of his offer. She'd already started the rumour: the damage was done. Kit and the princess would now be less likely to make the sort of slip that she could really hold over them, surely? She'd have to rely on the threat of invention, making up a story to blackmail them both with, something that would add to the impact of the gossip already in circulation, thanks to her.

Between them, for once, she and Valentine had played a bad hand.

Clemency picked up her cup and saucer once more, accepting a sugar-dusted confit from the plate Georgie offered. 'Perhaps you're right after all, Georgie.'

'I do think I am, darling.' She smiled, always so sympathetic.

Later, when callers arrived and Georgie was distracted, Clemency left them all and went out into the silent corridor, where light from the small window at the end cast distorted oblong patterns along the faded carpet. Letting herself into the deserted drawing-room and then the library, she sank into the armchair, breathing in the scent of an arrangement of fading roses that had been left upon the leather-topped desk in a copper vase, tallying what she knew.

To begin with, Valentine didn't just want her to ruin Kit and her highness, he needed it to happen. More puzzling, though, was that he hadn't just asked her to threaten them with slander or blackmail. Valentine never played a poor hand: she'd just misunderstood the nature of his game. She had never been meant to simply threaten the complete destruction of Kit and Nadezhda's reputations. He wanted her to actually wreak that damage, and so she had begun to, at least.

Clemency stepped carefully across the Turkey rug, opening the desk drawers one after the other. She found only collections of quills and reams of paper: Valentine was never careless, either she was wasting her time. She had to fight the urge to slap the leather-topped surface of the desk in sheer frustration. Looking up, her gaze settled on the oil painting hanging on the wall directly above the desk, a still life of bulbous grapes tumbling from a bronze dish. Only now did she notice a sliver of dancer wallpaper to the left of the heavily gilded frame. Had one of the maids knocked it whilst dusting?

People can be so idiotic, Valentine had said, long ago, tugging her into one of the curtained window embrasures at Boscobel Castle, feathering her neck with kisses as he slid the skirts of her gown right up, even though a servant could have come around the corner at any moment. *Look at Mama. She doesn't even see what's right in front of her own foolish face.*

No, Clemency had waited a long time for Valentine to make a mistake. Reaching out for the oil painting, she gave the frame a gentle push, watching as the letter that had been tucked behind it tumbled out and landed, noiseless, on the desk right in front of her. It was too easy to picture the self-satisfied smile on Valentine's face.

When Clemency unfolded the fragile sheet of paper, the first thing she saw was three black antlers: the crest of an old kingdom, the mark of the Kings of Württemberg.

The message wasn't even encoded, the height of foolishness or arrogance, likely both.

You promised to clear a path for me, and this has not been done. The letter was even signed, with a looping, confident flourish.

Charlotte.

41

Empress Marie-Louise was lucky with the weather: the hunt met on a clear dawn. An outdoor affair was always a risk with harried servants looking askance at striped tents rolled up around heavy larch poles still in the baggage train and the mothers of unmarried girls fearing rain and the state of their daughters' pin-curls. Already sweating in their livery, palace staff strewed a sandy clearing with strawflowers, larkspur and meadowsweet, long tables had already been draped with translucent linens for the feasting that would follow the curée. Stag and roe would be unmade and butchered on long trestles set out in front of the huntsman's cottage with all due ritual, and warm sweetmeats given out, and those who had distinguished themselves well blooded. Hot-house peaches and nectarines were piled in shining pewter bowls, and preserved Seville oranges arranged in honeyed slices on platters of chinaware. There were great heaps of glistening pastries, too, sugar-dusted and dotted with caramelised nuts, covered for now with muslin cloths.

Not far away, a quartet of violins and a harpist practised unfashionable Beethoven with bored competence, breaking off occasionally to tune up.

Nadezhda walked arm in arm with the tsar; Kit and d'Harcourt followed in conference with the imperial guard. Even so, she felt more exposed than a cockle pricked out of the shell. She glanced across the clearing, but people seemed to be avoiding her gaze. They were certainly giving her a wide berth. Was she the one they were all whispering about? Nadezhda could have sworn that girl in the emerald-embroidered muslin turned to speak to her companion just as she passed them both, actually laughing.

'The empress has certainly laid on the bounty.' Tsar Alexander spoke without looking at her. His languid gaze was fixed on the long table and the silk-clad women in feathered hats ablaze with military gold braiding, and men in bright regimental jackets not quite disguising their boredom as they waited to mount.

'In truth, sire, I'd rather have a bowl of kasha and butter,' Nadezhda replied in Russian. Wellington's last words revolved in her mind, unstoppable: *You must understand that nothing can be proven against Russia at this stage; I ask only that you remain on your guard and do nothing foolish.*

'Take care, my dear: it has taken them all six years to consider you acceptably English. I fear you must continue to profess a love for bacon and porridge until that English gold crowns your pretty head. Tell me, child: what do you think British intentions really are towards Russia?'

The ground shot away beneath Nadezhda's feet and a

shiver of fear spread between her shoulder blades. 'Sire, such affairs are beyond my comprehension. These are matters for the Cabinet, not for me.'

Alexander smiled again and turned to her, tilting her chin with one crooked finger so that she was forced to look up at him, just as her aunt Charlotte had done. 'Really, my Nadezhda, is this the girl with all that fire in her belly? What have they done to you in England to extinguish that?'

Nadezhda fought for words, aware that both she and her natural father were watched by courtiers of every nationality gathered at Fontainebleau: French, English, Ottoman, Persian, Prussian, Spanish; the most incisive and dangerous minds in Europe and beyond were at this very moment forming their own opinions on this little tête-à-tête. There would be nothing civil about the consequences. 'Sire, even just walking alone with you is enough to arouse suspicion. You must know that the English don't trust me and they never have: why else do you think I'm still uncrowned, that they won't place me on the throne without a husband they feel they can trust?'

Alexander released her and smiled again, the light of absolute authority in his blue eyes. 'Doesn't your marriage grow increasingly unlikely, with all this gossip?'

'I don't know what you mean.' Nadezhda looked down at the forest floor, but the leaf mould and moss spun before her eyes.

'Of course you don't,' the tsar said gently. 'I'm sure it's nothing but idle defamation, all this talk of you allowing Lieutenant Colonel Helford to defile your person in your own sitting-room, where I sat just yards away, with Countess Lieven and Joséphine. Did you find it amusing?'

'No,' Nadezhda said, catching her breath. She couldn't lie to him. She would have to arrange more lucrative bribery for the replacement footmen.

'Do you know,' Alexander went on, 'that in Russia, people who displease me are sent four thousand miles from my presence, to Siberia. We don't favour the rope, but perhaps the gallows would be a kinder end than that sort of living death. I do sometimes wonder, don't you?'

She said nothing: there was nothing, after all, that she could say.

'Ah well, a hunt at the very least is a chance for you to ride hard, my dear, using all your considerable skill. This must all be so very welcome after St James's: such a stuffy place, I always felt. I know how my little bird needs to fly free.' Tsar Alexander bowed, walking away, leaving her alone just as he had always done, so that she had nothing to do but twist her kid gloves in her hands and walk through the crowd until she found her servants with the black mare. Taking the lead, she walked her away and mounted, rearranging the skirts of her riding habit with savage economy. She looked up to find Louis Charles reining in his gelding alongside her: he had a light hand. His fingers were elegantly gloved in tan kidskin and he held the reins with competent ease.

'I look forward to watching you ride again, your highness,' he said. And then he just offered her what passed for a courtly bow from the saddle, and turned his horse away with a rather brusque movement. For a moment, all the bustle of the meet drained away and Nadezhda heard only the beating of her own heart, just like a hunted animal.

The English princess was nowhere to be seen. Jacques cantered among the throng of hard-faced aristocrats, fighting a hunter's instinct to draw the battered rifle from the tooled leather hunting-scabbard slung from the gullet of his saddle: not now. Riding around to meet the mounted courtiers and aristocrats, all feathered hats and fine-tailored riding habits with sweeping skirts, he and his lads might have succeeded in tracking down and flushing out the empress's prized white hart, but he'd failed in quartering his true quarry. The dogs circled around his legs, and he tasted their excitement: if this day went well they'd have their share of heart, lung or liver at the curée.

Picking up his pace as he walked through the trees and the darkness, Jacques suppressed a spurt of worry for his hound, his sweet lymer, hoping that her freshly healed leg would hold true. Porcelaine was a queen among hounds and today of all days he dared not trust the scenting of the hart to another, but it was better not to think on that, and the exact nature of what he'd been asked to do: it didn't feel real; it couldn't be happening.

Jacques realised he was now actually riding directly behind the Russian tsar in his magnificent gilded regimental jacket, gloved hands so light on the reins: he rode well, unlike some of them. Kings, emperors, queens and princesses, all of this felt like a strange dream, but the English princess wasn't among the crowd. He'd recognise that trim, boyish figure anywhere; neat in the side-saddle, she was, with the rich dark red superfine cloth of her habit. It'd be the white dress she wore underneath that showed the blood.

42

Nadezhda was ahead of him – too far ahead. Kit expected a shot to come from any angle: another attempt on her life here was a certainty rather than a possibility. Even d'Harcourt had raised his voice in the council chamber: it might be an insult to the French for Nadezhda not to ride out, but surely that was better than the alternative? Kit rose to a canter, steering the gelding between soaring beech trees and outcrops of rock draped in moss, sweat wicking through his shirt, his hair hot and damp beneath the cockaded hat. Less than a hundred yards away, d'Harcourt put his bay at a low outcrop of rock with effortless poise.

'Your highness!' Kit called out. 'We're too far from the rest of the hunt – the beaters are away to the west!'

Nadezhda turned to look at him with a flash of laughter in her dark eyes. 'Darling, do you really think I care?' And then she was away again, galloping the black Austrian mare hard through the trees, two creatures moving as one through shafts of dappled sunlight. Kit caught up with her;

there was something wild about her today, as if she really did genuinely no longer care what happened to her.

'Stay with us, for God's sake. This isn't safe.'

'Surely you haven't only just realised that?' Nadezhda pulled forward, the feathers on her hat torn back, low down over her mare's neck, swerving past a tree that she clearly hoped would have startled Kit's gelding. He took control, though, jumping the bay easily over the fallen tree; he risked another glance over her shoulder: d'Harcourt, thank God, had fanned out to the side.

'Never mind what game you're playing,' Kit shouted. 'Come on, Nadezhda, whatever damned maggot is in your head, this doesn't only affect you.'

In that moment, he was certain that she herself understood that she was riding for her life – away from him and d'Harcourt, and away from the court completely.

Nadezhda laughed then, the sound of it torn away by the speed of the hunt, all thundering hooves and the hot intensity of it. 'Stay out of what you don't understand is my advice to you, angel. And if you won't take it, well, I know everything that there is to know about your friend Miss Arwenack. Did you really think I'd consent to have a Mistress of the Robes without a few little secrets of her own?'

'Damn it, Nadezhda, I don't care.'

Nadezhda laughed again, still riding hard, turning to glance at him, those dark eyes alive with amusement. 'Perhaps you should, though. Perhaps you ought to know that she still receives Valentine Boscobel in her rooms, late at night, when she's foolish enough to think that no one has noticed, and that servants don't know everything about us all.'

There was little point in disguising the sickened shock he felt at hearing that.

'Come, can you actually truly not have realised?' Nadezhda said, with no trace of laughter in her eyes now. 'She's still fathoms deep an affair with him, Khristofyor. She's not worthy of you.'

Kit felt in that moment as if the entire forest spun around him in a green blur, and the gelding shied at another fallen tree; moving without thinking, he brought him rapidly under control, mane in his face, but by then it was too late. He had taken his eyes off Nadezhda for more than a second, and the princess was gone.

Back at the palace, Clemency sprinted up the marble staircase, holding her skirts out of the way with one hand and the iron balustrade with the other. At the Hôtel de Montausier, Thérèse de Saint-Maure's major-domo had just looked at her from the doorstep with the professionally bemused expression of a disapproving servant: No, his lordship was not at home. Madame de Saint-Maure was within doors with the little girl, and would mademoiselle care to be admitted to the drawing-room?

Hurrying away across the plaza, it had struck her for the first time that she would likely have to tell Kit, d'Harcourt, Lamorna and the Duke of Wellington about the message to Valentine from Princess Charlotte at the ball itself.

And yet how could she do that?

Pausing outside the state apartments, Clemency smoothed her hair before she approached the huge gilded double doors and the rigid, silent footmen leaning against the wall.

Think. She held proof of treason, implicating Valentine. If Valentine were arrested on evidence she'd provided, the Boscobels would ensure that she never saw her daughter or knew that she was safe.

Clemency walked on, the heels of her jean boots sounding out on the waxed and polished parquet. The only other sound she could hear was the beating of her heart pounding in her own ears.

Nadezhda's bedchamber was quiet, silent, a silver-gilt ballgown hanging on the armoire; the princess was apt to change her mind about the evening's gown at the last minute. Clemency knew she'd better have the terracotta and perhaps a gilded muslin ready, too, but all this would have to wait. She must choose accessories, too; perhaps the gold circlet for the muslin and a slender Grecian armband to accompany the terracotta silk. This was absurd, she was living two lives that ran concurrently, but that had been the case since the day she reached from her bed to the cradle in a dark, shuttered bedchamber, only to find cold linens.

Clemency crossed the richly carpeted floor to the concealed door leading to her own quarters; her satchel still lay tucked between her plain narrow bed and the bedside table. She pulled out the book block, creamy pages carefully sewn into one; all she needed to do was to glue the endpapers to the cover and screw the book into the little nipping press until the glue had dried.

Quickly, methodically, she set out her tools upon the plain tiled floor and unscrewed the press, laying it ready. Setting the book block carefully on the bedside table, she drew the letter from her bodice, sure that Valentine must be able to hear her from the forest itself. Gently, she smoothed the wafer-thin paper, slipping it between the marbled endpaper and the endpaper signature. With steady, practised care and her little pot of glue, Clemency concealed Charlotte's letter to Valentine between the double endpapers as best she could. Now, evidence of Valentine and Georgiana Boscobel's treason was bound in secrecy, hidden in this little book of her own creation. No one would ever know where to find it: no one except Kit Helford and his brother, and only when the time was right. She packed away her things in moments, her back slick with sweat even as she rang the bell.

Bluette came in, and Clemency set down the book, staring at her. She'd never seen Bluette overset before. 'What on earth is the matter?' She had to force herself to sound composed.

'Nothing, miss. Nothing at all. Would you like me to help with laying out the gowns for this evening?'

'That can wait. Come on, tell me – what's wrong?'

Bluette drew in a long, shuddering breath. 'I'm just being a fool, that's all. It sounds daft, with him being the huntsman, but I don't like my sweetheart being out there in the forest. I've just got this silly feeling there's something he's not telling me, and we're getting married next week. I don't like it. This court feels like a boiling pot with the lid on tight.'

Unease shuddered down Clemency's spine: when had Bluette shown anything other than complete and utter pert composure? 'I can't argue with that. Ten to one her highness will change her mind about what she wants to wear to the ball once this foolish hunt is over and done with. Come and help me hang up the silk, at least, or we'll have that sharp-faced maid and Dorothea Lieven both griping at us.' She glanced up at the clock on the mantelpiece, not fool enough to dismiss this sort of instinct. 'Look, you can have another afternoon out tomorrow. I didn't know you were getting married.'

'On Sunday; we have all the papers with the town hall.' Bluette looked up at her. 'Really, mademoiselle? I can go this afternoon?'

'Just this once. But don't make a habit of melodramas, will you?'

Clemency expected an acerbic response, but instead Bluette just held on to the window-ledge, looking down at her hands. 'Come on, out with it. There's something else, isn't there?'

Bluette reached into the pocket of her apron, pressing a crumpled handkerchief to her nose and mouth. 'It's worse than that, mademoiselle. If there's really something amiss, I don't know what I'll do, apart from losing him.'

'There's no earthly reason why you should lose anyone.' Clemency didn't have time for this. 'Look, I can't help you if you don't tell me the truth.' Which was more or less exactly the same as Lord Lamorna had said to her: he didn't begin to understand half the mess she was in, and maybe she was no better than him now.

Letting out a quick, sharp breath, Bluette turned to face her. 'All right, mademoiselle. I suppose you might judge me and turn me away. I just know in my heart that something is wrong. We're to be married at the town hall on Sunday, Jacques and me, but I'm with child already.'

On a white-hot flash of instinct, Jacques turned and caught a glimpse of wine-dark cloth just at the tail of his right eye. Reining in, he set off in pursuit, praying to God that he just looked like a palace servant doing his job, that no one who might be watching could possibly guess what he was about. The old grey gelding sensed his rider's disquiet; Jacques leaned forward to whisper calming words into his laid-back ears, his long, well-muscled neck quivering with tension. Jacques found himself admiring the princess's skill as she set that black mare through the trees, yards and yards ahead of him now; it was clear that she understood horses, just as he himself had always done. Perhaps they weren't so different, after all: they might be princess and lowly huntsman, but maybe, as he did, she preferred animals to people, finding them easier to understand.

What foolishness was he thinking? His life was worth nothing. They were no more alike than a white dove and a farmyard chicken. Scattergun memories chased one another: Porcelaine on the settle with Alie; Bluette's aunt in Avon handing him a terracotta bowl of steaming potage, chicken stewed with milk and egg yolk – *You'll have made arrangements for the marriage, I take it? People are starting to talk*; the princess's blood-red riding habit, so shockingly red against the backdrop of the forest, all brown, green and shafts of silvery light puddling between the trees.

If he got this wrong, Bluette and Alie wouldn't live out the week. Jacques knew enough of types like the slender young gentleman who had visited him in the forest to understand that.

Jacques slowed the gelding, unable to shake an unpleasant crawling sensation between his shoulder blades. Sun struck through branches, blinding: it was getting late in the morning. Soon it would be too late. He heard only the quiet sounds of the forest – wind shifting the branches above, the distant call of a woodpecker. He thought he could just hear the hounds in full cry, but so faintly it was only a reminder of how far the princess had strayed.

He should have dared take Bluette and Alie far away. It was a big country – the quiet, smiling gentleman might never have found them all, and they could have been safe. She burst into view then, the princess, riding hard across his path in that wine-dark habit without even a hat, so that her short, boyish curls were torn back from her head by the wind, and he saw the diamonds glinting at her ears. Raising his rifle, Jacques fired. He knew how to wing a creature without killing it, and in the end that was all he could bring himself to do; he caught her right in the arm, so that she was flung sideways in the saddle like a rag doll, although with terrifying speed she regained control, turning to look at him, her face so white against the brown and green of the forest. He'd take Bluette and Alie and they'd go far away from this place. There was still time, in all the commotion of her wounding still a chance.

'What the devil do you mean by it?' The princess spoke in perfect, well-taught French, hardly seeming to notice the injury to her arm, so that the gorge rose right up his throat. And then, as Jacques watched, she raised a pistol of her own and fired it right at him. The bullet bit hard, tearing through his lung, or so he guessed, with his huntsman's precision, from the sharp burning brightness of the pain as his mouth filled with blood; and the forest and the trees seemed to tip as he pitched sideways out of the saddle, dead long before the gelding he loved so much had panicked, dragging him behind with his foot tangled in the stirrups, crashing through the undergrowth so that the gelding broke a leg, and later had to be shot.

43

There were so many other times that Kit hadn't been fast enough, and now there was gunfire, when the hart was nowhere near. The forest flashed past in a blur of vivid greenery, and when he briefly closed his eyes he still saw the tracery of white beech branches against red darkness. He was riding hard, but he could do that with thoughtless ease, half of himself entirely at one with the horse, until on an instinct he reined in: Nadezhda was close by, he knew it. He heard himself call her name, his voice ragged, uncontrolled.

For the love of God, take a hold on yourself. Watching her ride away on that black mare across the spreading jewel-bright green lawn seemed like ten years ago, not merely the day before: the fact was, she didn't care. She didn't give a damn about what happened to him, or d'Harcourt, or Clemency as a result of her actions, but neither did she care what happened to herself, and that was exactly what had always made her so dangerous.

'Nadezhda!' he called, calmer now; the forest seemed to spin around him, a whirl of vivid green leaves, russet and brown leaf mould, and patches of hot blue sky visible between the thatch of leaves and branches high above. He dismounted, and clouds of hoverflies hung in the air; all was so quiet. Somewhere close by, a wood pigeon called out; he could hear his own breathing, of course, and the soft crunch of leaf mould beneath the horse's hooves as she shifted, uneasy, knowing just as surely as Kit did himself that something was wrong here. Looking down at his boots, grimed with dust, he saw the first dark and shining bead of blood. It was like finding lice: once you saw the first, you couldn't help but see the rest, crawling everywhere; there was blood all over the leaf mould, great shining droplets of it. That was when he began to run, and then he saw her at last, the black mare standing peaceably nearby while she lay curled up by the roots of a large oak tree, her wine-red riding habit thrown back and tangled in dead leaves, the white folds of her gown dark with blood.

Too late, he thought. Dismounting and running hard, he crouched at Nadezhda's side; she was still warm, and of course that would be fate at her most cruel – she'd be dead, but still warm, warm enough to hope against hope that she might yet be alive; and without daring to think he reached out and placed two fingers against the pale skin of her throat and felt warm, pulsing life.

'*Nadezhda.*' He crouched over her, realising that she'd been shot in the arm, not in the abdomen; with a slow, slight movement, she turned her head a little, just enough to face him, her dark, long-lashed eyes dim with pain.

'It's all right; it's going to be quite all right,' he told her, just as Crow used to say to him when he was a boy.

Her gaze softened when she looked at him, and tears sprang to her eyes; she opened her mouth to speak; it was so clearly hard to form the words. 'The huntsman tried to shoot me. I killed him, Khristofyor. He's dead.'

'Are you hurt anywhere else?'

'No, I don't think so. I'd forgotten how much it hurts. It's a long time since I was last shot.'

He returned her smile. 'The first night we met,' he said. 'A long time ago now.' He knew with a soldier's long experience that the gunshot wound in her arm wasn't serious enough to kill her alone: she wouldn't bleed to death or die of the shock, but fever held no respect for rank and it could just as easily be that which finished her. 'Come,' he said. 'You must try to stand. I'll get you back to the palace.'

She let out an odd little laugh. 'For them all to sneer at me? So that they can all whisper about us?'

'What do you mean?' Kit had just torn off a length from the bottom of her cloak to use as a sling, but he looked up at her now.

'No one has said anything to you?' She smiled. 'No, of course they haven't. You're a man, after all. Everyone's talking about our silly little kiss.'

'I'm sorry.'

'I'm not,' Nadezhda told him.

Kit said nothing else; now wasn't the time to hold himself to account. That would have to come later.

She allowed him to help her to her feet, both looking up at the slightest noise: a crackling of dried leaf mould. And then, as they watched, the white hart broke through the beech trees into a depthless silence. He was huge, a hart of ten at least, antlers spreading wide as dappled sunlight caught the glow of his pale hide, his old, wise eyes dark and long-lashed, his pale snout flecked with the occasional dark hair, pale flanks heaving. Kit could hear the great beast breathing now: a harsh, ragged sound; he had been running, after all, with the hounds giving tongue.

Neither said a word; in the back of Kit's mind he knew very well that the only way of quashing the scandal of being alone with Nadezhda in this way would be to create distraction and comment by shouldering his rifle now and shooting the white stag: he could do it; it would be easy. The beast was tired; he could make an end of it. He'd ride back with Nadezhda to the clearing by the huntsman's cottage and return with beaters who would tie the dead, great white hart across the back of a strong pony. The beast would be quartered and unmade before the curée, his own face daubed with the hart's blood, even though this was very far indeed from his first kill. He didn't do any of that; instead, he stood with Nadezhda in all her disarray, and they watched in ever-thickening silence as the white hart stood and turned his great antlered head towards them: he was as intelligent and knowing as Kit's own horse, and it seemed in that moment that all three of them understood each other. The white hart was prey just as Nadezhda herself was prey, hunted as she was with every step, moving with majestic ease and grace from one silvery stream of sunlight to another, cloaked by the sheltering trees that were his home, and Kit thought of the stories he'd heard in childhood of the white hart bringing messages from the otherworld.

I'm sorry. Without giving himself time to reconsider, he raised his hunting rifle and shot the white hart between the eyes, so that the magnificent animal was immediately felled, and in the spreading cloud of gunpowder, the weighty silence was broken by the unmistakable sound of riders approaching at speed. He heard Louis Charles before the smoke had even cleared.

'What an excellent shot, Lieutenant Colonel. And exactly the distraction we all need, I venture to suggest.'

D'Harcourt rode up behind him, the pair of them emerging from clearing smoke, Louis Charles calm and calculating, d'Harcourt wild-eyed with alarm.

'My dear,' Louis Charles said to Nadezhda. 'I'm so glad you're safe.'

He smiled, and Nadezhda looked at him, and d'Harcourt fell into step beside Kit as Louis Charles tossed Nadezhda up into his own saddle.

'They're saying it was the huntsman,' d'Harcourt said, quietly. 'But we still don't know who set off those fireworks, and he gave her the horse. Maybe it's not the Russians who've grown bored of the idea of an alliance with Britain. For all we know, the Austrians think they're better off with her out of the way.'

Kit said nothing; in unspoken agreement they rode back to the palace, never more than a few yards behind Nadezhda, now ensconced in the saddle before the Prince of Hungary.

44

It was dark in the cottage except for the fire glowing orange behind the grate. Alie sat on the settle, wrapped in the pretty old blanket that looked a bit like lace. She didn't let her feet dangle over the edge because she wasn't sure what might be under there in the dark, or in that spidery corner behind the big basket of morning sticks. Jacques was always telling Alie that she must never light the lamps or the tallow candles by herself, but now that it was dark and he wasn't here, her belly felt cold and tight with fear. Normally when there was a hunt she went with the beaters, and they were home a long time before mid-day, leaving all the palace people to eat pastries and roasted meat at the curée. But today Jacques had told her that she must stay here and wait and that tonight they were going away with Bluette.

She'd been a bit frightened about the idea of that, because if they left the forest where he was the huntsman, then how would they have any money? Jacques had said that she mustn't worry, and that everything would be all right. And then, as Alie watched, the door moved and she twisted her fingers into the blanket, wishing so much that he would come home. The door opened and although she tried to scream even as a log in the fireplace collapsed into sparks and darkness, no sound came out of her mouth, just exactly like one of those bad dreams when Jacques would sit up by her bed afterwards, except that he wasn't here now, and he wasn't coming back, because he would never leave her alone like this, hadn't he promised that he never would?

The door swung open halfway, and Alie wanted to hide under the blanket but she was too afraid. It was just Porcelaine after all: long and white and graceful, pushing the unbolted door open with her black nose and coming in, trotting across the floor to the settle so that her claws clicked on the cold flagstones, which only made the quiet seem deeper and thicker and much more frightening. Alie held out one hand and Porcelaine kissed it, pushing with her cold nose, eventually lying down on the floor just in front of the settle, and Alie knew then that it was safe to go to sleep.

It was still dark outside when Alie woke, but now the cottage was full of lamplight so that relief washed through her like a cool drink of ale on a hot day; Jacques must have come back, and he would tell her off for sitting up on the settle and getting so cold, and he would lift her up in his arms and carry her upstairs to the small bed. But then Porcelaine growled again; Alie could see her standing up now, hackles high, lips pulled back from her teeth because it wasn't Jacques, that dark shape by the fire casting long shadows across the floor, it was a strange lady. She stepped forwards into the circle of lamplight, and Alie saw that she was wearing a black cloak over a ballgown made of blue silk trimmed with bronze lace, and she had shiny fair curls all piled up on her head with a tortoiseshell comb. Alie tried to swallow but her throat was dry and closed up. When the lady smiled, she was very pretty, so it must be all right. Porcelaine didn't like her very much, though: she walked towards her, stiff-legged, growling again, and the lady stopped where she stood.

She was still smiling, and for a moment all Alie could hear was a strange, panicky whining noise between her ears, because why had a smart lady in a ballgown come all the way out here to see her?

'Goodness, what a nice dog you have!' The lady's voice was kind, but everything else about her was wrong and dangerous and out of place, like a fox let loose at a duck pond, and for the first time Alie noticed what she was holding: a pasteboard box tied with ribbon.

Alie didn't know what to say; she just wanted her to go away; she was so tired and hungry and afraid, and her stomach was rumbling. She should ask where Jacques was but that would be silly, because then the lady would know she was here by herself, and she was a stranger. If the lady asked, she would say that Jacques had gone outside to the jakes and he'd be back any minute. Slowly, edging around Porcelaine – she looked a bit silly doing that – the lady walked around to the table.

'It's very late,' the lady said. She was a bit older than Alie had first realised, and some of her maquillage was caked into the fine lines around her eyes. 'You must be hungry, waiting here alone all this time. It's lucky I bought these confits, isn't it? I think you'll like them. They're so pretty, too, aren't they?' She let out a strange, brittle laugh. 'Do you know, my son would be so cross if he knew I was here. But mamas must always look after their children even if they make silly mistakes, mustn't they? Somebody should be taking care of a little girl like you, at this time of night.'

Porcelaine let out yet another low, rumbling growl, so that all the lady could do was reach out and set the pasteboard box on the table beside the empty cup. There wasn't any milk left and she really would like something to drink. Alie clutched at the blanket, pushing her fingers through the lacy knitwork. *Please go away.* She didn't like this lady and she just wanted Jacques to come. Maybe he'd gone to see Bluette after the hunt? But if he'd done that, Bluette would have called him daft. *You can't leave the little one at home all this time, she'd say.*

'Don't be shy,' the lady said. 'You can smile at me, you know. What a pretty smile I'm sure you have, too. I just came to leave these bonbons here, and no one will ever know if you eat every single one all by yourself, will they? I know it's a bit naughty, but I should think you must be very hungry by now.'

She put the box down on the table and Porcelaine didn't move, so she walked backwards to the door with her hands held out before her; Jacques would be here soon, he definitely would. Everything would be all right then.

45

Nadezhda walked into the crowded ballroom with Clemency silent and rigid at her right hand in demure printed muslin; she was already too hot in her gown of light terracotta silk and with one bandaged arm on display. Why should she hide in her bedchamber like some child banished to the nursery, whatever anyone said? It was just so horrible that no one even bothered to hide the fact they were staring. Women gazed at her over their fans and one elderly Austrian diplomat even raised a quizzing glass to his eye as she passed, as though she were some underbred young girl who had committed a faux pas at a subscription ball, so that a hot, uncomfortable flush began to spread from her face down to her décolletage. Everyone she set eyes on was a stranger except her aunt Charlotte, surrounded by a chattering crowd near the grand piano. Charlotte was dressed in an awful gown of puce satin with too many flounces at the bottom, but no one else seemed to mind that, her whole audience tittering at everything she said. Even as Nadezhda looked across at them, some of the younger women openly stared back with frank hostility so that shame roiled within her.

She was intensely aware of Kit and d'Harcourt only paces behind, too: they kept her always within sight. Turning to glance at them both; she enjoyed a moment's savage satisfaction: there may not be a friendly face in sight, and she might not know which of the hundreds of people in this ballroom wanted her dead, but at least she had her men, her guards. They were both so handsome, d'Harcourt with his curling dark hair and Kit still dishing out that disintegrating smile to all and sundry despite the fury simmering beneath his well-bred carapace of good manners.

How in the devil's name should you be safe at a fucking ball, he'd demanded in the Russian she'd taught him, long ago.

Irrelevance is fatal, she'd retorted. He ought to know that. She couldn't allow herself to become a footnote.

The crowd shifted, men clad in glittering regimentals and beautifully cut civilian jackets, women in garish gowns and feathered head-dresses like so many tropical birds, and across the ballroom Nadezhda glimpsed Tsar Alexander in conversation with the Persian emissary. For a moment their eyes met across the mirrored ballroom, but then he just looked away without so much as a flicker of concern. She was nothing more than an abandoned project, an investment he'd decided to pull out of. Accepting a steaming ether-champagne cocktail from a footman, Nadezhda turned to smile at Clemency, who was after all the only person she had left. Even so, Nadezhda could not quite rid herself of the nagging realisation that apart from the footmen who had witnessed her kiss with Kit, and who had all been heavily bribed, there was only one other person who knew about it, and that was Clemency herself.

'What a wonderful evening it's going to be,' Nadezhda said to her, fighting a stupid urge to cry. She never cried. 'Dancing is the greatest tonic, isn't it? It would have looked so suspicious if I'd remained in my chambers for the whole evening as Wellington wished.'

'I don't wish to contradict your highness,' Clemency said, 'but I can't help thinking that it was too dangerous to come here tonight, after what happened. Countess Lieven certainly thought so: she isn't even here herself.'

Rats and sinking ships, Nadezhda thought wildly. 'Nonsense. Far better to be waltzing and showing how little we care for these pathetic attempts on my life. I'm going to talk to my aunt – she seems to be quite the centre of popularity this evening.'

'Your highness,' Clemency said, in a low, even voice, 'I definitely can't explain why, but if you'll take my advice, you'll leave Fontainebleau as soon as you can, and you won't trust Princess Charlotte at all. Please listen to me.'

Nadezhda felt a little dizzy with the dry sweetness of champagne still upon her lips. 'Why on earth should I do that, when I'm pretty sure that you're the very reason everyone is gossiping and staring at me this evening, Miss Arwenack – not that I can blame you. I'll own it was poor-spirited of me to rub that kiss in your face in the way that I did. Kit Helford is in love with you, you know – it's a shame that you decided to sell him down the river along with me.'

Clemency barely flinched. Oh, she was good. She was very good.

Nadezhda sipped her champagne again, even though her head was already spinning. 'Anyway, one good turn deserves another. You should tread carefully around Valentine Boscobel, you know. His emotions where you are concerned are quite complicated and interesting, in my opinion, as Mr Blakestock and Mr Walmslow found out when they offered for you.'

Clemency shrugged, but Nadezhda had her now: finally, the mask had dropped, and one saw every last agony on her face.

'I'm sorry. I don't know what you mean, your highness. Those men are hardly familiar to me – nothing more than vague acquaintances from my very first season. I can't even remember if Mr Blakestock was a banker or in shipping.'

'Come, can you actually not have realised?' Nadezhda said, with a conspiratorial smile. 'You had two offers in your first season, Clemency. Valentine Boscobel declined both of them.'

'He was my guardian,' Clemency said smoothly. 'Well within his rights to decline offers without my knowledge, and I'm sure he had his reasons. It would hardly have been my place to question his decision, even if I'd known about the proposals.'

She spoke without a single flicker of a change in her expression, even as Nadezhda sensed Kit tense behind her and saw that Lord Lamorna was walking towards them through a parting crowd, the resemblance unmistakable as it had always been; he had become distinguished in the years since she'd last seen him, his dark hair streaked with grey, impeccably dishevelled in his civilian's evening dress. He cut an elegant and well-practised route through the throng, and Nadezhda found that although it was in her power to simply walk away, she could not.

'Lamorna, how charming to see you after so long,' she said instead; despite everything, she was unable to help enjoying the fact that now he must wait to be noticed by her: Clemency Arwenack would have to be dealt with another time. If the girl wouldn't accept an honest warning given in the spirit of fair play, then it was no fault of hers. She'd done her best; she wasn't a bad person, not really, even if she was to be persona non grata at this awful ball.

'Your highness,' Lamorna replied, with a swift, perfunctory bow over her outstretched hand which he then completely undermined by a dismissive stare. If he was discomfited by Nadezhda's own appearance at Kit's side after having exerted himself on so many different occasions to ensure that they never met, he didn't show it. He turned instead to Clemency, with a rare smile of genuine warmth.

'Your very obedient servant, Miss Arwenack. How elegant you do look.'

Clemency dropped into a curtsey with a very uncharacteristic display of confusion that Nadezhda did not ascribe to Lamorna's own rather dangerous personal charms, which were just as considerable in their own way as his young brother's. No, Lamorna had simply greeted Clemency with the easy affection of old acquaintance.

'Your highness,' Lamorna said, carelessly. 'Do forgive my

imposition, but I must borrow my brother and d'Harcourt for a while, and Miss Arwenack, too.'

'She can't be left, sir,' Kit said, roughly, even as Clemency stared straight ahead with her usual gamester's poise.

'She won't be,' Lamorna replied, with a flicker of a glance towards the tsar, whom everyone was now pretending not to watch as he approached them all across the ballroom, so that Nadezhda could not actually breathe.

Kit said something in Cornish to his brother, who replied rapidly in the same tongue, and Nadezhda found herself facing Alexander once more.

He smiled, holding out one arm. 'My dear child,' he said, without ever tripping over the lie, 'after your ordeal today I wish to assure myself of your happiness. You will come with me.'

Nadezhda could do nothing but accept the tsar's arm and walk away with him across the crowded ballroom.

The antechamber was illuminated only by candelabra and lamps that caught the elaborate gilding on white-painted panelling; the crystal chandelier had not been lit and long shadows lurched about the room; Wellington stood before the fire in his mess jacket, impatiently jabbing at the glowing embers with one of the fire irons as if he were at home in Hampshire and not holding up his end of a disintegrating peace congress.

'I don't trust the tsar,' Wellington said, turning around to face them all. 'Surely it can't be safe to leave her with him, even in a crowded ballroom? She was shot only this afternoon, for the third time: this is absurd. The silly chit shouldn't even be here, making even more of a bloody figure of herself, as if all this gossip were not enough.'

Clemency swallowed a cold rush of fear: why had Lamorna borne her along so ruthlessly into this discussion? Wildly, she noticed odd details of the room: a tapestry hanging on the wall, a pewter bowl brimming with peonies and stalks of lavender, trailing strands of ivy.

'We don't actually need to worry about Russia,' Lamorna said. 'You'll see.'

'Russia was our own false flag, sir,' Kit said. 'My brother is omnipotent, as ever.'

Lamorna smiled at him, but no one else. 'Just a poor soldier in the Corps of Guides, still,' he said, which in Clemency's opinion was a typically laconic way of calling himself a master of spies. 'I do have a suspicion about what might help us now, though.' He turned his attention to Clemency herself, all merciless acuity, so that it was impossible to breathe. 'If everyone in this room were honest about the necessary limitations on their own behaviour, I expect this would be far simpler to explain.'

'Lamorna?' Wellington said sharply, and for a moment the room spun around Clemency in a whirl of gilded panelling and polished wood before she was able to turn and walk quickly away across the gleaming parquet floor; for a long time afterwards, she couldn't forget the scent of the roses outside the window.

46

Alexander held Nadezhda's arm in a light grip; the steaming champagne and ether cocktail sent her head spinning, freezing her lips; she felt sick, even though no one dared stare now that she was arm in arm with the tsar.

'Don't stop smiling,' he said, looking straight ahead, 'it won't be long now.'

She wasn't foolish enough to question him. Instead, she just tipped the rest of the cold champagne down her throat, tendrils of pain furling about the wound in her arm; Clemency was right after all: it had been a mistake to come here tonight, exposing herself to all these impertinent staring people. She glanced up and caught the eye of a debutante in garish frilled teal satin who only a few days before had been simpering and smiling as she waited to be introduced. Now, the girl's face froze in an almost comical grimace as she turned away.

Nadezhda was cold with humiliation, wishing she could break free of the tsar's inexorable grip on her uninjured arm. She wanted to run from the room, even if that would only complete her humiliation, a final admission of the fact that she had been outmanoeuvred. What did Russia intend for her now beyond a garrotting in the forest? It wasn't like Alexander to do his own dirty work, and she could count on the fingers of one hand the number of times he had taken a personal interest in her affairs.

They left the ballroom, chandeliers and silver branches of candlelight throwing lurching shadows across the intricately carved wooden ceiling, rich red carpet and marble beneath her slippered feet. People stepped back to let them pass, and Nadezhda felt she couldn't breathe, even once they left the stifling heat of the ballroom itself. Footmen opened doors before them one after another until they came into one of the smaller state apartment. Here, the white panelled walls were bright with intricate gilding and the chairs were all upholstered in green silk, and the Prince of Hungary waited in contemplation of a globe mounted on a brass stand. He wore plain black evening dress, cut with exquisite attention to detail across the lean expanse of his shoulders, and turned to face her, offering a slight bow.

'How do I know I can trust either of you?' The words flew from Nadezhda's lips and she was immediately afraid: to speak out of turn to the tsar was to wish for death, but perhaps she did wish for that. Perhaps there was nothing else: better to get it over with.

'Have I not always had your best interests at heart?' Alexander said quietly, in Russian, his blue gaze intent upon her. 'You were such a bright and sparkling thing, so much more alive, somehow, than my own lawful daughters. Have

I not always hidden you from those who would do you harm; do you not think that either of my brothers would have hesitated to have you strangled in your sleep had they known where to find you, in all these long years? Have I not put you in a position to take a throne of your own, as befits a mind such as yours – and what a mind – when such a thing would never have been possible in Russia?'

Louis Charles waited, examining the globe as if he could neither hear nor see them both, with such perfection of tact that Nadezhda didn't know where to place her next move.

'Yes,' Nadezhda said, because all of that was true, even if it was also true that Princess Charlotte had outplayed her, and she had no clear way of knowing who had helped her aunt on the way.

'Then my best advice to you – daughter – is to listen to his grace,' Alexander said, and it took Nadezhda half a moment to absorb the fact that Alexander had addressed her now in French, admitting the truth of their relationship to Louis Charles himself. 'Go safely, my little soul.' He bowed, all sincerity, and then left them in a room together with only a single glance over his shoulder, so that all Nadezhda could do was strip off her gloves, anything to have something to do with her hands, folding the silver-pearl satin fabric into a small, tight package.

'It's all just a mess, isn't it? I suppose you want to call everything off now,' Nadezhda said, her voice ringing out far louder than she had intended.

Louis Charles looked up, the globe spinning beneath his fingertips, his hands moving with slow grace in the candlelight. 'And I suppose I ought to be chastened by just how much you don't wish to marry me.'

She swallowed, and the room was very quiet, just her and him alone; it was too warm, the air heavily scented with flowers, roses, lavender and lilies rearing in profusion from a large Sèvres vase on a marble-topped table.

'How do I know whom to trust?' Her throat felt tight, and it was hard to speak; she fought another stupid wish to cry.

'You don't,' he replied, 'but you can either stay here and watch your reputation slide down into the nearest midden and continue to dodge attempts on your life, or you can come away with me.' Turning from her, he picked up a sheaf of papers from the table, holding them out. 'These are all the documents that we need to marry in a private ceremony in Paris as soon as we may, witnessed by respected attachés from the British, Russian, French and Austrian embassies. Would you like me to throw them into the fire?'

'Why on earth would I rush my endgame in such a foolish manner?' Nadezhda responded, setting her gloves carefully down upon the mantelpiece. 'And say that I agree to your proposal – which obviously has Russian approval, at least, unless between the two of you you're planning in reality to leave me dead in a ditch – what do you propose would happen next? Are we to work on the principle that possession is nine-tenths of the law?' Reaching out, she took the papers, unable to stop her hand shaking a little; she might walk out of here with him and feel the cold steel nub of a pistol-barrel at the back of her neck.

'My dear,' Louis Charles said, 'we can be married and

in London before your ambitious aunt Charlotte and her conspiratorial friends have any idea that we've even left France.'

She could almost have laughed, swallowing a quick, hot flame of excitement. 'There's quite a fair distance between where we stand now and coronation in Westminster Abbey, your grace.'

The distance between them both had closed, though: they stood less than a handspan apart. 'At the risk of sounding like an evangelical Lutheran preacher,' Louis Charles said, looking at her, 'every journey begins with a single step.'

Clemency made her exit in stunning quiet, leaving the two footmen to close the double doors behind her and d'Harcourt to punctuate the silence with a light cough. At the window, Crow just gave a tiny shrug, his expression shielded.

Kit spoke for him. 'For God's sake, Jack,' he said.

Crow looked at him with an unfathomable expression somewhere between irritation and affection. 'Somebody had to do something.'

Wellington leaned back in his chair with weary resignation. 'Would either of you care to enlighten d'Harcourt and me, or are we just left to make educated guesses about why you've driven Miss Arwenack to enact melodramas when, frankly, we've all had enough of them today already.'

'I'm sorry, sir,' Crow said, although as Kit knew too well he was very rarely sorry for anything. 'I have the greatest dislike of melodrama myself. Am I right in thinking that Commandant d'Harcourt needs no explanation?'

'How very behindhand of me,' Wellington remarked, with dangerous restraint.

D'Harcourt shrugged, conceding. 'Well, yes. Joséphine has always liked to know where the great and the good keep their illegitimate children, your grace. When the parents are English and the child is born in France in wartime, it draws attention.'

'It does rather.' Crow's gaze flickered dispassionately over Kit from head to toe.

'Where is the child?' Kit said, only just managing to speak with an assumption of calm.

'It doesn't matter,' Wellington snapped. 'Quite obviously, the Arwenack girl must be sent home before this gets out. God only knows there must be plenty of other ambitious females at this court to replace her. What other reasonable course of action is there? The last thing we need is a lady-in-waiting hiding a skeleton like that. Dorothea deserves the whip for this. The Arwenack girl was all her idea. Dear God, as if I have time for these affairs.'

Kit watched the realisation hit Wellington with the force of a blow: Dorothea had set Clemency into position just like a gaming-piece. Crow had told him everything outside, in rapid-fire Cornish.

'It matters.' Kit turned to d'Harcourt, savouring his brother's quite evident anger; it was still just as easy to rile him with poor manners as it had ever been. 'Thomas? You know something of this?'

Of course, they weren't friends. It was only natural that d'Harcourt should have concealed what he knew.

'I'm sorry, Helford, but I'm afraid I do,' d'Harcourt said, steady and sincere. 'The child was born just outside Paris, but taken away soon after that – to Peyrehorade originally, in the south. Napoleon granted the Château d'Orde to an order of Benedictine nuns: there were twenty girls with them at one stage. Payments from the Boscobels' steward first appeared in the order's records a little less than five years ago. Miss Arwenack has been under considerable pressure for quite some time.' He paused. 'The child was christened Adeliz.'

Adeliz: did Clemency even know her name? Kit let out a quick exhalation: Crow, who had once been so inviolate, was now just as easy to hit as the next man, and by God he deserved it.

'You didn't even know exactly what she was hiding, did you?' he demanded, as if no one else was in the room. 'You just gave them all enough rope, d'Harcourt included, and you bloody well tricked Clemency into giving herself away in front of us all, and then d'Harcourt into confirming all the sordid details—' He broke off, remembering all too well the white-hot rage at being so manipulated himself during the painful years of Crow's guardianship, led inexorably into his own punishment. 'Will you ever be anything but incurably contriving and dishonest?'

'Have you finished?' Crow asked. 'His grace and d'Harcourt are wishing themselves elsewhere, so perhaps we can finish this exchange of civilities later.'

Kit ignored him. 'What's the significance of it?' he said

to d'Harcourt. 'Is there any actual purpose to hanging Miss Arwenack's reputation out to dry?'

'We've suspected for quite a long time that the Boscobels were part of a move to disrupt the treaty,' d'Harcourt said. 'Valentine Boscobel places his business interests above all else, and he's not the only one.' He gave a wry smile. 'Unfortunately, he chose also to become involved in international politics, siding with a move to place Charlotte of Württemberg on the throne instead of Nadezhda Sophia. Charlotte's still remembered in Britain with some fondness as the princess royal, by older people at least, and now that peace is declared, her husband's alliance with Napoleon was deemed more likely to have been forgiven. Clemency Arwenack was drawn in at the sidelines: you know how she has operated – gaming, manipulation, threat. I'm confident that she meant to compromise the princess, but without fully understanding the Boscobels' rationale.' He shrugged. 'She's a charming girl, but even so. It's an irony, no? French, British, Austrian – all nationalities united in a desire for profit, even if not for peace.'

'The move to replace Nadezhda with Charlotte began in a certain faction at Whitehall,' Crow said, addressing Wellington. 'You'll know the one I mean, sir. It's not a Whiggish plot, but the Ultras.' He turned to the room. 'Highly conservative, if you don't know of them. The Ultras are more opposed to reform even than his grace's own party. You'll notice Dorothea has absented herself. She considers herself loyal to Russia, I believe, but not always to Alexander, when she feels that he is making a mistake. There are unofficial factions in both Petersburg and London who would have preferred this alliance had been scotched years ago – even if we only have intellegence, but no proof.'

'The whole affair bitched from the outset, then,' Kit said, even as Wellington walked away and stood for a moment by the fire in silent contemplation. 'And I take it you all realise the reason why Clemency has never confessed to this particular indiscretion? Why she allowed herself to be manipulated by the Boscobels for so long?'

Wellington turned and gave a thin smile. 'I'm surprised you of all people could be naive about this sort of thing, Helford. What girl would want something like this to get out? A child out of wedlock? She's ruined.'

'As if she cares for that,' Kit said. 'The Boscobels know where the child is, but Clemency doesn't, I'm sure of it.'

D'Harcourt shook his head. 'It was a cruelty. Perhaps they meant it in kindness. Sometimes such things are done.'

'They held it over her to ensure she did as they wanted,' Kit said. 'I'm going to Peyrehorade.'

Crow turned to him, his gaze flat, addressing him in Cornish. 'Take that line and you do realise that everyone will say the bastard is yours?'

'One to match the family collection, sir?' Kit replied in French, with savage courtesy.

'Either way, you didn't listen,' Crow said, expressionless. 'Commandant d'Harcourt used the past tense.'

'That's the difficulty, yes,' d'Harcourt said, swiftly. 'All payments sent to the abbess at the Château d'Orde stopped two and a half years ago.'

'Well, there you go,' Wellington said. 'Distasteful though it may be, the child is dead. The Arwenack girl must be told,

I suppose, for the sake of good order, but these things happen. Like or not, it was for the best.'

'I doubt Miss Arwenack would agree,' Kit snapped.

D'Harcourt shrugged, speaking into another silence. 'With respect, your grace, the situation is more complicated. Joséphine's interest was piqued when Miss Arwenack was given a court position: Joséphine lived in London herself, as you know, in the Occupation. She knows of all the usual families who might be expected to provide a daughter for such an honour. Miss Arwenack is not of such a house, and so Joséphine requested me to make enquiries, to understand why she was appointed. It was Countess Lieven's idea, which did create further interest. In fact, Adeliz Fideau was still alive when she left the nuns. She was moved to the care of a respectable widow in Paris, a Madame d'Arblay, but when Aurélie d'Arblay died two years ago, no one could discover what had happened to the little girl.' D'Harcourt paused, looking almost apologetic. 'If the child is still alive now, I'm afraid only the Boscobels know where she is.'

47

The pressure of Valentine's touch at Clemency's elbow was unexceptionable, light and warm, but still a firm reminder that he was in control: *they knew*. They all knew what she had done, what she was, a fallen woman, a mother with no child: Kit, Lamorna, d'Harcourt, even the Duke of Wellington, all of them understood her shame. It was bad luck she'd run into Valentine just moments after her headlong arrival back into the ballroom; she was going at this like a bull at a gate, letting the fear control her instead of controlling it.

She couldn't tell them all about Princess Charlotte, or Valentine, until she knew where her daughter was. She'd warned Nadezhda but that was as far as she dared go. They'd understand that, surely? And what could Valentine do to her, after all, at a ball, especially one so crowded as this? He was flushed, his handsome face glowing.

Walk with me, Button, he'd said, as if she had any choice. The ornately carved ceilings were high and vaulted, but still the heat was overpowering, so that it was hard to think straight. The corridor heaved with courtiers and she couldn't shake an uneasy certainty that there were too many people in the building. She felt like a marionette on strings, nodding and smiling as they stopped to speak to Valentine's acquaintances, strange and familiar faces blurring before her eyes. Relentless, he steered Clemency away, turning to her as they neared the Madame de Maintenon chambers, which the empress had ordered to be opened and used for card games. The orchestra was tuning up in the ballroom they'd left behind and discordant clamour rose up in a bubble of sound.

'Oh look, this is lucky. A few moments of privacy after all,' Valentine said; by now they'd reached a door manned by a pair of wooden-faced footmen in gold and white livery; she didn't miss the sneering look that passed between them. Her head spun as the doors were closed behind them with a quiet click. The antechamber wasn't that small, and they weren't alone, either – a set of chaises upholstered in green velvet was gathered around a fire at the far end of the panelled room, all occupied by turbaned dowagers and chaperones taking a break from the heat and crowd now that their charges had walked out for the first dance; Clemency was conscious of a waltz starting up in the ballroom.

'I don't know about you, but I find all that heat and the atmosphere a bit oppressive,' Valentine said, turning to her with his usual easy charm. He was so perfect, with his hair swept back à la Brutus, and his good looks, knowing only too well that those women gathered by the fire were surreptitiously watching him. 'Let's go over to the window; I've a fancy to breathe a little fresh air.' He smiled again as he spoke, but there was something relentless about it that made her want to tear her arm from his grip, even if everyone did stare. A woman gowned in ruby silk on the chaise nearest the fire turned with a sharp glance in Clemency's direction, looking past Valentine and directly at her.

'Some of these old tabby cats have a real sixth sense for impropriety, don't they?' Valentine's tone was conspiratorially low and cosy, but his breath stank of champagne. 'Sniffing out scandal at every given opportunity.'

'You promised, Val,' Clemency said. 'You said you'd tell me where she is.'

He looked wounded. 'All in good time.'

They were near one of the tall windows now, heavy curtains of silk embroidered in an elegant Mughal-style pattern of tumbling flowers and vegetation. She breathed in the green, watery scent of the enormous carp pool below and the gardens beyond: scythed grass in the dark, and the queer, metallic scent one often caught a hint of before a thunderstorm and the coming of rain – and was that also smoke? Tendrils of smoke, weaving up through the darkness outside?

Valentine smiled again. 'Shall we?' Pushing aside the curtains with one well-shaped hand, he stepped beside the window, taking Clemency with him. Even smoke-laced, the fresh air was a tonic, away from the oppressive heat. 'I'm sure you've been avoiding me, Button.'

'No,' she said. 'You told me I could see her. The princess is on her way to being ruined, and I've delivered your scandal. What more do you want? Where's my daughter? Our daughter?'

Releasing Clemency's arm, Valentine turned to face her, standing so close it was as if they were still lovers; she sensed the imprint of his touch on her bare arm, able to feel the heat of it.

'I just don't think we're ready for that,' he said, smiling, which meant he still had use for her.

She fought to compose herself; at the end of the day he was just a mark like any other.

'I've done what you asked, and in any case I'll be no use at court now, will I? Not if Charlotte replaces Nadezhda, which looks pretty likely from where we're all standing this evening. Look, you've gone too far now with all this, Val – why don't you just walk away before it's too late?' She glanced out of the window at the water glittering far below: they were directly above the carp pool and the muddy green stink of it rose up, unavoidable.

Valentine's eyes widened with hurt – he really believed she'd wronged him. 'I suppose I shouldn't be surprised that you've chosen to turn on the people who took you in.'

'When all is said and done, you still have Boscobel Castle, and a reputation.' She broke off, remembering how she'd walked into the great library at the castle on his arm, staring up at the array of gilded spines. *All of this can be yours*; that's what he'd told her, but in the end all he'd given her was the sharpest loss, simply because his mother thought he ought to aim higher when he chose to marry. 'Listen, this has gone far enough. Val, you weren't careful enough. I've proof that you've been acting on Charlotte's behalf to discredit Nadezhda, using me to do it. That's not going to look good, with all these investigations into the attacks.' She stared at him. 'Who knows, some people might even think that Charlotte only wanted Nadezhda ruined socially so that no one would miss her if she died. Take me to the child, or you'll lose everything.'

'Oh, Button, did I teach you too well?' Valentine reached out then, so gently, to touch her face; it was, she thought, the only honest thing he'd ever said to her. 'I'm sorry.' With a tightening of his grip on her wrist, Valentine pushed her, and Clemency fell into the darkness, her cry of shock lost to the night as she plummeted, silk and muslin skirts ballooning around her as she hurtled towards the embrace of the dark water. In the passages and gilded chambers beneath the ballroom, smoke billowed. The court began to run and scream.

48

The fire spread, hungry flames consuming ancient curtains, hangings and tapestries and dry wood panelling rich with oil paint; smoke bloomed into the crowded ballroom even as women tripped over their dresses, stumbling and running in clocked silk stockings and satin dancing slippers. Kit slipped into his battlefield self, issuing orders that were obeyed without question, working seamlessly alongside Crow and d'Harcourt to clear the ballroom until the vast room was empty of stragglers and tongues of flame began to lick along the ornately carved ceiling; he was distantly aware of d'Harcourt yelling at him, his face blackened with soot, even as smoke billowed, so that all three were coughing, their eyes streaming.

'She's gone: her highness is gone. Our duty's done. *Come on.*'

'I don't give a damn about Nadezhda.' Kit coughed, his lungs burning.

D'Harcourt swore, hacking into his elbow, sweat pouring

down his face, leaving pale runnels in the blackened patches of soot, and Kit felt a strong, familiar grip at his elbow.

'Don't be a damned idiot; she could easily have been missed outside.' Crow looked at him then with a flare of unfamiliar emotion in his eyes: unless he were looking at his wife or daughter, they were usually such a cold and austere grey.

'Go,' Kit said. 'Go and take Thérèse home. Morwenna will be afraid: she must be able to see the flames from her room. I'm not leaving here without Clemency.'

'Helford, what are you playing at?' D'Harcourt looked from one to the other, turning to Crow. 'Can't you stop him – look, we all need to get out of here. *Now.*'

'I've never been remotely able to stop him doing anything. Bloody fool,' Crow said and turned to Kit, even as the smoke billowed black behind him like a spill of ink in water; he spoke then in Cornish, with a faint smile. 'Get on with it, then.'

Kit smiled back through the smoke and went on without them both, pausing only to watch them run for the stairs; the only place they hadn't searched together was the Madame de Maintenon chambers. Half blinded by smoke, Kit ran alone up the corridor; it was dark, and he could hardly see, and all he could hear was the roar of the flames and the distant music of shattering glass as window frames buckled.

'Clemmie!' he yelled, but all he could hear now was the splintering of falling timbers and roof joists in the room below; if the joists went, he wouldn't have long before the floor caved in. '*Clemency!*' It was hard to breathe, but that didn't matter; if Hester had her boy it would make no difference to anyone if he didn't come out of here, and this was how he deserved to die, anyway: fire-setter, criminal. The heat was blistering, sucking the breath from his lungs, and looking over his shoulder he saw that the ballroom itself was consumed, orange tongues licking the bare stone walls and floor of the corridor leading to the Maintenon apartments, flame seeking fuel. His eyes streamed; he could barely breathe or see, but that was a human voice or he was out of his wits. Hauling his cravat up over his mouth and nose, Kit spun around and saw a huddled shape against the far wall. He ran, lungs burning, to find Valentine Boscobel crouching on the floor, overcome by the smoke.

Ow flog vian, Clemency called out as she slept. *My little child.*

'Where is she?' Kit swallowed a surge of hatred, shaking him. It would be so easy to punish the bastard for all that he had done, to leave him here to burn. 'Where is Clemency – I know she was with you. Where did she go?'

Boscobel could barely speak, his eyes streaming with tears as he choked out the words, his lips cracked with the heat. 'Outside.'

'Christ. Come on—' Kit broke off as a crash echoed from the ballroom, hauling the man to his feet: not even a cur like him deserved to die here, not like this. 'That's the roof. *Come on.* Cover your mouth and nose, that's it.' Slinging Valentine's arm over his shoulder, Kit surged back towards the stage, helping him along; she was outside, she was alive, and that was all that mattered, even if he never made it himself, and even as the smoke filled his lungs, and blackened his vision so that he could no longer see, and perhaps in the end this really was all he deserved.

Bluette sat alone on her narrow bed with Mademoiselle's little leather book clutched in her hands, listening to distant screaming and the roar of the flames. She rocked backwards and forwards and tears streamed down her face, but there was no point in saving herself. Long fingers of smoke probed beneath the door, and Jacques was dead, mixed up in stinking court business, and she was so angry with him for letting them do it, for not even asking to be helped, like a typical fool of a man. And now she was unmarried, with his child in his belly, and she would never see him again. The fire was growing; it had started below the ballroom, they all said, but it would soon spread to the state apartments and the servants' quarters here; they'd tried to get her to run with them, that young pair of footmen stationed at the door in her highness's chamber, but what they didn't know was that it was better she didn't escape.

She'd known there was something amiss, known that she ought to have questioned Jacques last night, but he'd ever been a stubborn man, and doubtless didn't want to burden her or some other such nonsense. They said the princess had fired the killing shot herself. Better that than the scaffold, but at least if they'd guillotined him, someone might have taken pity and let them wed from a cell. And so now she was sitting here, and the little girl must surely be in the forest alone, and if Bluette were a better person, less of a coward, she'd go to the child now and find some other way of ending her life when Alie was safe, but somehow it was impossible to get up from her bed, she couldn't make herself move. Bluette looked down at the leather book, her fingers white as she gripped it.

She'd promised, and Miss Arwenack had sworn to help her about the baby, even if Bluette didn't see how that was possible now.

Promise me you'll give this book to Lieutenant Colonel Helford. No matter what happens to me.

Bluette couldn't move. Without Jacques, there was no point to anything.

Clemency fell to her death. The night rushed past so fast and so hard that she couldn't breathe; the skirts of her ballgown ballooned in wild disarray and she plummeted, aware only of moonlight flashing on the water, the reek of smoke, and a pattern of branches against the night sky; there was the evening star, Venus, a bright point of light that she'd never see again. She struck the water like a cannonball, an explosion of agonised pain that blasted through her like sudden heat, and then she was underwater, out of her element, silk petticoats and fine muslin skirts ballooning up past her face in a confusion of slowly flailing limbs and a stream of silvery bubbles. *Still breathing.*

Clemency felt weed-slippery stone beneath one silk-slippered, sodden foot, and, acting on instinct alone, pushed upwards with all the strength she had, buoyed by an air-filled expanse of petticoat and the generous skirts of her gown. *Swim.*

She swam; long ago, Kit at her side, they'd dived beneath the waves at Marazion, she just a little too far out of her depth, swimming hard towards him in her pantaloons, her oldest gown, and an ash-smeared petticoat. Clemency swam hard now, too, the muscles in her arms protesting at the unfamiliar exercise and the shock of the cold water, green weeds tangling at her shod feet; one of the silk slippers slipped away, still tied at the ankle. With shattering clarity, she remembered bending down to knot the green ribbon earlier that evening. *No air.*

Perhaps it didn't matter after all, and she should just allow all this roaring water, bubbled silk and tangling weed to fade away into darkness. *So tired.*

Clemency rushed towards the moonlit surface of the water, unstoppable. She broke through from a watery underworld into cold night air, drawing in huge, desperate, life-giving mouthfuls.

She wasn't far from the marble-edged bank of the vast ornamental carp lake that spread out before the palace; weeds tangled around her feet, plastered her ankles, but with every last shred of strength Clemency struck out for the bank, reached it, and heaved herself up over the edge, the wet silk and muslin that had likely saved her life now dragging her backwards into the water.

Glancing over her shoulder at the bulk of the palace, Clemency saw first-floor windows lit up like a vision of hell, billowing smoke and streamers of bright orange flame; muffled screams tore at the night sky. There would be panic on the floor above, too; one of the second-floor windows which before had been lit up brilliantly for the night of the ball was now in darkness. She sat on the bank, putting back on her wet dancing slipper; it was hard to tie the ribbons with numb fingers that wouldn't stop shaking. Getting to her feet, she hauled herself up on to the raked gravel path, running hard and fast around to the front of the palace, where a panicking, weeping, coughing surge of humanity clad in evening dress spewed from every door and even from the ground-floor windows, women trailing long flounced skirts and bedraggled head-dresses.

Soaked to her skin and tripping on sodden skirts, Clemency pushed through the crowd, snatching at the arm of a dishevelled gentleman in a puce waistcoat with Prussian orders pinned to his breast, who turned to her with an expression of fatherly concern.

'Move along, mademoiselle. There's no place for a young lady alone in such a crush as all this.'

'Oh, never mind that!' Clemency said, breathless. 'Have you seen the English princess and her guard?'

'The tall one ran back inside to look for her lady-in-waiting, they say.' The Prussian gentleman shook his head. 'A brave young man, to be sure, but his friends will be sorry for it.'

Clemency stumbled on her gown as she stepped backwards, staring up at the flames now bursting from the ballroom wing of the palace. '*Kit Helford!*' she shouted.

She fought her way through the crowd until a palace

footman and an Ottoman courtier finally held her back, and all she could do was call his name into the night, knowing that she could never tell him how sorry she was.

49

Clemency watched the fire until the ballroom roof collapsed and sheets of flame poured out of the windows, and then, when a groan went up from those still bearing witness, knowing there would be no more survivors, she turned and walked away through the imperial gardens, stumbling past groups of shocked and frightened revellers until she sat by herself in the temple of Venus where Kit had cut her with all that lordly disdain, long ago it seemed now. She stared at the night sky between lichen-stained marble pillars, skeins of cloud stained orange by the flames. When it was light she might begin to hope for a place on the early morning *diligence* to Paris; the antiquated coach would leave Fontainebleau from the plaza, overloaded with passengers, baggage and corded packages strapped to the roof.

No, she wouldn't be on the coach. Five years ago, Valentine had taken her hands in the bedchamber at Boscobel Castle; she remembered such odd details: the gold tassels that tied back those heavy brocade curtains, and the blowsy pink roses on the silk wall-hangings that she hadn't been able to stop herself touching when Georgie's maid first showed her up to the room, for how could all this be hers?

She'd been naked, Valentine fully clothed.

God, he said. *I just love looking at you. Turn around.*

Obedient, she turned a pirouette before him; he was so handsome, and so kind, and he'd promised they'd be married.

I wish you could see yourself, he went on. *My own little country nymph. Such innocent perfection.* And he bent down to kiss her, which was always so exciting. He broke off then, though, and laughed.

What's so funny? she asked. *Come on, you can't tease me like this.*

Oh, nothing. Valentine kissed her back. *Just the old lady downstairs – she might meddle in my life all she chooses, but she doesn't know what's going on right in front of her own face, does she? Silly bitch.*

That was when she'd felt the first real sense of unease – weren't they to be married, after all? But he spoke about his own mama with such contempt that Clemency was shocked.

Right in front of her own face. Silly bitch.

Her baby was here somewhere, hidden in plain sight.

She heard footfalls outside, someone approaching; she froze where she sat, mouthing a silent and almost formless prayer.

Please.

Kit knew she came out here. It would just as likely to

be some drunken young diplomat's attaché from the ball, though. Glancing around in the darkness, Clemency knew she was trapped. She opened her mouth and tried to speak, but her throat froze even as the outline of a man gathered form and substance in the darkness at the entrance to the temple, backlit by the moon.

'*Button*,' he said.

Hours later, dawn light filled the plaza as ash drifted and flew in eddies like a fall of snow; men and women still in their formal ball-gear staggered arm in arm across the cobbles and Kit passed them all with only a dreamlike impression of soot-blackened faces and women with dishevelled hair, tangled ringlets and blackened feathers, diamonds catching the early morning light against sweaty, filthy skin. Thérèse's ancient major-domo opened the door and grasped Kit's hands as though he were his own child returned from the war. Clemency was gone. He'd found no trace of her; it was as if she had never set foot at Fontainebleau, and so Kit barely heard the old man's voice, relinquishing his grip as soon as he could do so without causing offence.

He ran up the stairs; his chest ached like the very devil, and he stopped halfway up to cough into his elbow, breathing in the scent of laundry soap and scorched linen. Thérèse's drawing-room was open as usual, but everyone in it was still clad in ruined ballgowns, dress uniform and evening-wear, Thérèse herself magnificent in maroon silk and an ugly set of Saint-Maure diamonds; d'Harcourt, Joséphine, Wellington and Crow were all present, along with various attachés and aides-de-camp; the only person not a picture of destroyed finery was Morwenna, who sat beside her father on the settle in a nightgown of broderie anglaise. She ran to Kit now in the wave of silence he had brought in with him, clinging to his legs. The quiet stretched on until Crow broke it, in his own inexorable fashion.

'Young idiot,' he said calmly. 'Someone get him a drink. Morwenna, sit. You won't be able to go around like a hoyden in Paris, you know. I don't know what your aunt has been teaching you.'

'You're quite cold-hearted, Lamorna, as well as a hypocrite,' Thérèse said, and Kit submitted to her embrace, breathing in her scent of orange-flower perfume and singed feathers, even as he gently prised Morwenna's fingers from his thigh. Crow rose from the chaise with all of his usual languor, sending Morwenna back to it with a single look; he came to stand with Kit by the window, waiting for him to speak.

'I couldn't find Clemency anywhere,' Kit said, in Cornish. 'I got Boscobel out, and he said she was outside. So why would she disappear from the face of the earth? I searched every inch of the palace gardens. Why isn't she here, Jack?'

'It's chaotic. You might have missed her.' Crow glanced across the room at their aunt, who was in serious conversation with Wellington, Joséphine and d'Harcourt. 'I'm taking Morwenna and Thérèse to Paris; the Duke wants attachés and Thérèse's social clout to lend some credence to Nadezhda's wedding. They'll be married out of the embassy before the end of the week unless someone cuts her throat first, but I don't fancy the chances of whoever might be foolish enough to try it. Either way, you've done your part.'

Kit stared out of the window at the cobbled plaza; the ash was still falling and he remembered Clemency at Nansmornow in the snow, long ago: *Dance with you? I suppose you think you're doing me a favour.*

Crow carried on talking, inexorable. 'Needless to say, your duty to Nadezhda is discharged; she's gone with her Habsburg and there's nothing more you need to do. You could come with us to Paris, d'Harcourt too. I'm sure she'd love the scandal of having you at her wedding, and it's bound to overshadow any remaining gossip about the Marquis of Dereham; he's alive, not that you've even asked about him once.'

'She never even knew the child's name,' Kit said, light-headed. 'What did you say her name was, Thomas, Clemency's child?' He turned away from Crow, who knew him too well for this to be borne: the truth was out now, anyway, so there was no point in pretending it wasn't.

D'Harcourt frowned, looking down at his own clasped hands. 'Adeliz.' He pointedly didn't look at Joséphine. 'To be honest,' d'Harcourt went on, with bald anger. 'I felt that Miss Arwenack should have been told where her daughter was long ago. It would have been a kindness.'

Joséphine glanced up from her conference with Wellington and frowned.

'Oh, Thomas,' Kit said, dimly aware of Morwenna running across the Turkey rug in her nightgown, with her bare feet; she was now tugging at her father's sleeve in a way that he could have advised was likely to end to her detriment. 'I think you've just talked yourself out of a comfortable position at court.'

D'Harcourt shrugged. 'I'm pretty sure that her highness and her prince have already manoeuvred us both out of that. I didn't like it much, anyway.'

'I suppose you'll return to your regiment,' Kit said.

'I suppose I will,' d'Harcourt said. 'And I suppose you'll continue to find yourself at the epicentre wherever there's a mess.'

Kit returned that with a sarcastic bow, and then Crow was at his elbow with a glass of cognac. 'Drink that,' he said, continuing in Cornish. 'Do you realise the one thing everyone at this damnable court has been gossiping about, apart from you and Nadezhda?'

'Yes,' Kit said, and he thought of those spreading flames in the cellar at Carlton House, long ago, and the dark shape of the noose, and the surging crowd all shouting at him to run. He'd ran, and yet all these years later found himself in the same place.

'Come with me to Paris,' Crow said. 'Out of sight, out of mind. Don't let the gossip gather any more strength or force, for God's sake.' He glanced over his shoulder at Thérèse and Morwenna. 'I'm getting them out of here this morning: the aftermath of all this is going to be horrific. Come to Paris. I've a caravel in Calais. Come home.'

'I can't,' Kit said, shrugging.

'*Papa!*' Morwenna's voice rang out in the sudden silence, and Crow replied to her with a few quiet, well-chosen words in Cornish that sent a violent flush spreading across her cheeks, so that she fled from the room in confusion, and

Kit left Thérèse and Crow to another sparring match and followed his niece out of the room. He found her alone in the corridor outside, her shoulders heaving; he knelt down before her: she had her mother's dark eyes and long lashes, but also her inimitable frank gaze.

'Papa is so cross with me, and I really don't like it.'

'Don't be upset, maid. It's been the very devil of a morning, you know. Your papa hasn't even been to sleep; you know how that makes us all ride rusty.'

'He wanted to know if you were alive so he didn't go to bed. I was only trying to say,' she said, flushed with mortification and a rare flash of defiance, 'I was only trying to tell you, and now Papa is angry with me.'

Kit held out his hands to her, but instead of embracing him she grasped his finger, looking up at him with a stern expression, her fair curls in disarray. 'My friend is called Adeliz,' she said. 'My friend from the stables. Well, she's called Alie, but that's her big name. And if you want to find her, then I know where she lives. But you'll have to listen.'

Kit got to his feet once more, noticing odd details: the liver and white spaniel in the portrait of his mother as a girl, a crack in the blue and white Delft vase on the window-ledge, a patch of frayed knotting at the edge of the carpet. 'I'll always listen to you, maid,' he said. 'Where is she?'

Leaving the Hôtel de Montausier without a word to anyone except his niece, Kit ran without stopping to the stables; elbowing his way through the chaos and delivering a stream of orders, he led out his own mare and mounted her bareback with only a bridle. Trotting through the gardens past the espaliered trees in a snowfall of tumbling white ash, he spurred the mare to a gallop the moment they reached the forest. Moving with her as one, he jumped over every moss-draped outcrop of rock and every fallen tree, just aware of the freshening air the further they got from the environs of the still-burning palace. Branches flashed past and in the slanting morning light he saw dappled roe deer standing silent and still; leaning over the mare's neck he spurred her on, and they went on like this for over an hour, the hair torn back from his face beneath the tangle of branches and fresh green beech leaves, and the hot blue sky.

The long tables were still laid out before the huntsman's cottage, but only the palest fingernail of smoke clung to the chimney, as if the hearth within was still banked down for the night. In all the chaos of the shooting, no one had come back to clear the platters, and all the sugared confections and baked meats of the curée were still laid out on gilded china; dismounting, he walked away, knowing the mare would wait for him come what may. All was quiet, eerily so: had the huntsman no family at all? Kit remembered him at the meet, a big, dark-haired man, the sort who exuded quiet competence, and yet Kit had seen too many of his men shot and blown to pieces to really believe that anyone was invincible. Doubtless Jacques Pelletier had seemed so to the child, though: *she's lived with him for a long time,* Morwenna had said. It was a good thing Nadezhda had killed him, a good thing it was already over, and there would be no imprisonment or scaffold, better perhaps too that the child wasn't able to say goodbye.

And yet no sound at all came from the cottage, no early morning grate-rattling or stacking of wood. Kit felt the web of acute awareness spread through him just as it had done since he was a partisan soldier.

He glanced down at the table; black flies clustered on a dish of honeyed cream left uneaten, hovering too around a joint of roasted beef studded with coloured jellies. A dish of jugged hare had been upturned on the table by some scavenging creature, leaving a trail of thick dark brown sauce on the white linen, now congealed.

Quickly, quietly, knowing that this was something he had better get over with, Kit walked to the cottage and pushed open the front door, ancient wood warm beneath his fingertips. Inside, he found just a single room: fireplace, wooden settle, patchwork coverlet abandoned on the floor, rough-hewn staircase off to one side leading up to a loft and a bed under the eaves. There was a table, too – a white pasteboard box lying open, sugar-dusted white confits scattered on the tabletop and on the floor.

Kit listened to his own spurs clink as he crossed the flagstones and picked up the blue satin ribbon, letting it hang from his fingers as his gaze travelled across the rag rug to the dead rat beneath the table. There was no one else here. No one alive, anyway. This instinct of his had never yet been wrong, but even so, he climbed the stairs and found a bed jammed up against a small window under the eaves: whoever had slept here had enjoyed lying beneath the covers and looking out at the rising moon. The coverlet was smooth and flat; the bed hadn't been slept in, not last night. Kit crouched and swept back a rough and ready curtain fashioned from a patched woman's gown, finding another bed: a child's sleeping place, really: no more than a pallet with a neatly smoothed coverlet. No one had slept here, either.

Running now, Kit took the stairs and went to the fire, but there was no reassuring sign of life here, no lamp still guttering. Swift-footed, wanting to get it over with, he went outside; the mare waited for him in the unending quiet, and all he could hear was flies hovering over the spoiled food. His horse had cooled enough to drink now, and he led her to the trough, one step at a time, managing the essentials. It was only when she bent her head to drink that he caught sight of a pale flash at the corner of his eye, and another frozen shiver of awareness slid through him. Turning fully, he saw them both lying in a patch of long grass just outside the back of the cottage, not far from a wooden outhouse painted in peeling whitewash: a child lying curled up among the couch grass and dandelions, a pale hound at her side. The child was absolutely still: stepping closer, he caught a glimpse of cheap cotton voile patterned with red cherries. The dog moved, though. In one fluid movement the creature woke and faced him with a snarl: a fine white hunting hound, a true porcelain lymer, collared with wide tooled leather.

Kit dropped to his knees, holding out one hand, speaking to her in soft Cornish, telling her that she had no need to be afraid, nothing to guard, not any longer. *I'm sorry, ow whegoll.* She came to him quite docile then: he'd always had this way with creatures – horses and dogs, it was all the same. Nudging his hand with her black nose, she whined, and he stepped closer, kneeling down at the child's side; God, her thin arm, the spray of instantly recognisable freckles across her cheekbone. Clemency's child, unquestionably.

50

Clemency awoke to a rocking motion in sweltering heat, the truth settling upon her before she was really aware of her surroundings. Kit was dead. He'd died in that fire, and for her own sake, when she had started the rumour that would have finished him before the first waltz had even been danced at that ball, to judge by the way everyone stared at Nadezhda.

Opening her eyes, she glimpsed a heavy drab blanket and a fur laid across her, and carriage curtains of faded watered crimson silk. The covers all slid from her lap as she sat up and she came face to face with Valentine. He held on to the leather strap, just watching her. He'd pushed her, let her fall. Clemency groped through a jumble of confused memories: the stink of smoke, a black sky stained orange, bubbles spewing from her mouth underwater; Valentine stepping towards her in the temple of Venus so that there was no escape from him. She longer cared what he might do to her, because there was only one person worth salvation now.

A mother's love is such a powerful thing, Georgie had said, *and so I'm afraid you simply can't marry Val, but don't worry in the slightest. Everything will be taken care of, darling.*

Valentine smiled at her. 'I'm sorry,' he said. 'You think I haven't been fair, don't you, but really I couldn't let you burn, sweet; how could I let you burn when I knew you could swim?'

He'd known about the fire before it had spread. She nodded: for now at least, he had to believe that she was too afraid to speak.

He reached out, letting one hand rest upon her knee so that her belly roiled in disgust. 'You've been really quite silly, Clemency, but you always come to bridle for me, don't you? We've been given a second chance. I should never have let that interfering bitch dictate things. This is our chance to be together. I always thought that if I couldn't have you, then no one else would, either. Kit Helford doesn't deserve you. He has no need for trade, to strive as hard as I must do. The Lamornas have always had everything handed to them on a silver platter. And yet he's nothing but a rebel and an arsonist who deserves to be punished. He should have hanged that day in London, don't you see? He ought to be eight years in a criminal's grave. Instead, he's considered a hero.'

Clemency knew then that Valentine wasn't just afraid of running away alone: Nadezhda's words rolled around in her mind like pebbles in a bowl.

You should tread carefully around Valentine Boscobel, you know. His emotions where you are concerned are quite complicated and interesting, in my opinion.

All this time she'd been afraid that the court would stumble on the truth about her child: a hound set to the wrong course all this time.

Valentine smiled. 'You're mine, Button. You've always been mine.'

She shut her eyes, trying not to shake, doing her best to remember those long-gone suitors: Mr Walmslow's damp hands as he led her down a polonaise at a late-season ball in London; the company so thin by then, carriages rolling away from select addresses in Mayfair every day, bound for country retreats. Perhaps. Had Walmslow thought she'd be desperate by the end of her first season, that she'd be grateful to accept any offer at all? He hadn't banked on Valentine.

She'd never know the shape of her child's face, the colour of her hair, or feel the warmth of her hand. If they ever met, the little girl would be afraid, confused; after all, she wasn't yet five years old. There would be no long-lost daughter falling into her arms: in any case, she'd be nothing but a stranger to a terrified child. Even if this was the last and only act of protection Clemency ever offered, Valentine Boscobel would never, ever reach their daughter.

Kit crouched down at the child's side: she lay silent and still on a bed of dead leaves, the resemblance so immediately obvious that it took his breath away, right down to the coppery strands in her plain brown hair. As he watched, the child's breath disturbed a frond of overhanging bracken, a vivid green tendril shifting against black leaf mould, so that he offered up an incongruous soldier's prayer: *Lord, I know what I must do this day. If I forget you, do not forget me.* She was alive. Unlike the rat in the cottage, she hadn't tasted those confits, dusted with white sugar, given to her in a pasteboard box tied with blue ribbon. Letting out one long, shuddering breath, Kit laid one hand upon her bare arm; she was so cold.

'It's time to wake up.' Kit heard himself speak as if he were listening to someone else, staring down at her in disbelief as she looked up at him with those wide, familiar eyes.

Clemency sat alone in the best bedchamber at the Chat Gris, facing the mirror as a maid combed out her hair. The room was crowded with knick-knacks: china shepherdesses on the mantelpiece, horse brasses on the ceiling beams. Floral glazed calico adorned the windows and the four-poster bed, and Clemency knew the door was locked.

'There, mademoiselle.' The maid smirked as she slid a final hairpin into Clemency's coiffure. 'A little respectable now, I think.'

She replied with a frozen stare that sent the maidservant out of the room: the girl would just have to console herself with the fact that she could dine out on this afternoon's gossip-fodder for the rest of her life. Valentine had no finesse at all, and it was obvious that the Chat Gris' experienced proprietor had immediately concluded he was hosting a rich gentleman and his trollop. She was sure they'd be turned away, until the moment Valentine smilingly produced a roll of banknotes. Still sitting before the mirror, Clemency put her hands up to her face and drew in a long, shuddering breath. Smoothing out the skirts of the fresh cambric gown, she ignored a memory of Valentine directing his groom to hand over a packed valise to the maid with a knowingly intimate glance at Clemency: how long had he been planning this? Her gaze travelled to the gable-end window, too small to climb out of. There was a scratch at the door, and another maidservant and a superannuated footman in tired livery came in bearing covered trays, which they set out on the round table at the foot of the bed. The maidservant dropped into a curtsey and fled.

Clemency got to her feet, holding on to the back of the chair, even as the footman stared straight ahead, maintaining professional servants' ignorance. 'I'm here against my will,' she said, swallowing a rising wave of humiliation. 'Please, I'd like to leave. Can you help me?'

The footman just looked her up and down as though she were a flyblown joint of meat on a market-stall and took his place by the table, waiting in silence, implacable. And then, even as she resolved to just walk out of the door and to run as fast and as hard as she could, in any direction possible, the pitted brass doorknob turned.

Alie had never ridden fast on a big horse like this before; the foreign seigneur held her tight about her waist as she sat in the saddle before him; they went at a proper gallop, the forest flashing past as Porcelaine ran alongside them, long and elegant she was, bounding over stands of bracken and past lichen-covered rocks. It was funny because the seigneur's face was dirty and smutted but his clothes were so glittering and magnificent, all golden and scarlet, and she'd wanted to reach out and touch the row of shining medals across his breast.

It's all right, he'd said, lifting her into the saddle as though she were lighter than goosedown. *I won't let you go.*

She wasn't meant to go off with strangers but if he was Morwenna's kinsman then it must be all right, although she didn't know why someone so high up and important was bothering with her, and Porcelaine was with them anyway, running alongside his horse.

I'd wager neither hell nor high water would stop you, my girl, he'd said, scratching her behind one ear. If he was a bad man, Porcelaine would have barked and growled and bitten him, and she hadn't: she'd licked his hand.

You stay away from that sort of people, Jacques always said, but he wasn't coming back anyway. *I'm sorry, child,* he'd said, leaving for the hunt, kneeling before her, and Alie felt cold inside: if she had a mother and father of her own this wouldn't be happening and she would be safe, even if Jacques was never coming back. She shouldn't have put on the new dress, really, the pattern of red cherries was all grimy around the hem. Would Bluette be cross when she found out about that, even though there wasn't going to be a marriage any more? But Bluette was gone, too, as if she'd been spirited away by the fairies.

Alie couldn't really remember much about the time before Jacques, just the big golden clock on the mantelpiece of the house in Paris, and the scent of clove pastilles; it had been Jacques's mother who was to look after her, she knew that much, because she'd been chambermaid at the house in Paris a long time ago, Jacques said, and now he was gone, and she couldn't even remember his mother at all, and Alie didn't know where she'd go next, or who with, because Bluette hadn't come to find her. She was too frightened to cry, even as the seigneur eased his mare from a gallop down to a trot. The forest itself gave way to the grounds of the palace, until finally they were riding along one of the smart gravelled paths on the way to the stables, and she felt a little rush of quiet tension pass through him as the Imperial Guards came around the corner and stopped in a row before them in those smart uniforms, white breeches, shiny black boots, blue jackets with carefully whitened kit-belts, so that Alie and the seigneur couldn't ride any further.

'It's going to be all right,' the seigneur said, his deep voice rumbling in his chest. 'You'll be quite safe.'

51

Watching the doorknob slowly begin to turn, Clemency fled across the room. Her fingers closed around cold brass, holding the door shut as the handle turned, slipping in her sweat-damp palm. She couldn't keep Valentine out. She gripped harder still, praying for salvation to St Cleer and the holy well at Liskeard, but Valentine had always been stronger than she was; the doorknob twisted in her grasp and Clemency could do nothing but step back as he came in.

'Silly girl,' he said, smiling at her, so handsome. 'There's nothing to be afraid of.'

Clemency fought swift-rising sickness, stepping away. Slowly – too slowly – he walked across the room towards her without consideration of the footman's presence, or his professionally averted gaze.

'You're beautiful.' He spoke so gently, looking her up and down, savouring the knowledge of what was beneath the cambric as if she were a gift, his to unwrap. 'You've always been so beautiful. This is our fresh start, Button. We can go wherever you wish.' He smiled. 'Vienna? Madrid? Venice? There's just so much of the world to see.'

It wasn't a cell, but Kit knew that the door to his own personal chambers at Fontainebleau was now guarded. Once an arsonist, always an arsonist. Siege towers, cannon-blasts, musket-fire, ambush, so many friends gone over the years: everyone he knew would be better off if he'd died in any one of those hundreds of engagements, all the way from Russia to Austria and into France. Instead, he'd lived through them all.

Even now, he heard the roar of the crowd, long ago: *Run, run, run.* And Kit had leaped from the gallows into a riot. In truth, he'd been living on borrowed time ever since. Standing at the window with his back to the room, Kit leaned his forehead on the glass. Knowing him as they all did, there were guards stationed in the ornamental garden below, too: he could hear them laughing, and Kit knew they were coming for him when he heard footfalls in the shaded corridor beyond his own chamber; men he knew by casual acquaintance were among the soldiers, all too mortified to speak or look at him; young Russell flushing brick-red as they all walked in silence to the Duke of Wellington's suite of rooms.

Kit found himself noticing queer little details as he was announced: Wellington's valet had cut him shaving, leaving a small nick along the prime ministerial jaw, and sunlight spilled across the polished walnut table, striking a brass vase containing a vast arrangement of delphiniums and roses that lent incongruous cheer to the room. Joséphine and d'Harcourt both sat at the table with Wellington: he supposed Dorothea had cut her losses and gone to Paris for the wedding. With all her machinations, she'd have some explaining to do if she wished to avoid a trip to Siberia. Like d'Harcourt and Kit himself, the duke still wore last night's dishevelled dress uniform. For a long while, nobody spoke.

Joséphine waited for him to sit down, then sat back in her chair, examining one of her own diamond rings. 'Oh dear, Christophe, darling – this is all rather a mess, isn't it?'

'Never mind that, ma'am.' Kit no longer cared about any of it. 'Where is Miss Arwenack, and where is the girl?'

Joséphine smiled, showing her blackened teeth – she was forever so well dressed that they came as a shock, but elegance had always disguised her true nature. Had Hester and Morwenna set foot on her home island of Martinique, they would have become property, thanks to the political actions of this smiling woman sitting here before him. Joséphine always acted in her own interests. 'Your concern for Miss Arwenack is quite misplaced, darling. Rumour and scandal make a capricious beast, but you ought to understand its habits by now. You know how it is: one rumour leads to another. It was Miss Arwenack who first started talking about your little indiscretion with her highness. It was she who spread the story, darling. After that, people were bound to start talking about fire-starting again – especially in relation to you.'

Kit stared out of the window at a flight of swallows wheeling and soaring in the hot sky above the palace gardens; he didn't deserve much better, he knew. His own dearest extortionist.

'It all went off like touchpaper, I'm afraid,' Joséphine said, tucking a strand of hair behind one ear. 'Anyway, none of this is exactly pertinent to our current situation, and the Boscobel carriage left Fontainebleau very early this morning: Miss Arwenack has gone away with Valentine Boscobel. I hear darling Georgie is furious – she always did have ambitions for him beyond a little bookbinder's granddaughter.'

Kit stood up, the room spinning around him, his relief that she lived outpaced by the desire to cut Valentine Boscobel's throat: he ought to have let him burn when he had the chance. 'I can't allow that to happen. Have her brought back.' Kit brought his hand down on the table so hard that the vase of flowers crashed to its side, spewing water and delphiniums. Vivid wet blue petals stuck to the polished wood.

'For God's sake, boy, that's enough,' Wellington snapped. 'If ever you wanted to prove yourself a hot-tempered irrational fool, you're doing a splendid job of it now. Control yourself.' White-faced with fury, he turned to Dorothea and Joséphine. 'Lieutenant Colonel Helford's military record is impeccable. Regardless of what his history might be, I see no reason to continue with this ridiculous charade. It's absurd that the fire should be thought of as having anything whatsoever to do with him. Do we not have enough fires that start completely by accident?'

It took every ounce of self-control for Kit to restrain himself now. 'What exactly am I accused of?'

Joséphine smiled. 'The trouble is, it's so difficult with your history. I hear that fire-setting is addictive, that the satisfaction is so great arsonists never only act once. With no war, no occupation, and a known personal grudge against my countrymen, could that urge no longer be ignored? Listen, I don't like that your career should crash to a halt like this, darling, and unfortunately very likely your life as well, but with your known antipathy towards the French, you must see that enquiries need to be made.'

'With due respect, ma'am,' d'Harcourt cut in, 'Lieutenant Colonel Helford has been nothing but warmly professional in his conduct towards me. And is he not half-French himself? Most of us suffered losses in the war, but times have moved on. We can't all bear prejudice towards an entire nation for actions committed in conflict, and despite Helford's reputation I don't believe he would do something as irrational as setting fire to a quarter of the palace containing thousands of people gathered for a ball. It was an act of unwarranted barbarism.'

Wellington looked up then. 'Of course he didn't do it. It's bad luck about the gossip, that's all.'

Joséphine smiled with brazen insincerity. 'Although if you hadn't set fire to Carlton House with me inside it, Christophe, there wouldn't actually be any incriminating gossip to cast suspicion, but we can't help that now, can we? It's a matter of reputation. The trouble is, it hardly matters who actually set the fire.'

'Look, Helford,' Wellington said. 'You're going to need to be able to prove where you were at every moment in that first hour of the ball.'

'I can't,' Kit said, simply. 'Thomas and I were there from the beginning, but I can't prove that I didn't slip away for the few moments it would have taken to go below stairs with an oil lamp. I can't and you all know it. And if you're going to have me shot then, for my family's sake, I'd prefer you did it sooner rather than later.'

'You can't just condemn a man on conjecture,' d'Harcourt said. 'This is absurd, if I may say so. What about all the attempts on the princess's life? Surely that's where we ought to look for an arsonist?'

Josephine sighed, going on as if d'Harcourt were less sentient than the brocade curtains. 'Napoleon is going to want to resolve this himself. It would have been a lot easier and less untidy had Lieutenant Colonel Helford confessed.'

'If I wasn't such a terrible liar then I would, to save you trouble, ma'am,' Kit said, with all the sweet venom he could manage. After all these years, it was a Frenchman who shifted to save his skin. He was damned if he'd give the rest of them the satisfaction of begging for his own life.

52

Clemency could do nothing but sit and try not to watch Valentine eat as she sipped at a glass of claret. Her gorge rose at the thought of what he might expect in return for his largesse once the afternoon wore on into night.

'You always used to have an appetite,' he said, his lips shining with grease. 'These missish, coquettish ways don't suit you.'

Clemency swirled the wine around in her glass. 'Think of your own reputation at home – if we run off together now, it's going to look so suspicious.'

Valentine leaned forward with his mutton chop, biting scraps of pale pink meat off the bone. 'You forget that I taught you everything you know. I know you don't give a damn about my reputation. Helford isn't worth your trouble, though. Didn't you know he's been accused of setting the fire? It's really amazing how one scandal feeds another, isn't it? You stoked the rumour about Helford and her highness – with admirable timing, I might add – and now there's been a fire here at Fontainebleau, everyone remembers London in 1817, and the young Helford arsonist.'

Clemency sipped her wine; it took all the self-control she had. He was alive. He hadn't burned to death in search of her. 'Oh, never mind Kit Helford.'

Valentine just laughed. 'Really? You almost convince me. But even if Helford isn't well on his way to an accusation of treason, you may be quite sure that he'll have nothing to do with you after this. The thing is, Clemency, that reputation is very much like virginity. It's easily lost and always impossible to regain.' He laughed. 'No doubt the world would call me a fool, but despite all your silly transgressions, I still want you. I'm even giving you the choice of where you wish to set up your establishment. Paris would be the most convenient, but I'd accept Brussels. I do frequently travel to both cities, as you know, so you'd never be deprived of my company for long. I'll take the little girl back to Boscobel Castle, of course. Her reputation isn't lost. Just yours.' He smiled. 'I'll have her all to myself.'

'I see.' Clemency reached for the joint of jellied beef; the footman had carved a few slices before he left, but he'd left the knife beside the plate.

In the council chamber, no one had picked up the flowers or the vase: water dripped noiselessly on to the Aubusson carpet. At Kit's side, d'Harcourt sat staring straight ahead with a fixed expression. No one believed him: worse, they hadn't even listened to him. Instead, they had just ignored him, even as the wide doors were opened by the footmen, who admitted Clemency's maidservant, Bluette. She clutched something in both hands; tears had left pale tracks on her ash-stained face.

Josephine looked her up and down in disgust. 'Who has allowed a dirty servant into my presence, in such a state of disarray as this?'

Wellington glanced at his young ADC, Russell, who had come in beside her; his hair was still damp from the morning washbasin, but there was a tideline of ash and filth around his jaw.

'I beg your pardon, ma'am,' Russell said, with a slight bow. He turned to Kit and Wellington. 'I wouldn't normally presume or allow this woman to intrude, but she was very insistent and I just had an instinct, your grace, that she's sincere and not encroaching or just mischief-making. She's insistent that Lieutenant Colonel Helford be given this book: it was found among the belongings of Miss Arwenack, who left instructions that this is what ought to happen should any accident befall her. I understand Miss Arwenack has gone away with Valentine Boscobel, and this woman has reason to believe that Clemency was afraid of him. It seems pertinent given the Boscobels' involvement, sir.'

'It sounds like nothing but a great Cheltenham tragedy to me,' Wellington said, even as Kit held out his hands to take the book from Bluette, remembering a firelit evening long ago in the attic bindery shop in Penzance, rain lashing against the windows. It was just a little leather-bound notebook with a tooled cover and beautifully marbled endpapers: she would have known how to do those by hand. Opening it, Kit saw that the pages were blank, yet to be written: a wide-open future.

'She made it herself, sir,' Bluette said, her voice ringing out into the silent room. 'Whenever she had a spare moment, not that there were many of those.'

He turned to d'Harcourt. 'Thomas, have you a knife?'

'I can hardly allow you to be given a weapon, Helford – not when you could fight your way out of here with a tooth-pick,' Wellington said shortly, gazing fixedly at a full-length portrait of the mistress of some long-dead king, as if he'd been forced to witness a marital argument in someone's drawing-room. Kit passed the book to d'Harcourt, who opened it with a small smile.

'What a beautiful piece of workmanship. Miss Arwenack is indeed a craftswoman.'

'I really don't see how any of this is in the slightest bit relevant,' Joséphine snapped.

'Open it and cut by the spine, please,' Kit said.

D'Harcourt raised his eyebrows. 'Here?' Kit nodded as d'Harcourt unsheathed his dagger and held it to the endpaper, near the spine, slicing through the marbled cerulean, ochre and green, passing the book to Kit across the polished walnut table once the cut was made. It felt like sacrilege to spoil such an object, but across thirteen years and over a thousand miles Clemency Arwenack was calling his name. He had to tear the endpaper a little: of course, she had only glued it around the edges; his hands were so dirty still, besmirching everything, but he pulled out the little scrap of paper all the same, smoothing it flat upon the table, and then passing it immediately to the Duke of

Wellington, the evidence against Nadezhda's true usurper signed in her own hand.

Charlotte.

53

Valentine spooned Chantilly cream into his mouth, never taking his eyes away from her.

'Why don't you enjoy yourself?' He got up, moving around the table, filling his glass of claret on the way. Clemency's heartbeat soared as he came to stand beside her: Valentine had never had as hard a head as she, his eyes were glassy and unfocused, his cheeks flushed in the gloomy candlelight; only a pale grey square of daylight was visible beyond the small window, and she remembered the first time he had caught her eye across the table at Boscobel Castle, a special smile just for her.

'Adeliz will be quite safe with me. There'll be nothing but the best for her,' he said, reaching out to stroke Clemency's neck, so that she had to bite hard on her lip to control a violent shudder. 'They named her at the nunnery. I think it's rather pretty. Perhaps every now and then we might be able to contrive it for you to see her, but I'm sure you'll agree how wrong it would be for such a young girl living under my protection to be corrupted by a fallen woman.'

Clemency found herself noticing odd little details: the pattern of blue flowers painted on the side of the bowl, a greasy mark on the lapel of Valentine's tailored jacket of superfine, brass handles on the fire irons at the grate catching the firelight; it was too hot, she thought desperately, no one needed a fire at this time of year anyway. Dimly, she was aware of hoofbeats in the yard outside: more witnesses to her disgrace, not that it mattered.

Valentine held out the spoon brimming with Chantilly cream, and with a jerk of horror she understood he meant it for her. She turned her head, pushing back her chair, but he moved with a burst of speed that was almost unnatural and the spoon struck her closed lips with a shattering burst of pain. She tasted blood; she dared not breathe.

'Come now,' he said, his breath stale in her face. 'Don't just sit there pretending to be Mistress Princum Prancum when we both know you're a hot little thing once you get started. The Helford bastard gets all your favours now, does he? The Lamornas shit into a chamber pot just like the rest of us, you know.' The cream-laden spoon jerked towards her again, glinting in the lamplight, and this time he forced it between her lips, the silver spoon ramming into her teeth and gums with another bright burst of pain even as she tasted the sickly sweetness.

Choking, Clemency took hold of his wrist; it was impossible to force down his arm – drunk as Valentine was, he was far stronger than she, and worse, he was enjoying her resistance.

'You're such a little wildcat after all,' he said. 'Perhaps I'll take you now, just the way I used to. You're mine anyway.'

Clemency tried to shout no without opening her mouth, but all that came out was a strangled moan; everyone in the tavern below would be listening to her struggle and perhaps even enjoying the entertainment. She spat out the spoon, gagging on sugared cream, fumbling blindly across the table until her fingers closed around the bone handle of a utensil of some kind, at least. Glancing down she saw that it was only a butter knife, quite blunt and useless, and let out a strangled, desperate laugh, even as she became aware of the fact that there were footfalls on the stairs outside.

She dared not cry out for help with Valentine so close; it might even make things worse, summoning any number of drunken men into the room; instead, she scrabbled across the tablecloth again, knocking over the carafe of wine; it splashed all over her fingers and wrist as Valentine leaned in to kiss her and she turned her head to one side as he begged her not to be shy.

She heard only the ragged sound of her own breathing, reaching across the table with her free hand until at last she touched the fatty cold roast beef, and with one final desperate snatch, her fingers closed around the handle of another knife, one that glinted bright and sharp in the candlelight. Taking it in her grasp, she wrenched her body around, away from Valentine and with all her strength she forced the blade of the carving knife into his belly, through his buttoned-up waistcoat and shirt as his face twisted with disbelieving fury. It gave her just enough time to push the chair back from the table and run backwards to the wall papered in wide stripes of crimson silk; holding the knife out before her with both hands, she watched, unable to breathe, as Valentine vomited blood, then snatched the entire cloth off the table. Tureens, plates, carafes and dishes smashed to the floor, buttered peas rolled towards her along the waxed oak floorboards, and the entire half-carved joint of cold fat beef hit the rug, rolling away towards the hearth, leaving a trail of grease.

'You little bitch,' Valentine said, uncertain on his feet as he moved towards her. 'It's really time you learned your lesson.'

He would never be anywhere near her daughter. Not ever again.

'Get away from me!' She held out the bloodied knife as if that could help her now; her hands shook so much that it twitched in her grasp like a live thing. Valentine spewed blood again, close enough now to snatch it from her grasp, hurling it across the room so that it struck the grate at the hearth.

'Bitch,' he said. 'Fucking little bitch. Too good for me now?'

Clemency tried to scream but no sound came out other than a strangled gasp, and in that sickening moment the door flew open and Thomas d'Harcourt came in, quickly followed by Kit, just as tall and beautiful as he had ever been, still filthy with smoke and ash. He reached Valentine in three long paces and before she could take another breath Kit had him on his back on the floor, his hands around Valentine's throat, even as d'Harcourt and Clemency both shouted at him to stop, Valentine's legs twitching and flailing as his windpipe was crushed.

'*Justice*,' d'Harcourt said. 'Let him face justice at someone else's hands.'

Kit looked up and laughed a little. 'All right. Since you ask.' He let Valentine loose like vermin caught in a trap.

'How dare you?' Clemency shouted, running at him, snatching hold of his jacket. 'First I thought you'd died in that fire. Then I was sure you were going to be shot for treason. He told me that you'd been arrested.' She broke off, incoherent. 'You mustn't frighten me like that. And I was the one who started rumours about you in the first place. I don't deserve you to be kind to me, not even remotely. I'm worse than you ever even suspected—' She could no longer speak for shame, but Kit just held her close.

'No, it's all right,' he said. 'Never mind it, Clemmie. You're quite safe.' He switched to Cornish. 'She's safe. The girl is safe. She's with my brother, and nothing can possibly harm her; he's taken her to Paris with Morwenna and my aunt. She looks just like you.'

She stared at him, expecting to read judgement and disdain even in that dear face she knew so well.

But Kit just looked straight back at her, his grey eyes steady. She couldn't move, couldn't speak; she had a profound sense of the world shifting around her, earth and sky spinning and her standing alone in the middle of it all; she'd taken a step out of her own life the moment she woke to find that empty cradle. Ever since that moment she'd just played a part in a play. It was time to step off the stage, with Valentine Boscobel's blood all over her hands. Dimly, she was aware of d'Harcourt kneeling over him, and servants streaming into the room, crowding around the injured man.

Kit bowed his head so that their foreheads touched. 'Come home with me. Please.'

Clemency let him go. *My baby*, she thought. *Oh God, my little child.* It was impossible to be with him now: how could she let herself feel anything for anyone else at all? She stepped back from him, and every shred of flesh in her body ached as the shock pulsed through her, echos of the labour pains she had endured with Georgie at her side in that dark bedchamber, long ago.

'I can't,' she said, her voice thick with unshed tears. 'I'm so sorry.' And then she turned and walked away from Kit Helford for good.

54

A week later, Clemency reached a rain-washed and bustling Calais, a fug of tarred rope, sodden canvas and pitch bubbling above braziers. She felt like a chemist's glass jar, volatile emotion surging within, but she couldn't allow that glass to shatter until they were safely home: no one in Cornwall need know that Jacques had died before Bluette actually married him, not afterwards. Bluette would be safe in the bindery shop with her growing belly, and Clemency would pull the dust-sheets off the furniture and the press, and light the old stove. Everyone who mattered seemed willing to believe that political conspiracy was men's work, not least with Georgie never mentioned by name in any of Valentine's correspondence. Clemency had heard variously that she'd fled to Venice, Rome and Athens; that Valentine would be hanged for treason; that he knew far too much about far too many people for those in power to risk the confession of a condemned man. There was still a voyage across the Channel to face, though, and more stagecoaches and taverns to navigate than Clemency could bear to even consider. She shaded her eyes with one hand, squinting towards the chaos of the bustling port, the near horizon a flock of masts and white canvas where privateers and caravels had already put out to sea. The cobblestones beneath their feet were slippery with greenish mud, spangled with fish scales that caught the light; somewhere nearby a brazier belched clouds of thick yellow woodsmoke.

'Come on,' she said briskly, and Bluette finished arguing with the coach driver about his hurly-burly method of dealing with other people's luggage. 'It's horrendously busy, isn't it? We won't secure passage if we're not quick, I shouldn't think. The coachman said that the diligence from Rouen is due in before long.'

'I've never seen such a crowd, mademoiselle,' Bluette said; she still had the glazed and wide-eyed look of a soldier returning from the battlefield. Clemency would make sure that Bluette kept her child, unbroken, unseparated. Surely it wouldn't be that difficult to secure passage across the Channel? But, one after another, every last enquiry was rebuffed with varying degrees of civility until they reached the end of the quay and the last purser that she could find shook his head, too.

'No, mademoiselle,' he said, not unkindly, 'I'm afraid there's nothing we can do for you, not unless you've written ahead and made an arrangement with the captain. Now, if you don't mind, the lads are trying to load Monsieur Giroud's quota of Chambord, although why that had to happen less than two hours before we'll miss the tide, it's really not my place to say.'

'But what about the next tide?' Clemency asked, desperate, even as he turned away. The slim roll of banknotes in her reticule would soon be depleted by unaired sheets and dishes of sour chops, and she was already calculating the cost of a night or two in Calais and passage for two women; if they could find a trader going to Plymouth instead of Dover, she might still afford seats on the coach from Plymouth to Penzance as well as bed and board in Calais.

'Not a chance, mademoiselle,' the purser said, with impatient kindness. 'All I know is every berth out of here is bespoken for the next week at least – the storms we've had have seen to that.' He turned away to shout instructions at a scurrying, tar-smeared ship's boy, and Clemency forced herself not to panic at the prospect of a week here, funds dwindling with every louse-ridden bed.

Bluette frowned. 'I don't think the inns so close to the port will be a wise plan, mademoiselle. There will be a lot of sailors – very rough men.' She broke off, turning back towards the road, squinting through the mist. 'Is that not Lieutenant Colonel Helford, mademoiselle?'

Clemency held her bundle tight to her chest, furiously ignoring the burst of longing and hope: he wasn't hers to miss. But when she turned, she saw not Kit, but Lord Lamorna with Thérèse de Saint-Maure on his arm, majestic in silk and ostrich feathers; Lamorna was hand in hand with his skipping daughter, who herself held hands with a younger child in a green pelisse and a neatly pressed gown patterned with flowers and cherries.

Bluette laid one hand on Clemency's arm, in silent communication, and Clemency could no longer breathe, the air drawn out of her lungs; she ought to look away – this could do nothing but harm. Everything else except the child – her daughter – spun away into a blurred mass of light and colour. Clemency saw only her child's thin arms encased in the green pelisse, and the plain brown hair so exactly like her own escaping from a matching bonnet, a small, familiar face flushed in the rain. The child turned as if they were connected by an invisible wire and there was no one else in the world, but when their eyes met across the wet cobbles, the little girl just looked at her with a brief, puzzled expression so that Clemency felt sure her own legs could no longer hold her, the light of recognition only dawning in the child's eyes when her gaze passed to Bluette, at which she stopped where she stood, plunging a thumb into her mouth.

'That's her,' Bluette said, stricken. 'Mademoiselle.'

Lamorna instantly turned to his aunt. With a swift word to her he left both girls clutching at her skirts, and walked up to them with the lazy, catlike ease that Clemency still found a little frightening. She dropped into a curtsey; Lamorna himself looked amused.

'You see, Lamorna,' Thérèse de Saint-Maure said. 'It is exactly as I have been telling you. The boy has not a modicum of the sense you assure me he was born with.'

'Well, I can see why you might sometimes think so, ma'am.' His gaze flickered dispassionately over Clemency's meagre luggage and Bluette at her side, addressing her without ceremony. 'You and your woman here will be pleased to sail to Cornwall with us, I believe.'

'There are no berths to be had until next week at least,' Clemency said; the little girl was looking at her now with an expression of faint puzzlement, and even though the child couldn't be harmed by her father now, Clemency knew all she'd lost. The first steps; her first words. They were strangers to each other, no matter what happened now. Years and years, gone for good. She felt as if she were balanced on the edge of a cliff, waiting to step off into nothing.

Lamorna considered her for a moment. 'There are no berths to be had, it's true,' he said. 'But the *Mawgan* is my own caravel, carrying a cargo of Burgundy directly to the quay at Lamorna Cove, and there is certainly enough room for you and your entourage.' He sighed, relenting. 'Perhaps we should walk for a few moments alone, so that you can tell me what you're really concerned about,' he said. 'Within sight of my aunt, of course.'

He offered his arm, and Clemency saw that she had no choice but to take it.

'Obviously my dear brother has made a complete melodrama out of what should have been, I hope, a happy ending,' Lamorna said, looking straight ahead. He still looked enough like Kit for Clemency's heart to twist in her chest. 'How on earth did you manage to prevent someone as hot-headed and irredeemably bloody-minded as Kit from following you?'

'I wrote him a letter before I left,' Clemency said; the memory of signing her name and handing it to the fascinated innkeeper at the Chat Gris still cut like a razor.

'Of course you did,' Lamorna went on, dispassionately. 'That's none of my business, however. But I don't like to leave an old friend's granddaughter alone in Calais with no passage to be had. You're not inconveniencing me, but I would like to know why you feel you're not able to accept safe passage home. You need not, of course, tell me anything more of a very personal nature.'

Safe passage. Clemency thought of Bluette's frightened face and her determined bravery, and momentarily squeezed her eyes shut.

'But I must be personal,' she said, meeting his calm gaze. 'It's the only way I can explain. Of course, you've guessed that Lieutenant Colonel Helford offered for me. He's forgiven all I've done, but your daughter is holding hands with the reason why I cannot accept, so it seems to me to be cruel and manipulative that you want to make me voice it.'

'And is it for you to say what I would or would not like?' Lamorna said. 'The situation you found yourself in at Boscobel Castle was damnable.'

She stared at him. 'What do you mean?'

'Exactly what you think I mean. You might have been a little unwise five years ago, Clemency, as we all are at times, but the blame for this doesn't lie at your door. You must understand.'

Clemency stared at the cobblestones, aware that her own daughter and Bluette had run to one another, Bluette gathering the child in her arms, whispering into her ear.

'Anyway,' Lamorna went on, relentlessly brisk. 'You're perfectly entitled to refuse my brother for whatever reason you like, but neither Valentine Boscobel's vicious behaviour nor Georgie's idiocy in enabling it ought to exclude you from accepting safe passage home with me, and although you're a woman of quite some mettle, and doubtless equal to a week in a Calais tavern, I'm sure you won't mind my pointing out that your maidservant looks on the brink of nervous collapse. The tide won't wait, so if you would be kind enough, we have a ship to board.'

That night, as the *Mawgan* tacked across the Channel, Clemency dined alone with Lord Lamorna, his great-aunt having withdrawn to her own cabin with a vial of smelling salts, a long-suffering personal maid and, as Lamorna assured her, a flask of really very decent brandy. Bluette sat in a chair beneath the porthole, knitting, and Lamorna kept up a stream of inconsequential conversation about the best methods of tooling leather for book covers, and how this was done in the ancient African kingdom of Meroë; he didn't face her directly across the table until the plates and dishes had been cleared.

'You're fortunate to have no tenant in the bindery,' he said, 'even if that was rather a misjudgement, when you could have been receiving rent all this time. I know I'm being odiously managing, but someone must, unless you choose to start facing the very real issues that now lie before you. What will you say to the child?'

In her seat beneath the window, Bluette briefly stopped knitting; then she resumed, the ivory needles clicking against one another in a silence that went on and on, shadows tossed around the cabin by the lamps that swung with every swelling roll of the caravel.

Clemency stared at him across her glass of claret: she'd never been able to lie to him. 'Must I say anything at all? Alie knows Bluette. It makes sense in her world that she should be with us, and she's endured so much already: she's lost everyone who ever looked after her. What have I ever done for her, except give her up? She doesn't need to know who I am. I'm sure it would only upset her.'

Unable to look at him, she pushed back her chair and went out up the companionway, out on to the deck where the sails were white in the moonlight, and the air tasted of salt, and all she heard was the creaking of tarred rope and the beating of her own heart.

On deck, she was vaguely aware of low voices in the cabin below, snatched out of her own hearing by the wind, and the night, and the crew calling to one another to let it away, gentlemen, and here where there was no witness except the night and the stars and a handful of uninterested seamen who passed her as though she were no more sentient than a coil of rope, Clemency let the hot tears streak her face until she felt nothing, washed clean.

Only then did she gather up the skirts of her gown and go below once more to the officer's cabin where her daughter slept with Morwenna and a maid – Alie, she must get used to that, although it was not the name she would have chosen; that would have been Mama's: Mary Alice. *Adeliz*, *Alie*. Perhaps it was not so far off, in the end.

Both girls were asleep beneath a voluminous tartan blanket in the single berth, Morwenna's maidservant, Sylvie, a silent heap of coverlets in a hammock strung by the sidescuttle. Stepping closer in the swinging lamplight, Clemency stopped just short of the bed, watching her daughter sleep for only the second time in her life; there was just the shadow of Valentine's handsome features, which was to be expected, and all Clemency could do was wish more than ever that she had not drifted off into a fretful sleep of her own after the pain and the shadows of her birth. In that moment, she was in a house far away from Cornwall and home, let alone safety, watching the vine-and-flower-patterned wallpaper seeming to shift in the lamplight as faceless people moved around the bed. She had to hold on to the companionway, forcing herself to breathe, to be here, now. In the narrow bed, Alie turned on her side, pressing her face against Morwenna's shoulder. Lady Morwenna lay sprawled on her back in utter security, but Clemency had to wonder if Alie would ever feel safe in the moments before she fell asleep.

'I won't leave you,' she said into the lamplit quiet. 'I won't ever leave you.'

55

A month later, in the last week of July, the great house Nansmornow sprawled among quiet green Cornish lawns, ancient stone buttresses golden in early evening sunlight striking off the Gothic window of the great hall. A scant few miles from Penzance, this southernmost tip of Cornwall had been spared the usual summer storms. Two horsemen came along the rutted lane from Newlyn. Together, they passed the track that led down to Lamorna Cove; they rode bareheaded and gloveless in the sunlight. Kit was laughing at something d'Harcourt said, his long fingers curled around the reins with effortless competence. The white lymer Porcelaine loped along at their side; she could run for hours. With the scattered houses of Rosemerryn on the right, and the crash of surf not far away to the left, they reached the gatehouse before a quarter-hour had passed, and stopped as Crow's lodge-keeper came out, obediently accepting both the cup of elderflower wine and a disrespectful instruction to get up to the big house as quick as they could. Kit never rode down the carriage drive at Nansmornow where the chestnut trees had been, and so they cantered right across the parkland where the grass had been left unscythed and full of wildflowers: it was easier that way.

Moving as one, Kit and d'Harcourt swung themselves out of the saddle in the stable-yard, handing their mounts and the tired hound over to one of the Trewarthen lads, and Kit felt the cool relief at speaking in Cornish after so many weeks of courtly French, breathing in the familiar scent of warm straw and linseed oil.

They went into the house through the flagstoned boot-room, Kit shrugging himself out of his Coldstream jacket and leaving it in a heap of gilding and crimson on the old wooden bench near his brother's gun cabinet, where the rifles and Hester's fowling-piece were kept. In waistcoat and shirtsleeves, he passed the scullery with d'Harcourt, laughing with smiling maidservants on the way. They loped by steaming clouds of lavender soapsuds and laundry airing on racks before a sulking fire; he supposed it had rained earlier in the day. He found Crow and Hester's butler and housekeeper waiting for him in the great hall where evening sun lanced in through the large window; making introductions, he shook hands with Hughes, and submitted to a hug and a scolding about the state of his boots from Mrs Hughes, who had known him since he was a boy.

'I'm sorry for all my mess, Catlin,' he said. 'How do the twins go on?'

'I should like to see the day, and they go on very well indeed, thank you,' she said, straightening his cravat, much to d'Harcourt's amusement. 'You'll find them all in the drawing-room.'

Kit heard the low hum of voices and went in to find a small group gathered on chaises drawn up close to a fire burning in the medieval hearth: Hester, Crow, Morwenna, Thérèse, in black and garnets as usual.

Morwenna was the first to reach him, getting up and bowling across the Turkey rug in her green satin slippers, crushing him in a breathless hug around his waist. 'You're home!' she cried out. 'And Commandant d'Harcourt! Are you going to stay?'

'You know very well that we are.' Kit swung her whooping up on to his shoulders. Hester was on her feet by now, too, round with the pregnancy, and she stepped swiftly across the room to greet d'Harcourt. She held Kit very close as she had done when he was much younger, only of course he towered above her now, even as Morwenna sat upon his shoulders.

'You rabble-rouser,' Hester said, reaching up to tidy his hair with a deft flick of her fingers. 'You're turning my daughter into a sad romp. Commandant d'Harcourt, what must you think of us?'

He smiled. 'I'm grateful for the invitation, Lady Lamorna.'

'You must stay for as long as you please,' Hester said. 'Kit tells me that you plan to remain in London for a while – searching for lodgings in the height of summer will be awful. It's much nicer here and we're so happy to have you.'

Kit caught his brother's eye as Crow deftly twitched Morwenna from his shoulders and on to his own, calling lazily to Hughes to bring champagne. Setting Morwenna down, resting one hand upon her ribboned curls, Crow glanced at the long window giving out on to the garden; later, they'd walk alone, but not now, not yet.

Kit and Hester were arm in arm in the rose garden his mother had planted; after Fontainebleau, he'd cheerfully never taste champagne again, so Crow had asked Hughes to bring up the amontillado from the cellar, and he sipped the cool sherry now, watching shadows lengthen across the scythed lawn.

'Crow and d'Harcourt have gone to play billiards,' Hester said, glancing up at him; save the growing belly, she looked more like herself again, and the sickness was over, at least. 'So you, my boy, are stuck with me.'

'I won't insult you by apologising,' he said. 'I made a bloody mess of it, Hets. I hope none of it comes your way.'

'It hasn't yet,' Hester said, 'but the fact that you came home a hero in the end, and that her highness is safely married, will mean Morwenna is still invited to play with other children, I would imagine.' She gave him one of her steady looks. 'Of course, there are some houses I would never let her go to, even if they did ask. It's not something you can mend by yourself. I've been to visit Miss Arwenack on a few occasions, you know. A very truthful girl, when it suits her. She admitted straight away that it was she who started a certain rumour about you. We had quite a long conversation, actually.'

'Did you?' Kit said.

'Yes. Luckily for all of us, Valentine Boscobel set fire to the empress's ball. Oddly enough, after that, all anyone could talk about was how many times you saved her highness's life, and how you ran back into a conflagration to look for her lady-in-waiting. Quite impressive, but I expect you're tired of it now, aren't you?'

'Very.'

'How long do you mean to stay in Cornwall? I've grown so used to only seeing you in London, when I see you at all.'

Kit let his gaze rest on the spreading lawn. 'I don't know. D'Harcourt has been invited to stay with the Wordsworths at some point – they've been corresponding for years. And Crow has told me about Borlaze – that it's mine, if I want it.'

'You're both very welcome here for as long as you want.' She smiled at him, then. 'Will the fact that you were once held prisoner in the cellar put you off Borlaze, do you think?'

'I don't know, but it is rather big as a place for a man to live alone, Hets.'

'Well then, don't live there alone,' Hester said. 'I don't think Miss Arwenack would find it too encroaching if you visited her this evening, you know.'

Kit drained the last of his amontillado, letting the little glass dangle from his fingertips, watching bees hover above the roses; the Ghislaine de Feligonde tumbled in abundance over the low box hedge and on to the gravelled path where they stood, densely packed petals intensely perfumed, variations of ochre-yellow through to white. He would have liked to paint them – perhaps he would, tomorrow.

His horse would still be foaming with sweat; he'd take one of Crow's.

Early evening sunlight streamed into the bindery workshop, striking off the finished books and the row of jars on the old wooden shelf, picking up the gilded spines of Aeschylus, *Castle Rackrent*, and collections of Shakespeare and the metaphysical poetry of John Donne. Clemency had her old striped apron on and the large press working. Having carefully glued a deep indigo cloth binding to the folios, she was now marking out and cutting the binding boards with her grandfather's old knife. A mop and bucket sat in the corner, still steaming. She and Bluette hadn't long finished chasing dust across the floor in the old circulating library downstairs. Soon Clemency would open to the town again, so that the dowagers could read the unsuitable novels they forbade their daughters, and mining overseers with an interest in chemistry could withdraw Davy's works on closed-lanterns, and retired admirals could read Lord Byron or mathematical treatises in translation from the original Arabic. It was wonderful, she thought, how very nearly all human knowledge was contained in the shuttered room below her, shelf after shelf. It was extraordinary too how, rather than shunning her for daring to live alone with only a pregnant French servant and a mysterious little cousin, her neighbours had, unannounced, left paper-wrapped loaves of bread on the doorstep, a basket of preserved pears in jars, once even a flitch of bacon. Although, no doubt it had helped to be very publicly delivered home in a crested carriage from the stables at Nansmornow, handed out of the landau by Lord Lamorna himself, and accompanied into the house by Lady Lamorna: there was no one who could stop her now.

Bluette and Alie came in from the yard, chattering and laughing downstairs; Alie liked sorting through the ribbons that she kept for making missal bookmarks. Alie and Bluette were such old friends and Alie still a little shy with Clemency herself, so that sometimes it was a struggle not to be jealous. But she had to think about now, and forget what might have been: no more daydreaming of a life where she had never let anyone take the child from her arms, and she had made it home to the bindery shop, cutting leather as her baby slept in a basket-cradle – an impossible life in which no one gossiped about Miss Arwenack's bastard daughter or turned away from them both in the street, or refused to serve her in the shops. This just wasn't a world where Alie could know who she was. It was heaven-sent that she was here at all; better that she faced enquiring glances as a distant cousin, not a child born out of wedlock.

Clemency was so absorbed in her task, and in the puzzle of how she and Alie would grow together, that she paid no attention to the rhythmic clatter of hoofbeats in the narrow cobbled street outside. Pasting, slicing leather and folding marbled paper, she hoped to go out before the sun set across the sea, and walk along the ramparts of the quay to look at Mounts Bay with Bluette and Alie, seagulls tossing in the grey skies above them, doing her utmost best not to think about everything that she had lost across that water. But Kit had never really been hers to begin with, and there was her own child at last, and books, and learning, and she had her establishment, and for now more than enough funds to live on. And some of it at least was thanks to the woman who would, according to the *Cornish Morning Post*, be crowned queen that autumn in London with a consort husband alongside her.

No, it had all worked out for the best, and it was foolish to feel such emptiness beneath this stupid happiness and content. Placing her knife with precision against the steel slide-rule, and slicing green leather for the binding, Clemency glanced across at the steaming glue pot on the little stove – she must be careful not to let it boil over. Spreading out the leather back-binding, she was unaware even that the door behind her had opened, and that Kit was leaning against the frame to watch her at work with his black hair tousled from the ride across the moors and clifftops from Nansmornow. She didn't see how his eyes lingered on the knot of linen where her apron was tied at the back, and how he smiled as she leaned forwards with competent grace to press the endpaper against the binding leather. She wasn't aware how long he stood watching, waiting so that he wouldn't interrupt her at work, but wait he did, until she had finished and stepped back from what she was doing, looking down at the finished work with her head cocked to one side in a movement so heartbreakingly familiar that he didn't know what he would do if he couldn't be with her.

'Miss Arwenack,' Kit said, and she turned, in that moment, to face him; he was leaning still in the doorway, bronzed from the heat of that frantic summer. He bowed, and she dropped into a curtsey, dizzy with the need to touch him, even though she could not.

'What are you doing here?' Clemency asked, her voice brittle. 'I can't be seen to receive men here at this hour of the evening.'

'If I had my way you wouldn't be single at all, you stubborn, infuriating maid,' Kit said, simply.

'Oh really?' Clemency said. 'And what gives you the right to be so opinionated about my affairs?'

'Hope?' Kit said, and Clemency did her best to ignore the fact that the air between them seemed to crackle with heat. For a moment, she was sure he was going to turn around and walk out, leaving her alone once more, but he didn't; he waited.

'Hope isn't enough,' Clemency said, because that was the simple truth, after all she had done to him.

'Well, then, because I love you, *caradow*.'

'How can you?' Her voice cracked. 'After what I did to you?' Clemency looked at the row of books before her, the gilded titles all blurring into one. Sunlight streamed across the ancient oiled floorboards, and the scent of the heating paste filled the air.

'That's right,' he said. 'I know exactly what you are. A scheming bloody baggage, brave as a lion.'

Clemency felt hot tears start to her eyes, even though she never cried, and when they kissed, his lips tasted of amontillado and his own sweetness, and with one swift movement he lifted her in his arms, and she wrapped her legs in a tangle of skirts about the lean expanse of his waist, and they kissed again, with her hands in his black hair, and his holding her close. He held her as if she were no weight at all, which wasn't true, walking in three leisurely steps to her workbench. She was dimly aware of him moving her work to one side, the ream of leather, Grandpapa's knife, deftly removing the crucible of paste from the heat. He set her down on the old oiled wood; they were of a height now, and Alie safe downstairs with Bluette, and so she had the cravat off him, unwinding starched linen as he watched her with that certain light in his eyes, which she had thought never to see again.

He smiled as she let it fall to the floor. 'Wicked maid,' he said.

'I know,' Clemency told him. 'But I do love you,' she said. 'And I always will.'

'You may have your own bookshop under my roof for all I care,' Kit said, and God how she really did love him. 'Clemency, it's your choice: I offer my name to you and to Alie. It's yours, if you'll take it.'

'Then I will,' she said, and he laughed.

'Oh good. That means I shall get you to church and then despoil you with real attention to detail. You'll see.'

'Not if I despoil you first,' Clemency said, and in the lamplight, they kissed again.

Epilogue

Borlaze, Cornwall, 1825

Blazing winter sun gilded the surf and the frosted bracken in the valley, and Kit lay among the crumpled linens in his wife's bed – Clemency had the sunniest bedchamber in the ancient manor house of Borlaze, where once, as a young insurrectionist, he had been imprisoned in the wine cellar. He lay watching the sun rise higher still as she slept with her head on his shoulder, one slender bare arm draped across his naked chest as shafts of brilliant light moved across the waxed and polished floorboards. This was home, but wherever she was would also be home, always. He sensed her wake before she even moved, and she rolled over to lie on top of him, sunlight hitting the copper strands in her hair as she smiled down at him.

'Good morning, soldier.'

He grinned, running his hands down her back, pushing her diaphanous nightgown out of the way so that he felt the warmth of her skin. 'Do you know, I really think you ought to be a bit more respectful. Less irreverent.'

She watched him with mock seriousness, reaching down beneath the covers. 'Of course, you're quite right, Lieutenant Colonel the Honourable Special Envoy to Bukhara.'

He laughed and kissed her then. 'What will we call you? Madam Special Envoy?'

'It sounds rather well, doesn't it? Perhaps they'll let me into the library.' Her eyes were bright with the thrill of it. With Clemency, it wasn't only the travel that thrilled her – to Petersburg by clipper, then Moscow, along the Volga to Saratov, where the Golden Horde had camped at Uvek, long ago, but also the possibility of seeing a treasury of books. It was one of those moments when his love for her felt so acute that it hurt in his chest. He kissed her again instead; they knew very well how to please one another, long and slow that morning, and had just finished very cursory ablutions and were back beneath the old crewel-work coverlet when their daughter came in like a shot from a cannon, fully dressed and holding her boots.

'Mama!' she said, climbing on to the bed and burrowing down between them both, even as her nurse called her back from the doorway, scandalised. 'Papa, you're so lazy, too. But you don't even know!'

'Know what, young baggage?' Kit said. 'What are you about, so early? You're very big with news, for such a small person.'

Clemency reached for his hand as she dropped a kiss on Alie's forehead, knowing so well that he had slept badly for nights, for fear of the coming news. But Alie was bouncing, not able to contain herself.

'It's Aunt Hester!' Alie said. 'She's had her baby, you know, *and* it's a boy, and really huge. And when Mr Hughes rode over from Nansmornow to tell us, he said to Bluette that Aunt Hester was up and wanting to walk in the garden in the sunshine, and that Uncle is beside himself and not wanting to let her, Mr Hughes said.'

Kit held Clemency's hand hard, grinning. 'Well then, we'd better go and wet my nephew's head, and tell his lordship not to be such a suffering fool, should we not?'

'I don't think you should do that,' Alie said, in all seriousness. 'But perhaps we could take them a Dundee cake? Morwenna likes it a lot, and there's a really good one in the kitchen, and I don't think they'll miss it.' She was just as gloriously practical as her mother.

'That sounds an excellent plan,' Clemency said, with equal gravity. 'And I think some lemon posset, too. He is the new Viscount Crowlas, after all.'

And so Kit and Clemency were dressed, and within the half-hour on horseback, laden with saddlebags and baskets, and Alie in the saddle before Kit: Clemency knew she would always be safe there.

Together, they rode along the clifftops, crossing heathered moorland within earshot of the Atlantic, the hair whipped back from their faces, coming first to the west lodge. Kit stopped then, Alie wrapped in her cloak before him, and so Clemency reined in, too, looking across at him, and in that moment he couldn't breathe, remembering.

'It's all right to go down the carriage drive, you know,' Clemency said, understanding him better than anyone.

'I know.' Kit didn't want Alie to guess at what he might be thinking, and so he spoke with a light ease that he didn't feel.

'You're here with us,' Clemency said, in Cornish that Alie didn't yet understand, walking her horse forward on to the carriage drive as it curved out before them both, finally reaching the front of the great house where the chestnut trees had once been. He rode at her side, and when they passed the three ivy-covered stumps that were all that remained of those trees, he took off his hat, but that was all.

'Here we are,' Kit said, and he dismounted, swinging Alie high in the air as he lifted her out of the saddle.

'You'll make a hoyden of her yet, if you're not careful,' Clemency said, but she was smiling at him.

'Just like her mother,' Kit said, taking her arm as they followed their daughter, running up the wide front steps to break their fast at Nansmornow.

Acknowledgements

First of all, I would like to thank my editor Rosie de Courcy who kept me going throughout the strange, dark and difficult year of 2020, and also for talking to me about these characters as if they are real people. I suppose to us they are. We gossiped about them all as though they were old friends, and if you've got this far then I hope that's how you feel, too. I'm indebted to my agent Catherine Clarke for her unfailing support, and to everyone at Head of Zeus, especially Anna Nightingale, Clare Gordon and Richenda Todd. I'm more grateful than I can really express to everyone who helped out with my research and in the writing of this book, but any remaining errors are definitely my own to claim! My sincere thanks are due to Stephenjohn Holgate for his thoughtful commentary, to Imogen for her advice at an early stage, and also to Janice Lobb for Cornish translation. In addition, I'd like to say a very wholehearted thank you to my writer friends, and especially to Emma Pass for reading *Scandalous Alchemy* just when I most needed it.

I'd also like to thank to Helen Louring Jensen and Sean Philips for assisting with the practicalities of falling from a window and into a lake whilst wearing a ballgown, and Ruth Frances Long for her advice about bookbinding. And last but very definitely not least, huge thanks to Lucinda, Chris and Stan for moving to France, just down the road from the Palace of Fontainebleau, and for having us to stay right in the nick of time, as it turned out. One day we'll have a glass of wine in that cobbled town square again.